URBIS

KINGDOM OF FAIRYTALES
SEASON THIRTEEN

You all know the story of your favorite fairytale, but did you ever wonder what happened after the fairytale ending? Well we know. Not all afters end up happily, sometimes the real adventure starts much later...

Following famous fairytale characters, eighteen years after their happily ever after, the Kingdom of Fairytales offers an edge of the seat thrill ride in an all new and sensational way to read.

Lighting-fast reads you won't be able to put down

Fantasy has never been so epic!

URBIS PRISON
SHIPLEY
BADALAH
THE VALE
AZREN
DESERT
KISBU
DRACONIS
ZHORE
MOSA
ELDER
ABORIA
AZURE
ENCHANTIA
AIRE
URBIS
EMERALD CITY
SKYLA
OZ
W
E
S
FLORIS
TULIS
THE FORGE
ARCADIA
RENAIS
MELFALL
ATLANTICE
ANTLA
KINGDOM
OF
FAIRYTALES

Copyright © 2021 J.A. Armitage
ISBN:978-1-989997-35-2
Enchanted Quill Press

This book is a work of fiction
Any resemblance to actual persons is purely coincidental

Contaact the author at www.enchantedquillpress.com
Cover by Enchanted Quilll Press
Interior Formatting by Enchanted Quill Press
Editing by Rose Lipscomb

KINGDOM OF ROYALTY

1ST JANUARY DERILLEN

I was dead. Or at least as close to it as anyone could come without actually being all the way dead.

Light interrupted the darkness. Light that I had not seen for so long, I couldn't even begin to guess the time frame. Years, most definitely, but how many?

I blinked, unused to the motion of my eyelids after so long. All I could see was white light, and yet, it filled me with joy. I'd seen nothing, felt nothing, been nothing more than a shadow, a whisper for longer than I could imagine—not flesh and blood, but something else. Now I had eyelids, and that meant I also had eyes, even if they were not used to seeing.

I cast my mind down my body and felt something take

shape. Something out of nothing. A torso, arms, legs. I tried moving my finger and was glad to feel it wiggle. It was touching something. It felt like...like grass, but it was brittle with the cold. I breathed in and smelled the scent of fresh air. I was outside, and it was cold. Very cold. My body shivered, making me want to wrap my arms around myself, but my arms weren't quite ready for something so difficult. Instead, I concentrated on the light, not quite white now, but with hints of darkness around the edges. I blinked again, and the white circle of the moon came into focus. Taking a deep breath, I turned my head to one side. I was in a forest of some kind. Why would I be in a forest? What was I doing here? A thousand questions flowed through my mind. If only I remembered something. My body shivered again, and I realized I was naked. Naked in the frost-covered forest floor in the middle of the night? The questions about how I came to be here would have to wait. I'd somehow been born again or come back to life, but if I didn't find something to cover myself, I would succumb to hypothermia and be dead again. But really dead this time and there was no coming back from real death.

I concentrated on my legs, willing them to move. My foot flinched with the effort, making a light cracking sound as it moved over the frost. Somewhere above me in one of the trees, I could now clearly see, thanks to the moon's light, a hooting owl take flight.

My breath floated like mist thanks to the freezing night air. Something about it gave me contentment as though it was somehow proof that I was living again. Not that I needed more proof than the stinging of the cold on my skin.

I pushed my hands to the ground and pulled myself up into a sitting position. My limbs were surprisingly supple for so long being unused, or not there at all. I still wasn't quite sure which, and yet, the cold sting did not abate. Now that my arms could move, I wrapped them around my body and rubbed the opposite arms, trying to keep what little warmth I had inside. Looking down, I saw a sliver of cloth, ragged and dirty, covering part of my stomach. It had the harsh stench of death to it. Once upon a time, it might have been part of my clothing, but the years had rendered it useless. I threw it to one side, where it fell into the undergrowth.

Holding onto a tree trunk for balance, I hauled myself into a standing position. In the distance, through the trees, I could make out a huge building, a castle of some kind silhouetted against the moon. A deep hatred, a wisp of a memory came to the surface, filling my throat with bile, and yet, I couldn't place it. Something to do with that castle had been my downfall. Beyond the castle, I saw the lights of a city or a town, but it was a long walk. Even longer if I factored in the fact that my legs felt as wobbly as a newborn lamb's. It would take me hours to walk there. Looking behind me, I only saw trees. I could chance it that there was a cottage nearby, but it would be a gamble. A gamble I couldn't afford to take. Getting lost in a forest would be a death sentence for sure. The castle was my only hope of survival, and yet, as I stepped toward it, an anger like I had never known filled me. The people living there had done this to me. I didn't remember why or how, but I knew it. I embraced the anger and turned it into determination. If they had hurt me, then they would also be my salvation. I walked out of the forest, treading lightly on the frozen grass. The castle was shrouded in darkness with only a couple of torches ablaze near the front, where I assumed the main gate was guarded. I would have to slip in through the back. A huge stone wall surrounded the castle, but as though I remembered it, I knew there was a gate in the back. I followed the wall, touching it with my fingertips, wondering if my intuition would be right. I was almost surprised to see the gate, but it was there. I'd used it before.

It was locked and covered in vines. No one had come this way in a long time. Holding out my hand in front of me to try and move the vines, I was shocked when they began to move back themselves, slithering like snakes away from the gate and to the wall. Had I done that? I was magic? Trying it again, I pointed my hand at the lock. A click inside the padlock told me I'd done it. I really was magic! Something about the revelation gave me strength. Of course, I was magic. I'd survived something unsurvivable. At least, I thought I had. I would worry about that later. Now, I needed to find clothing.

The trees in the garden were bare, thanks to the season, and the few shrubs that still grew in the winter months were covered with a thin layer of frost. My footprints would be noticeable as I crossed the lawn, but I'd be long gone before dawn, and maybe my footprints would disappear with the early morning sun before anyone noticed. The back of the castle was not as grand as I expected it to be. I couldn't make out much in the blue light of the moon, but I found a door that looked like one the staff might use. Perfect. Another use of my magic and the door creaked open slowly. I held my breath at the noise, half-expecting a hundred guards to descend on me, but they never came. Inside, I found myself in a small entrance hall. Boots caked with dry mud were lined up under a wooden bench along the side. Above the bench were a row of hooks, most of which were empty, but the last two held coats. Long, thick, fur-lined winter coats. Taking the nearest, I pulled it on and allowed myself to enjoy a few moments of luxurious warmth that seeped through my skin into my bones. I slipped my feet into a pair of boots that looked to be my size and headed back into the frigid night air.

The walk into town was not so bad now that I was warm. By the time I reached the outskirts, the first slivers of sunlight were beginning to rise over the horizon. During the walk, parts of my memory had started to come back. There was a blonde girl that kept coming to mind, but no matter how hard I wracked my brain, I couldn't place where I knew her or why she was so important. The same feeling I got when I saw the castle for the first time came over me every time I pictured her face. She had a beautiful face, of that there was no doubt, but I hated her. I hated her with every ounce of passion I had, and yet, for the life of me, I couldn't remember why.

The town was a strange place with buildings mostly made out of metal. Unlike the castle up on the hillside, none of this looked familiar. I wondered if I had worked there at some point, a maid, perhaps. I didn't feel like a maid. I had to be someone more important than a mere servant.

Despite the earliness of the hour, people were still in the streets. Most of them looked the worse for wear after a night of heavy drinking. I kept to the shadows as much as possible, trying not to stand on the streamers and after-party detritus that littered the sidewalks and streets. Someone crashed into me, almost knocking me from the sidewalk out into the street.

"Watch where you're going, fool!" I snapped.

He gave me a grin, doffed his hat, then stumbled away, clearly still drunk.

Looking up, I saw a sign reading Dragon Roost Inn. Inside the Inn, the strains of party music were still floating out. It looked like the whole town had been out to party the night before, and some of them were still making merry. For some reason, that annoyed me. What right did everyone have to be partying and drinking when I was left out for dead in a forest? Not that I could really blame them. I didn't even know who I was, so how could I expect anyone else to know about me? Part of me desperately wanted to head into the inn, grab a room for the night and some food and then pass out in a warm bed, but something in my gut told me that would be dangerous. I wasn't wanted here. I kept walking until I came to a town square, its cobbles barely visible under the layer of glittering streamers and scrunched up food wrappers, not to mention a thin layer of frost.

A few people were still drinking on a bench at one end, but largely, all that was left of the party was the mess—that and a food stand that seemed to be abandoned. My stomach gave a low grumble, reminding me how hungry I was. I made my way to the food stand, expecting to find nothing, but there were a couple of half-eaten pretzels left on the top. I stole them away, hiding them under my coat. Now, all I needed was somewhere warm to eat my meager meal. I was exposed, still naked under the coat. I didn't know who I was, nor where I was, and soon the sun would come up fully and I'd no longer be able to hide in the darkness.

Scanning the square, I noticed an old shop along one of the side streets leading away from the square. The sign that once hung there was dangling at an angle, and a thick layer of dust and grime coated the windows. It was perfect.

Getting inside was easy. I'd learned very quickly how to open doors with my magic. I slipped through the door, made sure to lock it behind me, and looked at the space.

Empty shelves covered in dust told me that this place had been deserted long ago. Behind the counter, I found another door, this one unlocked. It led to a set of steps, which, in turn, led to a small apartment. It was nothing spectacular and needed a damn good cleaning, but there was a bed, a stove, and a bathroom. It was far from perfect, but it was empty, and for today at least, it was all mine.

2ND DECEMBER
AZIA

I looked around the ragtag group of people collected from all of the kingdoms, marveling at my new family. Some were princes, some were princesses. Some were rich, some poor, some servants, and yet all were leaders, destined to take over in their respective kingdoms. Our newest recruit, Lyric, from the floating islands of Skyla, was the most enthusiastic of all. I watched as she sat at the campfire we'd made, talking animatedly about the adventures of her last few days in Skyla to the others.

Her face glowed with the light of the campfire, causing the golden ring around her irises to sparkle. A couple of rabbits cooked over the fire, emitting a delicious smell, and a handful of moths flew around attracted by the light.

"What about you?" Lyric enthused. "I've told you all about me, but how come you are all here and together? How did it happen?"

There was a sadness behind her excitement of adventure. She hid it well, but I'd become accustomed to the sadness that lingered in the eyes. The way people looked down and their smile faded when they thought no one was looking. Lyric hid it better than the others did, but it was there. We'd all lost someone. Lyric had lost her father figure, and unlike me, whose mother was under a curse, Lyric would never get Peter Pan back. He was gone for good. Dead, Killed by Captain Hook. I mentally added him to the list of our foes. I chalked up his abilities and his weaknesses as Lyric told us all about him. I knew them all. The people out to bring us down. I didn't know how they knew each other, but Hook was involved with all the others, just as Lyric was a part of us. I knew part of the story, how twelve siblings with superpowers came to be, but the people against us. Those that wanted us dead or in pain, those that wanted to take over in our kingdoms, I had no idea how they had gotten together, but they had, and the twelve of us—thirteen if my dragon friend Nyre was counted—were the only ones able to stop them.

"I started this adventure back in January," I began. It was pretty much the first thing I'd said to her since she'd joined our group the evening before, but if anyone should tell the story, it should be me, after all. I'd been the one to start it.

"When I turned eighteen, my abilities began to manifest themselves. I can talk to dragons. I can command them to follow my bidding."

With that, Nyre hopped down from a tree and settled beside me. I didn't mention to Lyric that Nyre was a wilful beast and would do whatever she wanted, whatever I said.

"Around that time, my mother became ill. She fell into a deep sleep, just like she had over a hundred years ago. Back then, it was a witch called Derillen that cursed her. Gaia found out that when we were all born, a burst of magical energy, healing energy, was sent out throughout the world."

Lyric looked confused for a second before her eyes settled on Gaia, and she smiled. I'd met them, all one by one, but I could see how difficult it would be to remember all our names in one go. I waited until Lyric's eyes settled back on me.

"Gaia saw our birth, or at least two of our births thanks to her Genie friend. She even traveled to the house in Urbis where the twelve of us had been given life. All born in one place at the same time, or should I say, one right after the other."

"I don't understand how that's possible," Lyric admitted. "I know you all think we are brothers and sisters, but how can a woman give birth to twelve children at once?"

"I didn't think it was possible either, but when Jakon was brought into the fold, he told us that his adopted mother, Dorothy, the previous Mayor of Oz, had been told that his real mother was actually a god. Aphrodite, the goddess of love, no less."

Lyric's eyes widened; then her mouth opened in comprehension.

"So we are born of a goddess? We are demi-gods. Well, that explains these," she said, patting her wings.

"So what can you all do? I know Azia can speak to dragons, and I've seen Castiel in his wolf form, so I know his talent. What about the rest of you?"

"Change appearance!" Fallon announced, holding his hand up. "Not that I use it much. Why would I want to change this face?"

Nyre giggled beside me as I rolled my eyes at his vanity. It had waned a little since he'd joined the group, but traces of it still showed through. He was totally deserving of it with his perfectly coiffed hair that never seemed to look out of place, despite the fact that we'd not been within a hundred miles of a barber in months. I secretly thought he'd stashed a pair of scissors in his bag and was giving himself haircuts and trimming his short beard in the night when we weren't looking. Either that or he was using his powers of appearance shifting to keep him from looking as bedraggled as the rest of us.

Next to him, Blaise nudged him in the ribs. "I can breathe underwater. My mother is a mermaid. Well, she sometimes has legs, just not now. That's kinda why I'm here. The sea witch got us." She ran a hand through her red curls and wiggled her toes the way she always did when talking about the water. I could tell she missed it.

"I can control fire," Gaia said, bringing the campfire up into a twirling display, involving embers sparkling and raining down on us, burning out before actually hitting any of us. When she had finished, she brought her hand down and let the fire settle.

"Woah," Lyric exclaimed, clearly impressed. "Who is after you?"

Gaia lowered her eyes, then brought them back up to Lyric. "My late grandfather's Vizier. He wanted to rule Badalah, but my father got in his way. I don't think The

Vizier ever got over it."

"Revenge and power seem to be a theme with these guys." Lyric's eyes passed over to Deon, who had his head down, face deep in another letter to his wife. I gave a small cough to get his attention.

"Sorry, what?"

"He likes to write letters," I mumbled to Lyric before turning back to Deon. "I think Lyric would like to know your powers. Why don't you show her?"

Deon carefully placed his writing paper and pen beside him, then concentrated on Lyric. At least, I thought it was Lyric he was concentrating on until she shot up in the air on top of a beautiful flower that had bloomed beneath her.

"I have the power to grow plants," he shouted up to where she flew off the head of the flower. She fluttered back down to earth, but the bloom remained, almost as tall as the trees surrounding it.

He gave a little theatrical bow without actually standing up. "I should tell Lilian about that. She'd get a kick out of it!" He picked up his pen and paper and began to write furiously again.

"Lilian?" Lyric whispered.

"His wife. I kinda interrupted his honeymoon, so he writes to her every day. When we come close to a post office, he posts the lot. I think his entire backpack is filled with writing paper."

"My gift is ridiculous," Halia said when it was her turn. "I can't fight, I don't know how to wield a sword like Azia, I can't control weather like Jakon." She strummed her guitar, and a robin landed on her shoulder.

"People are drawn to her music," I explained as another bird joined the first. "Birds too, so it seems."

"It's a bit lame," Halia conceded.

"It sounds lovely, though," Lyric encouraged her. "You have a real talent."

A growl sounded out behind me. In a flash, I was up with my sword out. The others followed suit as the growling intensified, each of us facing away from the fire. Whatever was growling, there was more than one of them. The sound echoed through the clearing. Then I saw one of them. Out from behind the trees, a wolf emerged, its teeth bared, and saliva dripping from its mouth.

"Castiel," I whispered, not daring to take my eyes from the angry beast for a second. "Could your friends have crossed the border?"

"These aren't shifters," he replied simply.

Dragon balls! While there was a chance that any wolf shifter we did happen to come upon could be carrying the curse, there was also a chance Castiel would be able to talk to them. There was no translating with real wolves. Not that their growls needed much in the way of translation. The pack was hungry, and we were food.

The wolf stared at me, its eyes focused on the kill. On each side of it stood another two or three wolves.

For a second, there was calm, and then the wolf leapt. Behind me, I heard the sounds of fighting, of Gaia's flames, of Jakon's mini-tornados. Shouts, growls, and yelps filled my ears as I held my sword out to the wolf in front of me. It was huge. Part of the reason I thought it might be a shifter. I guess living in a forest of a kingdom well known for its unicorns usually provided plenty of fresh meat. But this one hadn't eaten in a while. I could see it in its eyes.

Everyone was fighting the wolves except me. The wolf in front of me hadn't moved yet. Maybe it was waiting for me to make the first move. I was ready for this. I'd trained to use my sword. Images of myself and Milo in a clearing, not unlike this one, filled my mind. I'd beaten him on numerous occasions. I could beat this wolf.

"Come on," I whispered to myself. The thing was, I'd practiced a lot. I'd kept up with my practice on the road, but fighting a pretend enemy wasn't the same as fighting with the intention of killing. And killing the wolf was the only way out of this. Unless it killed me first, that was. I held my breath, waiting for it to make the first move. I needed that. I needed my first kill... only kill, to be something I had to do out of necessity. And then it pounced. My sword skewered its heart as it leapt onto me, knocking me to the ground. Not a fair fight. Not a difficult fight, but I'd done it. I pushed its body from mine and rolled over to see how everyone else was faring. Not as well as I had, it seemed. While I had only dealt with one wolf, the others were taking on two or three at once. Gaia and Nyre were fine. Fire versus wolves. Lyric was also fine, having wings. The others were not faring as well. I jumped to my feet and stabbed at a wolf that was about to attack Eliana. My second kill was much easier than my first. Ivy ran past me, firing makeshift arrows at another couple of wolves from a weird contraption she'd put together from things she'd found along the way. I let her pass, heading for Fallon instead. Fallon's gift of changing appearance was no use to him here. Grabbing his hand, I pulled him behind me as I fended off another couple of wolves. The wolf bodies were really piling up, but they kept coming. I wanted to ask Castiel how many wolves a pack usually held, but he was nowhere to be seen. And still, they kept coming. For every one that we slaughtered, another two or three appeared out from behind the trees, all intent on killing us for their dinner. The scene reminded me of the competition my father held all those months ago to find me a husband. Back then, it had been tigers and lions, but at least the people in the competition could jump over the barriers if they wished. We were surrounded. There was nowhere for us to go.

As I fought against wolves coming for me and Fallon, I saw another go for Kelis. She threw a spell at it, making it keel over.

"I don't suppose you can do that with all of them at once?" I asked as she bolted past me.

"I don't know how," she answered breathlessly. "I'm struggling to remember all my spells. Sorry!"

"Don't be," I yelled after her. "Just keep on doing what you're doing."

I sliced into another wolf almost without looking. It dropped to the ground, yelping. I'd missed its heart. It wasn't dead. This kill was an act of mercy. I put my boot into its side and ran my blood--covered sword down into its heart, killing it instantly. Beside me, Fallon struck out at a wolf that had managed to grab Nyre. He kicked so hard that the wolf's jaws opened in a yelp, and Nyre was able to fly up out of its reach.

"Azia!" Blaise screamed. I looked up from the dead wolf to see her arm dripping in blood, another wolf's teeth clasped around it. I wanted to go to her, but another three wolves had crept out of the undergrowth and were bearing down on me.

"Hold on!" I shouted back, moving my sword between the three. Behind, me Fallon yelled out in pain. We were overrun. There were too many of them.

A pretty melody rang out in the woods, and suddenly the wolves stopped. The thrum of the guitar got louder, and as it did, the wolves all forgot what they were doing and turned their heads to the source of it.

"Go to sleep, Go to sleep, Go to sleep, my baby," Halia crooned, the guitar in her hand. I yawned as the wolves began to drop to the ground. Not in death but in sleep. They rested their heads on their front paws and just listened to her.

I felt my own eyelids get heavy with the beautiful melody. I sat down with Jakon beside me, resting my head on his shoulder.

And still, Halia played. The famous nursery rhyme turned into something else. I only half-listened to the words, but with them, I was compelled to stand again. In a daze, I followed the sound of the music through the woods.

When it finally stopped, the spell was broken.

"Everyone ok?" Halia asked, placing her guitar back in its case.

I rubbed my eyes and yawned again. "What just happened?"

"I compelled the wolves to sleep," Halia said, pulling the zip closed around the guitar case. "You all started to fall asleep too, so I had to change the tune to compel you to follow me. We didn't go far. The wolves are about five minutes back on the path, and so is our stuff. I just wanted to get us all out of there in case my music didn't work. Some of us will have to go back and pick up our bags before the wolves wake up. I don't know how long my magic lasts."

"On it!" Lyric yelled, taking off into the sky before anyone could stop her.

She flew back less than five minutes later, laden with backpacks.

"They are still asleep, but my picking up the bags was beginning to rouse them," she said, doling the bags out. "I think we should make tracks quickly before they figure out where we've gone."

We set off after Blaise's arm was bandaged and after a quick check to make sure none of the rest of us was hurt.

"What were you saying about your gift being lame?" I asked, getting into step with Halia at the back of the group.

She gave me a self-confident smile. "I guess I do have it, after all."

We walked for hours, leaving the wolves far behind us. Eventually, we came to another spot to set up camp, far from the threat of the wolves. Gaia made a fire, and Deon, Lyric, and Blaise went hunting for berries while Castiel and Ivy hunted something more substantial for our dinner.

Standing up, I left the others to stretch my legs in the surrounding forest, Nyre flapping her wings beside me.

Vale felt surprisingly calm, but that didn't mean I could rest. I never rested fully anymore. There were too many people out to get us, not to mention the animals that called this forest home. The Vale had been the lair of an imp known as Rumpelstiltskin, an odious creep who thought it was funny to steal babies. He wouldn't find it funny when I slit his throat because that was exactly what I would do to him when I found him. Him, along with all the others that had come back from goodness only knew where back in January to disrupt the state of the entire world. My nerves buzzed with the thought that something could jump out at us at any moment and how unprepared we really were. The attack by the wolves had shown me that.

A branch snapped behind me. I ripped my sword from its sheath and turned, ready to slash whoever was following me. My nerves were on fire, my senses on a knife-edge.

Deon held one hand up and gave me a wry smile.

"Stars, Azia. Steady on. It's only me. I thought you might like some wild berries."

My heart pounded. I could have killed him. Another couple of steps closer and I might have.

"Sorry, Deon," I sighed, sheathing my sword and holding my hand out to accept the berries. In typical Deon fashion, they were wrapped up in edible leaves and presented like party food. I took the small bundle and took a bite. Red juice dribbled down my chin as the tartness of the berries mixed with the exotic minty taste of the leaves.

"Nice?" Deon enquired, his eyebrow raised.

I nodded my head and wiped the juice from my chin. "I don't know how you do it, Deon. We have the best chefs in Draconis working at the castle, and none of them make desert like you do."

Deon rubbed the back of his neck and looked down shyly. "It's only wild berries washed with juices from a Valean Citrus and a little bit of soft Ocean Ash Bark mixed with Appia Nut then wrapped with Candy Leaf."

"Well, it's heavenly."

"I don't want to sound like a bore, but..."

"I know what you are going to say, Deon, and you're right." He'd been telling me for weeks that I was too jumpy, too quick to pull my sword out at the first hint of danger, even when there wasn't any.

"I just don't want anyone getting hurt, including you."

I sat on a nearby upturned log and massaged one of my temples with my free hand.

"Milo taught me to fight, but he never taught me to

know when the time was right to fight."

"Sitting in the middle of a forest when your brother brings you dessert is probably not it," Deon mused aloud. He sat next to me, and I draped my arm over his shoulder. I loved having brothers and sisters. I missed Ash, Hollis, and Remy more than I cared to admit, but having this band of siblings with me, siblings that knew how to do magic and whose magic combined with mine, made me feel complete somehow. As though some part of me had been missing my whole life."

"You're probably right," I said, leaning into him.

We sat in silence for a while. In the distance, I could hear Lyric still talking and up ahead the faint strains of Nyre's breathing as she sat perched in a tree, no doubt eavesdropping on our conversation.

"Having those wolves attack us made me realize just how unprepared we are. There was no plan, no cohesion between us. I didn't know what I was doing," I admitted.

"We survived with only a few minor scrapes," he reminded me. "You saved Fallon's life a couple of times. Ivy saved mine at least twice with her crazy mechanical bow thing. It might not have looked like it, but we did work together."

"I was fine until Lyric joined us," I finally said, admitting the real reason I was feeling down.

"What do you mean?" Deon asked.

"Before she came, I knew what I was doing. I knew what my mission was. It didn't start out with me finding my real family, but after meeting Blaise and then Castiel, it became all I could think about. As if finding my siblings was the main plan all along, but it isn't, is it? The main plan was always to fight Derillen and save my mother from the curse."

"True, but now there are eleven of us to help you with that."

I sighed again and put my half-eaten candy leaf dessert on the branch next to me. "I know, but with that, there are now eleven more problems, eleven more people to fight, eleven more people with magic we have to figure out. I don't know where to begin. I was having a hard time figuring out how to deal with Derillen and Morpheus without everything else. Now we have sorcerers, sea witches, plagues, monsters, imps, wizards, and now, thanks to Lyric, insane pirates to deal with."

Deon chuckled beside me. "You left out The Queen of Hearts and her army of clockwork cards."

I rolled my eyes. He was joking with me, but it wasn't funny. What we were up against was insurmountable. There were too many of them and not enough of us. Although, after months of traipsing through kingdom after kingdom, it sometimes felt like there were too many of us too. Tensions were running high pretty much all the time, and I was tired. So, so tired.

"I just want to fly away, Deon. I'm jealous of Lyric because she has wings."

"You have wings too."

When I furrowed my eyebrows, he pointed up to Nyre in the tree above us. "You need a break, that's all. Why don't you take Nyre and scout up ahead? I'll let the others know you'll be back in an hour or so."

I kissed Deon on the cheek and whistled to Nyre. She was down from the branches in a shot. Without being asked, she grabbed hold of me and pulled me up into the sky above the treetops.

My fears and worries vanished as we soared over the canopy of treetops. Far behind us was Vale's shoreline, where we had met Lyric just yesterday, and beyond that, the floating islands of Skyla. In front, the forest stretched as far as the eye could see. It was both beautiful and terrifying because now we weren't heading out to find another sibling; we were moving toward our final destination, Urbis.

We would finally come face to face with those who had hurt us, who were still hurting us, and who were threatening all the kingdoms.

I took a deep breath and readied myself for the danger we would soon be facing.

JANUARY
DERILLEN

It didn't take long before my memories came crashing back to me. One night. One full night's sleep was all it took. I was Derillen!

To think that I'd wondered if I'd been a maid at the castle. Pah. Maid! I was the most powerful sorceress in all of Draconis. A witch they had called me. An evil witch. They didn't know anything. I'd been wronged by the royal family generations ago, and they'd wronged me again. It had been that prince. I'd watched him as he'd somehow gotten through my beautiful thorny masterpiece of enchanted brambles. He'd been nothing but a scrawny kid. But how? How had he managed it? And he'd woken her up. True love's kiss. What a joke!

I stumbled out of the dusty bed and ran my fingers

through my hair. Dust fell about me. I looked down at my naked body. I was a mess. This whole place was a mess. If I was going to find out what happened to me, I needed to look the part.

A swift wave of my hand and I was clothed in my usual purple and black. The long deep purple dress covered by a black cloak. Simply stunning. If only I'd have remembered the extent of my magic the previous night, I wouldn't have had to steal the old boots and coat. I pointed my finger to the offending articles and let a zip of magic erupt, engulfing both the boots and coat in a fireball. It was oddly satisfying watching them burn. They obviously belonged to a servant and not a member of the royal family, but knowing that something from the palace was burning gave me great joy. One day in the near future I'd burn the whole castle down with all the royals inside. First, though, I had some work to do.

Ten minutes later, thanks to my magic, the small apartment was sparkling clean, and the locks on the door had been changed. I had no idea who the shop and apartment belonged to, but the last thing I needed was them coming here and bothering me. I could get rid of them, of course, but killing people often led to questions. Easier to keep the doors locked. Besides, judging by the state of the place before I'd cleaned up, no one had lived here in a long time. Taking a peek out of the window, I saw the small alleyway with its cobblestoned street. This place was not good enough for someone as powerful as me. Not nearly, but for the time being, it would have to do.

Taking the steps down to the shop area, I stepped out onto the street. First things, first. I needed to find out how long I'd been gone for. It felt like forever, but the castle had looked much the same as it had the last time I'd seen it.

The streets were quieter now, despite it being the middle of the day. The drunken bums had finally made their way home or to wherever it was they had come from. Most of the shops were closed, but the odd one or two were open.

A young boy of no more than eleven or twelve with a cart selling papers stood at the corner of the large square, which was still a mess thanks to the party of two nights ago. I picked one up and began to read.

"Oy, what d'ya fink this is? A public library? You've got to pay for that."

"Oh, do be quiet," I said, idly pointing my finger at him and shushing him with a silence spell.

The headline of the Draconian Sentinel was some drivel about the New Year, which made sense. I flicked my eyes to the top of the page and the date.

"Is this date right, boy?"

The boy looked at me with fear in his eyes, his lips stuck together with magic.

"For goodness sake..." I pointed at him again and reversed my spell so he could speak.

"Is this date correct?"

He peered cautiously at the paper I was holding out to him. "It's the second of January, yes."

"Not the day, you sniveling imbecile. The year. Is this year correct?"

"Yes."

Dragon crap! Eighteen years. Eighteen years! I'd been gone, dead, enchanted, or whatever it was for eighteen years. It made no sense. No one in Draconis was more powerful than I. No one, and yet I'd been gone for eighteen years. Why? And why had I woken up now?

"Has anything happened recently? Anything

unusual, I mean?"

The boy shook his head, his eyes full of fear. He was of no use to me at all, and the second I left him, he'd be mouthing off all around town what I'd done to him. I needed to learn to keep my magic under wraps if I was going to find out what had happened to me.

Back in the alley, I changed my appearance. Gone were my beautiful robes. In place of them, I now wore a rather dull shift dress with a very ordinary coat over the top with high-top boots. Tying my hair into a quick ponytail, I headed back into the square. The boy had scarpered and taken his cart of newspapers with him. Not really surprising.

In the distance on the hillside, the castle stood as it always had with one small missing detail. My beautiful brambles were all gone. The brambles that had kept everyone away from the castle for over a hundred years. There was nothing but fields at the front and trees at the back, with the Fire Mountains completing the picture behind the forest.

My last memory had been of the young prince cutting through them and kissing Briar Rose. I still didn't know how he'd managed it, but I knew how to find out. I was back now, and I would make them pay.

The walk back to the castle was far more pleasurable than leaving it had been last night, the weather much more temperate in the daytime than it had been the previous evening. The frost had melted, and the only visible snow was on the very peaks of the mountains.

Something about it irked me. Draconis was far too pleasant for its own good. I knew it was childish, but eighteen years of anger was settling in my stomach, and I wanted everyone to pay. My powers had returned to me and, after eighteen years, were stronger than before.

“I wonder,” I murmured to myself, holding my hand skyward. Controlling the weather had never been my forte, but something told me that today I’d be able to do it. No snow began to fall, but the temperature became noticeably colder.

“Not bad, not bad.” I plunged my hands into my pockets and hiked up toward the forest behind the castle. The snow would come eventually. The magic was there. I just needed to perfect it.

The dragons living up on the mountain peaks would notice, but dragons and humans didn’t mix. I wasn’t worried about what they would do. I didn’t much care either. They could freeze to death for all I cared.

In the forest, I changed my clothing again to that of a palace maid. Getting in would be easy. I’d done it last night with no problem. There were enough servants in any royal household to blend in without being noticed. Getting information, however, would prove much more difficult. Even if I pretended to be new, someone was bound to get suspicious of all my questions. First things, first. Getting into the gardens again was ridiculously easy. I would have thought that they would have more security after what I did to the royal daughter. Briar Rose. What a disgustingly sugary sweet name. I really had nothing against the girl herself, but her parents, the king and queen. They had slighted me more than once, and if there was anything I hated, being made to feel less than I am topped my list. I would not be underestimated. My plan had been to slip into the castle the way I had the night before, but I’d barely taken two steps into the garden when Briar Rose herself appeared. From a distance, she looked different to what I remembered. She headed into the stables. Keeping to the shadows as much as possible, I followed and cracked the door slightly to see what she was up to.

She was talking to someone. Her father, the king...or at least he was dressed as the king, but this wasn't the king at all. It was the scrawny scruff who had chopped through my vines all those years ago. He was older now, thicker around the stomach. He was sitting on a horse dressed in the king's finest furs. And now I came to look upon her, the girl was not Briar Rose at all. So who, exactly, was she?

"Not really. I need to know who it was you wanted me to meet last night. Why all the secrecy?" The girl said, blocking the man's path.

The man sighed. "I didn't want to tell you like this, Azia, but your mother and I think it's time you settled down. I'm so very proud of you, my daughter, but you have your own ideas and plans; and while that is all well and good, it takes ambition and dedication to rule a kingdom. You are spirited, and that's what I love about you the most, but you need someone to guide you. To stand by your side. To help you on your journey."

Could this be the daughter of Briar Rose? Of course. Eighteen years had passed. Briar had married the scruff, and they'd had a daughter. Interesting.

It didn't explain how I'd come to be nothing for eighteen years and how the scruff had managed to get through my vines when no one else could, but it was good information to have. She waffled on like a petulant teen about not wanting to get married yet while her father talked about some man he wanted her to meet. Something struck me as odd about her. Something I couldn't quite put my finger on. It was only when she stormed out of the stables in a snit that I felt it. She didn't see me as she stormed past, but I saw her, and more to the point, I felt her. The power radiating from her was immense. She was magic. Not only that, but her powers were almost as strong as my own. Briar Rose and her parents had never been magic. That was why it had been so easy to enchant them. So where had this girl gotten her powers from? Her father didn't seem likely, but it couldn't be her mother either. I needed to find out about this family, and I wasn't going to be able to do it at the castle. Not with a power like hers around.

I turned away from the stables as the scruff rode out on his horse.

I was going to find out who the girl was and when I had, I was going to destroy her. There was only room for one powerful magic user in Draconis, and that person was me.

3RD DECEMBER
AZIA

Breakfast was a quick affair as it had been almost from the get-go.

"What can I do, Chief?" I looked up to find Lyric grinning down at me from the air. Behind her, Nyre flew a few feet above and considered Lyric with a bemused expression. I think she was a bit miffed with a new member of our group with wings. As if it made her less special somehow, and yet Lyric and Nyre were actually very similar with their impishness and eager-to-please attitude. Nyre also had the eager-to-be-a-pain-in-the-ass attitude at some points, a trait I hoped Lyric didn't share with her.

"Chief?" I asked, giving Lyric a half-smile as I dragged my backpack onto my shoulder.

"Yeah. You said yourself that you are kind of the leader."

I tried not to smile too much. Having Lyric along had made me nervous for all the reasons I'd told Deon the previous day, but it wasn't her fault. Her energy was like a breath of fresh air to the weary group. I glanced at the others as they went about our well-practiced task of getting ready for a day of walking.

"We'll be keeping to the forest for the first part of our journey," I replied to Lyric while packing my bag up. "I doubt we'll fall foul of any of the people after us, but we'll need to keep on our toes, just in case. The Vale is Rumpelstiltskin's stomping ground. Just because he was last seen in Arcadia doesn't mean he won't come back here. Could you fly on ahead, keeping low to the trees and keep a lookout for us? We'll be heading due east from here, so you can fly on ahead half an hour or so and then check in on us around midday."

"I'll keep an eye out for a good place for us to eat and see if I can find us a river or stream to replenish our water."

This time, I let the smile reach my eyes. It seemed that Lyric was going to be an asset to us, after all. Once she'd flown off, Nyre dropped to the ground beside me with a frown on her face. Seconds later, she'd transformed into her half-human self. With her beautiful iridescent scaly legs and her long dark hair, she looked beautiful as she always did when she shifted. She'd grown in the last year. She was sixteen now and becoming a woman. She was also naked.

"I wish you wouldn't do that!" I said, throwing a blanket at her. There was no point in searching through my bag for her clothes. She'd change back into her dragon form as soon as she had grumbled at me.

She wrapped the blanket around herself and pouted. "That's my job," she huffed, pointing to Lyric, who was disappearing over the treetops.

"True," I replied. "I just thought it would be nice to give Lyric something to do. And to give you a rest. Wouldn't you prefer to walk with us for a change?"

She tossed her hair in a way only a teenage girl could do. "Are you crazy? Be stuck down here in this spooky forest instead of soaring with the birds? Plus, I'd have to talk to grumpy one and grumpy two over there."

I looked to where she was pointing, unsurprised to see Castiel and Eliana getting their bags ready.

"Eliana isn't grumpy. She's lost her daughter. You'd be upset too. In fact I remember that you were upset when some of the people back home tried stealing a mother dragon's eggs."

Nyre considered this for a moment. "That was different," she said at last.

"Why?"

"Because they didn't have to deal with Castiel too. Honestly, one of them is bad enough, but both..." She pulled a face.

I shook my head and hoped that Castiel and Eliana hadn't heard Nyre. Not that Castiel would care one way or another what Nyre thought of him, but I knew Eliana already felt a burden to us. Her heartbreak was palpable, and because of our strange magical bond, we all felt it.

"Once we get closer to Urbis, you are going to have to be in your half-human form all the time. You know they are looking out for a group with a purple dragon, and you also know how rare purple dragons are outside of the mountains in Draconis. You aren't exactly inconspicuous. You may as well get used to it."

"No, thanks," Nyre said, throwing the blanket to the ground. Seconds later, she was flying high above me, and my blanket was covered in mud from where she'd thrown it.

I rolled my eyes and retrieved the blanket, tying it onto my backpack to dry rather than putting it inside.

I watched as she flew toward Fallon and Gaia, who were deep in conversation at the front of the group. She landed on Fallon's shoulder as I caught up with Blaise and Halia at the back of the group.

"Hey, Azia," Blaise said when she saw me. "We were just discussing Arcadia."

"Arcadia?" I asked perplexed. We were close to the Arcadian border over a small stretch of Elder land but had no plans to go over it.

"Each of us has someone that wants to bring us down. You have Derillen; I have the sea witch."

"Yes?"

"Well, Halia was just telling me that she didn't really have anyone like that."

I looked over at Halia. "What about Madam and her daughters?"

I'd heard the story. I'd listened over many a campfire to all their stories. It was difficult to keep track with so many of us, but I had the people after us and their abilities locked away in my memory. Once we got to Urbis, I was going to need all the information I could get.

"I have no doubts, Madam wants me dead," Halia replied in that beautiful voice of hers. "She'll be in Urbis along with all the rest of the villains, but she has no power. Not really. She has influence in Arcadia and is wealthy there, but she has no magic. She needed Rumpelstiltskin for that."

I thought about what she was saying. It was true that I didn't rank Madam as a priority to deal with, but I couldn't discount her. "From everything you've told me, she is the master of deception. She can lie and cheat and knows how to get what she wants. That will be valued in this group of theirs. Plus, there are ways to detect magic. She will be able to go places the others can't."

Halia nodded, deep in thought. "The thing I can't seem to get out of my mind is why these evil people would want to team up. They all seem to want power. Why share it with eleven others, and what exactly is it they are up to?"

I didn't have an answer for her. I just knew that whatever it was, it was going to affect everyone in all the kingdoms, and it wasn't going to be good.

After a quick lunch at midday, we set off again.

Castiel took the lead in his panther form, scoping out the ground. Lyric did the same in the air above the treetops, resuming her duties from the previous day. Nyre had mysteriously decided to keep lower to the ground and walk in her part-human form next to Ivy and Fallon.

Again, I took up my place at the back. Something felt off, although I couldn't put my finger on exactly what, so when Castiel offered to take the lead, I agreed. Along with his ability to shift into animal form, he also took on the senses of that particular animal. A panther seemed like a good choice.

As we walked, my feeling of foreboding increased. I felt magic in the air that was foreign to me, and I couldn't get over the feeling that we were being watched or followed. I looked behind us frequently, but there was nothing ever there. As the sun lowered in the sky, the feeling only increased, and I wondered if the wolves had somehow managed to track us or if Derillen had figured out where we were.

My nerves were raw by the time the sun set completely in the sky, and we stopped for a quick dinner of rabbit. I had a feeling the others wanted to set up camp for the evening, but the wolves were still on my mind. I needed to keep walking if only to tire myself out so that I didn't have this feeling of being followed anymore.

Directly in front of me, Eliana walked in small strides, the way she had done right from the start. Of all of us, she was the one that most looked like the princess she was. The rest of us looked...well, filthy. But Eliana made the effort every day to brush her long blonde hair and wash her clothes whenever possible. A few months back, I'd asked her why she cared so much about her presentation when we were literally seeing no one but ourselves and hiking through terrain ranging from muddy bogs to desert. She'd told me she wanted to look the way she'd looked when her baby had been taken so that her daughter would recognize her. Her words had nearly broken my heart, and I'd never asked her again.

"How are you holding up?" I asked, catching up with her. What I wanted to do was to acknowledge how close we were to her parents and her home, but I couldn't get the words out. Asking how she was, was the easiest option.

"I'm fine," she murmured quietly as she always did when anyone asked how she was. Of course, she wasn't fine. We'd all lost someone or something. Some of us permanently, but Eliana was the only one coping with the loss of a child.

"I was thinking of looking for an inn or somewhere

we could bathe soon. It's getting too cold for washing in lakes and rivers like we have done, and if I don't wash my clothes soon, they are going to start to walk all by themselves."

It was meant as an attempt at humor, but it didn't even raise a smile.

"I guess we could," she mumbled, "but how will we manage it without people knowing it's us? Our faces have been in all the papers for months."

"Actually, I've been thinking about this. We probably can't stop at an inn in The Vale because of your kingdom's newspaper."

"The Vale Echo," she interrupted.

"The Echo, right, but in a few days, we'll cross the border into Elder. There are no newspapers there. Castiel tells me that they like to keep to themselves and don't really pay attention to what's going on outside their own kingdom."

As though I was conjuring him up by using his name, in the far off distance, I heard a loud roar that could only be him.

"Castiel!" Eliana whispered quickly. The two of us picked up our speed from the slow amble we'd been doing to a sprint.

Small branches whipped at my face as I ran. It seemed Eliana and I weren't the only ones who had heard Castiel roar. The others had darted off ahead of us, leaving me battling through the undergrowth, not sure which way I was going, with Eliana right behind me.

Eventually, the trees thinned out. I raced out and crashed right into Gaia's back, sending her sprawling into a patch of Bluebells. The flame she'd been conjuring to light the path for us extinguished, and we were plunged into darkness.

"Sorry!" I muttered, holding a hand out to her as Eliana came crashing out of the trees behind me, almost knocking me over as I had Gaia. Gaia held her hand aloft and sent a flame up. It was only when I heard Eliana gasp that I thought to look up to see why we'd all so suddenly stopped.

My mouth dropped open, and I quite forgot I was supposed to be helping Gaia up.

There were many things going through my mind when I heard Castiel's roar. That he'd somehow tripped, fallen into a trap, or been struck by hunters. I even had Derillen pictured in my mind, just randomly sitting in a tree, waiting for us to come through so she could curse us.

What I was not expecting was Castiel, still in his panther form, wrapped around a small child.

JANUARY
DERILLEN

Humans were such easy creatures to mind control. Half a day of asking around town about the girl, and I'd found out rather a lot. Her name was Azia, and she was indeed the daughter of Briar Rose and that scruff who were now the king and queen. As it turned out, she was adopted, which explained why Briar Rose had had a child so soon after waking up from the enchanted sleep. Now at this point, it got interesting. Within days of her waking up, she and the scruff had announced their marriage, and at that point, the entire world had ceased to exist for me. Where I was and in what state, I doubted I'd ever find out, but it was not much later than that, that Azia had been adopted. Finding out where she was adopted from and why so soon after the royal marriage was much harder, but eventually, with a little probing and a lot of magic, I found out that she had been brought here from Urbis. A drunken man in the Dragon Roost Inn had parted with the information, not that he knew it. I'd read his stupid drunken mind and seen the carriage that had brought the brat to the castle when she was a baby. It had an Urbis insignia on it. Where in Urbis she had been born and to whom, I couldn't find out from anyone. It wasn't that people were lying or trying to cover it up; they genuinely didn't know. The scruff himself didn't even know where she had come from. Stopping him on one of his horse rides was all it took to probe his mind. He only knew that Azia had been delivered to the castle under the cover of darkness eighteen years ago. The fool didn't even know that his own daughter was powerfully magic.

Part of me itched to see Briar Rose again. To see what she had become. In truth, I'd never really disliked the girl. It was her parents that had slighted me. I'd only put her into an enchanted sleep to spite them, and now they were both dead. But seeing Briar Rose wouldn't help me. Her daughter was much more interesting to me now.

I booked a ticket on the first Urbis Express to Urbis, determined to find out what exactly it was I was up against. One thing I knew. She had something to do with me losing eighteen years of my life. Hers was the only magic I'd ever come across in Draconis that was strong enough to do such a thing.

On touching down in a busy cobbled square somewhere in Urbis, I inhaled, liking the smell of money, of power, of people. Even these people with their drab lives made me feel something I'd not felt for a long time.

I felt alive. In Draconis, I couldn't show my face. Not my real one for fear of someone recognizing me, but here, here I was free to be me.

Straight ahead, a busy road with shops bustling with people unnerved me. Yes, I enjoyed this new hustle and bustle, but it also served as a stark reminder that I didn't know anyone here, let alone anyone that could help me with my quest. And Urbis was not just a city. It was almost a kingdom all on its own, with the government overseeing everything. The kings, queens, presidents, and mayors of each kingdom had power, but they couldn't do anything without the permission of the government here. All laws had to be approved through the government building in the center.

Just seeing the place made me wonder if worrying about some child in Draconis was worth it.

I'd forgotten how large Urbis was. I was in the large shopping area in Middle Urbis. There was nothing here for me. What I wanted to see was the center of the bull's-eye as the locals called it. The very epi-center of Urbis where the richest, most powerful people in all the kingdoms lived. It was right there that I knew I belonged and right there where the only person I knew in Urbis lived.

As a witch, I had ways and means of traveling not open to mere mortals, but most were conspicuous, so I hopped on the first train that would take me to the very middle of Urbis.

The train itself made me think of a childhood game I'd played when I was young and still had friends, where one of us would hide, and the rest had to find them, then hide in the same place until everything became overcrowded and claustrophobic. My hand twitched with the urge to use magic to just get rid of these people.

There were so many of them. People on their way to work, people heading out for a day trip to take in the sights of Inner Urbis, people with shopping bags, and worse yet, people with kids. Nasty little sniveling brats, poking into everything and getting snot all over the place. But when the train pulled into the magnificent central station in Inner Urbis, my annoyance faded. The white marble of the station with its high ceiling and tall stained glass windows calmed me. This was a place for a queen. Much better than the mountainous hole of Draconis with its peasants and red dust everywhere. Not to mention the dragons. Inner Urbis was a sight to behold and, thankfully, free of dragons.

It had been so many years since I'd ventured here. I was a lot younger then, back when I craved the power of becoming queen of Draconis. I let myself let out a little laugh, which made one of the snot-nosed brats jump in fright. My villainous laugh was coming along nicely. How naive and shortsighted I was back then. There wasn't enough gold in the world that would persuade me to become the queen of Draconis now. From what I'd seen over the past few days, all the royals did was swan around and smile and wave at people. What a bore. No, there was something bigger I'd set my mind on now. The thought had been nagging at me for days, but it only just crystallized in my mind as we pulled into Inner Urbis. This is what I wanted. I wanted to rule Urbis. I wanted to build a palace fit for me right here and rule over the people. Granted, Urbis was not a kingdom as such. There might never have been a royal family of Urbis, but the time was right for them to accept me as their queen. I just needed a little help, and there was one person I knew that would be able to give me the power I needed. The only problem now was how to find him.

4TH DECEMBER
AZIA

Before I had a chance to really register what had happened, Eliana shot past me and scooped the little girl up into her arms. A quick check of my watch told me it had just turned midnight. What was a girl, little more than a toddler, doing alone in the middle of a forest in the middle of the night?

"It's ok, sweetheart," Eliana crooned, holding the little girl as tears fell down the child's face.

"Where did she come from?" Gaia whispered, brushing down her pants from her fall earlier. "We're miles from anywhere."

I did a three-sixty-degree turn. Apart from my siblings

and Nyre, we were completely alone. Beside me, Deon started to root around in his backpack. He pulled out a map of The Vale and laid it out flat on a rock.

"I think we are here," Deon said, jabbing his finger at a spot in the middle of a forest. It looked like we were about as deep in the forest as anyone could go without beginning to head out the other side.

"It's at least a two-day trip in any direction," I pointed out, but truth be told, it was a two-day trip for twelve demi-gods. A family with a small child like this would take much longer.

"How did she even get here?" Blaise asked, stroking the young girl's hair. The little girl snuggled into Eliana even more, hiding her head in Eliana's shoulder. The sobs were beginning to subside as Eliana half-sang, half-whispered a lullaby in her ear.

"And what reason would she have to be so deep within a forest?" Blaise continued. All around me, a sea of faces looked blank.

"Castiel? What happened?" I asked. Jakon quickly grabbed a shirt from Castiel's bag and threw it to him as he changed back into his human form. Castiel nodded gratefully and pulled the shirt over his head before grabbing his backpack from Jakon and extracting his pants.

I never quite knew where to look in times like these. Castiel was my brother and seemed to have no fear of being naked in front of others. He was almost as bad as Nyre in that respect, although he would dress quickly after shifting and not just stand there having a conversation without a stitch on as though it was the most normal thing in the world like my dragon friend tended to do.

I waited patiently for him to dress, then pulled him

away from Eliana.

"I found her like this," Castiel said, casting a furtive glance to where Eliana bounced the child on her hip.

"You roared," I pointed out. "We heard you."

"Yeah, I got the scent of other people. The roar was a warning. I found her sitting crying alone in the middle of this clearing. There was no one else around, so I curled around her to keep her safe and save her from wandering off into a thicker part of the forest."

"Did you get any other scents?" Gaia asked. "We could follow them and find her parents."

Castiel shrugged. "My sense of smell is much better as a wolf, but I didn't register anything other than the girl."

"Doesn't that strike you as odd?" Gaia asked.

I shrugged my shoulders. My entire life had been odd for months. Finding a girl in the middle of the forest was actually quite normal in the grand scheme of things.

"It's getting late," Deon said. "The girl looks well cared for. I say we settle down for the night. Make sure she's fed and warm. Castiel, can you change into a wolf and see if you can find the scent of the girl's parents?"

Castiel nodded, throwing his clothes to the ground and shifting once more. Seconds later, a beautiful wolf stood before us. It seemed that whatever Castiel shifted into, he looked magnificent. He bounded off into the woods ahead of us as we all began to unpack.

I gave a sharp whistle, and both Nyre and Lyric appeared in the sky above us.

"Ready to bunker down?" Lyric asked.

Nyre headed to the center of the clearing where Fallon and Kelis were busy building a fire. They stood back and let Nyre blow fire onto the kindling.

"Boss?"

"Sorry, Lyric. Yes, we are done for the day. Would you mind just having a quick flight over the surrounding area? We have a bit of an issue."

"Sure thing. What am I scouting for?"

I nodded toward the girl who was still wrapped in Eliana's arms.

Lyric's eyes widened. "Who's she?"

I shrugged my shoulders. "That's just it. We don't know. Castiel is out in his wolf form looking for her parents, but it would be great if you could do the same from the air."

Wordlessly, Lyric nodded. She unfurled her wings and took to the sky.

A tap on my shoulder took my attention away from her disappearing above the canopy. I brought my gaze down to find Gaia and Ivy.

"Hey, what's up?"

Gaia looked to Ivy, who nodded. "We think there is something fishy going on with the girl. This forest is hundreds of miles in either direction. You know that from when we walked through it the first time to reach the shores of The Vale to meet Lyric."

"I do know that. I've just sent Lyric to have a scout around for her parents."

Gaia flicked her eyes skyward then brought them back down to mine. "When we were traveling in the other direction, we saw no signs of human life after the first couple of miles. The trails we've taken so far are made by forest animals. There is no reason for a small child to be here."

"There's a road that circumvents the forest," Ivy added. "It's a longer route, but with a horse and carriage, it would knock days off the trek. We didn't take it only because we didn't want to be seen."

"Maybe the girl's parents didn't want to be seen either," I maintained, ignoring the feelings that had been plaguing me all the previous day.

Neither of them looked convinced.

"Ivy and I were wondering if she'd been left here on purpose."

I looked over to the edge of the clearing, where the little girl was now playing a game of pat-a-cake with Eliana. The pair of them were both giggling. It was the first time I'd seen Eliana smile since I'd met her.

"It's certainly strange," I conceded. "Let's go and see if she'll tell us what happened to her."

Eliana pulled the girl close as the three of us headed toward her. It was almost as though she thought we were going to steal the child away from her.

"Eliana, we were just wondering if we could talk to her." I said gently.

Eliana strengthened her hold on the child. I hoped either Castiel or Lyric found her parents soon before Eliana bonded with her too much. We couldn't take a child into the battle we were facing. Just the hike out of the forest would be an ordeal for such a young girl.

"Roberta. Her name is Roberta."

I bent down so I was at the same height as her. She pulled back further into Eliana's lap.

"It's ok, Roberta," Eliana soothed, stroking the girl's curly hair. "This is my sister, Azia, and these are my other sisters, Gaia and Ivy."

I got a little thrill every time someone referred to me as their sister. It still hadn't quite sunk in that I had eleven real siblings. The feeling was short-lived as the girl glared at us in a way that sent a shiver down my spine.

“Roberta,” I spoke softly, trying not to frighten the child. “I’ve asked my other sister and one of my brothers to look for your parents. Do you know where they are?”

The glare left her eyes, turning back to the fear I’d seen when we first found her wrapped in Castiel. Maybe I’d imagined the glare. The girl was so small, she was probably terrified.

She shook her head and brought her thumb to her mouth.

“Did they bring you into the forest?” I probed.

She moved her light brown eyes to Eliana.

“It’s ok, honey. You can tell them. They only want to help.”

Roberta nodded her head.

“That’s a yes? Your momma and papa brought you here?”

Another nod

“Do you know why they brought you here?” Gaia asked, lowering herself next to me.

The girl shook her head. This was getting us nowhere.

“Can you tell us where you are from? Are you from The Vale?”

A nod.

“Eliana, can we have a word with you?” I said, standing up.

“I’d rather stay here. Roberta is scared, and I don’t want to leave her.”

“I’ll look after her,” Gaia volunteered, but Roberta refused to let go of Eliana. It seemed that Roberta had bonded to Eliana as much as Eliana had bonded with her. This was going to get awfully messy if neither Castiel nor Lyric could find her parents soon.

We slept for a few hours until the sun rose in the sky. Roberta slept huddled up right next to Eliana in her blanket.

I barely slept at all and was glad when morning arrived. As the others went about packing up for the day, I took the chance to speak to Roberta again. All I could see of her was her small face peeking out of Eliana's blanket.

"I'll bring you both some food when it's ready," I said, nodding to the campfire where two wild birds roasted on a spit. "Is that ok? You hungry, Roberta?"

The little girl nodded. Eliana smiled and wrapped her arms around the girl.

I left them and took my place around the fire next to Ivy and Halia.

Deon handed us some roots that he'd chopped and placed on a large leaf for each of us.

"An appetizer until the birds are cooked."

I took the berries and snuck a quick look at Eliana and Roberta. Neither was paying any attention to me. "I wanted to talk to you all about the girl," I began quietly. Everyone's eyes turned toward me, and once again, I felt as though everyone expected me to be in charge as if I had some wisdom that they didn't. "She says that she doesn't know where her parents are, but they must have brought her here. She is either unable or unwilling to tell us much more. Eliana is looking after her for now, but the question is, what are we going to do with her?"

"We can't take her with us," Fallon said, taking one of the birds from the fire and replacing it with one of the uncooked ones.

Blaise shot him a look of irritation. "We can't exactly leave her, Fallon. She's like, four years old. She'd be dead within a couple of days."

"I wasn't saying leave her here," Fallon protested. "I

just meant, she can't come with us once we get out of the forest."

"So, what do you suggest?" Blaise asked.

Fallon pulled a piece of the meat from the bones of the cooked bird and handed it to Nyre, who was sitting next to him. "We drop her off at the nearest town. Deon, do you have the maps?"

Deon looked up from the bark he was whittling into powder. "There's a village we passed when we first entered the forest when we were heading to the shore. We walked around so as not to be seen, but it's on the map. If you remember, there were a number of cottages in the forest itself for the first kilometer or so."

Blaise shook her head. "I can't believe this. We can't just dump her with the first person we meet."

It was rare for Blaise to be angry, and it took me by surprise.

I turned my head to see Eliana cuddled up with the child. I had a feeling Eliana wasn't going to let the child go to a stranger either.

I'd let them talk. Now it was my turn. "We won't be leaving this forest for a couple of days. If Castiel and Lyric can't find her family, we take her with us. We can knock at some doors in the cottages at the edge of the forest and see if any of them are missing a child. Maybe she wandered off alone from one of them."

Even to my own ears, it sounded ridiculous. A child so small would not have been able to survive long enough to get to where we found her on her own.

Deon sat forward, tipping all his bark shavings onto the ground in the process. "And what if we don't find her parents?"

I had no idea. I only knew that we couldn't take her with us to Urbis and that Eliana wasn't going to give her up to anyone but her parents.

JANUARY DERILLEN

Much of Urbis looked the same as I remembered it from when I first came here as a young woman. The clean streets, white marble everywhere. The rows of expensive townhouses, four and five stories high, each with a brass nameplate with the surname of the occupants inside. The whole place reeked of wealth and power. The Urbis Tower dominated the skyline from a distance, but in the very center of Urbis, the long Government building next to it overshadowed everything, even the magnificent library that took up one end of the massive cobbled square.

Yes, in the daytime, little had changed, but the nighttime was a different matter.

The nightclub where I'd first met Morpheus had

been turned into a boutique coffee shop that closed at 8pm every night. Morpheus wouldn't be seen dead in a coffee shop. It wasn't his style at all. Not that he would be seen dead anywhere in the literal sense. He was a god, an immortal. He was also one of my oldest friends.

I'd met him for the first time when I was a young woman of nineteen or twenty. He had many women. I wasn't fool enough to think I was special to him, but we fell into something. Not quite a friendship, not quite a relationship. As a young woman away from her home kingdom for the first time, I was mesmerized by him. He was impossibly beautiful, and the magical power emanating from him drove me almost insane. But I could only spend time with him when I could find him. There were many nightclubs in Urbis, and he never went to the same one two nights in a row. Sometimes I went months without seeing him. It almost killed me being away from him, but he was a god, and I was a witch, a not very powerful one at that.

Eventually, I'd returned to Draconis, realizing I had no future with Morpheus. I'd put him to the back of my mind and tried to start a life without him. I'd even fell in love again. It wasn't quite the same passion I had for Morpheus, but then I knew nothing would compare to the breathless beauty of the man-god. The man I'd fallen in love with had left me for the princess of Draconis. She was no prettier than me, no more intelligent. In fact, she didn't hold a candle to me in any way except for one thing. She was the daughter of the king. It was then that I had realized power was everything. I had a little magic, but I had no rich parents. I had no parents at all, growing up as I did in an orphanage. And if power was everything, I was going to fan the flames of my magic and go out there and get it. So at the age when the few friends I had were settling down and having children, ten years after my first visit, I took my second trip to Urbis with the intent of seeing Morpheus again, but that time it wasn't for pleasure,. It was all about business.

It had taken me almost six months to find him, but find him I did. He was in the private room of a very exclusive cocktail bar, surrounded as he usually was, with women.

By then, I'd honed my magic skills so getting into the private room was a lot easier than it had been ten years previously. Morpheus was not particularly surprised to see me. He was the God of Dreams, which meant he knew exactly what I'd been dreaming about if he so desired to take a look. And I dreamed about him often. He was impossible to exorcise from my mind. I didn't harbor any expectation that he'd thought about me since I'd left ten years previously, so I was pleasantly surprised when he threw the other women out and asked how I was coping with the loss of my boyfriend to another woman. Yes, he'd known. He'd been keeping up with my dreams after all

He was the one surprised when I'd spoken of revenge. Even more so when I'd asked for his help.

I still remember how he'd laughed at me until he saw how serious I was.

"Derillen," he'd said, passing me a cocktail. "You've never been the jealous type. I was with scores of women when I was with you, and you didn't mind. What's gotten into you?"

How wrong he'd been. I'd tolerated the other women because I had to if I wanted to spend time with him. I could hardly tell him that seeing him with other girls tore my heart to shreds each and every time.

"He was mine. She stole him. Apparently, she's pregnant with the new heir to the throne."

I'd almost spit the word out, thinking of her with my ex-lover's baby.

Morpheus had sat back, clasping his hands together. "I'm the god of dreams, not war, not vengeance. What is it you wish me to do? Make her sleep? Give her nightmares?"

"You can do that?" I'd asked. He'd been joking, but something had struck a chord with me. Putting my ex-boyfriend or his new wife into a cursed sleep would only hurt one of them...but if I did it to the child. That would bring them both to their knees.

"I wasn't being serious, Derillen. Yes, I make people dream. I can lure them in their sleep to my dreamscape and make it so they don't escape."

"What about a baby?"

It was the first time I'd seen him look at me as though I was crazy. Maybe I was.

"I'm not doing it to a baby!" He'd sounded so firm on the subject.

"Ok then," I'd murmured, running my finger down one of his exquisite legs. "What if I waited until they were older? Seventeen, perhaps? I could make it worth your while..."

Truth was I had nothing to give him, but he was a sucker for beautiful women, and I'd been practicing my abilities to shift my appearance. I was still the Derillen he'd known ten years previously, but my hair was shinier, my waist slimmer, my skin unflawed. I was the best version of myself I could be, and I was perfect. I knew Morpheus well enough to know what he liked and thus the deal was sealed. In exchange for being his girl-du-jour and hanging on his arm at all the exclusive events, not to mention other favours, I was granted one enchanted sleep for the baby. On his or her seventeenth birthday, Morpheus would come to them in their sleep and take them into his dreamscape. Seventeen years would be enough for me to figure out a way to make sure everyone knew it was me that had conquered the castle and everyone in it. And I'd done it. I'd made it known to all of Draconis that the little boy or girl would become enchanted on their seventeenth birthday. No one needed to know about Morpheus. They would all think it was me. I'd concocted some rubbish about a spindle and they all believed it. The massive bramble bush that surrounded the palace. That was all me. It had been great until that scruffy oaf had come along and kissed her. That was over eighteen years ago and now there was another brat to deal with.

And so I was here again, in the middle of Urbis, looking for Morpheus. I wasn't twenty anymore. I wasn't thirty either. Over a hundred years had passed since I'd last seen him but my abilities were stronger than ever. I much preferred to look like myself, but Morpheus wouldn't want to be seen with an old woman, not even one as beautiful as I was.

I shook my perfectly shiny hair, smacked my red lips together, throwing the doorman a wink, and stepped into the first nightclub I'd found in the hope that Morpheus would be there.

5TH DECEMBER
AZIA

I woke up to the first morning where the weather was so cold, I could see my breath. The light had just begun to filter through the trees marking yet another day in the forest, but instead of thirteen of us, there were now fourteen.

I searched the ground for Roberta. She was tucked up in Eliana's arms, her thumb in her mouth. She really was a cute kid, but after a night of tossing and turning over the problem, I was no closer to solving it. Castiel hadn't sniffed out her parents, nor anyone else. Bizarrely, he'd managed to smell our lingering scents from when we'd passed through in the opposite direction over a week previously. Strange then that he couldn't smell anyone else. Not even the child on the path in either direction. It was as though she had appeared from nowhere.

Around me, the others slept. Castiel had taken to sleeping in his wolf form over the past few nights as it kept him warmer. It was great in one way because it meant we had an extra blanket to share, but it also meant he woke up starving and had to eat before he'd do literally anything. His appetite was twice that of the rest of us when he was constantly changing between forms. Nyre was always hungry too, but most of the time, she hunted her own food.

"I don't like it," Castiel grunted as we began our day's trek through the forest. Eliana was walking just behind Jakon and Halia, so she was well out of earshot. "She wasn't brought there. I would have smelled it." It was a recurring theme of what he'd said to me the day before after Eliana had curled up with Roberta and gone to sleep.

"I agree with Castiel," Gaia added. "It's a little too strange for my liking. If someone left her, Castiel would have smelled them. If she'd somehow managed to survive for nights and nights on her own and walk hundreds of kilometers..."

"Which is unlikely," I butted in.

"Impossible," Castiel corrected.

Gaia waited for us to be quiet, then continued. "If all that had managed to happen, Castiel would have smelled her scent on the track at either side of the clearing."

"I know all that," I said, feeling a little picked on. "I spent all night turning it over in my mind. I don't understand it either. I began to wonder if she'd somehow fallen. Unicorns fly in this area, don't they?"

"The best person to ask about Unicorns is Eliana,"

Gaia pointed out. She was right, but it didn't make me want to ask Eliana. I wasn't sure how she'd take the theory of Roberta being dropped by a unicorn. Besides, if the girl had fallen, wouldn't she be injured in some way? I'd not looked at her too closely, but she appeared to be perfectly healthy.

"I'm not sure what to tell you. I can't leave a four-year-old girl alone in the middle of the forest to die."

"If that's what she is," Gaia replied cryptically.

"What do you mean?"

"Things are not always what they seem. You should know that better than anyone. Look at us. We all look human, and yet we all have our powers. Some of those are the power to change the way we look. Fallon and Castiel here, for example."

"She's a little girl!" Eliana spat, making the three of us jump. She'd slowed down and let the others pass her so she could listen to our conversation, guessing rightly that it was about Roberta. "Stop talking about her as though she is some kind of monster."

"Eliana," Gaia said, her voice calm and even. "I'm not saying she's a monster. We just don't know how she got to the clearing, that's all. It has me worried."

"I know. You all talked about her last night, but there is no need to worry. I'm looking after her."

I raised my eyebrows.

"She's with Jakon right now," Eliana answered my unasked question. "She let him carry her while I came back to talk to you."

"We were wondering if she might have fallen from a unicorn somehow," I said. "Did she mention unicorns at all? It would explain everything."

"She hasn't spoken at all," Eliana replied.

"Not at all?" I said, confusion rippling through me.

"She told you her name."

"Actually, she didn't. I guessed it."

"You guessed her name?" Gaia asked. I could hear the disbelief in her voice.

"I went through a list of traditional Valean names, and when I said Roberta, she nodded."

Gaia and Castiel exchanged a look.

"How about I go and walk with Roberta for a while?" I said. It would give me a chance to keep an eye on her.

The little girl was sitting on Jakon's shoulders, squealing with joy as he produced teeny tiny tornadoes in the palm of his hands.

When she saw me, she gave me the same menacing look that she'd given me the night before. It morphed back into a smile when she saw Eliana next to me.

"Mama!" she cried and leaned over to her.

Jakon had to almost grab her to stop her from falling off her shoulders as Eliana took the girl into her own arms.

"Mama?" I whispered.

Eliana beamed with joy. She'd never heard her own daughter call her by that name, and I could see she was lapping it up. I also noticed that she didn't contradict the girl.

Something about the child concerned me no end, but now that she was in Eliana's arms, she looked like any other kid. She was as cute as a button. With one hand, she gripped onto Eliana, gripping her around the neck as she balanced on Eliana's hip. With her other, she put her thumb back into her mouth. My younger brothers back in Draconis were not so much younger than me that I remembered at what age they stopped sucking their thumb, but this girl looked a little old for it. Almost as though she was trying to look even younger than she was.

There was just something about her. It hadn't gone without notice that she looked like Eliana with her blonde hair and big eyes. Maybe she looked like Fae would look when she was older. It was all a little too perfect, and in that case, it wasn't perfect at all. If she was just a little girl who had been left in the middle of the forest somehow, taking her with us would slow us down and, worse still, put her in danger.

Eliana was a demi-god, so carrying a small child was easy for her, but I could see that she was tiring after carrying the girl for so long.

"Would you like to walk?" I asked Roberta. I figured she was old enough to walk alongside us for a while.

The way she looked at me, her eyes narrowed, made my blood run cold.

"I'm fine carrying her," Eliana said, glancing over her shoulder to me."

I let them walk ahead until Gaia caught up with me.

"We need to keep an eye on her," was all I said.

The walk through the forest was uneventful. I'd come to treasure the days like this because I knew how short-lived they were. Once we were out in broad daylight again, steering clear of the main roads and the towns and cities, every day could bring us into life and death situations, and despite my own personal feelings on the girl, I'd hate if anything happened to her because of us.

When the evening came upon us, we once again set up camp, the way we had done hundreds of times. The clearing we found was not as big as the one the night before, but it was ample for us all to sleep in.

This time I asked everyone to sit around the fire.

"I'll take Roberta and sit over here where it's quiet," Eliana said.

"Actually, I was hoping you'd join us tonight." I turned to one of my brothers. "Jakon, would you mind watching Roberta for us. We'll bring some food over for the both of you."

Eliana was reluctant to let Roberta go. When the little girl screamed out for her the second Jakon picked her up, I saw the pain in Eliana's face. Roberta screamed 'Mama, mama over and over again with tears streaming down her cheeks and her little face going red with the effort.

She'd been fine with Jakon earlier, but now she fought to get out of his arms. I'd picked Jakon to watch her because he had so many younger siblings. He was used to dealing with small kids. As I watched, I saw him trying to soothe her, but nothing was calming her.

Eventually, she quietened as Jakon sat her on his knee at the edge of a clearing and began producing snow above their heads. It was his new trick, one he'd been practicing for a couple of weeks, a pointless one as there would be plenty of real snow soon enough.

Eliana visibly calmed down when Roberta stopped screaming, but I noticed her eyes flicking over to her often.

"I'd like to discuss Roberta," I began. "I know you've all had your own thoughts, and I know she came to us under mysterious circumstances, but the truth of the matter is, we can't take her to Urbis. It's way too dangerous."

"She can come home with me," Eliana blurted out. "When we reach the edge of the forest, I'll call for Zacharina, and she can fly us both home." Zacharina was the unicorn that had made most of the journey with us. She'd only left when we entered The Vale so she could visit her own daughter, Epiphany.

"No!" Blaise, Deon, and Halia chorused.

"What do you mean, take her home with you?" Ivy asked. "What about the reason we are on this trip. What about Fae? You can't have forgotten about her, surely."

Eliana stood, and I braced myself for her anger. She showed it so rarely, but when she did, it was fierce. "Of course, I've not forgotten about Fae, I've thought of nothing but my daughter since the day she was born, but I've been walking for months. That's it. Just walking. Following you all from one place to the next, not getting any closer to finding her. We've not had a single lead. Not one. She's gone. We might never find her. She's probably dead by now."

Tears flowed down her face, and she began to look a little like Roberta had just minutes before, but her eyes were ablaze with anger, the gold in them like a halo around her irises.

"She's not dead, Lia," I said, calling her by her nickname. "I can feel her thread of magic. It binds her to us."

"Yeah. You told me that the first time we met. So where is she, huh?"

I didn't know what to say. I had no clue where Fae was any more than she did, but I knew she was alive and out there somewhere. I believed we'd find her in Urbis, but there was no point bringing that up again. she already knew my thoughts on everything.

"Roberta is a little girl who needs her parents," I reminded her. "They are out there looking for her."

Ok, I had no idea if that was true, but I had to have her see sense. Roberta couldn't be a surrogate daughter to take the place of Fae. On top of that, we needed Eliana. We were the strongest when we were all together. With each of us that had joined the group, our strength had increased. Take one away, and our power would be diminished.

"You know what it's like to lose your child," I continued, hoping I wasn't fanning the flames of her anger. "You know the pain in her parents' hearts and what they must be going through. If you take her to your palace, they might never find her."

"My father will put up posters all over the kingdom," Eliana said, uncertainty in her voice.

"What about Fae? Are you giving up on her?"

If she went ahead with her plan and left us at the edge of the forest, she would never find us again. We'd become very good at keeping away from people. Her father only had so much power, and even then, only in The Vale. Once we left the forest, it wouldn't be long before we crossed the border to Elder, where we would enter the forest once again.

"I can't save her," she whispered, then strode over to where Roberta and Jakon were sitting.

"What are we going to do now?" Castiel huffed.

I shrugged. "We can't force her to come with us. We are all here of our own volition. If she wants to take Roberta back to her home, then I think we have to let her."

I saw the disappointment in many of their eyes. I could see that they were expecting me to come up with some plan to keep Eliana with us, but the truth was, I couldn't think of one. If anything, it might be the best solution. If we took Roberta from her, she'd never forgive us. We'd have to get through this without her, and with any luck, find Fae for her. If she did find Roberta's parents, then that was a bonus.

"Do you think it's safe to let her go home alone?" Gaia asked, twirling her long braid through her fingers

I sighed. “We’ve wasted so much time. We can’t change our plans and trek north to The Vale’s capital city. She is putting herself in danger, but she will get there quickly with Zacharina. Her parents have plenty of guards that will protect her once she’s there.”

Castiel lifted a brow. “Like they did when Fae was kidnapped.”

“What do you want me to do, Castiel?” I snapped back, thoroughly sick of the whole situation.

“I don’t know,” he said, running his hands through his hair and standing up. “Just something. She can’t leave.”

“I don’t think she can stay either,” I responded, but it was pointless. Castiel didn’t want to hear it. He pulled his clothes off quickly and changed back into his wolf form before galloping into the woods.

“He’ll be back,” Halia assured me, putting her arm over my shoulder. I hadn’t realized how shaken I’d been over the whole thing until Halia’s soothing tones sent calmness through my body.

“I know. He just needs to let off steam.” I pulled my legs toward myself, hugging my knees. “We should probably plan our next course of action once Eliana leaves. It’s starting to get really cold at night, and I was thinking of sending Fallon into the town at the edge of the forest to buy us all some blankets.”

“Stinging nettles, Azia! Won’t that look a little suspicious?” Deon asked. “Even if he does change his appearance. The people will be on the lookout for things like people bulk buying blankets. We need a better plan.”

I hated it when everyone questioned me. It wasn’t as though anyone else was coming up with anything else. We had to come up with something more intricate, that was true, but I was tired and all out of ideas.

Castiel came back later with a young deer, which we skinned and ate. It was the best meal we'd had in weeks and a far cry from the rabbit and wild birds we usually ate. While we filled our bellies, I listened to the others discussing our next move and concocting an elaborate plan to get us the supplies we needed to get us through the next couple of months. It really hit home just how difficult our lives were about to become.

It was only when we were cleaning up our plates, that I noticed Roberta watching us. She was not in the circle, but she was close enough to hear every word we said. I wondered if she'd been listening the whole time. The self-satisfied grin on her face told me she had. It also made me wonder why a four-year-old child would care.

JANUARY DERILLEN

It took most of the night, but I found him in a small club for the powerful and elite. My powers were much stronger than they had been the last time we met. After all, it was over a hundred years ago. It was because of my magic I found him. Everyone's magic had a trail, and his was no different. I'd not been able to sense it all those years ago, but I could now. I could almost taste it, a lingering taste of hot spices, vanilla, and the bittersweet, delicious tang of magic. I followed it from club to club until I found him.

Before I was escorted into the club (Thanks to a little magical hoodwinking of the door staff), my stomach gave a little flutter.

I took a deep breath and gulped it down. I wasn't

a young girl anymore. I wasn't even a thirty-year-old. I'd been around a long time. I was too old for flutters. I didn't want Morpheus anymore. I needed him, yes, but only for his power, not for his body. Those days were long behind me.

I stood up tall and followed the doorman through to a private lounge. The lights were low, and the little I could see was softened by cigar smoke.

What I found surprised me. I'd barely ever seen Morpheus without a bevy of scantily clad women hanging onto his every word, but the only women here were seated at the table as he was. They were his equals, or as close to equal a god and a mortal could ever be. Cards. Poker if I were to guess, but I'd never been the gambling type. I liked to have the odds stacked in my favor in all things, and gambling meant there was a possibility I could lose. I didn't like to lose. Standing at the door in the shadows, I recognized a couple of the people at the table. One of the women was a prominent politician; one of the men was a famous actor that refused to perform anywhere but in the Urbis Central Theater, the biggest and most famous in all the lands. And so he was cast in absolutely everything whether there was a part for him or not. The others I didn't know, but the whole place stank of power and influence and money if the giant stacks of the stuff were anything to go by.

But I cared for none of that. My eyes fell on one person and one person only. Morpheus. He hadn't aged a day, and I'd forgotten how breathtakingly beautiful he was. I'd not prepared myself for the way my pulse started to race at the mere sight of him. I'd thought I was over him a long time ago. It turned out, I was wrong. When he looked up from his cards and laid his eyes on me, my breath hitched in my throat, and his stare cut through me like a knife.

He gave a smile that I was sure wasn't good for poker and laid his cards out on the table.

"Ladies, Gentlemen. I fold. Have a good evening."

I'm pretty sure the other people around the table were astonished by their sudden good fortune. I didn't know poker, but I felt the excitement around the room as the biggest stack of gold was now up for grabs.

"Not a good hand?" I whispered as he grabbed my hand and pulled me out of the poker room and into a dark corridor.

"A Royal Flush but friends are more important."

"Friends?" I asked, raising an eyebrow as he pinned me to the wall. His breath warmed my cheek, and his lips flittered so close to mine I could almost taste them. Who was I kidding? Morpheus had me weak at the knees even now after all these years.

He grinned lazily, his hand on the wall above my head, and his eyes teasing me. "I've missed you, Derillen," he whispered, his voice husky. He pulled back and took my hand again, leading me along the corridor and into a private room. A lone chaise lounge sat at one end of the room, and apart from the large chandelier in the center, which was currently unlit, and an exquisite rug on the floor, almost certainly from Badalah, the room was quite empty. A faint red light glowed from somewhere, making it almost womblike.

Morpheus held his hand out and gestured to the chaise. I sat upon the velvet softness and folded my hands on my knees. To do anything else would show the slight tremor in them. I couldn't show him any weakness. Not even the type that told him I was still wildly attracted to him. I hated how my lips suddenly felt too dry, causing me to have to lick them. I hated how the flutter in my chest was back and now, like the flutter of a butterfly's wings, felt like it could cause hurricanes. I hated that only five minutes ago, I'd been a mature, confident woman, one of the most powerful women in Draconis, whose magic was barely surpassed, and now I felt like a gauche schoolgirl who couldn't seem to get enough air in her lungs.

I needed to get a grip!

"It's been a long time, Derillen. I didn't think I'd see you again."

"Nor I you, Morpheus," I lied. He knew I'd be back to him like a moth to a flame. I couldn't stay away. A hundred years meant nothing when you were a god.

He smiled and kissed my cheek, sending a shiver down my spine. "How have you been? I heard that your scheme didn't quite pan out the way you wanted it to."

"No," I admitted, trying to regain my composure. "That's why I'm here. The curse was supposed to last forever. No one, but you or I should have been able to break it."

He looked at me with an almost bemused expression. "Are you suggesting I had something to do with your downfall?"

Urgh, I hated how he knew everything through my dreams that I had no control over. "No... I..."

"I'm joking, Derillen. I have an idea what caused your problems, and I assure you it wasn't me."

I sat forward, closer to him, our hands almost touching. I batted down my ridiculous feelings and concentrated on what he had to say. This was the reason I was here in the first place.

"You know how that scruffy man-child got through my thorns and woke Briar Rose?"

He laughed, which irked me.

"I don't see why this is funny, Morpheus. I was banished. At least I think I was. I don't know what happened to me. It was like I wasn't there anymore. I've been nothing...less than nothing for the past eighteen years."

He raised an eyebrow at this. It was clear it was new information to him.

"By scruffy man-child, I'm assuming you mean the King of Draconis. Briar Rose's father gave him the position as a thank you for saving the kingdom."

"But how did he save the kingdom?" I asked, trying to keep the irritation from my voice. "He was a nothing. He was barely more than a boy. My brambles were infallible!"

"Clearly not."

"Mmm," I growled, to which Morpheus laughed.

"He had help, Derillen. The man-child was only ever that. A man. A normal man."

"Who helped him?" I demanded. "Who is more powerful than me?"

He held his hands out and smiled, lifting an eyebrow over one of those gorgeous cerulean eyes of his with a ring of gold around the iris.

"Ok, apart from you." I smiled back, trying to match the cocky way in which he looked at me so I didn't turn into a puddle at his feet. This was not going the way I'd planned. Not at all.

"I'm not the only god, Derillen. You know that. There are many of us."

Now it was my turn to be surprised. "A god helped him? Why would a god help a guy from Draconis?"

"I doubt it was intentional. If I'm right in my thinking, the person who helped him didn't even know him. She was a newborn baby."

If he wasn't so utterly beautiful, I'd have walked out right then and there, but I couldn't bring myself to move from the chaise, let alone walk out the door. He was teasing me. Or was he? "You've lost me...and I need a drink."

He waved his hand, and a couple of drinks appeared in his hands, one of which he handed to me.

I took a sip. Neat whiskey.

"I'm a god," he started.

"I know."

"I've made mistakes. Being immortal does not mean I'm infallible. I'm also not the only god that comes into the mortal realm occasionally. It is rare, but sometimes, some of the others do too. Rumor has it that on one such occasion, the goddess Aphrodite came to this mortal land for the first time after having an argument with her father, Zeus. I heard whispers of a pregnancy between her and a mortal. She kept it secret. Her father would have banished her from the realm of the gods had he found out. He would have killed her child had he known. Of course, I only heard this from mortals, so it could be nothing more than malicious gossip, but it fits."

"This child was the one that helped the King of Draconis? Why? How? I still don't understand." I downed the glass of whiskey and let Morpheus fill it up again. I couldn't for the life of me figure out what some goddess and her half-mortal child would have to do with the royal family of Draconis.

"Not quite. Aphrodite is the goddess of love. She's also the goddess of fertility. One night. One drunken mistake. She became pregnant with twelve children. Twelve demi-gods."

I goggled at him. I couldn't even begin to imagine the physics involved in such a thing.

"Go on..."

"It was unprecedented. And no one knew—at least, none of the gods. I'm not sure how many humans knew. Anyway, as long as Aphrodite stayed in the human realm, she would stay safe and keep her children safe."

"How did she keep the birth of twelve children secret?" I never thought I'd ever have to ask such a ridiculous question.

"She gave birth in Outer Urbis. People there tend to keep to themselves."

Well, that made sense. I could imagine an immortal coming to Inner Urbis where everything was beautiful and perfect, and the people were wealthy and attractive. But Outer Urbis was hardly on the vacation list for anyone with any class, let alone gods. It was the perfect spot to hide a burgeoning belly.

"I still don't know what this has to do with me or Briar Rose. Nor does it tell me how you know all this. If it was such a big secret, how did you come to know?"

He slowly swirled the whiskey around in his glass. "When a god is born, an incredible amount of power is released. These children are only demi-gods, but there are twelve of them. I felt the power ripple through Urbis the day they were born. Even the mortals felt it, although they didn't know what it was. At the time, I didn't know of Aphrodite's situation. I barely knew Aphrodite at all, prefering as I did to keep to the human realm and my dream world. I'd heard a rumor that some guy had come into a bar drunk, boasting that he had slept with Aphrodite herself. Of course, I dismissed it as the drunken ramblings of an idiot, but after feeling that ripple of power course through the world nine months later, I put two and two together. The idiot mortal didn't know what he'd done, but I understood power like that. It was then I headed back to the realm of the gods. Aphrodite hadn't been home in months. Nine, to be exact. Finding her was easy. Back in this realm, I followed the epicenter of this new power. It radiated out in waves. I found Aphrodite and her babies in a small house in Outer Urbis. She begged me not to tell Zeus or any of the other gods. I kept my promise. You are the first person in eighteen years that I've told that story to." He downed his whiskey in one gulp.

"I still don't understand what this all has to do with me."

"Don't you get it yet?" he said, leaning in closer to me. "Can you not work it out from the timing?"

I shrugged my shoulders, suddenly feeling foolish. I'd never met Aphrodite. Morpheus was the only god I'd ever met. How should I be able to figure this all out?

"When those children were born, the power they gave out took all the bad from the world. I'm not ashamed to say they diminished my own power for a while. That's why your Briar Rose was able to be woken by a kiss. That's why the king of Draconis was able to get through your brambles. It was nothing to do with you. It never had been. This thing affected everything throughout all the kingdoms. It affected everyone. You were collateral damage, so to speak. If you are looking for the person who banished you, you will have to find the children."

My mind struggled to take in everything. I'd been made into nothing by a bunch of newborns? It would have been bad enough to find out it was another powerful witch or sorcerer that had done that to me, but twelve babies who had only just taken their first breaths? I despised snot-nosed babies at the best of times.

"Where are these children?"

Morpheus laughed again, and I hated him for it. It was okay for him. So he'd felt a diminishing of his power. Big deal. I'd completely ceased to exist.

"You surely don't care?" he asked lazily. "They didn't do anything to you on purpose. Besides, they won't be children anymore. This all happened eighteen years ago."

"They almost killed me," I screeched. "Worse. I had no mind, no body. I stopped existing. Where are they?"

"I don't know," He replied, holding his hands out, palms upward. He looked like he was telling the truth, but then again, I'd just taken him from a game of poker in which deception was the name of the game. "I have no fight with Aphrodite. I only went to her out of curiosity, no more. I kept her secret, and that's it. I only know she returned to the realm of the Gods not long after the birth and has been there ever since."

Anger and frustration bubbled up inside me. "You must know where they are! If they are not in the Gods' realm, then they are here somewhere. They could be in Inner Urbis, right now!"

Morpheus stroked his chin. "They could be, yes. After the massive burst of power that allowed me to track them to Outer Urbis after they were born, everything changed. All the kingdoms were filled with light and beauty. People were happier. Wars, feuds, squabbles, they all came to an end. The world has known peace for eighteen years. Their power diminished and was spread out not long after they were born. Within a few weeks, I couldn't feel it anymore. but..."

"But what? Tell me!"

"I've felt it returning. It's not strong enough for me

to find them, and to be honest, Derillen, I have no compulsion to do so, but they are getting stronger. They are adults now. They are Demi-gods. Their power will far outshine yours. I sense they are apart, but if they get together, they will outshine all of us. Even me."

"If you won't tell me where they are..." I started, standing up.

"I can't tell you, Derillen. I don't know where they are. I've not known what became of them since the day they were born."

"So tell me where they were born."

Morpheus sighed. "Thirty-eight Maplechase Drive. What exactly do you plan to do, Derillen?"

"I don't know yet, but I can't have a bunch of kids out there thinking they can defeat the mighty Derillen. I'm going to stop them if it's the last thing I do."

And with that, I turned my back on Morpheus for the last time. If he wasn't going to help, I'd find someone else that would.

6TH DECEMBER
AZIA

The wind sent my hair flying out behind me and filled my lungs with crisp cold air. The treetops appeared as though they were nothing more than tiny bushes from this height. They spread out n the distance as far as the eye could see behind us, but in front, almost a day's hike away, the trees came to a stop, and the easiest part of our journey would be over. I'd elected to take a flight with Nyre with the excuse that I needed to scope out where we were heading, but the truth was, I'd heard nothing but squabbling all morning. Up until now, the others had trusted me. Every time I'd met a new sibling, they'd instinctively known who I was. Our connection was undeniable. But in the last few days, the monotony of the walk, compounded by Roberta joining us, had created dissension within us and slowed us down, making everyone cranky. Even Eliana, who was usually by far the kindest one among us, had become unbearable and snappy. It was like the longer she carried Roberta, the moodier she got.

After flying as long as I could get away with, I asked Nyre to take me back to the group. It wasn't too difficult to find them. I could hear their raised voices rippling through the forest.

"What's going on?" I demanded as Nyre dropped me down in the middle of the group.

A quick count told me that at least half of them were missing.

"Why don't you ask her," Halia screeched, pointing at Gaia.

Gaia growled. "I didn't do anything. It's hardly my fault that you weren't looking where you were going."

"Looking where I was going? Your sash, or whatever it is, was trailing on the ground, and now I have scratches on my arms." Halia lifted up her arms to show me to prove her point.

"I said I'd use some ointment on it, but you didn't want me to, so you may as well shut up about it," Gaia retorted in a very un-Gaia-like manner.

I massaged my temples and suppressed a sigh. Gaia never usually talked like that. And Halia, like the rest of us, had suffered her fair share of bumps, bruises, and scrapes over the past few months. This was the first time she'd ever complained about it.

"Who's carrying the first aid packs today?" I asked, feeling like I'd just landed in a school playground.

"Deon has one, but he went off in a snit over something or other, and Ivy has the other, but I don't know where she is either," Halia replied sulkily.

As well as Halia and Gaia, Fallon, Jakon, and Blaise were among the group. Eliana was also there holding onto Roberta as though she was a newborn instead of a four-year-old child, perfectly capable of walking. Something about the way she held her annoyed me, though I couldn't put my finger on why.

"We are supposed to stick together," I said. "Being apart is dangerous."

"Says the woman who went for a pleasure flight this morning," Fallon snapped, folding his arms. "How come you always get to do what you want, and the rest of us have to follow along like puppies?"

"Because you don't have a dragon, pretty boy," I snapped back irritably. "Find yourself one, and you can fly whenever you like!"

It was a ridiculous thing to say. Not even Nyre would be able to fly once we were out of the forest. We couldn't afford for her to be recognized. Irritation bubbled through me as Fallon turned on his heels and stormed off along the path. Nyre shot me a look of contempt and flew after him. What had gotten into everyone today?

These small arguments were all well and good while we were hiding in the forest, but once we were out in the open air, these little things could be the difference between being caught or saving all the kingdoms. We couldn't work if we couldn't stick together and work as a team. The old adage that we were only as strong as our weakest link was all too true, and in our case, our weakest link at the moment was Eliana. It was she who demanded we take Roberta with us. I turned my eyes to the little girl. She grinned back at me, and I wondered why she found all this squabbling so entertaining.

I let them all go on ahead while I waited to see who

was behind us. Lyric was flying ahead, and Castiel was doing his job of keeping to the front in his wolf form. As for Deon, Ivy, and Kelis, I had no idea where they were. I should have whistled Nyre to come back so she could go look for them in case they were injured, but she had taken Fallon's side over mine, and I was past the point of caring. I'd done so much for them all, and all they ever did was complain. When the others were out of sight, I took up the rear, purposely keeping back so I could walk alone. Who cared where Deon, Ivy, and Kelis were? They were adults. They could figure out where to find us. They knew we'd be setting up camp before we hit the edge of the forest.

As it was, it turned out I was last to hit the camp, and Deon, Ivy, and Kelis were already there.

Everyone was there doing what they had to do, but the silence as they worked was palpable. Usually, we chatted as we did the tasks needed to set up camp, but the only sounds were the sounds of the forest—small animals skittering through the undergrowth and birds nesting in the trees above.

Ivy, Blaise, Jakon, and Kelis sorted out the beds and blankets, putting them around the fire as Nyre lit the small pile of branches in the center. Castiel and Gaia skinned some small rodents that Castiel had, no doubt, caught for our dinner. Fallon sorted berries and leaves under Deon's watchful gaze. Halia, Lyric, and Jakon set up basic traps on the path ahead to alert us to any intruders in the middle of the night, and I began doing the same on the path we'd just come from.

Eliana sat watching us work as she played with Roberta. Yet again, she was not helping, so the rest of us were picking up her slack. Roberta stuck her tongue out at me, and it took everything I had not to return the gesture. Above me, something rustled the leaves of a tree. For a second, I thought I saw the shape of a man, but I blinked, and it was gone. An owl flew from the branches and took to the sky. I was so tired; I was seeing things that weren't even there.

"I don't know what's happening to me," I whispered to Nyre as she landed beside me. "I'm irritated by everything and everyone. I'm just so tired and sick of everything."

Nyre gave me an expression as if to say "welcome to my world," but she didn't shift into her half-human form so we could have a real conversation. In this whole journey spanning nearly a year, this was the first time I felt alone. Even with Nyre beside me and my eleven siblings working together nearby, I had no one to talk to. Every single one of them was getting on my nerves. I missed Milo. I missed him so much it hurt. I missed my parents, my brothers. I even missed Caspian. He was an insufferable ass, but at least I could converse with him. When I didn't want to kill him, that was.

Forgoing dinner, I lay down on my blanket and pulled it around me so it covered my head. I was behaving like a petulant child, but I wasn't the only one. Usually, dinnertimes were our time to chat, to make plans, to tell each other of our individual histories. Halia would play her guitar and sing, bringing the woodland creatures out to listen. Kelis would give us a light show with her wand. Tonight though, no one spoke beyond Deon complaining that he'd misplaced his journal, and it wasn't long before I heard them all crawl into their own blanket beds.

An owl hooted, jerking me awake. Our makeshift alarms were nothing more than bits of string across each path with bells tied to them. Simple but effective.

Sure, they'd woken us a few times when they'd been set off by animals or the wind, but that proved they worked. I listened out for the telltale jangle of the bells, but all I could hear was the sounds of various soft snores and the gentle breathing of my siblings. And yet the hair on the back of my neck tingled. I sat up and narrowed my eyes to try and see anything amiss in the dim light of the stars. The fire had long since burned out, and the dusty glow of fading embers was not enough to cut through the dark. Behind me, a twig snapped close by. I jumped up, grabbing my sword, and spun on the spot. In front of me, stood a dark figure. I almost plunged my sword right through her before I realized it was Kelis. Her eyes widened as she caught sight of the sword between us.

"Kelis!" I hissed. "You almost gave me a heart attack. What is it?"

She beckoned me away from the group to a fallen log just outside of the clearing upon which she sat.

"I had a dream!"

If any of the others had said that, I'd have rolled my eyes, but Kelis's dreams always meant something. She'd only been with us just over a month, but her dreams and visions had helped us more than once. She'd seen a bobcat in a vision, enabling us to ready ourselves for it. She'd predicted we'd meet Lyric on the shores of The Vale rather than in Skyla itself.

"What was it?" I whispered, deliberately keeping my voice down. I didn't want to wake the others.

"It's Roberta." There was fear in her eyes as she spoke.

I knew it. I knew there was something weird about her and the way she had just appeared from nowhere.

"What about her?" I asked, casting my eyes over to where the little girl slept in Eliana's arms. They both looked so peaceful.

"Someone kills her. I saw her with a sword in her belly. There was blood everywhere. Eliana was covered in it. And her screams! They will haunt me, Azia!"

Whatever I was expecting, that wasn't it.

"Who kills her?" I asked a little too loudly. One of the others stirred. Kelis waited until all was quiet again and whispered back.

"I don't know. I didn't see. Eliana was absolutely destroyed by it."

"And Roberta was definitely dead?" I swallowed back thickly, feeling sick at the thought of it. And by a sword. That meant a person was going to do it to her.

Kelis nodded. "I'm pretty sure she was."

"What about Eliana? Was she hurt?"

"I think the blood was all Roberta's, but it was hard to tell. Eliana was definitely alive in my dream. She was holding Roberta in her arms, and the sword was still sticking out of the girl. I didn't see anyone else in the dream."

"Does this happen soon?" I asked, not really wanting to know the answer.

Kelis nodded slowly. "We were still in the forest."

I looked back over to where the little girl slept soundly. If Kelis was right, she had less than two days left to live.

JANUARY DERILLEN

This part of Urbis made me want to vomit. The houses built higgledy-piggledy with no thought to style or structure. It was as far away from the beautiful architecture of Inner Urbis as Draconis was, but at least Draconis had the majestic mountains and fresh air. The air in Outer Urbis was far from fresh. Swishing my purple cape over my shoulders, I walked over the cobbles of a street, laughingly named Maplechase Drive. The street was much rougher than the name suggested, and though there was the odd maple tree, it would have suited the name Falling-into-Disrepair Road, or Stinks-Like-Lack-of-Money Boulevard.

This couldn't be right. No goddess in her right mind

would choose to give birth in a place like this. Not with all the power that the gods possessed. This Aphrodite goddess could have chosen literally anywhere to have her children. The famous Urbis Maternity Hospital, for instance. Considered the best in all the kingdoms, it was where most of the rich and famous chose to have their children.

As I walked down the street, the suspicion that Morpheus was teasing me somehow, that this was his idea of a joke, began to dwell upon my mind. He knew how I felt about places like this. But Morpheus wasn't one to joke. This actually had to be the right place. A man with a beard and glasses peered out of one of the windows as I passed. And then, I came to the address Morpheus had given me. A dirty brick terraced house that looked just like all the others on the street. Bland and barely still standing. Upon me knocking on the door, an elderly lady opened it. Her grey hair was tied in a bun, and she wore thin, silver-rimmed spectacles.

"Can I help you?" she asked. I caught the mistrust in her beady eyes. She was not long until the grave by the looks of her and even closer to needing a bath.

"I hear you helped...a friend of mine give birth a few years back."

She narrowed her eyes. "I was a midwife. I helped many women give birth."

"Ah, but this one was special," I said, pushing past her into what looked like a kitchen. She tried to stop me, but she was so decrepit she'd have had trouble stopping a gust of wind from entering.

As soon as I was over the threshold, I felt the remnants of magic. Even after all these years. It had faded, and not many would be able to feel it, but it was ingrained into the very walls of the place.

"Look. I don't know who you are, but you can't just come barging in here. This is my home."

"It's delightful," I lied. "My friend gave birth to twelve babies. Her name was Aphrodite."

She didn't even look surprised. I had a feeling she knew this day was coming.

"That's impossible." She didn't even flinch. I had to give her credit. She looked weak, but she wasn't going to give up the information I needed easily. Fortunately for me, she was human, and humans were easy to crack. A little bit of magic, and she would tell me everything.

I looked right into her eyes and hit her with magic. Her eyes unfocused. Easy!

"What happened to the children?"

"She wanted to keep them." the old woman said in monotone. "But her father would have killed them. Zeus, you know."

I vaguely remembered Morpheus mentioning his name. The only god I knew or cared about was Morpheus. The rest of them were less than useless as far as I was concerned, swanning around in their god realm.

"I don't think she realized how special they were. Oh, she knew they would be powerful. They were demi-gods. But there were twelve of them. Together, they had twelve times the power of one. It was only a couple of days after their birth that things began to change. I saw it in all the newspapers. It was like order and light had come to the world."

"Uh-huh," I encouraged, trying not to barf. I knew all this. She had a smile on her face as though she was remembering them. Stupid old crow.

"Eight girls and four boys. Each cuter than the last."

"What happened to them?"

"She couldn't keep them," she continued. "I

persuaded her that they needed to be kept safe away from here. Of course, twelve babies at once were impossible to keep secret, so we had to separate them. The only way that Aphrodite would agree to give them up was to give them to the people that would give them the best lives, so with her magic, we traveled to every kingdom. It was serendipity, really. Twelve kingdoms, twelve babies. One for each kingdom."

I closed my eyes and inhaled deeply before coughing.

If they'd been taken to all the kingdoms, I would never find them all.

"Azia was the first. She was such a feisty one. Did you know that Aphrodite named them in alphabetical order? I'll never forget the names. Azia, Blaise, Castiel, Deon, Eliana, Fallon, Gaia, Halia, Ivy, Jakon, Kelis, and finally, little Lyric. So beautiful."

I'd already stopped listening. I'd heard the name Azia before. Where? And then it hit me. Azia was the name of Briar Rose's daughter. The king and queen of Draconis had adopted a demi-god, and if they had, it stood to reason that the other kingdoms' leaders had too.

I knew exactly where I'd find the twelve monstrosities. I'd have to find help to kill them, of course, if they were as powerful as I'd been led to believe, but I knew some people.

The old woman came out of her trance while I was distracted.

"Oy, what do you think you are doing? I'll call the police."

Killing her was easy. One wave of my hand and she was dead. Her body upended some pots and pans on her table, sending them clattering to the floor as she fell.

7TH DECEMBER
AZIA

"Stay with them both. Do not leave their sides at all!"

Castiel nodded his head, apparently deep in thought. "Won't she notice if I'm suddenly walking with her instead of racing off ahead and checking out the route for danger?"

"You've been doing that for a while now. Today we will be entering the part of the forest where some humans live in cottages. The trees thin out. I'll tell her that a wolf will cause suspicion if it's alone. You were never going to be in your wolf form around people anyway. I've sent Nyre and Lyric up ahead and asked them to stay low so they can see the path. Jakon is taking the lead today. With his powers, he'll be able to whip the wind around anyone who tries to cross our path. I've got Gaia walking alongside you just in case, and I'll take the rear."

Castiel nodded again and pulled his shirt off, flinging it at me. When he'd shifted into his wolf form, I picked up the rest of his clothes and packed them into my backpack.

Apart from Castiel, Gaia, Jakon, and Kelis, no one else knew what Kelis had told me, least of all, Eliana. I watched as Castiel trotted up beside Eliana.

Roberta squealed and giggled. "Doggy!"

Eliana gave her a small smile but didn't question why Castiel was suddenly walking beside them. Gaia took her place just behind them and gave me a grim smile and a small thumbs up. As the others began the journey that would lead them back to civilization, I made sure my sword was within easy reach. Today was probably going to be the first time I'd need to use it on something other than a wild animal. This was what I'd trained for, what I'd spent years watching my brothers do and the reason for the hours I'd spent practicing with Milo in the woods behind the castle.

Nerves rattled through me as I followed behind the pack. Practicing swordcraft with a man who was in love with me was not exactly the same as killing someone who wanted to kill me. Or Roberta.

The sun's rays filtered through the branches making it seem warmer than it was. Deon complaining about his missing journal was the only thing taking my mind off our upcoming situation. Deon usually kept his calm, but his journal going missing was really grating on him.

"Has anyone packed it accidentally?" he moaned, rifling through his bag as he walked.

"No one has it, Deon," I snapped, passing him on the

path. "It'll turn up. Have you checked all the pockets on your bag?"

"I thought I had," he mumbled. He carried on searching as I walked on ahead. I'd listened to enough complaining. Deon's journal was of little concern to me compared to what was going to happen to Roberta.

By the time we settled down for lunch, nothing out of the ordinary had happened. If anything, we'd made good time. Tonight we'd be close to people, and that was when our problems would begin.

While we ate, Castiel made a quick dash ahead on the path. Half an hour later, he was back. I raised my eyebrow in question, but he just shook his head. If anything, that made me feel worse. If we knew what the enemy was, we'd be able to prepare, but all we knew was that the enemy had a sword and had no problems with killing children.

The trees thinned out further as we continued our trek. In the late afternoon, I whistled Nyre back. I had to wait back and let the others go on a little way ahead of me so they wouldn't see me talking to her. If they suspected something was wrong, I'd have to tell them, and that meant having to tell Eliana too. The fewer people that knew what was going to happen, the better.

"Have you seen anything?" I asked her. Using closed-ended questions that only required a yes or no answer was slower, but it also meant she wouldn't have to change into her part-human form.

She nodded.

"A person?"

A shake of the head.

"A house or cottage?"

She nodded again then blew out five smoke rings.

"Five kilometers away?" I guessed. She nodded.

After I'd thanked her, she once again took to the sky, her giant wings flapping wildly. This would be the last day she'd be able to fly freely as a dragon. Tomorrow, she'd be walking with the rest of us, which she would hate, or we'd have to travel at night when no one would see her.

I jogged to catch up with Ivy, who was the last one of the group.

"Everything ok?" she asked, eyeing me curiously.

"Fine. I just thought I heard something."

Although none of us really had a gift for telepathy, our magical bonds were strong, and lying to the others was virtually impossible. She knew I wasn't being honest with her, but she let it go.

As we made progress through the forest, my feelings of unease grew. With careful glances, I kept a check on the path behind us, but there were no signs of us being followed. Though I could see neither of them, I knew Lyric and Nyre would be taking it in turns to check the forest around us.

The group ahead had barely stopped when Kelis came running back to me. She grabbed my sleeve and nodded quickly, her breath coming out in quick spurts.

"This is it!" she hissed. "From my dream. This is where it happens!"

"I think this is as good a place as any to stop," called Jakon from up ahead. It was a small clearing, just big enough for us to set up our camp. I vaguely remembered it from the journey here. We'd purposely stopped here, just after the cottages and houses had stopped.

"Right," I called out, waving to him. "Set up camp as normal. Castiel, please go on ahead and make sure everything is safe." I tried to put enough emphasis on my words without sounding suspicious.

I began to help set up the blankets, making sure mine was right next to Eliana's. My eyes were on her the whole time as she sat and played with Roberta. In the past couple of days, Roberta had become a little more talkative, although she still hadn't explained how she came to be in the middle of the forest alone. In fact, she'd not said much about herself at all, but she liked to ask Eliana about where we were going and hear about the adventures we'd already had.

"Tomorrow? Tomorrow?" the little girl asked.

I pretended to be straightening my blankets as Eliana explained that we would be heading out of the forest, and then, they'd both fly away to a magical palace on a unicorn. Eliana's palace was not magic beyond its stable of magical flying unicorns, but to a four-year-old, it must sound like a wonderful place.

"Others?"

"The others?" Eliana said, looking up. Her eyes fixed on me, and I gave her a smile. She smiled back.

"The others will continue their quest. Once they leave The Vale, they'll go into a completely different kingdom. Have you ever heard of Elder?"

Roberta shook her head, and her blonde curls bobbed around her shoulders.

"It's a big kingdom with lots of trees. A lot of the people live in the trees. There are lots of wolves there too."

"Casti?"

Eliana grinned. "That's right, Roberta. Just like Castiel, except these poor wolves are changing into bad wolves because they are sick. Everyone is heading to Urbis, where the bad people are to make things better. You remember what I told you about the bad people?"

Roberta nodded solemnly.

"My brothers and sisters will have to travel at night so no one sees them. Fallon over there can change his appearance when he likes so he can go into shops without being found out."

"Wanna go with others!" Roberta demanded as only a small child could.

"You are coming with me, remember? I'm going to take you to my castle on a flying unicorn."

"No! Go with others," she pouted.

"Can I have a word?" I looked up to see Castiel standing over me. He'd shifted back into his human form and was wearing a pair of pants that looked suspiciously like Jakon's. It was then, I remembered that I packed Castiel's clothes in my bag. I pulled his clothes out, handed them to him, then followed him down the path that would lead us out of the forest.

"Ten minutes' walk down that way, and there is a cottage. I saw no signs of life, but the smells were strong enough to know someone was either there or had been there recently. I saw another couple of cottages a little farther beyond too. One of them had smoke coming out of the chimney."

"Thanks," I said, wondering how the information was going to help. Living in a cottage in the forest was hardly an illegal activity. We'd have passed those very same houses on the way here without anything happening.

"I know you don't want to, but I think you've got to tell the others. We'll all need to be on alert if someone is going to come in for the attack."

I sighed, knowing he was right. There were twelve of us with powers beyond that of any human. We also had a real fire-breathing dragon.

"Kelis's vision might not have been right. I've been thinking of this all day. Anyone with any kind of magical powers wouldn't need to use a sword, but anyone without magical powers wouldn't be able to get through us."

"We still need to tell everyone. This shouldn't have been kept a secret at all. We are supposed to be a team."

Back in the clearing, the fire had already been started, and a dinner of roasted fruits was already underway, filling the air with a sweet smell. I did a quick count, seeing that we were all there.

"Hey everyone," I began, loudly enough for everyone to stop what they were doing and look my way. "We have a bit of a problem. Kelis had a premonition that we'd see danger tonight."

"What kind of danger?" Blaise asked.

"We are going to be attacked. I think by only one person, but I'm not sure. They'll have a sword with them."

I left out the part where Roberta would be killed. I was going to do everything in my ability to stop that from happening. The little girl was wrapped up in Eliana's arms, sucking her thumb, seemingly oblivious to the danger she was facing. I glanced over at Kelis, whose eyes were boring into me. I gave her a slight shake of the head. There was no way I was going to let Eliana know the full extent of the premonition.

"Tonight we are going to take it in turns to sleep, half on, half off, changing every couple of hours. Some of us will stay here in camp ready to fight if needs be, and some will check the surrounding area for anything suspicious."

Everyone listened intently as I split them into two teams. I made sure Eliana was on mine because there was no way I was going to sleep tonight, no matter what team I was on. I pulled my sword from its sheath and settled down next to it in my blanket as the first team began their job. Next to me, Eliana snuggled up with Roberta. I watched them as they both closed their eyes. It was shaping up to be an interesting night. I only hoped that the both of them would make it through.

JANUARY
DERILLEN

Finding most of the monsters, as I'd come to think of the demi-gods, was easy. So easy, it was ridiculous that no one had noticed it before. Inner Urbis's huge records building held the newspapers from all the kingdoms going back hundreds of years in some cases. Almost all of the leaders of the kingdoms had either adopted a child out of the blue or "given birth," to a child in mysterious circumstances. The kingdoms were all coming out of war of some kind eighteen years ago, so the weird coincidence had gone largely unnoticed.

Some of the monsters were a little harder to find. The king and queen of Floris, for example, had a daughter that did not fit either the timeline or the name of any of the monsters. The kingdom of Elder had neither a royal family nor a newspaper. But I'd find them. I'd find them all, starting with that little brat, Azia. I already knew how to hurt her, and it would be the sweetest revenge.

"I won't do it again, Derillen."

Morpheus blew cigar smoke rings lazily into the air. I'd promised myself I'd never see him again, but here we both were. He was different to me now. Something had changed, and I didn't like it. I wasn't hiding my age. That probably had something to do with it. I looked young. All witches looked much younger than they actually were, but I didn't look young enough. I could pass for a human woman in her late fifties, maybe, but I'd never be the girl I once was. Maybe that's why Morpheus had lost interest in me. Maybe it was because he didn't give a damn about Aphrodite's monsters parading around the world as though they owned it. Of course, he didn't care. He was a god. He could do anything he wanted, and power was not something he'd ever cared about. All he wanted was pleasure. Fine wine, exclusive clubs, and young, beautiful women. The last one was my way in.

"I can start the curse without you," I wheedled. "I just need you to shut the doors to your sleep world so she can't escape."

"And why would I do that?"

"Because we were friends... because we'd once been more than friends, because I'd do it for you... Because she's beautiful, Morpheus. So beautiful that she was known as the Sleeping Beauty. Every man in Draconis wanted her. Many risked their life just to be the one to wake her. Many perished in the process. You could have her. You locked her in your sleep realm before, but you never went in there to see her. This time you could. The most beautiful woman in all the kingdoms will be yours and yours alone."

Morpheus waved my words away. "I've heard the story of the most beautiful woman before. It was said that the queen of Enchantia was the most beautiful, then her daughter, Snow White."

I mulled the information over in my mind. I knew of Snow White. She was the current queen of Enchantia and also happened to be the adopted mother of one of the monsters.

"How about I promise you Snow White too? The two most beautiful women in all the kingdoms, and they will both be yours to do whatever you want with."

Interest suddenly sparked in his eyes. It was quite remarkable how easy he was to manipulate, even as a god.

"I'll curse them both to sleep," I promised. "Once they are in your kingdom, you make sure you keep them there. I'll need them as a distraction."

"A distraction from what?" Morpheus asked his greedy eyes boring into mine.

I lifted my glass of expensive champagne and gave him a wink.

"That's for me to know, my dear Morpheus. You just do your job, and I'll make sure to do mine.

8TH DECEMBER
AZIA

Midnight had come and gone without incident. The other group's two hours were up, and the group I was in was due to rise again. Gaia gently shook my shoulder to wake me, though I was already awake. I'd not slept through two sleep turns and wouldn't until we caught the person or people responsible for planning to hurt Roberta. A quick glance at her showed me she was sleeping peacefully, one thumb in her mouth, long eyelashes sweeping her cheeks.

"Any news?" I whispered.

Gaia shook her head. "Nothing. Jakon headed to the nearby cottage. There was a light on in one of the windows but no noise."

That was interesting. They were still awake after midnight? Plotting something? Did they know we were here? My mind had turned over a thousand possibilities, but the nearby cottage was my number one priority. They were the closest people to us.

After Gaia lay down to sleep, I woke the others in my group. Castiel, Lyric, Fallon, Halia, and Ivy were up and ready quickly. Their skin glowed orange in the firelight. Usually, we doused the fire after dinner, but on this night, there had been a vote to keep it going. It meant we were easier to spot, but it also meant we'd be able to see when we were attacked.

I beckoned the small group to the edge of the clearing and began whispering instructions.

"Castiel. You wanna be a wolf or something else? We need something quick and strong."

"How about this?" He pulled his clothes off and began his transformation. I'd seen him turn into a wolf on many occasions, so I wasn't expecting the golden fur or the shaggy blonde mane that covered his head. A lion would stand out a mile in The Vale, but we needed him to protect us. It was a perfect choice.

"Head out to the cottages. If anyone even thinks about leaving one in the next two hours, roar at them. If they have a sword, eat them!"

"Don't you think that's a bit excessive?" Ivy asked, adjusting the hat she always wore.

Seeing Castiel head off into the woods brought a flashback of lions at the competition to marry me all those months ago. They had viciously torn some of the men limb from limb.

"Maybe a little," I conceded. "Can you go in that direction too? Halia, you go too. Check out all the nearby cottages. Not just the first one. I'll send the signal if I need you."

Unlike every other night, we'd not set up the string and metal signals around the camp. Instead, we were patrolling it. "Lyric. Can you check out the path behind us and keep flying around the camp in general? Stay quite close."

"Yes, Boss!" She gave me a quick salute and soundlessly took to the sky.

"Fallon, you stay here with me. I'll stay near Eliana; you patrol at the other side of the camp."

I stood up and stretched out. The air was thick with tension and cold, but there was nothing particularly out of the ordinary. No weird noises, no hordes of sword-wielding beings ready to attack. It was like every other night in the forest, except the promise of danger was there. My body was tingling with anticipation. Kelis had not told me which night this would happen, but this was the only night we would be here. If it was going to happen at all, tonight was the night.

"What do you want me to do?"

I almost jumped at the voice, then checked myself. It was only Eliana. Officially she was in the group that was meant to be awake, but I'd purposely not woken her. She still didn't know exactly what danger we were facing.

"You watch Roberta," I whispered, bending down to where she lay on the blanket. "Keep a hold of her. Don't let her go anywhere without telling me. No toilet trips without letting anyone know, ok?"

She smiled and nodded. This was her dream job. Looking after the child.

"What's happening, mama?"

"Nothing, sweetheart," Eliana soothed, running her hand through the little girl's curls. "We are going to sit tight here together. Would you like me to sing you a lullaby?"

Roberta nodded and snuggled in further to Eliana. I picked up my sword and began walking around my half of the camp. It was a short walk. Fallon did the same at the other side, stepping around the blankets laid out in a circle. I gave him a small wave, which he returned.

The first tendrils of sunlight began to peek over the horizon, brightening the sky slightly. We were in the home stretch. In a couple of hours, it would be light, and we could set off, proving Kelis's prediction wrong. I believed Kelis entirely, but this premonition had been in dream form. There was a possibility it was just an ordinary dream—a bad one, but a dream nonetheless. In the heightened state of anxiety we were all in, being away from our homes, everyone looking for us, we'd all been having nightmares. It was natural.

"Hey Azia."

Halia appeared from the forest at the other side of the clearing. I beckoned her over to my blanket, and the pair of us sat down. Roberta looked at her curiously, but then turned her attention back to Eliana, who was playing some childish game with her that involved quietly clapping their hands together and singing in whispers.

I laid my sword down next to me as Halia sat down. "Any news?"

Halia shook her head. "The others are still patrolling, but no one has come out of the cottages. The lights have been turned off on the closest one, and the other two a little further on were quiet too. Castiel traveled to pretty much the edge of the forest next to the village, but he said he saw nothing out of the ordinary. Everything is quiet. I've left Ivy and Castiel. I just wanted to let you know. Anything happening here?"

I shook my head and stifled a yawn. "Nothing. I'm beginning to think it was just a dream. The sky is lightening. It will be morning soon. Give it another hour and then come back. We'll pack up early and move on from this place before breakfast. Maybe Fallon will be able to score us some hot food in the village."

Halia stood up and reached out a hand to help me up. She gave me a quick nod and raced back into the forest.

I massaged my eyes and yawned. I'd been awake all night, and it was beginning to catch up on me. Roberta gave a little giggle as she whispered something to Eliana. It reminded me what we were doing all this for. When we got to the village, Eliana would call her unicorn, and the two of them would fly away to safety. Tomorrow night, I'd be able to relax.

Fallon gave me another wave from the other side. I walked over to him.

"I'm beginning to think this was a pointless task. There's no one here."

Fallon shrugged his shoulders, then lifted his eyes to the sky. "You are probably right. Didn't Kelis say that this attack happened at night? It's almost dawn."

"Halia just told me that everything is quiet at the cottages and the village. I've not heard from Lyric yet, but..."

I was cut off from my train of thought by an ear-piercing scream. My heart began to pound as I realized I'd left my side of the camp, and therefore, Eliana and Roberta alone. I turned quickly, trying to see the foe, but there was no one there. I searched the trees behind Eliana for any sign of an attack or what it was that had made her scream like that, but everything was how

I'd left it. The others began to wake as I took my first steps back to Eliana. Before I'd taken any more. Eliana reached forward and grabbed the sword I'd left on my bed when Halia had come to talk to me.

Who was she fighting? An invisible foe? I'd never heard of invisibility being possible.

As if in slow motion, she lifted the sword above her head and screamed again before plunging it right into Roberta's belly. The little girl's blood splattered everywhere, covering Eliana. With terror in her eyes, she caught Roberta's body and stood.

There was a crazed look in her eyes, and that's when it dawned on me. Magic was being used. Someone was using mind control. Kelis hadn't seen Roberta being murdered; she'd only seen this.

I couldn't move. Disbelief had me rooted to the spot. Someone else screamed at the sight. I think it was Blaise, but I couldn't be sure. No one moved as Eliana took a few paces forward toward the fire.

It was a terrifying sight: Roberta with her head lolled back and unseeing eyes reflecting the red light of dawn and the dying fire, and Eliana, her white nightdress, soaked with red.

"She's under a spell!" I yelled as a warning. If she could kill the little girl she'd fallen in love with so easily, then she wouldn't hesitate to rip the sword from Roberta's lifeless body and attack one of us.

"There's no spell," Eliana whispered. "I did this myself."

"There has to be a spell," I insisted, my brain foggy with confusion. I couldn't tell what Eliana was thinking, but I knew she wasn't capable of this.

"To perform mind magic on someone, you have to be close by," Kelis reminded me. "If anyone made her do this, they would have to be very close."

"Spread out everyone!" I said, panic filling my voice. "We need to find them."

Just then, Halia, Ivy, and Castiel bounded back into the clearing.

"Castiel! Use your Lion senses to find the killer. They are controlling Eliana."

I had no idea if Lions were as good at smelling as wolves, but if there was anyone in the trees around us, Castiel would find them.

"I told you. I did this." Eliana repeated, this time more loudly.

I walked slowly toward her. Her whole body shook. This wasn't right.

"Why, Eliana? Why did you kill her?"

She dropped the girl's body and looked at it as though repulsed as it landed at her feet. The sword was pushed further through Roberta's middle with the force of hitting the ground.

Bile came into my throat, and I had to fight hard to keep it down.

"Him. Why did I kill him?"

I furrowed my eyebrows. "What are you talking about?"

Eliana looked into my eyes, tears dripping from hers. "That's not a little girl," she choked out, "It's Rumpelstiltskin, and he's been listening to every word we've said for days."

As though she'd said something magic, the body erupted into a puff of purple smoke and dissipated into the sky. The blood covering Eliana faded away, and my sword clanged to the ground.

"Can someone tell us what's going on?" Jakon shouted, coming up behind me as I reached for Eliana's hands. She was trembling so much; I could hardly keep her still. Her breath was coming out in long sobs. She wouldn't be able to speak for long.

"How do you know?" I asked her, trying to keep my own panic from my voice.

"I found Deon's journal in my bag earlier. I hadn't taken it." She sucked in another breath. "He began to sing a song. I'd only ever heard one person ever singing that song. It was him. He'd been using me to spy on us. That's why he chose to be a little girl who looked like Luka."

"Luka?"

"Fae's father. He looked like me, and Luka, and like Fae might look when she's older. He played me like a fool. I'm so sorry."

She collapsed to the floor in an agony of grief. She'd lost Fae already. This would only compound that.

Jakon was by her side in a second. She clung to him as I faced the others.

"It was Rumpelstiltskin," I announced to those that hadn't heard Eliana. "They've found us. He's been listening to every word we said for the last few days, and he's read Deon's journal."

"But he's dead," Ivy pointed out, her face pale with shock. "Surely, that's a good thing?"

I shook my head. "If he was dead, his body would still be here. This was all an illusion. Wherever he appeared from, I think we can assume he went back there. He used the power of teleportation to stay close to us, controlling the illusion of Roberta."

"No," Castiel said. "I would have smelled him. I checked the path both before and after us regularly. There is no way Rumpelstiltskin was close enough to do that."

Above me, Nyre landed on a tree branch. I looked up to see her sitting there. "He was in the trees, I announced, piecing it all together. He could teleport from one tree to the next above our heads." I groaned. I'd seen him. I'd actually seen him and dismissed it as an over-active imagination.

"They are getting stronger, and they are getting clever. From now on, we can't let our guards down at all. We must assume that every person we meet is one of them."

Gaia shook her head, her eyes blazing with fire. "How will we even get to Urbis if they know where we are and where we are going? Rumpelstiltskin will be back there telling them all our plans."

I looked around at my brothers and sisters. They all had shock in their expressions, but underneath that, I saw strength. "I don't know, Gaia, but we will. Even if it means changing all our plans, we'll do whatever we have to do."

And as the night came to an end with the arrival of dawn, we once again set off through the forest and out into the rest of the world.

KINGDOM OF POWER

9TH DECEMBER
AZIA

"Dragon shit!" I exclaimed as I dropped my glass, spilling beer all over my top. The fact that I had a glass of beer at all was little short of a miracle, but after yesterday's nightmare when Eliana had pushed my sword through a four-year-old's stomach, I'd had enough of everything and booked us into the first inn I could find. As the little girl had turned out to be Rumpelstiltskin and had somehow managed to survive a hole right through his middle, I figured that the bad guys already knew where we were, so we might as well have a little comfort to regroup and re-plan. It was already midnight by the time we had booked in, but a lot of money thrown the way of the innkeeper was enough for him to prepare us some food and promise his silence on ever seeing us.

My room had two beds, both of which smelled faintly of cat pee. The flowery wallpaper was beginning to peel, but anything was better than sleeping outside in the crisp winter air with only threadbare blankets for warmth. I sat on my bed against the pillows, my brother Deon perched on the end of Blaise's bed.

"Do you want me to write that down?" Deon asked, his eyes twinkling as he held his pen to paper.

I shot him a withering look and mopped up the beer with a blanket from the bed. I was paying for the room for the night; I might as well make the most of it.

"Derillen is the ringleader," I said, watching as Deon wrote it down. "She's a witch. She can create brambles; she can shift her appearance like Fallon. She can cast glamours and compel people to do her bidding...she can..."

"Put people in cursed sleep?" Deon volunteered, rubbing the back of his neck with his hand and yawning.

I shook my head. "No, don't write that. I don't know if she really can. I think that's Morpheus's domain. I really think she knows him somehow."

Deon waited for me to continue, his pen poised.

"We need to write down Morpheus as a separate entry," I continued. "He is the one that can keep people in his dream world. I think we can assume that Snow White is in there too. He can manipulate dreams. I'm not sure what else at this point."

"Morpheus... dreams... Got it. I wonder why he is doing this, though. He's a god, like us. Surely he's more likely to be on our side than a witch's?"

I shrugged my shoulders and refilled my glass from the pitcher on the bedside table. I'd invited Deon to come to my room so we could list all the magic we were up against, but so far, Deon had declined to drink, preferring to work completely sober. This might be the last beer we got in a while, and I was planning on enjoying it.

"We have Blaise's sea witch," I continued after taking a swig of the somewhat flat brew. "She can breathe underwater. She can command weird sea creatures, I forget what they are called, and she can fly."

"The way Blaise described it, it was more like floating than flying," Deon reminded me.

"Floating, flying, whatever. They can hover over the air, and they aren't real. Just put down whatever you want," I responded irritably. It was too late for this, and I was exhausted, but if we didn't figure out a plan and exactly what we were up against, we might as well give it all up.

"Castiel's issue is a plague," I mused. "I'm not sure who we can blame for that. We'll have to ask him."

"I have a witch too!" Deon said, holding his hand up.

"They get everywhere, don't they?" I replied with a wry smile on my face. "What is it about witches being insane?"

Deon laughed. "I don't think they all are. Look at Enchantia. It's full of witches. I'm sure most of them are lovely. In fact, I know a couple of witches in Floris, and they are perfectly respectable."

I sipped at my beer, remembering drinking beer at the Dragon Roost Inn with Milo. It had been so much better than this witch piss sold as ale. I nodded at Deon. "Fair enough. What can your witch do?"

"Beyond killing everything slowly, I don't know. I guess you could call her a maker of disease except unlike Castiel's wolves, hers killed plants and my mother-in-law's hair until she was sick too."

I stood up and took a deep breath. The room was small, with only the two beds and a wardrobe with the door hanging off. The Draconis Royal Hotel it wasn't. It was also dark and dingy, even with the small lamp flickering away in the corner. "Rumpelstiltskin seems to be one of the strongest. He can read minds to shift and appearance, and he can survive being stabbed. He can teleport too."

I sighed as Deon wrote down everything I said. They had so many powers. Powers that we didn't possess, and we weren't even halfway through the list yet.

"He can't survive being stabbed. I'd bet money on it." Deon said, looking up from his notebook.

"But he did," I argued. "We both saw it."

"We saw something. I think he can project himself or whatever he wants us to see."

"Oh, great!" I replied, shifting position to my knees. "That's so much better." I rolled my eyes.

"It is, actually. No one could survive what happened yesterday and then disappear like that. If he was somehow projecting or making us believe he was there, then that means he's not invincible. He's flesh and bone like the rest of us."

I was too tired for this. It was way past midnight, and my eyelids were drooping.

"Let's come back to him. What about Fallon's guy... Edward... Eddie."

"Edwin," Deon corrected me.

"Edwin. He can turn people into beasts." I pointed at Deon, happy that I'd remembered something with my brain as foggy as it was. Maybe a whole pitcher of beer had been a bad idea. "Not sure if he can do anything else. The sorcerer Gaia was fighting can fly using a carpet. He can produce fire. He seems like an all-around badass. Halia only had her stepmother, who wasn't magic, but she persuaded Rumpelstiltskin to help her, so we can't count her out. Who's next?"

"Ivy. She had the Queen of Hearts to deal with and her army of mechanical cards. She said there was something to do with a clock, too, although she didn't know what it was about."

"Right. I'd forgotten about the clock. Jakon had the Wicked Witch of the East. Another witch who presumably can do what she wants."

"Don't forget her flying monkeys," Deon said, writing it down.

"How could I forget the flying monkeys?" I said with a grin. It was so ridiculous the sheer amount of magic we were up against and the number of people involved. What with the sea witch's army of creatures, the Queen of Hearts' mechanical cards, and the Wicked Witch of the East's monkeys, we were out-numbered by a long way. We only had each other, and a dragon, and a unicorn, and the unicorn in question hadn't been seen in a number of weeks.

Deon continued writing as he spoke. "Kelis had another witch, but you said earlier that you thought Derillen helped her or at least introduced her to Morpheus, and lastly, there is Captain Hook."

"At least, he doesn't have any magical powers," I said with a sigh.

"No, just a group of homicidal pirates and flying ships."

"Is that all?" I giggled. "I was beginning to worry for a second that we didn't have enough to cope with."

"Maybe we should call it a night and go downstairs to join the others," Deon said, folding his book and taking my beer out of my hand.

I closed my eyes and took a deep breath, inhaling the musty smell of the room combined with the cat-pee-stinking mattress.

"Yeah. I could do with some fresh air."

We found everyone outside seated on benches, which had been placed there by the owners of the inn. Right on the edge of the forest, this place would probably look nice in the summer. But with dark cloudy skies above us and little attempt by the owners to provide anything beyond the minimum at this time of year, it was miserable and unwelcoming. Perfect for a group of outlaws that didn't want to be found.

I wrapped in the blanket I'd brought outside with me and sat next to Ivy on one of the benches. Either Gaia or Nyre had set up a fire in a pit. A quick look around told me that Jakon, Eliana, and Blaise were missing.

"Where are the others?" I asked Ivy, who pulled my blanket around her so we could share the warmth.

"Blaise and Jakon are doing laundry for us all. They pulled the short straw. Eliana is sewing the clothes that need fixing. I think she's in her room."

I wasn't surprised that she was away from the rest of us. She'd blamed herself for Rumpelstiltskin learning our plans, and no amount of trying to persuade her otherwise was helping.

"We need a new plan," I announced. "Deon and I have been writing down all the people that are out to get us and their powers. It's a disturbing list and what's worse is they know our next move thanks to Rumpelstiltskin. I don't think we can go through Elder anymore. I think we have to go through Arcadia instead."

"Hang on a minute!" Castiel said, his long hair still dripping presumably from a bath he'd had. It was the first time I'd seen him look truly clean in months. "We need to go through Elder. I need to check on my family."

I chewed on my lip. Castiel was the stubbornest one of all of us, and though he was right most of the time, this time, he was thinking with his heart rather than his head. "Eliana couldn't go home even though we are in her kingdom, and neither can you. It's too dangerous."

Castiel steepled his fingers and leaned forward on his bench. His voice took on a gravelly timbre as he spoke, putting me on edge. He only spoke like this when he was angry. "Actually, I remember Eliana saying she was going to go home. You were ok with that."

"Eliana was going to go home and stay home," I pointed out. "You want to go home just to see people. It would add at least a couple of weeks to our journey."

"And going through Arcadia won't?" he growled. "Deon. Pass me the map."

Deon dug around in his bag and produced a map that showed all the kingdoms, which he passed to Castiel.

"See?" Castiel said, walking over to me and pointing at the map. Azren is up there, but if we go south, we'll be walking around the border, which will also take time. You'll still have to cross some of Elder to get to the border of Arcadia anyway."

"Yes, but only a little. It will take less time this way," I argued. "Maybe a week more than our original plans rather than the two weeks you'll add by going your way, and that's not including the time you want to spend with your family and friends. We can't risk it. What if our families are being watched? You'll put us all in danger."

Castiel emitted a low growl from his throat. "Look how heavily wooded Elder and then Aboria is," Castiel said, jabbing his finger at the tiny trees that depicted forests. “We can get almost all the way from Azren to Urbis by going through forest. It’s the perfect cover.”

Looking at the map, I could see that he was right. Derillen and her cronies would be expecting us to walk right through Elder in a straight line. Either going up to the capital of Elder or going south into Arcadia would not be what they would expect, but then again, Rumpelstiltskin had managed to find us in the middle of a forest in The Vale. So what did it really matter? It didn’t, but Castiel’s way was longer, and I was already sick and tired of this journey. I needed it to be over.

“We are going through Arcadia,” I maintained. “I have a hunch that’s the right way to go, and I can’t add a week to our travels just because you want to see your family. We all want to see our family, Castiel. It’s not just you.”

His expression changed slightly, and his eyes flashed with anger. “Your mother is cursed, but she’s alive,” Castiel grunted. “My friends are dying. One by one, they are either dying of the curse or are killing each other because of it. Don’t tell me how I feel, because you have no idea. We didn’t all grow up in a castle with servants on tap. Some of us had to survive in the woods. My friends can’t even do that.”

I looked him in the eye and held my gaze steady. “I’m sorry, Castiel, but my mind is made up. This is why we are on this quest. Adding an extra week to it will only prolong your friends’ suffering.”

Castiel glared at me in a way that reminded me he sometimes had fangs. “Fine. Go whichever way you like, but don’t expect me to be with you if you go through Arcadia. I’m done.” He left our circle and slammed the door of the inn behind him.

“We weren’t planning to go as far north as Azren in

the first place!" I said, trying to justify my stance to the others.

Ivy wrapped her arm around my shoulder. "He's in a bad mood. He'll come around by tomorrow after a good night's sleep. Going through Arcadia is the better option."

"Is it, though?" I looked at Halia, who knew more about her home kingdom than any of us.

"It's more built-up than Elder and Aboria," she said, drumming her fingers on her guitar. "It will be harder to hide, but maybe hiding in plain sight might be our best bet. Villages and cities are the last places they'd expect us to be."

She strummed a slow tune on her guitar producing enough magic to calm me down. She was a whizz at controlling emotions with the thing. It came in very handy at times like these when all I wanted to do was throttle Castiel for being so utterly selfish.

Later, after much discussion, I headed back to my room with Blaise. Everything weighed heavily on my mind. Eliana, whom I'd barely seen since we got to the inn, Castiel who had threatened to leave us, and the long, long list of magic the other side had that seemed insurmountable to beat. It was one thing having a plan to get to Urbis, but quite another to have one once we were there. I still had no clue how we were supposed to beat an army of witches, sorcerers, and all-around mad creatures.

I fell into bed and into a fitful night's sleep that not even sleeping in my first bed in months could help.

Hours later, Blaise and I met the others in the inn's small dining room for breakfast. Just like the rest of the inn, it was built using logs, which made it oppressively dark in the winter months. The couple of lamps lighting the place barely cut through the dark.

Everyone was sitting at a long table, which was just three smaller tables pushed together. Not that it mattered, we were the only guests.

I felt a wrench in my gut as I noticed Castiel wasn't among them.

"Where's Castiel?" I asked, trying to appear nonchalant as I took a seat near the end of the table next to Ivy. The expressions on the faces of my siblings already answered my question.

Jakon was the one who put it into words. "He wasn't there when I knocked on his door this morning. I think he stuck to his guns and has gone home."

"No!" I cried out. I'd made him leave. We were only strong when we were together. Without one of us, our powers diminished. I closed my eyes and felt into myself to the core of my magic, trying to feel his strand of magic that had been inside me since we'd all turned eighteen. He wasn't nearby. His strand of magic was less defined than those of the others.

"He'll never be able to find us once we leave here!" I said, panic lacing my voice. "We need to stay here for a couple of nights to see if he comes back."

Jakon shook his head and reached across the table to place his hand on mine. "You know we can't do that, Azia. The detour through Arcadia is already going to add time to our journey, and every day we take getting to Urbis, the stronger they get."

I held my head in my hands. I'd spent almost a year gathering up my siblings only to lose one at the last minute. Tears pricked at my eyes, and for the first time in months, I let the tears fall. If I couldn't perform the simple task of keeping my brothers and sisters together, how could we even begin to defeat all our foes?

I felt a warm hand on my shoulder. Every part of me wanted to shrug it off, to cry in peace, but when I heard the voice of the person touching me, I looked up and wiped my eyes.

"We are still strong," Eliana said. She was pale, but there was a strength in her I'd not seen in weeks. "We can do this. If Castiel really wants to find us, he'll figure it out. He's our brother."

I gave her a watery smile as she placed a pile of freshly laundered, freshly mended clothes on the table next to me. "Now, let's get our fill of food because this might be the last time we have a hot meal in quite a while."

The food was mediocre, but there was lots of it. The innkeeper, buoyed by the extra money I'd passed his way, had even made up lunch bags full of sandwiches to last two or three days, with snacks and fruit for us all.

As the others began piling the food into their backpacks, I wandered outside.

The place looked almost the same in the day as it had at night. The sky was dark and heavy with snow that was yet to fall.

Something moved behind me, making my heart thump. Turning quickly, I almost butted into the muzzle of a unicorn.

"Zacharina!"

She lowered her eyelashes as I stroked my hand through her hair. It had been a while since we had seen her. When we first got to The Vale, she had flown north to visit with her daughter, Epiphany.

"I know someone who will be over the moon to see you."

Eliana's face lit up with a wide smile when I knocked

on the window of the inn and pointed out Zacharina. She came barreling out and practically launched herself at the unicorn. Just like I had a connection with Nyre, Eliana had the same with Zacharina. The magical creatures would find us even when we couldn't find each other.

I wrapped my arms around myself and looked up the dirt road that would take us to a crossroads with one way leading north, one leading east, and the other leading toward the southern border. In my heart, I hoped that Castiel would change his mind, but seeing wolf tracks imprinted in the mud left me in no doubt he was gone. And if he was gone, that meant he was gone for good because I wasn't planning on getting found. Not until we got to where we were going.

JANUARY
DERILLEN

Getting into Draconis Castle was easy. They really needed to pay more attention, but they didn't, and as a lowly maid, I was pretty much able to go where I pleased without any problems. Morons. All the guards they had and their biggest threat was right under their noses. Putting Briar Rose under a curse would be a much more difficult prospect. There were certain potions that could put someone into a deep sleep, but there wasn't a curse that would do that. I needed to make sure that when I gave her the potion, Morpheus would be there at the other side of sleep to lock her in the dream world. Otherwise, she would wake up the next morning with nothing more than a headache. Because of that, I had to organize an exact time of sleep. I'd given myself a few days to get ready. It would have been the easiest thing to just let her fall asleep and let Morpheus take her, but I wanted to play with her first, play with the king, her daughter. Making her sleepy involved a little potion in her food delivered by the brand new maid every day. Me being the maid, of course. It was hilarious seeing the distress over Her Majesty's sudden illness. If only they had looked to the shy young woman who'd been given the job of delivering food and drinks to her. But of course, no one did. I'd made myself look as dull as possible, and that, combined with the maid outfit, had made me almost invisible to the royal household. It was disturbing how easy it all was. The brat was too busy being sullen about some guy she was supposed to marry. The guy was a creep, so I wasn't surprised, but still. The girl had no class at all.

The guy himself, Casper, or Caspian, or something, was a faerie, which meant he was my biggest obstacle. Magic senses magic. If I got too close to him, he'd know what I was immediately. That was if he took his head out of his ass long enough, which didn't seem likely, but I wasn't about to chance it. I didn't need to be at the castle day in and day out to slip the queen the potion, so I only came back at mealtimes. Besides, I had other parts of my plan to deal with. Namely, meeting the monster brat alone and seeing exactly what I was up against. I just needed to engineer a reason to meet her.

The girl was so easy to manipulate. In the end, she actually came to me. I didn't need to go find her at all. I cast a glamor over the shop I was living above to make it look like a wool shop. It turned out to be a genius idea, and the spindle in the window, a moment of inspiration. My plan had been to have the shop displaying the spindle for a few weeks, thinking that the news of a spindle in the village would eventually filter to the royal castle. It was ridiculous how many people still believed that Briar Rose had been put to sleep by pricking her finger on a spindle all those years ago. As if a machine for making wool could ever put someone in a curse. But people are stupid and believe what they want to. That had been one of my finer moments. Before Morpheus would take Briar Rose into his sleep kingdom the first time, he'd made me promise that I'd wait until she was seventeen years old. At the time of the promise, she wasn't even born yet, and I didn't want my revenge to be served cold. I wanted it served up hot. So on the day the royals held a party to announce her birth, I promised them she'd die from a spindle on her seventeenth birthday. All I had to do after that was watch as the queen and my ex-boyfriend destroyed Draconis's wool industry by burning all the spindles in the kingdom. It was such a pleasure watching them go up in flames. The myth of cursed spindles was still going strong, it seemed, because the brat came into my store on the very first day it opened.

Her cheeks were rosy with the cold weather, but her lips were pale. She was beautiful. Not as beautiful as Briar Rose, but then no one was. The magic radiating from her took my breath away, but I could see she didn't even know she had it. She picked up a pair of mittens and placed them on the counter.

"Is that it, my love?"

"What?" The poor girl looked dazed. I almost felt sorry for her until I remembered what her grandfather had done, what her father had done, and what she herself had done. Three generations of royals, all of them against me, all of them causing me pain.

"The mittens, dear. Is that all you want today?"

"Oh, yes,"

I could see that the mittens were only an excuse. Her eyes kept moving over to the spindle in the window.

She was the one that brought it up, telling me that it was illegal. It was almost fun watching her being drawn to it as though it was something magical.

"What harm can it do?" I said, "Go and take a closer look. You can see for yourself how harmless it is."

I stepped toward it and urged her to touch it. I used all my powers, everything I had to control her mind, to make her touch the spindle. It wouldn't have done anything even if she had touched it, but I needed to see if I could control her mind. She held her finger up toward it but wavered. Even with literally every ounce of magical strength I had, she still fought against it. Then her stupid father came in and broke my concentration.

She was stronger than I had realized. If I didn't squash her like a bug, squash all of the monsters, they'd be the end of me, and I wasn't planning to go down without a fight. In fact, I wasn't planning to go down at all.

10TH DECEMBER
AZIA

The first flurry of snow began to fall as we hiked along the old dirt road, reminding me that before we did anything else, we would need to stop in a nearby village for supplies. The blankets we had were threadbare, and not even Eliana's sewing skills could make them good enough for the upcoming winter. We'd spent the previous night in a copse of trees that had offered us next to no protection, and my bones ached with cold.

The map showed that the road that would take us southeast to the border went right past a village that was marked Leodis in tiny letters.

I walked ahead, taking the place that had been Castiel's for the past few weeks, and led the group along the dirt track. The imprint of horses' hooves still showed in the mud where the snow had not quite covered them, telling me that this road was used occasionally although we'd seen no one in the past day and a half of walking. On either side of the road, dry stone walls separated it from farmer's fields that seemed to stretch on endlessly like a desert of snow.

The road eventually took us to the crossroads marked on the map. Going southeast would take us past Leodis and then to the border, slightly lower down, which was the way I wanted to go. Once in Elder, we'd go south for a short while, curving back west around the coast and end up in Arcadia. Looking down the road, I could see the small town of Leodis in the distance.

"We need to split up," I said, gesturing for Deon to come forward. I pulled the map from the side pocket of his backpack and laid it out the best I could on the top of a wall. "I don't want all of us to stop in Leodis. We are way too conspicuous, especially with a dragon and a unicorn. Fallon, you go ahead with Halia and Eliana. Change your appearance and buy as much as you can. Blankets, tents if you can. Take Zacharina and load her up. She'll need to wear some kind of head covering so her horn doesn't show. Deon, Ivy, and Gaia go next. Head down this road. Past the village, it looks like farmland most of the way to the border. The rest of us will follow on. Then we can cross through into Elder tonight before crossing over to Arcadia tomorrow. There seems to be a ruin here just a little way past the village," I said, pointing at the map. "We'll meet up there once we are past the village and have lunch."

"Sounds like a plan," Deon said encouragingly. He placed the map back in his bag and passed handfuls of envelopes to Fallon, each with Lilian written on it and the address of the Floris Palace. "If you see a post office, can you post these for me, please?"

Fallon nodded. "You are making me look bad, man. I've barely written to Veda since I set off."

"She knows you love her. Besides, I know I'm a little over the top about it." He rubbed the back of his neck and gave a shy smile. He was just too cute for his own good. He rifled in his bag and pulled out a blank sheet of paper and an envelope, which he handed to Fallon along with a pen. "For Veda."

Next to him, Nyre scrunched up her nose as Fallon pocketed the paper. I wasn't sure, but I was beginning to suspect she had developed a crush on Fallon after all these months of walking together.

"The rest of us will follow along in a couple of hours," I said, interrupting the love fest. "Nyre, you are going to have to change."

The dragon blew smoke rings from her nose in disgust, but as the first group set off into the village, she changed into her half-human self. I threw her some long pants to cover her scaly legs and a sweater to keep her warm. The nine of us that were left hopped over the wall and sat on the other side, partly for shelter and partly so that no one passing on the road would see us. Half an hour after the first group left, Deon, Gaia, and Ivy headed down the road that would take them past the village.

I sat with my back against the wall. Once again, a feeling of unease engulfed me. I looked over to Kelis to ask if she'd had any premonitions about today, but she was deep in conversation with Blaise and Lyric and seemed perfectly happy. The further my siblings walked away, the worse my feeling grew. This was the first time we'd stopped in a village for months. Who knew how widespread the knowledge of us was by now. That was something else I hadn't considered when I'd decided we'd all go through Arcadia rather than Elder. Elder had no newspaper. The people and wolves of Elder didn't much care about the outside world. Yes, our foes would expect us to head that way, but what about everyone else? Keeping us all incognito would require a miracle.

At last, the time came for us to move on. When I was sure it was clear, I hopped back over the wall, closely followed by Nyre and the others.

"This sweater is itchy," Nyre complained as we started along the dirt track. It was now completely covered in fresh snow, and the only tracks that showed were the slowly disappearing tracks of the others that had gone on ahead.

The village itself was quiet, largely due to the weather, I suspected. We kept to the road that skirted it, moving quickly toward the ruins shown on the map. The houses at the edge of the village showed it was not a wealthy one. The cottages we passed to our left were made of stone and all needed repairs of some kind. Paint flaked off old window frames and garden gates hung precariously from the fences that surrounded the houses like forgotten doll's houses that young children had not quite figured how to play carefully with yet. To our right, beyond another stone wall, was a snow-covered field with a small woods beyond it that ran the length of the dirt track we were on.

After an hour or so, I spotted the ruins from the map. The village was far enough behind us for me to feel a little safer, and we'd managed to get around it without any problems. I'd expected the ruins to be from some kind of temple or place of worship, but as I got closer, I saw that they were what was left of an old castle. It was nowhere near as grand as my home in Draconis, but the tower and part of the ramparts were still standing. If Fallon and the others hadn't managed to find tents for us in any of the shops in the village, this would do for one night. Some of the roof looked to be keeping the snow out. I was feeling a little more optimistic as we diverged from the road and crossed the field to the castle. Even better, I could just about make out the tracks of the others that had gone on ahead. They'd found the place alright.

"Bit spooky," Blaise exclaimed as we came upon the old outer wall, which was mostly just rubble now.

"It's awesome!" Nyre cried, running toward the one tower that was still standing.

I followed the footsteps to what would have once been the great hall, but now was barely more than a broken mosaic tiled floor and one wall with a huge fireplace that had partially caved in. Beyond it was a doorway, which looked like it would lead to the tower. Smoke curling into the sky from somewhere told me that the others had already started a fire.

I found them, not in the tower as I'd expected, but in another room to the side. There was a hole in the ceiling blowing in flurries of snow, which lay in a pile at one end, but it was mostly intact and dry enough at this end for us to eat our lunch without getting wet. When Deon saw me, he ran over and threw his arms around me, almost knocking me over.

"The others aren't back yet," he whispered into my ear. "I thought they'd be here before you."

I looked around, and sure enough, Fallon, Halia, and Eliana were missing, along with Zacharina.

"They'll be here soon," I said, not entirely convinced.

"Let's eat our sandwiches and wait for them. I was hoping to get to the Elder border by tonight, but if they aren't here soon, we'll have to sleep here. I'll go back to the village after lunch and see if I can spot them."

We sat in silence as we ate sandwiches that had been prepared for us by the Innkeeper the day before. I watched as Deon twisted his vine shaped wedding ring on his finger and kept glancing toward the doorway as though the others would walk in at any second.

An hour later, and it was apparent that they weren't coming back. Something had gone wrong. I could feel it in my bones. Just as I had felt something missing when Castiel left, my magic power felt diminished now.

I stood up. "I'm heading into the village to find them."

"I'm not sure that's a good idea," Blaise piped up, dropping a half-eaten apple onto her lap. "They could be back any minute."

I pulled my cloak around my shoulders. "I think we all know they are in trouble. They left hours ago. Even if they bought up a whole store of blankets, they should have been here by now."

Deon stood beside me and rested his hand on my arm. "Just because they are not here yet doesn't mean they are in trouble. They didn't have a map. Maybe they just took a wrong turning."

"That sounds like trouble to me," I replied, although we both knew that wasn't the trouble I'd been talking about. Not that it mattered. They weren't here, and I was going to find out where they were. I pulled him away from everyone else. "I know you think they are in trouble as much as I do," I said, keeping my voice low. "I saw you fidgeting with your wedding ring. You only do that when you are nervous."

"I'll come with you," he offered, grabbing his coat

from the ground.

I was about to protest but going alone scared me more than I cared to admit. "Fine," I conceded gratefully.

"The rest of you stay here and wait. We'll be back soon."

Snow swirled around us in thick heavy flakes. Our tracks from the road to the ruin had already been covered with a fresh load of it. It was beginning to get deep, which made it harder to walk, but it covered our footsteps.

We walked in silence up the track until the edge of the village came into view.

"What's our plan?" Deon finally asked.

I shrugged. "I don't have one. You?"

"I'm not sure what we can do beyond walk around the village and try to be inconspicuous."

"Great plan," I said without a hint of sarcasm. It was no worse than anything I'd come up with, which was nothing at all. I didn't know Leodis, and I didn't know what we'd be facing once we were there. My sword hung at my side, concealed by my cloak. I only hoped that I'd have no cause to use it.

After all my fear that the town would be full of dangers, I was pleasantly surprised to find it was a pretty picture-postcard village with winter festival lights decorating the village square illuminating the glittering snow that cascaded down in front of them.

"Where first?" I whispered.

As we walked slowly through the snow-covered square. A delicious smell of warm cinnamon filled the air, making my stomach rumble.

"Let's get a coffee at the bakery and review our options," Deon suggested pointing to the source of the cinnamon smell. It sat in between two shops. An outdoor equipment store called Wagner and Cox sat on one side with a flower shop called Fleur Occasions on the other. The flower store was closed, but Wagner and Cox had an open sign in the window.

We didn't have many options as far as I could see. "We can't go to the bakery. We need to find the others. Why not try in there?" I said, pointing to the outdoor equipment store next door.

"I'll get us a coffee and cinnamon roll to go. My fingers feel like they are about to fall off with the cold. We'll check out Wagner and Cox right after."

I nodded gratefully. It was painfully cold, and our clothing was threadbare and barely fit for any purpose anymore, even with Eliana's constant darning and mending of it. My gloves had holes in most of the fingers

Inside, the bakery was empty except for a young girl behind the counter. Deon ordered our coffees as I looked for somewhere to sit and wait.

I found a seat at a corner table away from the window and let my hood down for the first time since setting out. As Deon ordered two coffees and two cinnamon buns, I picked up a copy of The Vale Echo that had been left behind. Our photo was on the front cover. I held my breath as I read the headline.

REWARD INCREASES IN SEARCH FOR OUTLAWS

I pulled my hood up quickly, grabbed the paper, and stood up. As the girl prepared our coffees, I took hold of Deon's arm and practically dragged him from the shop. The snow had abated slightly, but the cold bit into my exposed skin as we ran.

"What's the matter?" Deon asked as I pulled him into an alley behind the shops.

I spread the paper out on a low wall after dusting the snow from it, and the pair of us read the article.

The twelve murderers who escaped from Urbis Prison last month in what has become known as the prison's biggest breakout since it opened have been spotted in The Vale. One of them is Jakon Gale, who escaped the month before and is thought to have orchestrated the whole breakout. His earlier companions are no longer with them, and it is currently unknown where they are. He and his current companions have been seen with a small purple dragon.

A source who wishes to remain anonymous told us that they spent the night at the Forestside Inn in the south of Vale. They were overheard discussing the route they were planning on taking on their way to Urbis, but our source said that he didn't hear their exact plans. He did say they set off with bags full of food and that one of the male members had left earlier than the others, probably to scout ahead. The group is thought to be armed and dangerous. Some of them carry weapons, and the dragon is known to be able to breathe fire. The group is also known to have magical abilities, which makes them more dangerous than the average criminal. If you see them, stay away and head to the nearest police station immediately. Because of the nature of their crimes, the reward for capture has been increased to ten thousand Urbis Dollars.

"Murderers?" I murmured.

My breath caught in my throat at the lies in the article, but what caused me the most alarm was the fact that we'd been spotted in The Vale. We needed to get out of here and fast. My plan of spending the night in the relative comfort of the ruins was dashed. The border to Elder was close by, and if we kept on walking through the night, there was a chance we'd get to Arcadia before the morning.

"We need to find them now! If everyone knows we are in The Vale, we'll have no chance of hiding. Damn that innkeeper. I gave him so much money."

"Calm down," Deon murmured quietly. "It could be worse. He could have gone to the police when we were there and collected a reward, but he at least waited until we'd gone."

"What a great guy!" I replied, my voice heavy with sarcasm.

Deon pulled the paper from the wall and rolled it up. "The village is small. There are only a few places they could be. Let's walk around until we find them. A unicorn is going to be easy to spot. We'll find them."

"Fine," I conceded, "but we need to be quick. Everyone will know what we look like by now." I pulled my hood low and headed back out into the square. At least, the weather was on our side. Very few people were out and about in the swirling snow.

We retraced our steps back to the entrance to the village and methodically walked up and down every street. The houses in the inner part of the village were all the same, made from weathered stone with tiny gardens out front and smoking chimneys atop snow-covered roofs. I imagined they would be so pretty in summer with red roofs and flowers coloring the gardens, but with the white snow, gray stone, and heavy sky, the whole place was bleak and soulless. It was a far cry from the red soil of Draconis. A pang of homesickness hit me as we turned back into the square where we had started. A couple more people were out braving the cold, but there was no sign of Fallon, Halia, and Eliana.

"They aren't here!" I said, feeling defeated. I could feel their magic, but it wasn't strong enough for me to follow.

"Azia," Deon cautioned, pulling me into the shadows. "Look."

My eyes followed the line of his finger. It took me a few seconds to see what it was he was pointing at. At the road leading away from the square were a number of tracks in the snow. More than a few people had walked out of the village and toward the road that would take us back to the ruin.

"The tracks must be theirs," I said as we came to the road past the town. The tracks indeed headed back to our hiding place. I heaved a sigh of relief and once again mentally berated myself for panicking too early. It was beginning to become a bad habit. One that wouldn't suit me well.

"I don't think so," Deon said, grabbing my hand to stop me from racing off down the road.

"What do you mean?"

"Look at the tracks. None of them belong to a unicorn. And there are more than three people's footprints."

With dismay, I saw that he was right. The prints we'd made walking into the village were now almost entirely covered with fresh snow. These prints were new, but they were indistinct, already being covered by the heavy snow. It was impossible to make out how many there were and in what direction they were going.

I fingered my sword as I always did when I was nervous. Feeling the shape of the engraved dragon reminded me of Nyre. I wished I'd brought her with us. She could fly over the ruin and tell me what was going on. As it was, our only option was to head down the road and see for ourselves.

The weather picked up again as we dashed through the snow. Ferocious winds blasted the bitterly cold snow into our faces making it hard to see anything at all.

My nerves increased as we came to the small path leading from the road to the ruin. The almost covered tracks led right there.

Pulling my sword out of its sheath, I held it aloft as the snow swirled around me. A crash of thunder echoed in my ears as I stepped into the ruin.

"Stay behind me," I whispered. Outside, the snow blew in a gale, and thunder pealed once more. My heart thudded as I turned the corner to where we'd eaten lunch. There was nobody there. They'd all gone and left all their belongings behind.

"There was a struggle," Deon murmured, taking in the scene before us.

Ashes of the fire had been kicked over, creating a black mess over the floor and driven by the wind to the other side of the room. The blankets were strewn around the room, some in the dry end, and some had been kicked to the snow-covered side. It was a mess, but at least there wasn't any blood.

"We should have followed the prints from the village to the source rather than down here," I said, turning to head out.

"Not now, Azia," Deon said as his face lit up from a flash of lightning. Seconds later, another crash of thunder blasted through the sky.

"What do you mean, not now?" I hollered. My voice sounded eerie in the sudden silence that followed the thunder. "The prints will be covered by the morning, and we won't be able to find them."

He pointed to the window. The sky was dark as night, and the snow was so heavy that I couldn't see more than a few feet. I'd never seen a storm like it.

"The prints will be covered already. If we go out

in this, we'll be dead of exposure long before we find them. We might be demi-gods, but I'm not taking the chance to check my mortality. We'll head out first thing tomorrow when the storm is over."

Anger turned my stomach. I'd made a mistake again. Last week it was allowing Rumpelstiltskin into our camp and giving him all the information he needed to pass on to Derillen and her people, and this week, I'd managed to lose everyone. First, it was Castiel I'd driven out, then Halia, Eliana and Fallon, and now, everyone else. I turned to Deon, wanting to shout at him because he was the only one there, but it wasn't his fault. None of this was. He was the only one I had left.

"Come on," I said. Let's get those blankets out of the snow. I had a feeling we were going to need them.

JANUARY DERILLEN

Looking down at the list I'd made, I saw that the next monster was the daughter of the King and Queen of Atlantice. Having already taken care of Briar Rose, my next move was to head there. The royals of Draconis were so wrapped up in their own problems that the queen getting sleepier and sleepier had barely registered with them. Oh, they'd noticed, and they'd had discussions about it, but thanks to the brat's bizarre new romance with her guard and the faerie moping all around thc castlc about it, not to mention the dragons deciding that the top of the mountain wasn't the place to be anymore, there were plenty of distractions for a maid to administer sleeping draughts to the queen and make sure she'd be asleep when the time was right. A little vacation for a few days wouldn't hurt my plans. Not at all.

On the Urbis Express, I pulled out the notes I'd made after reading all about the monsters. The Atlantice brat was called Blaise, and as far as I could tell, she actually thought she was the real daughter of the king and queen. For descendants of gods, they really were stupid creatures—nothing like Morpheus. But then again, no one was quite like Morpheus. I allowed myself a sigh as I thought of his beauty and his power. If he'd only chose to be with me, this would be oh so much easier, but no. He was a selfish man. God or not, he was still a man, and though he could be manipulated, I knew that not even I could get him to give up his partying ways. More's the pity. We could rule all the kingdoms together, and I wouldn't have to resort to traveling on these darned airships like a normal person to get around.

The history of Atlantice was pretty straightforward. Before the brats had come into the world, the kingdom was overrun by some sea witch and her minions. Just like me, she'd not been heard from in over eighteen years, but I was willing to bet she was still out there, and I was further willing to bet that she was as angry as I was. Perhaps she didn't understand what had happened to her, but thanks to me, she soon would.

The airship landed in Urbis at the same station it had on my earlier trip, but this time, I wasn't planning on staying. The thought of Morpheus being only a train ride away had me almost heading to the train station, but what was the point? He'd made me a promise, and I knew he'd stick to it. Going to him would only disappoint me further. I knew I'd find him in some club surrounded by young women. My heart couldn't stand it.

“Stop being ridiculous,” I hissed to myself as the airship once again took to the sky, heading back to Draconis. I watched it from the ground, concentrating on the beauty of the workmanship of it. From the elegant passenger ship below to the red and gold balloon above that carried it. I watched it until the words Urbis Express written in gold on the side were too far away to read. Anything to keep from thinking of Morpheus. I wasn’t a child. I was a woman. An old woman, at that. I had no time left for romance. Power was what I wanted. It ate away at me, and as I stepped onto the next airship, which would take me to Atlantice, I knew I deserved better. I deserved to be in the royal cabin that was reserved for the leaders of the kingdoms. I deserved it all.

Atlantice turned out to be a strange place. Having never visited it before, I was taken aback by the narrow streets and waterways that wove through the cities like snakes weaving through the undergrowth. The Urbis Express landed in the capital city of Antla in a cobbled square similar to the one in Urbis. I stepped out and breathed the fresh air. The slightly salty smell of the sea wafted on the breeze, although I couldn’t see any hint of the ocean. The only water in sight was a canal, which had a great number of small rowboats, each manned by one person. I watched how the other passengers all gravitated to these boats, paid the oarsmen, and hopped aboard.

“How quaint,” I murmured, following the others. As I stepped toward the bank of the canal, a young woman in a red boat pulled up. Her long hair was tied back in a braid, and she wore a red woolen hat that matched the color of the boat perfectly.

"Need a ride, miss?" she inquired, giving me a friendly smile.

I didn't care for the title of miss, but the idea of floating into the city had its own appeal. I accepted her offer and hopped into the boat to a small bench seat opposite her. As she rowed backward, I was afforded a view of the town in front of me.

"My name's Ella. Where would you like to go, miss?" the girl asked.

There was only one place where I knew I'd find a witch of the sea.

"I'd like to procure the services of a sea captain. Do you know where I might find one?"

"Any of the bars in the village probably," she replied with a slight grin on her face. "That's where most of them head when they are back on land. Wanting to do a bit of sightseeing around the coast? It's beautiful this time of year and not too many tourists. It gets busier in the summer."

"Something like that," I replied, matching her smile. "Do you know of anyone who'd be able to take me out to sea? Someone who would be sober at this time of day? I'm willing to pay good money."

I swear the young girl's eyes lit up as I brought out my purse and showed her the notes in there. It wasn't the currency of Atlantice, but she'd recognize the Urbis notes anywhere.

"I have a sailboat," she offered eagerly, eyeing up the pile of cash. "It's not much, but it's good enough for a day trip."

I summed up her offer. My plan had been to find

some old seadog who obviously didn't care much for the royals and would tell me what I needed to know, but the look of eagerness on the girl had me reconsidering. She would be an easy mark for obtaining the information I wanted.

"Tell me, do you know much about the history of Atlantice?" I asked, leaning forward. "Specifically, before the young princess was born? I would like a real tour with a guided history if I'm to hire anyone."

She rested her oars on her knees as she thought. "Princess Blaise is the same age as me, and I don't remember that time, but I know all about it. Her birth was something of a surprise because the king and queen had kept it hidden. It wasn't long after their wedding either. That's probably why they hid it."

She picked her oars up when she noticed we were drifting slightly and in danger of crashing into one of the buildings that flanked the canal.

"What about before the princess was born? I heard stories of a sea witch."

Ella lowered her oars in the water and skillfully maneuvered the boat until it was floating in a straight line again.

"It was a dark time by all accounts," she began. "My father told me that I was born at the right time. The witch was more problem to the merfolk than to humans, but she did enough damage on both sides. If you like, I can tell you all about it as I take us around the coast."

She was a salesperson by nature, and she knew what I wanted to know.

"I'd like that," I said, handing over a pile of cash. It was nothing compared to the money I'd have once I was the supreme ruler.

She pocketed the money quickly and picked up her oars again.

"She was awful," Ella said, beginning her story as she rowed. "Some say she was beautiful, and some tell the tale that she was ugly. There's no definitive answer on that. It depends on who you speak to."

I raised an eyebrow. Ugly and beautiful? Could she shift her appearance like I could? Intriguing.

"What was it she wanted?" I asked. If I knew her motivation, then getting her on my side would be easier, especially with my powers of persuasion. "I mean. What was her reasoning for being so...awful?"

Ella shrugged, missing a stroke of the oar and almost sending us in a circle.

Another boat passed us, and the passengers waved. I gave a half-hearted wave back, then turned my attention back to Ella.

"Who knows why people do these things?" she said wistfully. "As far as I know, it had something to do with the royals, but I don't know what."

That piqued my curiosity. "The royals. What can you tell me about them? Apart from the mysterious appearance of their daughter?"

Ella shifted in her seat and seemed quite happy to be talking about Atlantice's history. Of course, her enthusiasm could be linked to the giant wad of cash burning a hole in her pocket.

"King Ermias and Queen Antonella were married at a young age. King Ermias was heir to the throne with or without marriage, but one day Antonella appeared. No one knew who she was. She wasn't a princess from another kingdom, nor was she from one of the noble families of Atlantice."

"So a queen that appeared from nowhere and then a

child that no one knew about. Interesting kingdom you have here."

She nodded, her eyes almost twinkling. "It wasn't customary for a royal to marry a commoner, but marry her he did. As I said earlier, they had their daughter, Princess Blaise, not long after. Shotgun wedding much? Mind you, they are still together and still doing a great job, so maybe it was meant to be. Maybe it was love at first sight. Kinda romantic, don't you think?"

"Hmm, a beautiful story indeed." Vomit inducing. "What happened to the witch?"

She shrugged her shoulders. "I don't know. One minute she was trying to take over, and the next, she just disappeared. There's been no sight of her since around the time Blaise was born. I guess she died. It would have been a much more interesting story if the king had killed her in a huge fight, huh?"

"I don't know," I mused. "I'm finding this very interesting. You say you know where she used to hang out?"

We pulled up to a quay, and Ella tied the boat up next to some others.

"There's not much to see as she lived under the ocean, but I know where she was seen coming to the surface the most." She hopped out of the boat and held her hand out to help me.

The sea breeze hit my face as we walked the short way from the canal to the seafront. We crossed a cobbled road leaving the buildings behind us. To our left, on the seafront, there was a restaurant with tables and chairs outside and just beyond was a low sea wall spattered with sea spray. A couple of dolphins frolicked in the sea beyond a pier. They had what looked like bags on their backs.

"Are those dolphins carrying something?" I asked as the girl led me along the jetty where the sailboats were moored. These were so different from the boat we'd just left. Many had cabins, and one or two were big enough to live aboard.

"They are mail dolphins. Most of the houses and businesses in Antla are connected to tunnels that the dolphins swim through to deliver the mail. It takes the pressure off the road system."

I raised an eyebrow. The use of mail-carrying dolphins was a strange concept, but if it worked, it worked.

Ella was almost apologetic when she showed me her boat. With no cabin, it was barely bigger than the boat we'd just come from, but it had a sail, and that's all I needed.

"Sorry, it's not much," she said, helping me down. I sat on another bench seat, but this time, she sat next to me rather than opposite.

"The wind is good. I should be able to get us there quickly. I have to warn you, though, that there isn't much to see. One part of the ocean looks pretty much like every other part. I can take you over the undersea kingdom if you like. If the tide is low, you can sometimes see the top of the underwater palace."

She hoisted the sail, and immediately the wind took us away from the shore.

"The royal palace is underwater? How do the royals breathe?"

She laughed, making me feel uneasy. I should have been more prepared. Being laughed at by a commoner was not something I enjoyed, not even one as useful as this girl.

"King Ermias, Queen Antonella, and Princess Blaise live over there," she said, pointing to a huge palace at the edge of the shore in its own private cove.

"The palace underwater is the realm of the merfolk."

Ah, now I knew a little about Atlantice's merfolk. The kingdom was known for them.

"I didn't realize they had a palace. I thought they just...swam about."

"They do, but they have homes down there, despite the AML trying to destroy their way of life."

"AML?"

"Anti-Mermaid League. It's a bit pointless, really, but they like to think they are better than sea dwellers. Do you want to see the palace? It's just over the reef?"

As much as an underwater palace interested me, it wasn't something I'd come for. If the sea witch didn't live there, I didn't need to know.

"Actually, I'd prefer if you take me to where the sea witch lived."

She gave me an odd look as though she couldn't imagine why I'd even want to see it, but her thoughts on the subject were no concern of mine. I only needed her to take me to the sea witch, not have an opinion as to why.

We sailed for an hour or so before coming to a stop. "It's here," she said, pulling the sail down.

We bobbed on the surface of the ocean, not moving in any direction. She checked some kind of maritime instrument and nodded her head.

"What's here?" As far as I could see, there was nothing here: nothing but water. I couldn't even see the land; we'd come out so far.

"This is where the sea witch was spotted coming out of the water more than anywhere else. There were many stories from both sea captains and merfolk that this was the place."

"But there's nothing here," I grimaced, feeling furious. I was not about to be fooled by a young girl.

"Yeah, I told you. She lived below." She gulped as she pointed downward, dipping her finger in the ocean. "The sea is deep here."

I peered over the side and found myself looking into nothing but darkness. A couple of strands of seaweed floated on the top giving the whole area a decidedly disgusting fishy odor.

Frustration rippled through me. I bit it back and plastered a smile on my face to hide the anger I was feeling. "How did the people call her to the surface?"

The girl furrowed her eyebrows, and I saw fear in her eyes.

"No one called her. She came of her own accord to wreak havoc."

I took a deep breath and dropped the smile. Who cared what the girl thought of me? It wasn't like she could run away. "But if anyone wanted to call her?"

"Why would anyone want to call her?" Ella bleated. "She was a witch. She liked hurting people." She began to pull the rope that would put the sail up again. "Maybe we should head back to the mainland. It's getting late."

"And maybe she just needed a bit of bait?" I said, standing up. The girl didn't have a chance. I pushed her backward into the water as the boat began to take sail once again. I didn't need it to go far, just far enough that she wouldn't be able to clamor aboard while I planned what to do next.

The girl could swim, but it was doubtful she'd be able to make it to the shore. It was too far away. On the other hand, I didn't have all day to wait for her to drown to see if that would make the sea witch appear.

I conjured weights above the girl's head and let them

drop. Seconds later, she disappeared under the water, and I was alone.

11TH DECEMBER
AZIA

I woke up in darkness. The smell of earth and dirt filled my nostrils, and course fabric scratched against my cheeks. I felt myself being hauled to my feet, and beside me, I heard grunts from Deon, who, presumably, was being manhandled in a similar way.

My hands were grasped tightly behind my back, making it impossible to grab my sword or to throw a punch, but I still had my feet. I kicked out blindly behind me, feeling the heel of my new boot hit the leg of my attacker. An oof came from him as I began to struggle against him. He tightened his grip and mumbled something. Another one mumbled back. The sack over my head blocked out most of the sound, so I couldn't hear what they were saying, but I could guess the gist of it. I twisted against the attacker's grip, causing him to let go of my wrists and, instead, clamp them to my side by putting his arms around my middle. It wasn't what I intended, but it gave me an idea. I let him drag me easily across the cold stone floor, feeling the ashes of the fire crunching beneath my feet. From the direction we were taking, I guessed we were heading toward the grand hall. My attacker remained silent, but it wasn't him I needed to hear. Deon shouted my name, giving me a general idea of where he was.

"I'm here," I shouted back. "I'm ok."

"So far, you are," my attacker grunted loud enough for me to hear. "Do what I tell you and keep it that way."

He didn't see it, but my middle finger was most definitely extended. The hilt of my sword brushed against the tip of my fingers but grabbing it wouldn't help me if I couldn't pull it from its sheath.

"Deon?" I shouted again, needing to hear his voice.

"I'm here."

He was closer now, almost within reaching distance. In one swift moment, I lifted my legs, bearing all my weight on my attacker, and kicked out ahead. My feet connected with someone in front of me.

"What the..." My attacker said as I brought my head back sharply. The sack might have muffled his words, but the sound of his nose breaking as it connected with the back of my skull came in loud and clear, as did the agonized scream that came from his mouth. He released me, and I dropped to the snow. Pulling the sack from my head, I assessed the situation quickly. There were two of them. The one that had been holding onto me was on his hands and knees, clutching his nose as blood streamed from it, turning the snow a bright red beneath him. The other, a younger man with dark blond hair and a weasel-like face, recovered from my kick quickly. I pulled my sword from its sheath and held it out in front of me, but he was too quick. He managed to knock it out of my hand with a baton. It fell into the snow in a soft thump. He raised his hand to bring the baton down on me, a sneer on his face, but before he could, the vines that coated the walls of the ruins writhed up his body, wrapping around it and effectively tying him up, including his hand that still held the baton.

"Come on, let's go," I shouted, grabbing my sword from the snow and Deon's hand. We pelted out into the field away from the castle and to the copse of woods behind it. The first man chased us, blood still dripping from his nose, but there was no way he could keep up with two demi-gods. Losing him was easy. Staying lost would be hard.

"Nice magic!" I huffed to Deon as we pelted through the trees. The snow had stopped at some point in the night, but it was still bitterly cold, and my breath showed in front of me as I spoke.

"It was nothing. The vines were already there. I just repositioned them."

"What now?" I wheezed as we exited the small woods and climbed over the low stone wall to the road. I could just about see the ruins in the distance to our right. The men wouldn't be far behind us, and as far as I could see, we had little in the way of places to hide.

"The way I see it, we have two choices," Deon said, bending over and holding his knees to catch his breath. "Either we follow their footsteps back into the village to see where they came from, and maybe the others will be there. Or, we wait here and let ourselves get caught."

I wrinkled my forehead and narrowed my eyes at

him. "Why would we do that?"

Deon cast a glance back toward the ruins. "Because if they catch us and they do have the others, they will probably take us right to them."

I thought about it for a second. "Great plan, but if the others are imprisoned, then surely we will be too. Let's go with plan A."

He nodded, standing up straight. We walked up the road, following this morning's footsteps of the two men to their source in the hope that everyone else would be there.

"How do you think Derillen's henchmen found us so quickly?" I asked as we came to the houses on the outskirts of the village.

"They weren't anything to do with Derillen," Deon stated. "They were locals. I could tell by their accents. They both held police issue batons. My thought is that they saw the article in the paper yesterday and decided to cash in on the reward."

"So Derillen doesn't know we are here yet?" Relief ran through me. Something about knowing that Derillen wasn't involved yet made me feel a whole lot better about things. A couple of greedy local cops, I could deal with. An army of magic-wielding insaniacs was another thing entirely.

"I doubt it," Deon replied, walking briskly through the thick layer of snow last night's storm had produced. "She'll know approximately where we are, thanks to Rumpelstiltskin and the newspaper article, but exactly where we are? No. Those two idiots we just left behind will, no doubt, have sent a messenger on the Urbis Express to Urbis yesterday, though."

"So if Derillen doesn't know yet, she will soon."

"Exactly," Deon agreed, picking up his pace until he

was almost running. "We need to find the others and get out of here fast."

If Deon was right, the logical place to find them was the police station. We'd passed one yesterday in our walk around the village.

"I saw the police station at the top of the village, north of the village square."

Deon nodded, then slowed. I shivered at the sight of all the fresh tracks in the snow on the road into the village. There were only ours when we'd set out yesterday, now it looked like hundreds of people had walked into the village.

"Why are all these tracks here?" I questioned as we cautiously followed them. "The weather is barely any better than it was yesterday."

"Shopping?" Deon guessed, but I knew he was wrong. Why would so many people come out today if no one had come out yesterday? The storm had started later in the day.

The further we walked into the village, the greater my anxiety grew. Something wasn't right. The second we rounded the corner to the main square, my fears were founded. It was full of people—a shouting, angry mob of people.

Deon grabbed my hand to stop me from going any further and pulled me into a small alleyway between two shops where we could see the square from the shadows. At the front of the crowd were a number of posters, all of them featuring the picture from yesterday's newspaper. Everyone's face had been crossed out except Deon's, Castiel's, and mine. The only three that hadn't been caught yet.

My first thought was to stay back and listen to what was being shouted, but I didn't get the chance.

Someone at the back of the crowd happened to turn around and see us. She let out a bellow, and seconds later, a bell rang out through the village. The group descended on us. I turned on my heel and began to run with Deon beside me. I knew we could outrun them, even a whole village of people, but where was there to run to? The village was small, and the only other place I knew nearby was the ruins. Neither was safe. In the snow, they'd find us eventually.

"This way," Deon said, pulling me around a corner. We ran down the back of a row of shops, jumping over boxes and garbage that had been left out in the snow. Veering quickly to the right away from the shops, we found ourselves in another alley, this time behind the pretty cottages. A group of the villagers appeared at the other end of the alley.

Ducking into someone's snow-covered yard, we managed to hide without being spotted, but it was only a matter of time before we were. It was a small village, and it looked like everyone in it was in the lynch mob.

"Why couldn't I have been given the gift of invisibility?" I quipped quietly. "What's the use of calling dragons if the only one nearby that will be able to hear me is more than likely locked up in jail?"

"Your gift will come in soon enough. For now, though, you also have your gift of swordsmanship."

"It's not a gift. That came from practice. I don't see how it will help us now, though. I'm okay one on one, but a hundred on one might be a little out of my depth."

"I'm not saying we slay the entire village," he whispered, gripping the back yard gate we were up against. "I'm pretty sure the lure of ten thousand Urbis dollars is what's getting them out of their houses. That's ten year's wages in a place like this."

"How do you know what people in The Vale earn?"

"I read."

I rolled my eyes. "Show off! So you still haven't told me what I'm supposed to do with my sword if you don't want me to stab someone with it."

"Nothing," a voice boomed from behind us. I turned quickly to find a steely, old woman with sharp eyes looking down at us. A pair of glasses hung around her neck on a chain. "My winter roses are difficult to grow, and I wouldn't want anyone accidentally lopping their heads off. If you're looking for a place to hide, why not come into my house. No one will come knocking on my door, I assure you."

I glanced at Deon, who shrugged his shoulders. The sound of the mob was getting closer, and our choices were limited. She opened her back gate, and the two of us ran through her yard and through the open door of her house. We came into a room that was immaculate with walls lined with shelves of books. A simple rug covered the floor. The furnishings consisted of two armchairs, a small sofa, and a side table. The side table was covered with what looked to be newspapers.

I peered out of the window through net curtains as the mob ran right past the garden gate, not giving us a glance. I let out a breath at how close a call it had been.

"Thank you," I heard Deon saying to the woman. "We really appreciate it."

"It's quite alright," she said with a hint of efficiency in her voice. "I do so hate the mentality of the people around here. I doubt they know the significance of the people they are chasing. They just see dollar signs. Would you both mind taking your boots off. Cleaning this rug is such a time-consuming endeavor, and I value my time tremendously. "

"You know who we are?" I asked, pulling my boots off and placing them next to Deon's by the back door.

She smiled and pulled her glasses up onto her face "Yes, Your Highness. I know who you are. And you too, Mr. Deon. I've read enough in the papers to work out that you are wanted—you and the other heirs to the thrones of the kingdoms. What I can't for the life of me figure out is why. I don't believe for a second you are murderers, and I furthermore don't believe any of you were in Urbis Prison. Please take a seat. I don't like to stand on ceremony here."

I sat on one of the sofas next to Deon. Stacked on the floor beside the side table were more stacks of newspapers, not only the Valean Echo but papers from other kingdoms. I made out copies of the Draconian Sentinel, among others.

"We don't know exactly," Deon started. "It's something to do with our history. We..."

I nudged him in the side. Neither of us knew this woman. She could be Derillen or Rumpelstiltskin for all we knew. Both of them had the power to change their appearance at will.

"We are powerful people," I said, interrupting Deon. "Our families are powerful, I mean. Politically speaking."

It didn't really answer her question, but she didn't question us further.

"Indeed. Well, it is a pleasure to have royalty in my house. I'll make us some tea. I'm afraid it's only the cheap stuff, but it's the best I can get around here. Leodis is not known for its culinary delights, and I have to make do with what I can order in from nearby towns."

"I'm sure it will be lovely, thank you."

"What was that for?" Deon whispered once she was out of the room.

"Everyone wants to kill us or capture us. Just because this woman hasn't done it yet, doesn't mean she won't. Remember last week when we thought a four-year-old girl was helpless and needed saving?"

Comprehension dawned on Deon's face. "Right!"

My eyes skipped over to the piles of newspapers again. I was itching to grab one. I stood and took the top one from a pile of Draconian Sentinels, hoping for some news about my family. The front page was filled with an article about the dragon shifters. I scanned the article for a mention of Vasuki and Emba, Nyre's parents, but the article was very general and spoke about a meeting between the dragons and my father to talk about dragon/human relations. My heart leapt at seeing his name mentioned.

The woman bustled back in with a tray of tea and homemade cookies, so I folded the paper and placed it beside me.

"Something is happening everywhere, and I think you two know what," she said, her steely eyes boring into me. "I appreciate that you don't want to tell me, but I happen to know that Princess Eliana is currently in the village jail. I know that you are with her, and I know you want her out, along with the other heirs. I want her out too. I have great respect for the royals of this kingdom. Her Highness, the princess, has been through a lot in the last couple of years, and I don't wish to see any more harm come to her. It's my personal belief that she doesn't deserve to be locked up, nor to have a price to be on her head."

"She doesn't," I replied, planning my words carefully. "She's done nothing wrong. Do you know how we can get her out?"

The woman sighed. "I'm afraid not. You have seen

what the people of this village are like. It's a poor village, and they are all after the reward. None of them have enough brain cells to think about why there is a reward or to care. I wish I could help." She passed me a cup of tea and a saucer with a slice of lemon and a sugar cube resting upon it.

"Thanks. There must be some way into the jail?"

"Only through the front door of the police station," she replied, passing a cup and saucer to Deon, then taking one for herself and sitting in the armchair opposite us. "It is not high security, just a couple of jail cells and two desks. The sheriff of these parts and his deputy are not particularly bright and aren't beyond corruption. I'd say offer them a bribe to let their prisoners go, but unless you are carrying over ten thousand Urbis dollars in cash, I'm not sure they'll be swayed—not when they have the promise of that coming their way, anyway."

"I assure you, we don't have anything like that amount of money on us."

The woman smiled sadly. "I assumed you didn't. You could try and fight your way through, but with the whole village out to capture you, I doubt you'll get very far. I have a horse and cart I could hide you in to get you out of the village, but there is no way I could take it to the police station. The sheriff and his deputy might be stupid, but they are not that stupid."

"We had a run-in with them this morning," Deon said. "They came off worse than we did."

The woman gave an impish grin that brightened up her face completely. "Good for you."

I glanced over at the stack of papers again. She had hundreds of them, all in neat piles.

"What exactly do you know about our situation?" I asked, holding up the paper I'd picked up earlier.

The woman smiled broadly and sat back in her chair. "It started with you, actually. No one around here reads the papers other than The Vale Echo, but I like to keep up with things. Your mother's illness was written about in the Draconian Sentinel, but none of the other kingdoms had much to say on it. I didn't think much about it either. I mean, people get sick, right? Except you went on vacation not long after. It seemed strange to me that a young princess would leave her home while her mother was so sick. Then in Atlantice, there was another mysterious illness. The Conch spoke of an uprising against the Merfolk and that Queen Antonella had become one of them. Then, Princess Blaise also disappeared without much fanfare."

She sipped at her tea and placed the cup back on the saucer. "After that, I kept an eye out for something similar happening, but nothing did for a long while. I thought that maybe it was all a coincidence, and I was reading too much into things, but then about three months after Princess Blaise went missing, Eliana did too. Right after the abduction of Princess Fae. I knew something was up. I like to keep up on the royals, and I know that Eliana would not leave without just cause right after her baby had been taken. I went back through my newspapers and looked for other things that were odd. Elder has no newspaper, but I did find a couple of small articles in other papers about a problem with the wolves, and I wondered if that had something to do with all this. After that, Princess Lilian of Floris married. I expected to hear about her leaving next, but of course, she never did. It was never mentioned that her new husband had gone, but I later saw you in the wanted posters and recognized you from a photo of your wedding. Actually, I did see something unusual in one of the photos. Let me see if I can dig it out."

She rifled through the stack of Floris Observers and pulled one out. It had a photo of Deon and his bride dancing at their wedding reception. The look of love in their eyes was beautiful, but it wasn't what the woman pointed out. There, in the background, chatting with each other were Blaise and I. We were slightly blurred as the photographer had been intent on capturing the happy couple, but there was no mistaking us. I could just make out Castiel sitting on my other side, half-cropped out of the photo.

It had only been eight or nine months since the photo was taken, but it felt like an eternity ago. Deon's wedding was one of the last days I'd felt true hope.

"When I saw you and Princess Blaise at the wedding, I knew something was amiss. Neither of you were with your parents, and by all accounts, you were both still on some mysterious vacation. In fact, neither the Sentinel nor the Conch had mentioned either of you in months."

I looked over at Deon, who had taken the paper from the woman's hands. I could see by the wistful smile on his face that it wasn't Blaise or me he was looking at in the photo.

"At first, I don't think anyone else noticed things changing," she continued, "but by the time things were happening in The Forge, the kingdoms' newspapers had begun to take note."

She pulled her glasses off, gave them a wipe, and let them hang around her neck before carrying on with the story. "It was about that time that there was a new president elected in Urbis. She somehow managed to bypass the whole process of getting elected. One day no one had heard of her; the next minute, she was running Urbis. Once she was in, she brought her own people to the cabinet."

"She?" I asked, my heart rate increasing with the thought of what I was about to hear.

"She's called Derillen. No surname. I can see by the rather sickly look on your face that you know of her?"

"You could say that," I replied.

She frowned. "Since then, Urbis has been printing pictures of you in all the papers. The reward keeps increasing. They really want you."

I rubbed my temples and sighed. Everyone knew about us. Getting to Urbis was going to be impossible.

"That's where we were headed," I said, forgetting that I was supposed to be keeping quiet about our plans.

"I'm afraid you've got no chance," she replied. "Urbis has completely shut its borders."

"What?" I exclaimed, my pulse throbbing in my ears.

"The borders have been closed since early September. There's no way in and no way out."

"How is that possible?" I asked, thinking of the sprawling city, almost as big as a kingdom.

She sighed. "The gates to the city have been closed for months, and there is a magical shield up stopping anyone of magical means trying to break through. The only way in is the northernmost gate, and it's heavily guarded. Only those personally vetted by the President or her new cabinet are allowed to pass. I heard that she's using the basement in the parliament building as some kind of prison, so she can torture people she doesn't like, but of course, it's all hearsay. I never had any desire to go to Urbis. Too busy, but now, I doubt I'll ever go."

This was worse than I thought. My head hurt with the obstacles we faced. What had seemed extremely difficult before now felt impossible.

"You both look exhausted. How about I make you something more substantial than cookies to eat, and we can try and come up with a plan to get Princess Eliana and your friends out of jail."

It was only early afternoon, but she was right. I was both hungry and tired. There was no point trying anything with my head reeling the way it was. I accepted her offer gratefully and wondered how we were ever going to get out of the village, let alone across all the kingdoms to Urbis when almost everyone wanted us dead.

JANUARY
DERILLEN

"What are you doing?" I asked, pursing my lips at the creature in front of me. She was a mess of mossy green from her hair to her body that curiously ended in a tail like that of a seahorse.

"Nothing," she mumbled, munching on a bloody bone, presumably of Ella, whom I'd pushed over the side of the boat, not half an hour before.

I rolled my eyes at the hideous creature. "Did you or did you not have something to do with the kingdom of Atlantice a number of years ago?"

"Atlantice!" She spat, sending bits of flesh out into the sea. "Full of humans. I hate them."

"Hmm," I muttered, feeling rather nauseous at the

sight of her bobbing in the water like an over-inflated beach ball. Maybe I'd picked the wrong person to help me. She was a pitiful creature and ugly as sin. Blood dripped down her mouth as she continued to chomp noisily.

"Did they do something to you?" I queried. "By which I mean, did you...not exist for a number of years?"

For the first time, she looked at me, curiosity filling her bloodshot eyes. "How do you know about that?"

"I happen to know that the daughter of the King and Queen of Atlantice did it to you. Someone did the same thing to me."

Her eyes widened, and she bared her teeth. The sight of blood dripping from her green and blackened pointed teeth turned my stomach. "Queen of Atlantice!" she spat. "She'd have been nothing if not for me. She was a mermaid before I gave her legs. I got her where she wanted to be and then nothing. I was forgotten about. She owes me!"

"I know the feeling," I replied wistfully. "You really gave a mermaid legs?"

I began to wonder if I hadn't made a mistake, after all. That was a gift I didn't have. "You can do that?"

"Legs, better hair, bigger boobs, different face. Whatever people ask for. It's not all I can do!" She spoke animatedly now. She shook her head, making her jowls wobble and her wet hair flick around her face. As it settled around her shoulders, it dried to a vibrant purple color. Her face thinned out, and the mossy complexion dropped away to reveal perfect skin. Her body changed to that of a much younger woman. She still had the seahorse tail, but the difference between what she had been and what she had become was remarkable. I could shift my appearance to look more youthful, but this woman was a master at it. I made a mental note to keep her away from Morpheus. He'd never mentioned any predilection for merfolk, but this woman would turn any man's head.

As I told her the history of the monsters and how we'd been made into nothing, thanks to the burst of magical energy when they were born, I began to think I might just be able to do this after all. The sea witch was very persuadable. Blaise's adopted mother had done to her what Azia's grandparents had done to me. We'd been messed with and pushed aside as though we were nothing, less than nothing.

"I'm going to head to one of the other kingdoms," I explained after getting her on board with my plan to rule all the kingdoms. "It's not just us that this has happened to. Other magical beings have been treated badly by humans thinking they are better than us. Can I leave you here to deal with things?"

"What exactly do you have in mind for me to do here?" The sea witch asked curiously.

"I don't care," I bellowed. "Just make sure you end the princess. She's trouble. She might not know her legacy, but if you don't end her, she'll end you. Mark my words. Once you are done, get to Urbis. I'll meet you there."

She frowned. "What are we going to do in Urbis?"

"Oh, my dear. I have so many plans. Don't worry. You and I, plus a select few, will climb from the depths where the humans have thrown us and rise to our rightful places. Do you think you can kill the brat?"

She shrugged. "My powers aren't what they used to be. I'm weak."

I remembered the feeling well. "I was the same. Give it a week or so, and your powers will come back, stronger than before."

"And which kingdom will you go to next? Enchantia? There's plenty of magic there."

I shook my head. "It's on my list, but I have a young man to deal with in Elder next."

She nodded then dove back into the water, leaving me alone to get the boat back to land. It was then that I realized that I should have kept Ella alive, but I'd needed bait, and she was all I had available. Hoisting up the sail and adjusting it so that it took me toward land, I pondered my encounter with the sea witch. We'd spoken so briefly, and I wasn't convinced she was the right person for the job, but she was the only person in Atlantice I knew of who had the ability and motivation to do this. Killing the monster child of the king and queen was a start, but it wasn't my entire reason for getting the sea witch on my side. She'd cause trouble for the whole royal family of Atlantice, and though I had no beef with them specifically, I knew that they were part of the problem. Humans who thought they were better than the rest of us. If I could start conflict within each kingdom and then between all the kingdoms, taking over all of them would be easier. They'd be begging for a new leader by the time I was done. It would be like picking ripe berries from a bramble.

12TH DECEMBER
AZIA

A night in a warm bed and a couple of hot meals had done wonders for clearing my head. My fears that the woman, who'd finally introduced herself as Ms. Clarington, was going to turn into Derillen or Rumpelstiltskin and murder us in our sleep, had proved unfounded. She'd put us in the spare room in twin beds. Flowery wallpaper filled the walls, and the brass bedstead creaked every time I moved. But it was heaven compared to all the other nights I'd spent on this mission so far.

"You awake?" Deon whispered across to me.

I rubbed my eyes and looked over to the other bed in the room. "Yep. Come up with any ideas about what we are going to do?"

"I fell asleep straight away. I hadn't realized how tired I was."

"Come on," I said, swinging my legs out of bed. "We need to get the others out of the police station today, and I think I smell bacon cooking."

I almost ran to the bathroom and pulled off the nightgown that Ms. Clarington had lent me the previous night. After a quick wash, I began to put it back on before seeing two piles of washed and folded clothes—mine and Deon's. I inhaled the sweet scent as I pulled my own clothes on. It had been a long time since I'd worn truly clean clothes. Washing them in lakes and rivers didn't quite have the same effect.

"Here, you might want this," I said back in the bedroom, throwing Deon's clean clothes down on the bed.

He pulled his blanket up further so that it went right to his chin.

"I'll see you downstairs in a couple of minutes," he said. I gave him a curious look and headed out the door and toward the delicious odor of frying bacon.

Ms. Clarington stood at her stove cooking breakfast, her grey hair in a neat bun, and her glasses perched on her nose.

"Sleep well?"

"Very well, thank you," I answered as she passed me a plate of bacon and eggs.

"Did the nightgowns I lent you fit ok. I know they aren't very masculine, but they are all I have. I figured that Deon wouldn't mind if it was just for one night."

Nightgowns...plural? No wonder Deon had been so coy this morning. He'd already been in bed when I finished getting washed the night before, now that I came to think about it. An image of Deon wearing a flowery nightgown came to mind, and I let out a snort.

"It's quieter out there today," she said, nodding toward the window. "The snow has started coming in again, and I think it's putting a lot of people off going out. Plus, I might have spoken to a friend who called on me this morning and let her know that I saw a couple of strangers running across the fields toward the Elder border last night. She's a bit of a chatterbox, so I think the rumor will have gotten around half the village by now."

She didn't smile, but I could see she was pleased with herself. I would have kissed her, but she didn't seem like the type that would like that. Instead, I thanked her as Deon walked in through the door, wearing his own clothes.

She placed his plate in front of him as a knock came on the front door

Deon and I exchanged looks.

"That will be my friend again." Ms. Clarington said. I'll just be a minute.

She closed the inner door between the kitchen and the hallway.

The outer door opened, and I heard a man's voice.

"Ms. Clarington told me her friend was a she," I whispered as I left my plate of food and tiptoed to listen at the door.

"Maybe she has another friend?" Deon whispered back, joining me with his ear to the inner door.

"I assure you, I don't know what you are talking about." Ms. Clarington spoke unnaturally loudly. "I've not seen them, and I don't carc for putting my nose in matters that don't concern me. I suggest you put the taxpayers' money to good use and solve some crimes rather than chasing kids around the countryside, sherriff."

"Sheriff?" Deon mouthed at me.

The man spoke again, and this time, I recognized his voice. He was the man who had tried to grab me at the ruins the day before. "I'll just come in and take a look if you are sure you don't know anything about their whereabouts."

"You most certainly will not," Ms. Clarington thundered. "You cannot invade my home without just cause."

But it was apparent he'd already done so. Deon bolted for the back door and unlocked it as I began picking up the plates.

"What are you doing?" Deon hissed as he opened the door. I slipped my feet into my boots as I shot through it and sidled close to the house where the snow was shallower.

"Follow me!" I whispered to Deon as I hopped onto the wall that separated Ms. Clarington's backyard from her neighbor's.

I made sure I pushed all the snow from the wall with each step in the hope that the sheriff wouldn't make out our footprints.

Deon closed the door quietly behind him and followed in my path. When we'd gotten to the alley where Ms. Clarington had found us the day before, I handed Deon his plate and knife and fork.

"You wanna have a breakfast picnic now?" he asked with a frown.

"No, but if they'd found three plates, they'd have known Ms. Clarington was lying."

"Ah, good thinking!" He grabbed the bacon from his plate and stuffed it into his mouth before leaving the plate by Ms. Clarington's back gate under a bush. I followed suit, ducking behind the low wall just as the sheriff opened Ms. Clarington's back door.

Ms. Clarington's smooth tones echoed out. "See Mr. Busby. I told you I had no one in my house."

"Sheriff Busby," he corrected her. "What's knocked the snow from that wall there?"

I stiffened, wondering if I'd left a footprint after all.

Ms. Clarington's terse tones cut through the silent morning. "How should I know, sheriff? I'm too busy to be peering out of my windows and keeping a watch on what knocks snow off my wall. Although, if I were to hazard a guess, I'd say next door's cat. It really is a nuisance, and I've told my neighbor a thousand times that I don't like it peeing on my hydrangeas, but does she listen?"

"Well, it had better be a cat for your benefit," Sheriff Busby snarled, clearly upset about being thwarted. "I have a lot of money riding on catching the last of the outlaws. I've had word that The President of Urbis herself will be here in a couple of days, and I don't doubt she'll be upset to know if you have been hiding them."

"I'll bear that in mind, sheriff. Now, if you'd like to come back inside, may I offer you a cup of tea?"

I heard the sound of the back door closing.

"Come on," I whispered, motioning to Deon. "We need to get out of here."

Deon and I ran along the alley to the back of the shops in the square, where we hid behind some snow-covered garbage.

"What now?" I hissed, panic lacing my voice. "Derillen's coming the day after tomorrow. If we don't get them out, she'll..."

"She'll take them back to Urbis," Deon responded

calmly, resting his hand on my arm. "It might be the best thing. We were going there anyway. This way, we won't have weeks of hiking through snow to contend with."

I thought about what he'd said. I wanted to get to Urbis, but doing it already imprisoned by Derillen was not the way I had in mind when I started this venture.

"What if she doesn't plan on taking them to Urbis? If she only wanted us in prison, she could keep them here, right?"

Deon shrugged. "I doubt the two small jail cells here will contain magic enough to stop demi-gods."

"They already do," I pointed out. "If they didn't, the others would have escaped by now."

"Good point," Deon conceded. "But why would a small police station in the middle of nowhere have magic means to hold prisoners? There aren't any magical jails in Floris as far as I'm aware. We send any prisoners that use magic for their crimes to Urbis Prison."

"We do too."

"Well, something is keeping them locked up. Something magical."

"I hate it when you are right." I sighed and folded my arms against the cold.

Deon almost smiled. "Believe me, on this occasion, so do I. We can't go back to Ms. Clarington's house. It would only put her in danger. I don't exactly want to spend the day hiding in amongst garbage either."

I screwed up my nose. "So, what do you suggest?"

Deon shrugged.

I stood up and felt snowflakes settling on my head. "I say we go and break them out. If we get caught too, then so be it. At least, we'll know what we are up against."

"Aye-aye, captain," Deon said with a grin.

"Oh, shut up. You are beginning to remind me of Lyric."

It was a light moment in the middle of a harsh reality. We were heading into the viper's den with no plan and very little chance of winning. At least, Derillen wasn't here yet, and it was that thought that I held onto as I pulled my hood up over my head and stepped away from the garbage and back out into the alley.

With the snow swirling down around my ears, I walked with purpose along the back alley of the shops. Sneaking around was a sure-fire way to get caught, but if we walked like we belonged, we might get away with hiding in plain sight. Ok, it was a long shot, but it was all I had.

The square was much quieter than it had been the day before, but there were still people out and about. Turning abruptly away from it, Deon and I headed to where I remembered the police station to be using the back streets. The lack of footprints told me that the streets were barely being used. When the snow had first fallen, I'd been worried, but now, it helped us by showing us the quietest route.

The police station was a small brick building with a blue sign above the door. Silver letters on it read Leodis Police.

I hesitated by the front door. There was no one around, and a quick peek in the window told me that the reception area was empty.

"There's no one in there," I said, turning to Deon.

Deon joined me at the window and peered in. "There must be. We are the most wanted criminals on the planet. No one would leave the others unattended."

"They would if they knew there was no chance of them getting out," I pointed out. "Ms. Clarington mentioned the sheriff and his deputy. She never mentioned anyone else. It's a really small village. What if they are the only people that work here?"

"And what if we could just walk in there and find some keys on the desk and let them out," Deon answered, his voice dripping with sarcasm.

"You don't know unless you try," I said, striding to the open front door of the station.

"Azia!" Deon hissed. "I was kidding. What are you doing?"

I turned back to face him. "The way I figure it, we have no choice. If we can't find a way to outsmart a couple of bumbling policemen, how are we going to be able to fight the most powerful witches and wizards on the planet? I'm sick of hiding. Now is the time to take action."

I stepped inside before he could tell me what a huge mistake I was making.

Except, I'd been right. I was as surprised as Deon to find that the station was empty, or at least the reception area was. Grey carpet, worn down with years of use, covered the floor. At one end was a tatty leather sofa with posters pinned to the wall above it. I was wholly unsurprised to see the biggest was of us. The others looked old and were for various misdeeds such as sheep rustling and petty theft. No wonder Busby and his deputy were excited about us being here. We were the most exciting thing to happen to Leodis in a long time if the wanted posters were anything to go by. At the other end was a desk and directly behind that, a door. The desk was empty except for a pen. Striding across the room, I turned the handle on the door to the back of the station.

"Locked," I said, turning to Deon. "Do you know how

to pick a lock?"

Deon took the handle and wiggled it a few times as though that would work. "Ivy tried showing me once, but without an actual lock to practice on, I'm not sure I really understood the concept. It involved a hairpin. Do you have one?"

I shook my head impatiently. A year ago, I might have had a hairpin, but having not been to a hairdresser in twelve months, my hair had grown out into a straggly mess. One I held back exclusively with a bit of string or ribbon if I could find one.

I folded my arms and looked on impatiently. "Are you a demi-god or not?"

"I make plants do things. I'm not sure how that's going to help in this situation."

"Remember when you practically launched Lyric into the air last week when you grew a massive flower under her? Can't you do the same with this door?"

He appeared thoughtful for a second, then closed his eyes. I kept a watchful eye on the main entrance as he worked his magic.

Less than a minute later, vines grew up from the ground, punching their way through the worn carpet and winding their way through the lock. Another few seconds and there was an audible click as the lock mechanism gave way.

"Impressive!" I said with a grin as the vines fell away to the ground and then shriveled up to nothing.

Deon wiped his hands together. "All in a day's work."

As soon as we stepped through the open door, something happened. There was nothing visible, but my magical link to my siblings was abruptly cut. I stopped and caught my breath, feeling suddenly cold and naked as though the magic that surrounded me had been keeping me warm all these months.

"Azia, Deon!"

I didn't need the magical link to them to see my siblings. All of them were in two cramped cells that filled the end wall of the police station. I ran to the closest only to be met with shouts of "no!" from all of them. I skidded to a halt, but it was too late. The second my fingers touched the bars, a sweeping sensation came over me, and my body contorted itself into an unnatural position, squeezing impossibly small until I found myself looking out of the cell from the other side at a rather sick-looking Deon.

"There is a magic inhibitor on this room," Fallon explained just a tad too late, "but the magic on the bars was set by Derillen. Her magic is the only magic that can work in here."

"They knew we were coming," I sighed. "That's why it was so easy."

"I think we can assume that's why the main door was unlocked," Deon added. "With magic on their side, they didn't need to be here. They could be out looking for us knowing that if we came here, we'd basically imprison ourselves."

"You are on the outside," I pointed out. "Look for some keys or a crowbar or something."

Deon looked at me as though he wasn't sure I was being serious. I waved my hand at him, and he set about looking through the drawers in a desk in front of the cells.

"How did you find us?" Eliana asked. I looked around my cell. As well as Eliana and Fallon, it also held Gaia, Blaise, and Ivy. Nyre, in her dragon form, sat grumpily with her arms crossed on a bench, which seemed to be the only piece of furniture in the cell apart from a bucket in the corner. In the next cell over, everyone else stood watching Deon as he rifled through the drawers.

"Derillen came here to set up a magic jail?" I asked, trying to wrap my head around it. "There must be tens of thousands of small jails like this dotted all over the kingdoms. Not even Derillen could visit them all."

"Don't worry," Fallon said, draping his arm around my shoulder. "She's not been here. The only people we've seen are the sheriff and the deputy. We were told that she'd sent something months ago. Of course, they won't tell us what, but some kind of magical device is being used. Apparently, it inhibits other people's magic and does that weird thing with the bars. It's a one-way ride, unfortunately." Fallon touched the bars as if to prove his point.

"We need to get out," I warned. "We need to get out now! Derillen is going to be here the day after tomorrow."

Beside me, Eliana gasped and bought her hands up to her throat.

"How do you know?" Gaia shouted across from the other cell.

"I overheard Busby talking about it." I turned my attention to Deon. "Forget about keys. Look for the magic artifact."

Deon looked up from the drawers. "What does it look like?"

I turned to the others and was greeted with a round of shrugs.

"I guess we don't know, but it will be out of place."

Ivy jumped up and wrapped her fingers around the bars. "Look for a metallic object. Something like a watch, maybe."

"You won't find it."

Deon stopped what he was doing and turned to the

doorway we'd come through only minutes before.

Sheriff Busby stood there, his hands on his hips and a grin covering his face. His broken nose had set at an odd angle, and both of his eyes were black thanks to the head butt I'd performed on him only a day ago.

"I know you won't find it because I happen to have it." He pulled a framed certificate from the wall and grabbed something from behind it, holding it aloft for us to see. It was a small metal shield with a coat of arms on it, too small for me to make out exactly what it was. He slipped it in his top pocket and buttoned it closed.

Deon lunged for him, but Busby was ready, and what he lacked in speed, he made up for in size and brute strength. He blocked Deon's attack and made to grab him around the neck, but Deon was too quick. Unfortunately, so was the deputy who had just appeared behind Busby. The pair of them each grabbed one of Deon's arms and held them behind his back.

With a quick shove, he hit the bars of the cell, and like I had, just moments before, his body contorted, and he slid through the bars.

"Magic sure makes everything easy," Busby laughed. "What do you say, Larry?"

"Makes my job of keeper of the keys a bit redundant," the deputy grinned. "Still, more time for drinking tea and planning what to do with our reward."

The two laughed loudly at their joke and left, locking the door behind them.

We were all trapped with no way out and with Derillen on her way.

Our mission was over before it had properly begun.

APRIL DERILLEN

"You really are something else, Derillen," Morpheus laughed, swirling his whiskey around in his glass. "You can't just announce you want to become the President of Urbis and expect to be, just like that. The current president spent years working his way up."

"I don't have years, as you well know, but it doesn't matter. I have it all in hand. I've managed to recruit some people to help me. They will be arriving shortly. Anyway, enough about me. How are you faring with Briar Rose?"

"She's a remarkably beautiful woman," he mused, staring off into space with a sickly look on his face.

"Oh, do snap out of it, Morpheus. You are far too old

for her."

He knocked back his drink. "I was too old for you once, but that didn't stop us having fun, did it?"

I gritted my teeth at his use of the term *once*. "What am I now? Some old bag?"

"Oh, come on, Derillen. Have a drink." He poured a whiskey and passed the glass to me before pouring another for himself.

I sipped at the whiskey and wished it had ice in it. This wasn't going the way I'd planned. "I need help, Morpheus."

"What? Again?"

"Yes, again. It's not as if you are not enjoying playing with Briar Rose or whatever sick games you are doing with her in your dreamscape."

"I'm the perfect gentleman in there."

I snorted whiskey from my nose. "You've never been a perfect gentleman. Are you going to help me or not?"

Morpheus licked his teeth and sat on the question. "I'm not your go-to boy when you need help, Derillen. I have my own things to do."

"Briar Rose being among them, I suppose. I promised you Snow White too, remember? I'm planning to go to Enchantia in a few months, and then she, too, will be yours. Think about it. The two most beautiful women in all the kingdoms, and they will both be yours for the taking."

Bile rose in my throat at the thought of what he would do with them, but I swallowed it back. I couldn't let him see me as weak. If he did, I'd already lost.

"Ok, what is it I can do for you?"

"There are rumors of an imp in The Vale. His name is Rumpelstiltskin. I've heard he is powerful, but I've scoured the whole kingdom and have yet to find him.

Do you know him?"

"I don't associate with imps. Not even powerful ones."

I could see by his eyes that he wasn't telling me the whole truth. "But, you've heard of him?"

"There have been mentions of him in some of the clubs I frequent. Usually, someone drinking to forget him."

I leaned forward, curious. "Why?"

"From what I've heard, he has a habit of ruining people's lives. He does it for the fun of it."

"So, how do I find him?"

Morpheus shrugged and sat his glass down. "Go back to The Vale. Head to the seediest bar you can find and complain loudly about some problem in your life. He'll show up sooner or later."

There were hundreds of bars in The Vale. It was a big kingdom. "Thanks a bunch for all your help, Morpheus," I said sarcastically, putting my unfinished drink down on the table and standing up. When I got to the door, he called out my name.

"What?" I shot back.

"Don't agree to anything he offers you. He's a wily character."

"Thanks for the advice," I muttered, heading out and slamming the door behind me.

13TH DECEMBER
AZIA

"There must be a way out!" I said, gritting my teeth. I'd said it so many times in the last few hours that even I was beginning to get tired of my own voice. But if we didn't get out, that would be the end of us. We all knew Derillen wanted us, and though we didn't know, for sure, exactly what she had in store for us, it wasn't going to be good. So I'd spent the last few hours examining every part of the cell, going over and over it again in case I'd missed something.

"Are you sure you can't get through this lock?" I asked Ivy as I prodded the keyhole.

Ivy opened her eyes and rubbed the sleep from

them. “I told you. Those locks are notoriously difficult to crack. Cells like these are made to keep in thieves who know how to pick locks; they’d be pretty useless otherwise. I tried for like an hour before you showed up, and I couldn’t get it to budge.”

If only we could use our magic. We were faster, stronger, more capable than most, and yet we’d been caught by a couple of dopey policemen and a simple spell by a witch.

“Nyre. You are small. You might be able to fit through these bars.”

Nyre opened a lazy eye and folded her arms, not even dignifying me with an answer. Lots of help, she was. Although to be fair, I had spent an hour the night before getting her to blow fire at the bars in the hope the heat would make them more pliable or weak, but after a few burnt hands and about a thousand complaints from Nyre, I’d given up on the idea and only had blackened bars to show for her efforts.

Midnight had long since passed, and every minute I spent trying to find a way out and failing was another minute that we came closer to Derillen arriving. Our magic was stronger than hers, I was sure of it, but without it, we were sitting ducks.

As the sun began to creep up into the sky, I finally sat down and closed my eyes.

I was awakened what felt like a few moments later by Nyre nudging me. I’d somehow fallen asleep on her shoulder. I wiped the dribble from my chin and looked around. Angry voices floated in through the tiny barred window to the outside. Pulling myself up, I stood on the bench to see what was going on.

Hundreds of people stood outside. The second they saw me looking out, a ripple of excitement ran through the crowd. I ducked down.

"What's going on outside?" I whispered to Nyre, who was in her part-human form.

She bit her nail and spit it out on the floor before answering. "Something about it not being fair that PC Plod One and PC Plod Two will get the reward for our capture. I think everyone wants a bit of it."

I rubbed my hand down my face and felt the anxiety I'd felt last night begin to well up again. Getting out of the cell was proving hard enough, but to do it and then get past hundreds of people would be impossible.

"Dragon Shit!" I exclaimed.

Nyre gave me a funny look. "In that bucket? Er, no. I haven't been for days. I'm so bloated."

I gave her a withering look. "It was a figure of speech, dumbass."

"Just trying to lighten the mood," Nyre replied petulantly.

I stood up and paced the cell, wondering if I'd missed anything, but the walls were solid.

"Did anyone come up with any ideas for us to escape?" I asked, hopefully.

A sea of blank faces stared back at me.

"Getting out of here is going to be difficult," Gaia replied. "We spent hours trying on our first night in here, but with our magic stripped, we'll have to figure a way out that doesn't use it. Kelis tried reversing the spell with her wand, but the universal rule of magic is that only the spell caster can reverse it. Because of that, and our lack of time and escapology ability, I see two options."

I perked up. "Great! What are they?"

"Neither is perfect," Gaia admitted, "but at the moment, I can't think of anything else. The first involves taking the guards out once they let us out of the cell. Of course, we'd have to plan it down to the split second because there will be very limited time, if any, between them letting us out of this area and handing us over to Derillen."

"She'll be in the next room," Ivy pointed out. "We'll be jumping right from the frying pan into the fire. The only way out of the station is through the front doors. We'd have to take Derillen on too."

"That was actually my second plan," Gaia said. "Wait until we are handed over. There are twelve of us and only one of her. We are Demi-gods. She's just a witch."

While Gaia's plan sounded like it would work, I wasn't convinced. There was no way Derillen would walk into the police station unprepared. She knew we were stronger than her in every way except when we didn't have our powers.

I grabbed hold of one of the bars and rested my head on it. "If she puts a spell on the outer room before we come out, we'll be in the same position we are now. Expanding the no magic charm from this room to the reception area would be enough. She would be able to kill us with a killing spell the second we get out of the no magic zone."

"Not if Kelis goes first and uses a killing spell first."

"Hey!" Kelis cried out, suddenly interested in the conversation. "Why should I go first?"

"Because you are the only one who knows how to do a killing spell," Gaia reminded her. "Your magic is more generalized than ours, remember."

Kelis scowled and crossed her arms. "Do you know how much practice it takes to learn a new spell? Before a few months ago, all I knew how to do was make my hair straight without a hairbrush. I've hardly had a lot of experience with killing spells. None to be precise."

"It was only a thought," Gaia said kindly. "I'm sorry. I didn't mean to upset you. If we all went at once, we could simply overpower her. Twelve of us, One of her. We could kill her with our strength alone."

"I don't think they'd let us out all at once," Fallon pointed out. "I think whichever plan we come up with, Derillen has already thought of it. She'll have been planning something like this for months. We've only been thinking about escaping here for a night or two."

There had to be another way. I wasn't going to let her beat me like this. Not inside a prison cell in the middle of goodness knew where. If Derillen killed us, it would mean my mother would be trapped in her sleep forever. So would Kelis's mother. Baby Fae would never know her mother. She'd never come home to The Vale.

"I'm not letting it end like this," I raged, standing up and gripping my hands tightly by my side. My hand hit the hilt of my sword. I'd forgotten I still had it on me. Everything else I owned was still back at the ruins along with everyone else's things, but my sword was still attached to my belt. I was just thinking of a plan of skewering the two policemen when another angry voice filled the air outside. This one much louder than the others.

"Let me through, I say!"

I jumped back onto the bench to see what was happening outside, but I didn't need to see who it was. Eliana had jumped up next to me on the bench.

"Mother!" She almost pushed me off the bench to get to the tiny barred window.

Outside, the crowd still jeered, but I saw nothing of the Queen of The Vale.

"Are you sure that was her?" I asked.

"I'd know the sound of my mother being bossy anywhere. I've had eighteen years of it!"

I jumped down from the bench as the voice sounded out from the reception area.

"I demand to see my daughter immediately!"

The two policemen had been quiet all night, but the queen's voice was coming through loud and clear.

"I'm afraid that's not possible, Your Majesty," Busby replied. He sounded terrified. I almost giggled at the thought of his face. To be caught between Derillen and ten thousand dollars and his queen was not a position I'd like to be in. "She's a wanted criminal."

"Criminal?" the queen shrieked. "Criminal?"

"Woah, mother sounds angrier than when she found out I'd gone outside without her blessing. I don't envy those policemen," Eliana said with a huge grin on her face.

"Shh," Blaise barked, holding her finger to her lips as the queen continued her tirade. "I wanna hear this!"

The Queen of Vale continued, "My daughter is a princess and the Heir to The Vale's throne. How dare you accuse her of being a criminal. What evidence do you have?"

"Urbis has issued a wanted poster," Busby blustered. "It plainly says that she is a criminal. See. It's on the wall."

"I don't give a unicorn's behind what is on your wall. You are telling me that you are holding her without any evidence...Without knowing what her crime is even?"

I caught Eliana's eye, and she winked at me. Her mother might just be our ticket out of here.

"Err. Yes, but she must have done something, or there wouldn't be such a large reward, you see." I could almost hear Busby's desperation not to lose the reward he'd been promised. I almost felt sorry for him.

"Without a crime and without any evidence of a crime, you are legally not allowed to hold her."

"Urbis says, I can. The President of Urbis personally asked for their capture," he replied, sounding a little more confidant this time. "The Echo said they'd escaped Urbis Prison and that they are wanted for murder. Murder! That's a crime. A very bad one at that."

I shuffled closer to the bars, trying to hear every word.

"The law regarding prisoners is that they can be kept twenty-four hours without any evidence. The law that was passed in Urbis many years ago. How long has she been in your care?"

Busby mumbled something.

"I'm sorry, I didn't hear you," the queen said.

"Two days, Your Majesty."

"So the law says that she can be released, and I, as your queen, say she can be released. I don't think we have anything else to discuss, do we?"

"The President of Urbis will be arriving tomorrow!" Busby sputtered. "I believe she'll be passing a few different laws soon."

Footsteps sounded out, coming closer.

The queen spoke again. "And when she does with the backing of the parliamentary board in Urbis of which my husband, the king, is a member, I will be keeping to the laws as I am today. Let them out immediately."

"She'll be here in twenty-four hours!" Busby cried, losing any semblance of dignity. I could hear the pleading in his voice.

"I said, let them out immediately, or I'll have you fired."

"Your mom is awesome!" Nyre whispered to Eliana

with a grin on her face.

Seconds later, the sound of keys turning in the lock had everyone standing to attention.

Busby came through the door first, looking absolutely miserable. I didn't know what a rural policeman made, but I was willing to bet that ten thousand Urbis dollars would go a long way. Even if he split it half and half with the deputy.

"Mother!" Eliana shouted, gripping onto the bars next to me.

The queen walked forward, tears in her eyes, and held her arms out to her daughter.

"Stop!" I shouted as she neared us. "The bars have a spell on them. Anyone who touches them gets sucked inside."

"That only works on people with magic, remember?" Eliana reminded me.

"You told me that Rumpelstiltskin gave your mother the magic to weave straw into gold. What if the tiniest bit of that magic is still lingering inside her? Do you want to chance it?"

"That was years ago," Eliana said with uncertainty. "Before I was born."

The queen stepped forward again, careful to stay a couple of feet from the bars.

"Let's not make things more difficult than they have to be, eh?" She turned to Busby. "Open the doors, please. To both cells. I believe these are all your friends, Eliana?"

"They are my brothers and sisters. You remember Azia, Blaise, and Deon?"

"Oh, yes. Come on, let's get you all out of there. We have a lot of catching up to do."

Eliana practically bounced on her feet as Busby

fumbled with the keys. I knew she was desperate to ask if there'd been any sighting of Fae, but she remained quiet. There would be time for that once we were out.

Busby found the key he was looking for, but as he went to put it in the lock, he spun on his feet and grabbed the queen.

"What do you think you are doing?" the queen cried. Beside me, Eliana screamed.

The deputy ran forward and helped Busby restrain the queen.

"Put me down immediately!" she said, kicking out, her skirts flying upward. She missed by inches, but that did not stop Busby

"Not a chance," Busby snarled, slapping her in the face. A red hand-shaped mark appeared immediately on her cheek.

Beside me, Eliana pushed toward the bars as though they would yield to her, but they remained solid.

The queen spat in Busby's face as Larry held her arms behind her back. He wiped off the spit with the back of his sleeve, then punched her in the stomach, causing her to sag.

"You've not seen your daughter for a long time," he snarled at her. "I think it's time for a family reunion."

He grabbed the top of her arm, causing Larry to release it.

As Busby pushed the queen toward the bars to test them to see if they would suck her in as they had Deon and me, she fought against him.

He brought his baton from his belt and raised it above the queen's head. Eliana screamed.

With a split-second thought, I pulled my sword out and thrust it through the bars. It hit Busby, slicing him right through the heart. He dropped to the floor without a word and was dead before he hit the ground.

A scuffle beside me took my thoughts away from the fallen sheriff. Fallon had the deputy in a neck hold through the bars.

"You've got a choice now!" I said, holding the sword to his neck as Fallon held him.

My hands shook at what I'd just done, but I kept my voice clear.

I held my mouth close to his ear. "You either agree to let us out without any trouble, or I stab you through the heart like I just did to your boss."

"You know the second Fallon lets him go, he'll be off into the next room," Deon pointed out from the other cell.

"That's fine," Nyre said. "Because I have the keys. Busby dropped them when he fell." She twirled the keys around her finger and smiled like a cat that had gotten the cream. Or the dragon that had gotten the keys.

"I guess your options have changed, " I whispered to the deputy. "Either run or end up in a puddle of your own blood."

Unsurprisingly, he chose the option to run, leaving the outer door open, saving us the trouble of opening that one too.

Once both cell doors were open, Eliana fell into her mother's arms, and the two of them sobbed onto each other's shoulders.

A growing puddle of red coated the cell floors. A feeling of dread crept up into my stomach, and it was all I could do to hold what little food I'd had down. I was a murderer. I'd killed a living person. All my training with Milo had been to do just that, but nothing in my training had readied me for the shock I'd feel after I'd done it.

"Any news?" Eliana asked her mother, breaking me out of my trance.

The queen shook her head sadly. "I'd hoped you would have news."

"I have so much to tell you," Eliana said, "but nothing about Fae. We think she's in Urbis."

"Urbis is a political nightmare at the moment," the queen sighed. "There is a new president, and she's been making some very questionable changes. The whole city is locked down, and we've not been able to get in. Not even your father."

"She's the one after us," Eliana exclaimed. "She's also the one who has Fae. Rumpelstiltskin is working with her."

The queen blanched at the mention of Rumpelstiltskin, and the color drained from her face.

"There's no time to chat," I asserted urgently. I wiped the blood from my sword on Busby's uniform, trying not to look at the pool of red underneath him. "Dcrillen will be here tomorrow, and we still have to get out of The Vale."

"How are we going to do that?" Blaise asked once we'd bustled through to the reception area. "There are hundreds of people out there, and they don't look too friendly."

"We might not have had magic in there," I said, pointing to the room with the cells in it and trying not to look at Busby's body. "But we have our magic back now. I think it's time we used it."

"Let me do this!" Fallon said, holding his arms out. His face began to contort until Busby stood before us. He'd been able to change his appearancc since I met him, but only recently had he been able to extend his magic to the clothes he wore too.

I gulped as Fallon smiled at me through Busby's eyes. They still sported the bruises I'd given to him. Something about having a man I'd just murdered grin at me turned my stomach.

"Extraordinary!" the queen remarked, having never seen Fallon's ability before.

I pushed Fallon to the door. "Go outside and do whatever it is you have in mind. Just do it quickly!"

I held my breath as he opened the front doors to the police station and stepped out. The crowd went quiet for a second, seeing something was happening. It didn't last long.

"We want the reward too!" someone shouted out, followed by a number of jeers.

Fallon's voice, sounding like Busby's, shouted out. "I'm sorry to announce that the reward has been canceled. The crime of which the people in the cell have been accused of has been found to have been committed by someone else. They are free citizens. I ask you all to move back and let them through."

"Not a chance!" the same voice as earlier said. "How do we know you aren't lying?"

Fallon cleared his throat. "I just told you I was letting them go. Would I do that if there was still such a large reward on their heads?"

"I didn't see the President of Urbis pass through the doors," someone else shouted.

I held my breath, wondering how Fallon was going to answer.

"Yes, she's not here yet."

I let my breath out and almost cried. I knew exactly what the next question from the crowd was going to be.

"Then how do you know that someone else committed the crime?"

“I, er...” Fallon stammered, and I knew we had lost.

“Come on,” I said, pulling my sword out again. It looks like we are going to have to wing it, as usual.”

I opened the door and stepped out into daylight.

“Let us through!” I shouted to the crowd, holding my sword aloft and wishing I’d left Busby’s blood on it, after all. “We are armed and dangerous. We are also magic. We don’t want anyone getting hurt, but if you don’t let us through, some of you will be.”

My brothers and sisters lined up beside me. Within a second, the crowd started toward us. They were also armed. With sticks and farm equipment, but there were about fifty of them to each one of us.

Everything happened in a blur.

Gaia shot a fireball out into the crowd, dispersing them. Screams rang out as people struggled to get out of the way of the fire.

“It’s the illusion of fire,” she whispered in my ear. “It won’t hurt anyone, just scare them.”

All around me, chaos reigned as my brothers and sisters used their magic together for the first time. Deon waved his hand, making flowers shoot up through the cracks in the cobbles. Each flower was as tall as the one he’d made for Lyric, but unlike Lyric, these people didn’t have wings. Those unfortunate enough to be in a spot where each one grew up got catapulted into the air.

Zacharina appeared out of nowhere, catching them and lowering them one by one to the ground safely.

“Zacharina!” Eliana shouted out, waving her hands to the unicorn. It flew over, landing just beside me as I waved my sword at anyone that dared to get near.

“I missed you!” Eliana said, clutching Zacharina round the neck.

"No time for that!" I said, hoisting her up to the unicorn's back. Behind her, the queen jumped and grabbed her daughter round the waist. "Head to the ruins!" I said quietly. "We'll meet you there." Eliana nodded, and the three of them took to the sky.

Seconds later, Lyric followed with Deon in her arms. Nyre threw her clothes off, not in the slightest bit bothered that she was naked in front of hundreds of people, and changed into her dragon form. She plucked Blaise from the crowd. They soared above the people in the direction of the ruins, leaving the rest of us to fight our way out.

"Come on," I said, grabbing Ivy's hand and pulling her through the crowd. Some of our magic was pointless in this situation. Ivy was a miracle worker with machines. It wouldn't help her get through a crowd out for blood. My sword, however, helped, keeping everyone back. So far, it looked like no one had been hurt, and I wanted to keep it that way.

Fallon, still looking like Busby, followed close behind us.

I couldn't see the others as we fought through the crowd, but the fireballs whizzing past my head were enough to tell me that Gaia was getting through ok. I'd not seen Halia or Jakon since the chaos started. Hopefully, they were together somewhere. Jakon would be able to whisk them both away in a tornado.

Once we'd gotten past the chaos, we ran at full pelt toward the edge of the village and the road that would take us to the ruins. My heart strained at the speed we ran as the crowd chased behind us.

"I bet this is the most excitement they've had in years," I panted to Ivy, who ran alongside me.

"Yeah, great fun!" she replied. I couldn't tell by her

tone if she was being sarcastic or not.

I checked behind to see if Fallon had heard me, but he'd gone, disappeared into the crowd.

"Damn!" I hissed under my breath, but we couldn't stop. Fallon would have to help himself.

"If we head straight to the ruin, they'll see which way we've gone," I huffed, hitching a thumb over my shoulder.

Ivy looked back. "We are way ahead of them. They can't keep up. We just need to lose them."

"How?" The village was small. Even with speed on our side, we'd be caught eventually.

"There!" Ivy cried, pointing to the sky. A small, purple dragon headed in our direction, soaring downward in a sweeping motion when she spotted us.

A quick look over my shoulder told me that we were far enough away from the village and the people for Nyre to take us without being seen. She clenched her talons into the back of our shirts, pulling us both into the air at once and dropping us in the small woods that ran right down to the back of the ruins

"Are the others back yet?" I asked her after she'd turned back into her half-human form. Once again, she was naked, but the cold didn't seem to bother her at all.

Nyre took off through the woods, her bare feet cutting through the snow and her naked ass disappearing into the trees. "Most of them," she called back as Ivy, and I took off after her. "We are still waiting on Gaia, Halia, Fallon, and Kelis."

"Fallon was right behind us," Ivy exclaimed as though she'd only just noticed he wasn't still with us.

"He got lost in the crowd," I explained as we caught up with Nyre. A small woodland creature, not yet hibernating, ran across our path, causing us all to stop for a second.

"Want me to go look for him?" Nyre asked anxiously.

I shook my head. "No, turn back into your dragon form and fly back to the ruins. Tell everyone to get everything packed up and ready to go."

"We aren't staying there tonight?" Ivy asked.

"It's too close to the village. Someone is bound to go check it out, sooner or later. We are going to have to walk through the night and get to Elder. If we can sleep there, we'll be able to make it to Arcadia by the end of the next day."

Nyre nodded and jumped up into the air, changing form and spreading her wings as she did.

The run back to the ruin took half an hour, even at full speed. I was glad to see Gaia, Halia, and Kelis there already waiting for us. I did a quick headcount.

Thirteen. That was right...except it wasn't. I'd counted Eliana's mother as one of us. Someone was missing.

"Where's Fallon?"

"I don't know," Gaia replied. "I thought he was with you?"

"Dragon shit!" I murmured. "I knew I should have gone back for him."

APRIL DERILLEN

"Whiskey with ice," I demanded of the bartender. He slammed it on the filthy bar, sloshing the whiskey out of the glass, and went to serve another customer.

The whiskey was watered down so much it tasted like barely more than flavored water. Still, I was not here for the drinks nor the atmosphere, which was just as well as the place was a complete dive.

"Can I buy you a drink?" a grizzled old man said, taking the seat next to me at the bar.

"I already have one," I said, holding my whiskey water up and tinkling the ice cubes on the side of the glass.

"So, I can buy you another," he slurred with a leer.

"You're beautiful, you know that?"

"Yes, I do. Now, kindly leave me alone."

I shot him with a blast of magic, making him fall off his chair. He pulled himself up and staggered out of the bar.

I downed the whiskey and decided to call it a night. I'd spent way too many nights wasting time in the worst bars of The Vale. I had more important things to do than sit around, waiting for drunken imbeciles to try to pick me up. I'd already made a little headway with my plans to take over Urbis. I'd found four helpers already, but without me watching them, who knew what was happening? I'd asked them to introduce discord amongst the presidential party and the staff at the government building, but who knew what they were up to? Without me to lead them, they were a mess.

"Your glass is empty," a voice next to me said. I readied myself to shoot another spell, but when I saw the man sitting in the seat next to me, I hesitated. He was the spitting image of Morpheus. There were slight differences. The man's eyes were black instead of the rich brown of Morpheus's, and there was no gold circle around the iris marking him as a god. This was just a human being that happened to be exceptionally good-looking—too good-looking, in fact!

"Can I buy you a drink?" he offered. I was just about to accept when something nagged at me.

"How about I buy you one instead?"

"I can't let you buy me a drink without offering something in return," the man said. His mouth turned up at the edges in much the same way Morpheus's did when he was flirting. I'd seen it enough times.

"Your company will suffice," I said, hailing the bartender. "I'll have another whiskey and Mr. ..."

I waited to hear his name.

"I'll have the same, thank you."

The bartender dropped two whiskeys in front of us, and I paid using a note from my purse.

"You looked upset earlier. I was wondering if there was anything I could do? I don't like to see a young lady in distress."

Oh, he was smooth. A bit too smooth. Other women might fall for it, but I wasn't other women. He thought he was reeling me in, but he was the prey here, not me.

"I can look after myself. Tell me, Mr. Rumpelstiltskin. What is it that you do?"

His eyes widened for a second, then he smiled. "You know who I am. Interesting. Not many do. I like to keep my life private."

"As do I. I have a proposition for you."

He licked his lips in a way that Morpheus would never do. "Propositions are my favorite thing of all."

"So I've heard, Mr. Rumpelstiltskin, so I've heard."

DECEMBER 14TH
AZIA

My plan had been to go back for Fallon, but the others hadn't let me. I understood why. I'd only get caught up in the mess as Fallon was, but yet again, it was my fault that someone was gone. I should have kept a closer eye on him.

As soon as we'd noticed Fallon missing, we'd headed beyond the woods and managed to find shelter for the night huddled together in the back of an abandoned wagon. It was far from ideal, and after a fitful night's sleep, I wasn't feeling any better about our situation.

"I should have gone back for him," I complained for the tenth time as I felt around in my bag for anything resembling food.

Ivy put her hand on my arm. "There was an angry mob chasing us. You couldn't have done anything. Let's eat quickly and get ready to go. We can head to the ruin and see if he made it back there. He'll be fine."

Beside Ivy, Nyre sat chewing her fingernails, a habit she'd only picked up recently. "I could go and get him!" she offered to a resounding no from pretty much everyone.

"I'm not losing you too," I murmured. "If anyone goes to the village to look for him, it will be me."

Nyre sat back against the side of the wagon and went back to chewing her nails dolefully.

Our food rations were slim—just a few apples and granola bars we had left over from the inn. My stomach was hungry, but with every bite I took, it only served to make it hurt more.

"Don't do it," Deon warned, whispering in my ear.

"Do what?" I asked, surprised. I'd been doing precisely nothing for half an hour beyond picking at a granola bar. Gaia, Blaise, and Halia had taken the first go at standing guard. The rest of us were eating.

"Don't take all the blame. Fallon will get back. You know he could charm the legs off a centipede, that one. If anyone can figure out how to get away from a group of angry people, it's Fallon."

I rubbed my eyes and massaged my temples. "What if he doesn't? You are always telling me to look on the bright side, but what if there isn't one? What if they caught him? We are murderers now. I'm a murderer. All those posters with our picture on them are everywhere. They are true now. We really are criminals."

I could see out of the corner of my eye that everyone was watching my rant. I usually kept my fears to myself, but that was before I'd stuck my sword through a human being and lost two of my brothers.

"It was self-defense."

I looked Deon right in the eye. "You know it wasn't. He was on the other side of the bars from me. He wasn't even touching me."

"He was beating up the Queen of The Vale! He was going to give us all up to Derillen. If she'd caught us, we'd all be dead now."

"Derillen!" I shouted, jumping up. In all the madness, I'd forgotten about her.

Fallon was still in the village, and Derillen would be there by now.

"Where's the nearest Urbis Express station?" I asked urgently.

"What? Why?"

"Deon. I know you have all your maps and timetables for everything in that bag of yours. I need to know where the nearest station is."

I began rummaging through his bag, pulling out all the papers he had. I piled them up haphazardly next to me on the back of the wagon.

"Stars, Azia, hang on." Deon took the bag from me and took out the rest of the papers, stacking them neatly by his side.

"The nearest station to us is actually across the border to the east in Elder," he said, pointing to the map.

"Ok, and what time does the airship come into that station from Urbis today?"

He flicked through his papers and pulled out a leaflet with a picture of the Urbis Express on the front. Opening it out on his lap, he ran his finger down a list of stations until he came to the one he was looking for.

"There are two due in this morning. One at seven

AM from Floris and one at nine from Urbis."

I looked down at my watch. It was just after eight.

"How long would it take to get from the station to here, say on a horse or in a carriage?"

"I don't know," Deon said, looking up from the leaflet. "About an hour, probably."

I threw my half-eaten granola bar on the ground and began running.

"Hey!" Deon shouted after me. "Where are you going?"

Without turning, I shouted back. "I'm going to get Fallon. Everyone stay here and get ready to go at a moment's notice. If I'm not back by nightfall, head to the Elder border without me. Do not follow me! Cross the border. I'll find you."

I expected them to stop me or to chase after me, but none of them did. I picked up my pace once I was back on the road in case they changed their mind. Whether I was a leader in their eyes or not, I felt responsible. I'd lost Castiel. I couldn't bear losing Fallon too. At least, Castiel wasn't in danger. Fallon had the entire village to contend with, not to mention Derillen, who'd be there at any second.

The ruins looked exactly as they had the previous night before we'd headed through the woods. It meant that the townspeople hadn't come looking for us there, and it also meant Fallon wasn't there either. There was only one other place I'd find him, and that meant heading back to the village.

The edges of the village were quiet and devoid of people, but I could hear them chanting. The sound came from the village square where I'd left Fallon behind. I slowed my pace and walked cautiously along the snow-covered cobbles. I pulled my hood low over my face and rounded the corner.

My heart nearly beat out of my chest when I saw the reason the people were chanting.

Derillen was already there, standing in all her glory upon a table that someone had brought out for her so she could talk over the crowd. Her long purple dress hung over the back of the table, as did her black high-collared cape.

I held my breath, keeping to the shadows at the back, and listened to what she had to say.

"I have traveled a long way to come to this village, and you all have the audacity to tell me that the prisoners have escaped. I cannot begin to tell you how displeased I am. How much you have let your President down. I, however, am not a person that holds a grudge. No, not at all. You are all my subjects and deserve the reward I promised. In fact, I'd like to double the reward to twenty thousand dollars."

A cheer went up, and the chanting began again. This time I could hear it clearly. They were chanting her name. Just hearing it turned my stomach.

"Of course, I cannot just give out my money in exchange for nothing. I need the criminals. They are highly dangerous. I have heard that they headed north. They will be quick and had a head start. To the first person to bring them back to me, even just one of them, I will grant the full twenty thousand dollar reward." She swished her cape in a flourish as they started chanting louder.

"Go on then, imbeciles. What are you waiting for?"

As if they'd all just realized that chanting wasn't going to catch us, they began to race out of the northernmost entrance to the square, tripping over each other as they ran, trying to be the first to get to us. I wondered who had told Derillen that we had gone north. Perhaps one of the villagers chasing Ivy and me the previous day. We'd started going north before Nyre had picked us up. Not that it mattered. All that mattered was that I found Fallon and got to the Elder border before Derillen found us.

I scanned the retreating crowd, waiting to see if Fallon would appear. If he was hiding among them, surely he would wait until they'd all gone north and then sneak south to the ruin. The people were practically fighting each other in their desperation to get out of the square. Derillen watched them, an evil gleam in her eye.

I was just considering if I could race across the square and kill her with my sword when one of the village folk that hadn't managed to get completely out of the square turned and pointed at me.

"There's one, there!"

"Dragon balls!" I hissed and turned. Within seconds I had the village people after me...again!

I sprinted across the square, looking behind me to calculate how far away they were. I'd managed to run away before; I could do it again. I turned back to see where I was going, but suddenly the world spun as my foot caught in one of the stems of the massive flowers Deon had produced the day before.

I fell flat on my face giving the villagers enough time to catch me.

A couple of them hauled me to my feet as the rest crowded around.

I was completely at their mercy. My sword was squashed against my leg and my arms pinned to my sides.

My breathing increased as the crowd parted.

I struggled with my captors to no avail. Derillen

moved between the crowd, eyeing me up and down. I'd never felt so much hatred for anyone as she walked toward me.

Her eyes were full of malice as she stopped mere inches away from me.

She cast an eye at the two men holding me. "Good job, men. Head to the police station and write down your names and addresses so I can send your reward to you. I have her."

She reached forward and gripped my arm tightly as the men let go. I struggled against her, but her grip bit into the flesh at the top of my arm.

"As for you," she sneered, her features turning up into a malicious grin. "You'll be coming with me."

"I'm not going anywhere with you!" I spat back.

She wiped the spit off with the back of her sleeve and glowered at me.

"Oh, I think you will because I know something you don't."

I strained against her grip, knowing it was pointless. If she let go, I'd still be in the middle of a few hundred-strong crowd. "I don't give a dragon's ass what you know."

She leaned closer to me. "Oh, I think you will!" she replied, lowering her mouth to my ear.

I was poised, ready to draw my sword. I was still surrounded by people, but with the two holding me gone, I had enough space to grab it. I'd probably not get out alive, but then again, neither would she, and that was all I cared about. As she began to whisper in my ear, my fist clasped around the hilt.

"Azia, it's me. I'm doing good, huh?"

My heart almost stopped beating as I registered the words, the accent. Fallon?

He pulled back and positioned his features in a way that was all Fallon with one eyebrow raised and a smirk on his lips. A split-second later, he was back to being the evil witch. He turned to the few villagers that were left. "The rest of you head north and see if you can catch the others. I'll give twenty thousand dollars per criminal that you catch. Make sure you bring them back to the police station when you find them."

They didn't need telling twice. The promise of so much money was more than enough to have them racing off, leaving no one in the square but Fallon and me.

"That was magnificent!" I whispered, sure not to show my joy too quickly.

When I was sure the last of the villagers had gone, I threw my arms around Fallon, pulling him into a hug. "I thought you'd been caught. When I saw the villagers, I hoped you'd turned into one of them. I never expected this." I gestured to the clothes.

He smirked again in a very un-Derillen like manner. "Let's get out of here before the real Derillen turns up."

"I couldn't have said it better myself." I took Fallon's hand and began to walk out of the square in the opposite direction to the way the villagers had gone. We'd just passed the bakery when the sound of horses' hooves clip-clopping over cobbles had me pulling Fallon into the nearest shop. I peered out of the window to see the real Derillen stepping down from a carriage.

"We need to get out of here now!" I urged, turning around to see if there was a back entrance to the shop.

The storeowner frowned. "Can I help you?"

My heart skipped a beat, thinking we were caught, but the man's eyes were firmly on Fallon, who still looked like Derillen. I pulled my hood further over my eyes and stood behind him.

"I was wondering if you could tell me if there is a back door to this place?" Fallon said, his voice high and haughty. He sounded nothing like the real Derillen, but then, he'd never heard her speak. Hopefully, this man hadn't either.

"I do, but it's only for staff. It's not for customer use."

I peeked behind me to see Derillen looking around with a confused expression on her face. It wouldn't take long for her to find us if she made the decision to check the shops. There were only so many to choose from.

"Do you know who I am?" Fallon said, walking forward and slamming his fist down on the counter. Behind him, I jumped with the force of it.

"Unless you are a paying customer, I don't care who you are."

A quick look around me told me that this was Wagner and Cox. Shelves of outdoor boots lined one wall, with rolled-up tents, sleeping mats, and other camping equipment taking up a table in front of the wall.

"We are!" I said, grabbing a pair of boots in my size and placing them on a counter. "If you let us go out the back, we'll buy more boots and some tents too."

His eyebrows shot up. "Don't I know you from somewhere?"

"No," I replied a little too quickly. I'd figured that if he didn't know what Derillen looked like, he'd not recognize me either. I pulled my hood down over my eyes as I grabbed a tent and dropped it next to the boots. Nudging Fallon to grab more, I pulled my secret cash stash from my pocket and threw everything I had at the shopkeeper. It was more than enough to pay for the couple of tents and pairs of boots we'd picked up. Without waiting for him to count it, we both ran behind the counter, through a door, and along a corridor until we came to the back door of the shop.

Pulling my old boots off, I threw them to one side and slipped my feet into the new ones. The supple leather and lined insides immediately brought warmth to my cold and aching feet.

"Ready?" Fallon asked, changing back into his normal self.

I nodded, and he heaved the back door open. Snow fell lightly in my hair as we raced down the alleyway past the back of Ms. Clarington's house. Without glancing backward, I ran until the very last house before the track that would take us to the ruin. Fallon, a little way ahead, stopped suddenly, then without warning, bounced back, falling into me, knocking us both to the ground.

"Sorry, Azia. you ok?" Fallon stood up and held his hand out to help me to my feet.

"What was that?" I replied, gingerly feeling the back of my head where it had hit the ground.

"I don't know. Some kind of invisible field."

I held my hand out and felt what Fallon had crashed into. Almost like rubber, but completely invisible, it blocked our path back to the ruin. A slight hum of magic filled the air. "Derillen!" I said. "We'll have to go another route."

I didn't like the idea of heading back into the town to try another road out, but there was no way we were going to get through here.

Before we had a chance to take another step, a voice I recognized immediately boomed out, "People of Leodis! I have created a magical field around the town. No one will be able to get in, and no one will be able to get out. Do not fear. Once the criminals are caught, the magical field will be removed, and you will be free to go about your day. To aid in the capture of the criminals, I will be sending a signal out. I ask that you do not be afraid. It cannot hurt you, and you will not feel it when it passes through you. It is merely a detector of magic."

Fallon's mouth fell open. "What now? She'll find us in no time. We can't get out of town!"

Panic filled me at the predicament we were in. The others would be safe down at the ruins, but Fallon and I had no way of escaping. A sound filled the air, like the purring or low humming of an engine.

"Let's head back to town. If she's putting all this magic out, there's no need for her to come looking for us. She's letting her magic do the work for her. We'll have more space to run."

"I think it's too late," Fallon shouted, pointing to a green wall of magic that was cutting through the houses at the side of the alley. It moved slowly, coming in a straight line and moving in a circle from the center of town, probably from the town square where we'd last seen Derillen.

As it closed in on us, the humming became louder, and the air began to crackle.

"We'll never get to the end of the alley in time," I yelled as the hair on my arms began to stand on end.

Fallon grabbed my arm and began to run, but it was clear that we weren't going to make it. The center of the circle and the beginning of the alley had a much smaller arc than if we'd run the other way, but the other way was blocked by the magic field. The row of houses had no gaps for us to run through...except...

"This way!" I yelled, pulling Fallon into the first garden we came to. Without knocking, I opened the door of the cottage, and the two of us ran through.

Green light gave the kitchen an eerie glow reminding me how close we were to getting caught. A family sat in the front room of the house. A father was playing with his young child on a play mat. They looked up as Fallon and I crashed through.

"Sorry!" I shouted, hurling myself through an open window at the front of the house. Seconds later, Fallon joined me.

The front of the house had a small garden with a low fence enabling us to easily jump it.

We'd managed to outrun the green light so far, but how long could we keep running? The road we came out on was flanked by houses on both sides, but the opposite side had much bigger houses with bigger gardens and gaps between them. We ducked between the houses, putting more distance between ourselves and the magic detector. Ten minutes later, and we were still running.

"I wonder if she'll stop, once she's done a full rotation?" Fallon huffed. "If we keep running, we might be able to outrun this thing, and she'll give up."

In theory, it sounded easy, but when it came to Derillen, nothing ever was.

"She'll keep looking," I wheezed back. "If she doesn't find us on the first rotation, she'll do another. Maybe faster and faster until we can't outrun it anymore."

Fallon glanced back over his shoulder, then stopped.

I stopped too. "What?" I asked, glancing nervously behind me. We'd managed to run so far ahead of the green light that I couldn't see it directly anymore, but the clouds above it reflected a green haze. We wouldn't have long before it would appear through the houses directly behind us.

"We can't keep going like this. Not if she's going to

run us into the ground. If there was somewhere we could hide, we could head there, but the light goes right through brick walls. There isn't anywhere. We might as well turn ourselves in and deal with Derillen face to face."

"I'm not giving up," I huffed. "If I have to run all day, then I will."

"Okay," Fallon replied, "come on then. Let's do this."

The green light appeared through the houses behind us, prompting us to start sprinting again. Each road we took had to be carefully calculated, so we didn't end up trapping ourselves. Effectively we were running in a huge circle as close to the edge of town as we could. With every road we turned down, we had to make sure there was a way forward out of it.

My lungs ached, and my muscles burned with the exertion, but stopping was not an option. Giving in was not an option. If Derillen caught me, then so be it, but I wouldn't go down easily.

We turned this way and that, racing through town, not spotting anyone on the way. Most were probably still out of town on the northern road searching for us. The rest, no doubt, were hiding in their homes.

"Azia!" Fallon warned, grabbing my arm, forcing me to stop.

"What?"

He pointed ahead. Directly in front of us in the distance, another wall of green light was heading in our direction. Looking over my shoulder, the first was still there. We were trapped.

"No!" I cried out. This couldn't be it. We'd gone through too much to get caught now. I'd endured sleeping in the cold, being fooled by an imp pretending to be a young girl, and then spending a night in a prison cell, all in the last week and a half.

"Oh!" An idea flashed into my brain. One that would save us both from being caught if it worked. "I think I can save us. It's a long shot."

"Better than no shot," Fallon responded. "But whatever it is, it had better be quick. Look."

The green light behind us was almost upon us, and the one coming from the front was getting nearer. Turning quickly on the spot, I got my bearings.

"This way. Quick!"

We raced, running as fast as our legs would carry us. The two green lines of magic were closer now, and our small section of town was rapidly decreasing.

My lungs felt like they were on fire as I pulled Fallon into the police station.

Thankfully, it was empty, and the doors had been left open. I pushed Fallon through to the back room and leaped in behind him as the first green wall of magic lit up the reception area.

The stench of death filled my nose, making me feel sick. I held my breath, trying not to look at the corpse of Busby that had been left to rot on the floor where he had fallen.

The light passed through the reception area and moved slowly through the back room. Fallon pulled me into one of the cells, but he didn't need to. The green magic washed right over us, carrying on without anything happening.

"What just happened?" Fallon asked, looking around him. "Why didn't it work?"

"This room inhibits our magic, remember?" I said with a relieved grin. "Busby had the artifact that stopped it. It must still be in his pocket. If we have no magic here, the magic detector will pass through us harmlessly."

I glanced quickly at Busby and the dark brown bloodstain beneath him. My stomach heaved, and I had to swallow back the bile.

Looking back at Fallon, I saw the look of amazement on his face.

"Did anyone ever tell you that you are a genius?" Fallon gasped, pulling me into a hug as the second wave of green light passed over us. Like the first, it didn't detect our presence.

"Can you see if you can find the artifact?" I asked. "I don't want to go near him."

I nodded at Busby's body. Fallon gingerly felt in Busby's pockets, pulling out a small silver shield with an emblem I didn't recognize on it.

"Is that it?" I asked as he passed the shield toward me.

"It's all he has in his pockets unless you think a pack of gum might be it?" he replied, holding up a small pack of gum.

The shield felt heavy in my hands. I ran my finger over the molded D with brambles entwined behind it. There was no doubt this was Derillen's.

"If only we could use this to get out," I mused aloud.

Fallon called back from where he'd moved to on the bench in the cell. "Not a chance. It only inhibits our magic, not Derillen's. Keeping hold of it will only put us at risk."

We did need all the magic we could get, but I couldn't help feeling that this object would come in useful one day. I slipped it into my pocket and joined Fallon on the bench where he was gazing out of the small barred window.

"It's gone awfully quiet out there."

The green still lit up the sky, but both walls seemed to be moving away from us. There was nothing we could do now but wait for whatever it was Derillen wanted to do next.

Hours passed as we sat in that cell along with Busby's body. Every time I caught sight of it, my stomach heaved, but moving wasn't an option. Ironically, the only place either of us was safe was in the small jail cells as the green magic circled back to us time and time again. Outside, the sky became dark and heavy with snow. No one came to look for us, and no one came to visit the police station. It was as though no one had cared for Busby in life, and no one cared about his death. He was a horrible man, but no one deserved to decompose in a prison cell—not even Busby.

As the snow began to fall outside, only visible in the lights of the nearby houses, I stood up and ventured into the main part of the police station and then outside.

"What are you doing?" Fallon hissed from the doorway.

"I'm going around to the back of the station to see if I can find a shovel. I'm going to bury Busby's body."

Fallon glared back at me. "Are you completely insane? Derillen is still out there."

I shrugged my shoulders. I couldn't explain my actions. I'd killed Busby, and though I was defending the queen at the time, it still sat heavily on my heart.

"She's not going to come looking for us herself. She believes her magic is infallible. The green walls of magic are nowhere near us. She's not caught us yet. Are you coming to help or not?"

Fallon hesitated, then threw up his hands. "Fine, but as soon as we see the green heading our way, we are going back inside!"

"Deal!"

At the back of the station was a small shed full of junk. Propped up against one of the walls were a couple of shovels. The earth behind the station was hard with cold, and the work was backbreaking, but a couple of hours after we'd started, there was a hole big enough for Busby. We buried him by the light of the neighboring houses as the snow fell around our ears. By the time the village clock struck midnight, his burial site was completely covered with snow, almost as though he'd never been there at all.

"People of Leodis," Derillen's voice echoed out into the night. "The wall has now been taken down. You are free to come and go as you please."

I held my breath, waiting for more, but nothing else was said.

"Come on, let's get back to the ruin. I told the others to go on ahead without us, so it's likely they aren't there. It looks like we are going to have to walk through the night if we have any hope of catching up with them."

"Or finding them," Fallon replied. "They will be well hidden."

"I'll always be able to find Nyre, and Nyre will be with them. We'll be fine."

I spoke with much more confidence than I felt, and as the snow came down around us, I wondered if we were walking right into a trap.

JULY DERILLEN

"Mr. President, there is discord among the kingdoms. The King of Badalah himself is missing, and they say there is a sickness there that is making people quite mad."

President Elm shook his head and massaged his temples. The stress was really beginning to show, and he'd aged considerably in the few months I'd managed to sidle in as his chief of staff. He'd been fearless back then. In a few short months, he'd turned from a lion into a mouse, mostly, thanks to me.

Any bad news I heard was fed directly to him, and when the news wasn't sufficiently bad enough, I made some up. Every day there was something else. The missing princes and princesses, the problems in the kingdoms, the breakdown of trade.

“People are scared, Mr. President, and so they should be. Everything is falling down around our ears.”

“Now, now, it’s not that bad. So, some of the kingdoms have a few problems. It can’t all be smooth sailing. I’m sure this will all work out.”

I shook my head forcefully. “That’s not exactly the attitude a leader should have, is it now, Mr. President? The media don’t want to know that this will all work out. They want ideas and leadership.”

The President sighed. Months of me wearing him down had done wonders. The man could barely decide if he wanted sugar or lemon in his tea anymore.

“I know what they want, but without any way of knowing what is going on, how can I be expected to deal with it? It’s not helping that those people you hired are not listening to a word I say. I swear the pretty mermaid one changed appearance yesterday. For a second, I swore I saw her looking like an old hag in the government fountains. Her hair was green.”

“Now, I know you are tired,” I said, ushering him to a chair. “She’s quite the beauty.”

“I don’t really understand why we need a mermaid anyway. All she does is sit in that fountain all day and brush her hair.”

“I told you, mermaid rights. It’s important now more than ever after what went down in Atlantice.”

The president rubbed his eyes.

“Just a suggestion. Why don’t I go out and talk to the media about what’s happening in Badalah? I have all your notes. You can stay here and rest. I’ll tell them you are feeling unwell.”

“You’d do that?” he asked gratefully.

“Of course,” I smiled. “We have to let them know the

truth, don't we?"

DECEMBER 15TH
AZIA

The town was deathly silent as we made our way through the streets, being careful to keep to the shadows and away from the town square. Being just after midnight, I didn't expect to see many people, but the lack of Derillen unnerved me. I kept expecting her to jump out of the shadows at any moment.

As we approached the road to the ruin at the very edge of the village, I began to think that we'd made it after all, but the low voices of two men talking had Fallon and I hiding around the corner of the last house.

"It's a bloody nuisance, is what it is," one complained. I peeked around the corner to see both men in thc Urbis Guard uniform in front of a temporary roadblock made up of a couple of logs. Both men rubbed their arms to keep out the cold.

"Tell me about it. I told our Rita that I'd be back in a day or so. Ms. High Almighty said it was a done deal, that they were in jail. No one said anything about keeping guard."

I turned to Fallon and whispered to him what I'd just heard.

"We'll have to go through the woods and circle round."

I shook my head. The woods would be guarded too. Derillen wasn't going to leave here until she had looked everywhere for us. I only hoped that the others had done what I asked of them and left without Fallon and me. "I have a better idea."

Ms. Clarington's eyes widened as she opened her back door in her flowery nightgown. She hastily pulled the glasses hanging on a chain around her neck up to her face and peered at us.

"Well, well, well. I wasn't expecting to see you again." She peered left and right out of her door and then stood back so we could come in.

"I'd better make us a pot of tea, and you can tell me what's been happening. Word is that the queen herself is in town."

"She was," I replied, taking my boots off and placing them neatly by the door. "I'm hoping she got away before Derillen caught up with her and the others."

"Others? I notice the lovely Deon isn't with you. Is he safe?"

"I hope so. I honestly don't know. I told them to cross the border into Elder, but they don't often do as I say."

Ms. Clarington smiled wryly as she poured the tea. "And this must be His Highness, Prince Fallon of Aboria."

"The one and only. It's a pleasure to meet you."

If I hadn't known better, I would have been sure Ms. Clarington's cheeks colored slightly as Fallon took her hand and kissed the back of it.

"I'm assuming you need my help," she said in a fluster. "Whatever it is, I'll do it. I'm very devoted to my queen."

I gave Fallon a grin, and he offered a wink back. "You mentioned that you'd take us to the border with your hay cart. There is a roadblock, and I'm pretty sure Derillen's men will be checking the woods on the edge of town."

"Of course, but we can't go now. A hay cart in the middle of the night will look awfully suspicious. We'll set off at dawn. The pair of you look exhausted. You know where the bedroom is. Go and get some sleep, and I'll see you in the morning."

I downed my tea and headed upstairs gratefully. I wanted nothing more than to head out straight away to find the others, but I was grimy and worn out from burying Busby.

I stripped off in the small bathroom and showered off the dirt before putting on one of Ms. Clarington's frilly nightgowns. I ventured into the bedroom to find Fallon dancing around the room in another nightgown, this one patterned with flowers.

"Look at this," he said, his eyes wide and with a smile on his face. He gave me a twirl.

"Yeah, gorgeous, you goof. Get into bed!"

He jumped on one bed as I took the other. I'd thought I wouldn't sleep, but when I opened my eyes, morning had already broken, and the scent of breakfast was wafting up the stairs.

"The cart is not here, obviously," Ms. Clarington

said as she dished up a hot breakfast for Fallon and me. "I think getting to it is going to be interesting with the Urbis Guard in town, but we'll see what we can do."

After breakfast, the three of us set out. Once again, the thick snow was our friend. The sky was heavy, and seeing more than twenty feet ahead was almost impossible.

Ms. Clarington led us through the streets until we came to a small stable. At the front, under a canvas cover, was an empty cart.

"I use it to go to nearby towns to pick up food and antiques. There's a much wider choice the further you go," Ms. Clarington explained as we hopped in the back. The guards won't know that, and I can tell them I'm a merchant of some kind. Unfortunately, if you cover yourself with just hay, they'll no doubt search it. We are going to have to find something that they won't want to search." She screwed up her face slightly. "The only thing I can think of is manure. There's plenty of it, and it will keep you warm. The cart is not particularly well made, so you'll be able to breathe through the small cracks in the bottom."

"No!" Fallon said, folding his arms. "I'm not lying down under a pile of horse shit."

I rolled my eyes. "If you don't and Derillen takes over, we'll all be in deep shit. Just get in."

Fallon didn't waver. "No. I can't. I'll throw up. I feel sick just thinking about it."

"Fallon. This is our only way out. I can't say I'm too happy either, but rather this than dead."

"I'd rather be dead!"

"You'd rather be dead, huh?" Ms. Clarington said, bringing out a horse and beginning the task of hooking it up to the cart. "That gives me an idea that might save both your nose and my cart. It's the only one I have, and to be honest, I'd prefer it not to have the odor of horse manure. Hop up, and I'll see what I can do."

However much I hated the idea of hiding in a pile of horse poop, going out into the town with no disguise worried me far more. I shot a glare at Fallon as I pulled an old blanket I'd found in the back over us.

"If we get caught now, I'm not going to be happy," I hissed as we moved through the streets. The horse's clip-clops came to a sudden stop and my breath caught in my throat. "I swear to all the gods, I'm going to kill you myself if Derillen doesn't do it first."

"Just don't mess up my hair when you do," Fallon whispered back, only infuriating me more.

We stayed where we were as Ms. Clarington talked to someone. I held my breath, trying to make out what they were saying, wondering how long it would be until the blanket would be pulled back, and we'd be discovered. I grabbed the hilt of my sword, my fingers ready to pull it from its sheath, waiting for the moment we'd be discovered. When the blanket was finally pulled back, I was ready. My sword was at the neck of the man before he had time to blink.

"This is Mr. Parson, Azia." Ms. Clarington said, putting a finger to the end of my sword and pushing it away from his throat. "He's going to help us."

I opened my mouth to apologize to the gaunt-looking man, but Fallon stepped in front of me and offered his hand. "Pleased to meet you. I'm Prince Fallon of Aboria, and this is Princess Azia of Draconis. She's a little jumpy."

I shot Fallon a look, then shook Mr. Parson's hand.

"How exactly are you going to help us?" Fallon enquired.

Mr. Parsons wordlessly leaned down and lifted up a box, which he slid onto the back of the cart.

"Oh, no," Fallon mumbled as a second box joined the first. "No way."

I almost laughed at the look of terror on his face. "You should have gone with the manure," I said, opening the lid of the first coffin and jumping in.

Ms. Clarington stepped forward. "Mr. Parsons has drilled some air holes in the side. I'm sure you'll be very comfortable. He tells me that these are his premium models."

"Lovely," Fallon replied, his face turning a sickly shade of green as he opened the lid of the second coffin.

"Just get in and close the lid," I smirked.

"Mr. Parsons will put a couple more coffins on top in case the guards want to open them. The top coffins will contain real bodies. They'll be heavy, so you won't be able to open yours until Mr. Parsons and I move them at the border."

Fallon's face went from green to grey. "Did I ever mention my fear of small spaces...and dead bodies."

Ms. Clarington pushed him back. "I'm sorry, Prince Fallon, but this is your only option. Now, lie back so we can close the coffin."

I snickered as the lid of Fallon's coffin was lowered until I couldn't even hear his low moaning anymore. Then it was my turn. Everything went dark as the lid was shut tightly above me. The only light I had were the few drilled holes in the side of the coffin. I shifted slightly as the other coffins were lowered on top of us and placed my mouth as close to the air holes as possible. As confident as I had seemed to Fallon, being trapped in a space I could barely move in, knowing a dead person was mere inches above me, had my heart palpitating. I took in a few deep breaths and closed my eyes as we began to move, the coffin bouncing slightly as we clattered over the snow-covered cobbles.

My eyes remained closed the whole journey until we came to a standstill. Putting one eye to a drilled hole, I could just about see a dry stone wall. My heart began to beat quickly again as the voices of the two guards drifted in. I tried the deep breathing trick again if only to hear what they were saying over the thrum, thrum, thrum of my heart.

The cart lurched a little, and I figured one of the guards had jumped on. Seconds later, there was a small scream, and the cart lurched again.

And then we were off. I saw one of the guards through the drilled hole throwing up on the road. The fool must have opened one of the upper coffins. I gave a mental high five to Ms. Clarington for her ingenuity and made a note to send her and Mr. Parsons a gift once this was all over.

We finally came to a stop again, and this time, my coffin lid was opened,

"The border is just over that wall," Ms. Clarington said, pointing to another dry stone wall, this one taller than the others, about ten feet or so high. It was unremarkable, and I wouldn't have known it was even a border wall if Ms. Clarington hadn't told me. Every hundred feet or so was a set of wooden steps that would take us to the top of the wall, and presumably, another set would take us down to Elder on the other side.

"Thank you for everything," I said, hugging Ms. Clarington. Her body tensed up as though she wasn't used to hugging, but she relaxed and put her arms around me.

"It's been a pleasure, Azia. I do wish you all the best,

and I hope we'll meet again someday."

"I'd like that." I handed her Derillen's shield. Taking it with us would strip us of our magical abilities, and that was a risk I couldn't afford to take. "Please, can you mail this to Urbis? I don't know if mail is getting through, but I have a friend there who will look after it. It impedes magic." I gave her the address Charlotte had given me all those months ago when she'd invited me to stay with her and Caspian.

After a final farewell, Fallon and I turned to the wall. Over the other side was Elder and beyond that, the border to Arcadia. As I took the first step up behind Fallon, I thought about the others. I had no way of knowing where they were. I only hoped they'd listened to me and started the journey last night rather than waiting at the ruin. They were a stubborn lot, but the feel of their magic was much dimmer than usual. Almost nonexistent. It could have had something to do with the shield I'd just given to Ms. Clarington or, more likely, they were already a long way ahead of us. Fallon and I would have to hurry to catch up with them.

Another forest awaited us as we made it to the top of the wall, a forest with the chance of sick and crazy wolves, insatiable with bloodlust. If we walked during the daytime when the wolves returned to normal and hid high up in the trees at night, we'd be fine. Castiel had told me as much. I wished he was with us as I took Fallon's hand to jump down the other side of the wall. Below us was a drop of ten feet or so onto a patch of grass. We jumped together. I'd expected our landing to be soft, but when my new boots made a clatter, I saw that the ground here was stone rather than grass. Confused, I looked up. The woods were no longer there. I found myself in a huge stone room with arches. To my right and left, I could just about make out small arched windows, too narrow for anyone to climb through. Beyond them, there was nothing but dark sky. Turning quickly, I found the wall still behind me, but now it rose up to the arched ceiling. My shadow danced upon it in the flickering candlelight. The air was thick with the smell of burning candles and the stench of something else that made me turn my nose up in disgust

"Where are we?" I whispered

"I think we fell through a portal," Fallon muttered. "A really big one."

I shook my head, trying to get my head around the concept. "I thought portals were like doorways. Actually, I thought they were a myth."

Fallon shrugged, his usually beautiful features contorted with confusion. "I guess they aren't."

The candlelight flickered across his features, giving him an eerie look. A shiver ran down my spine, and I fought the rising panic within me. Wherever it was, it wasn't Elder. For a second, I wondered if I'd fallen into Morpheus's dreamscape, but I'd been very awake when we'd jumped across the border. This place, as terrifying as it was, was at least real, and if it was real, it meant there was a way out of it.

"Let's get out of here," I murmured, but before I'd taken more than a few steps, hundreds of ghostly figures appeared out of the shadows. We were trapped, and there was nowhere left to run to.

KINGDOM OF FAIRYTALES

DECEMBER 15TH
AZIA

A night trapped in an underground building with hundreds of other people was not what I had in mind when I crossed the border from The Vale to Elder, but here I was, along with Fallon. It hadn't taken long to find out where we had ended up. Enough people had been willing to tell us. It didn't take a genius to figure out who had magically brought us here either.

Lit by only a few candles, the cavernous space jangled my nerves with its dancing shadows and dark corners. I'd barely slept, waking an hour before dawn to check through the people again to make sure I'd not missed any of my brothers and sisters.

"Where did you cross again?" I asked a middle-aged

woman named Sally, whom I'd met the night before. With smart clothes and an expression of despondency on her face, it was hard to remember why I'd thought the people here were something more than they actually were. When I'd first seen them coming out of the shadows, my mind had flown to something scary, something other-worldly, but they were just people. Prisoners like Fallon and I had become.

"I was going to work," Sally answered with a grimace. "What kind of a crime is that? No kind of crime is what. I live in The Forge, but I work just over the border in Oz. Now, I know we aren't supposed to cross the border, any border. It's been illegal for a while, but my family is starving, and I needed to work. How was I supposed to know that if I crossed, I'd end up here?"

I nodded politely. It was one of a hundred stories I'd heard since ending up in this vast prison.

"You'll be fine," a gruff voice cut across us. I turned to find an older gentleman with thick auburn hair and beard, both of which had streaks of white through them.

"Every day at dawn, there is a sweep of the prison. All those with magic get left behind. Those without magic are marched to the North Entrance of Urbis and told to go home."

Sally grimaced. "Which is all well and good if you live just beyond the North Entrance in Badalah. How am I supposed to get home from there? I have no money."

The old man shrugged as though traveling hundreds of miles on foot wasn't such a big deal. "You'll figure it out."

"Great," Sally huffed, crossing her arms. "And just how am I supposed to cross the borders I need to cross to get home? I'll end up back in here the second I step foot outside of Badalah."

The old man raised a finger. “Ah, that’s where you are wrong. You’ll be given a magical broach that lets you cross any border without being scooped up by the magic portals.”

Sally brightened up immediately. “So, I’ll be able to work?”

The old man nodded. “I dare say you will.”

“How do you know all this?” I asked.

He grunted, then cleared his throat. “This is not my first time here. I’m from Draconis. I have a sister in Urbis. The first time I got caught, it was quite by accident. I thought I’d be fine to hop over the border, but I was wrong. I ended up here. Terrified, I was. Thought I was going to be hung. Anyway, no one was interested in me, once they knew I wasn’t magic. They gave me a broach and sent me on my way. But I hadn’t seen my sister see, so I threw the broach away and skipped the border again. Of course, I ended up here again. After a few hours, I was let go, but this time I ducked out of the line of people waiting to leave Urbis by way of the North Gate and went to visit my sister. Now, every time I want to visit Urbis, I hop the border and end up back here. It’s cheaper than a ticket on the Urbis Express, and because there are so many people being sent out, the North Gate has plenty of people with carriages willing to take you home.”

Fallon and I had spent the night in the giant prison, along with hundreds of others. I’d spent my first few hours here searching for our siblings, but whatever had happened to them, they hadn’t ended up here. I‘d listened to the stories of other people trapped here like us. The old man was the first to offer any clue as to what this place was about. Everyone had just arrived here, like us. Fallon and I had moved more than once to accommodate the growing number of people still arriving.

I shifted closer to the old man. "Can you tell me exactly what happens? How do they sort the magic from the non-magic people?"

He checked his watch. "You'll see for yourself in a couple of minutes. It's nearly dawn."

"I need to know now!" I urged.

The man licked his lips. "They sweep a green light over everyone. It's some kind of magic detection thing."

"Dragon shit!" I hissed under my breath. Exactly like the one in Leodis except there, I'd had Derillen's magic impeder. I'd given it to Ms. Clarington to send to Charlotte and Caspian only the night before.

"It don't hurt none," the old man said, mistaking my distress as worry about pain.

"What happens if you are magic?"

He stroked his chin. "They throw the magic people in the cells there," he said, pointing to a row of empty cells along the center of the room. "There are plenty of people who are magic that fall into the same trap as the rest of us. Take the Enchantians, for example. They are all magic. It's not a crime."

"Neither is going to work," Sally piped up, "But that didn't stop me from getting stuck in here."

The old man tutted. "I've met more than a few Enchantians on my travels back home. They told me that they were brought up in front of some of the governors to be checked more thoroughly. I think they are looking for those criminals on the loose." My cheeks heated as he peered at me more closely. "Say, you two look a little like them."

I turned my head away from the old man.

"Thanks," I murmured, standing up. Fallon followed

me to the darkest corner.

"You can't talk to any more people," Fallon admonished. "It's a miracle no one has recognized us already. Let me change, and I'll go and see if I can find the others."

"The others aren't here," I whispered. "We'd have found them already. You heard what that old man said. If they'd have come here the day before yesterday, they'd have already been caught. Derillen is probably sitting upstairs somewhere just waiting for you and me, knowing we'll be here soon."

"You don't know that."

I huffed and wrapped my arms around my knees. "I wish I'd brought Derillen's shield now. It protected us once; it could have done it again."

Fallon shook his head. "We don't know the range of that thing. What if it had taken everyone in this room's magic. I think the guards might have sussed something was going on when literally no one showed up on their magic detection scan."

Frustration filled me. "What are we going to do?"

Fallon shrugged. "I don't know."

Almost as soon as he'd gotten the words out, a green light appeared at the other side of the room. It moved slowly toward us, passing through all the people. It stopped, and an alarm sounded. Seconds later, a number of Urbis Guards ran to those setting off the alarm and dragged them to the cells in the center of the room just as the old man had said.

The green light continued its journey, getting closer and closer to us. Every time it stopped, the magic people in question were lit up, making them easy to find for the guards.

I could only watch on in horror as the hundreds of

people were split into two groups. Most were ushered outside, but the cells were filling up fast.

The old man turned to us as the green light passed right through him. He gave a wave of his hand before heading off to join the line to the exit.

The green wall of light moved closer and closer until Fallon and I were the only two people left. He grabbed my hand as the green passed through us.

It had barely touched us when the alarm once again went off.

Two guards ran over and pulled us to the cells. Neither of us fought against them. There was no point. The place was full of guards, and as far as I could tell, there was only one way out.

With my hood pulled as far over my face as I could get it, I took a seat on the floor next to a sobbing man. He wore once white robes that were now filthy with the dirt from the prison floor. Looking around, most of the people wore white, marking them as Enchantians. There were others dressed like us, but they were few and far between.

"What now?" I whispered to Fallon as the cell gate was closed and locked behind us.

Fallon shook his head. In the darkness, it was barely perceptible, but he'd changed his appearance. He no longer looked like Fallon. His clothes had lightened to a dirty white to match the clothes of many of the others, and his hair receded into his head until he was bald except for a few wisps of white hair at the sides.

"That's okay for you," I huffed, "but I don't have that ability, remember?"

"Yeah, but there is more than one way to disguise someone."

I raised my eyebrows. "I'll just check through my bag

for a disguise, shall I? Dig around through my collection of wigs and pull out my extensive theatrical makeup collection." I folded my arms and stared through the bars at the hundreds of people pushing toward the only exit—non-magic people, who would soon be heading to the north gate of Urbis and their freedom.

He grabbed my bag and started rummaging around in it before he found one of my shirts and a stack of cash. I watched as he glanced toward the guards to make sure they weren't watching and then wordlessly passed both to the sobbing man. Except he wasn't sobbing anymore. He looked downright cheerful as he counted the cash and put it in the pocket of the shirt of mine he'd just put on.

He passed me his robe in exchange. I pulled it on and tied it tightly over my hooded jacket, making sure my sword was hidden beneath it.

"I don't think this is going to work. I still look like me."

Fallon spat on his hand then dragged it across the floor of the cell. In one quick motion, he brought it to my face and coated my chin with the wet dirt.

"What are you doing?" I hissed, spitting grit from my mouth.

"One last thing!" He brought out a knife from his own bag and grabbed my hair.

"Stop struggling. I don't want to hurt you." A second later, he held my messy ponytail in his hand. "There."

I gritted my teeth and resisted the urge to pull the knife from his hand and stab him with it. He held the knife up in front of me and tilted it so that my reflection was visible. With the dirt on my chin acting as stubble and short hair, I looked like a young man. It was possibly the worst disguise I'd ever seen, but in the dim light, it might just pass.

"This had better work!" I whispered as the last of the non-magic people left the large room. When they had gone, a guard opened the cell door and instructed us to line up against the wall.

I followed the others, standing near the end next to Fallon. My heart pounded, and my throat felt dry.

A woman with heavily lidded eyes stepped into the room, her high heels echoing through the empty space. There was something about her that made my blood run cold. A shiver ran up my spine as she began to work her way down the long line of people.

Her long black curly hair was the exact shade of her eyes, and she wore black to go with both—a tight wrap-around dress with high heeled boots and long black gloves.

She walked upright, her nose in the air as though there was anywhere she'd rather be than under the government building.

"Is this all of them?" she inquired, her voice deep and haughty.

I stepped slowly to my left away from the closest candle, keeping to the shadows as much as I could.

"This is today's lot, ma'am." The chief guard replied. "Of course, we'll have more coming in. We always do."

She rolled her eyes. "Let's get it over with then," she snapped. "I have better things to be doing than wasting my entire day down here."

"Yes, ma'am."

"Cordel. You know my name. Use it."

"Yes, Cor...ma'a...Cordel."

She smiled, raising her dark lips up at the edges in a way that made my skin crawl. This was one of Derillen's people. I was sure of it, but which one?

She barely looked at the people as she strode down the line, giving each person only a perfunctory glance. Her lack of interest in her job was hopefully going to be our way out of here. I held my breath as she dismissed the people in front of me. She stopped short when she came to Fallon. Something about him piqued her interest. I hastened a quick look at him. He'd taken on the appearance of a total stranger, so what was it that Cordel saw in him? Could she sense his magic? Inside my boots, I tapped my toe up and down and gripped the hilt of my sword. Killing her wasn't an option. There were too many guards, but I liked the way it calmed me.

"It's none of them!" she announced with a swish of her dress. She turned on her heel and marched out, taking the stairs up to the main level two at a time in her haste to get out.

"Alright, you heard the lady," The chief guard shouted. "Get out of here."

We were ushered up the stairs to a small waiting room and handed a broach with a D emblazoned on it, just as the old man had said we would.

"You have all broken the law," the chief guard announced. "Our kind and merciful leader understands that the restrictions are hard on everyone, so she is giving you these broaches to allow you to cross borders to get home. You may have heard that these will allow you to move freely throughout the kingdoms, and until last week, that was true. However, a great number of people were abusing our leader's generosity and using them to do whatever they pleased. We cannot keep the people safe if everyone goes about doing whatever they like. There are still a number of criminals out there yet to be caught, and we cannot do that if we are wasting time with the lot of you. Therefore, these broaches will only allow each one of you to cross one border to get home. On your second attempt to cross a border, these broaches will put you to death instantly."

An angry chatter grew among the crowd. "What about me," one asked. "I live in The Vale. That's more than two kingdoms away."

The guard sneered at the man. "That is not my problem. We've been more than generous. I suggest you find a new home until the criminals have been caught. Now, if there are no more questions, our guards will accompany you to the train station where you'll be taken to the North Gate."

It was clear there were plenty more questions, but we were ignored and pushed out into a long corridor.

I hid in the middle of the crowd, trying to be as inconspicuous as possible. I might have passed for a man downstairs in the dimly lit prison, but up here, it was well lit, and my disguise was flimsy at best. The corridor walls were filled with gold-framed paintings of the previous presidents of Urbis until about halfway down where the frames changed. Each one was different. The first had molded metal playing cards framing a painting of a busty woman with a red corset dress and a small heart-shaped birthmark painted above her lip. Below it was a sign that read, "Queen of Hearts" in gold ink and below that, her title, "Commander of the Urbis Army."

"There isn't an Urbis Army," I whispered to Fallon.

"There wasn't," Fallon corrected me.

I recognized these people as our foes. Blaise's sea witch, looking beautiful with flowing purple hair, Rumpelstiltskin in his normal form as an imp, and a woman with a hooked nose and green tinge to her skin named Momba. The title she'd been given was

Keeper of the Jails and Chief of Urbis Prison. Even in her painting, she looked faintly bored as though she'd rather be somewhere else.

Fallon stopped suddenly, causing someone behind me to crash into me.

"Sorry," I said, giving the person a brief smile before turning back to Fallon and pulling him along. "What is it?"

He nodded at the painting we were passing. "Edwin. Veda's father. I knew he'd be here, but seeing it shocked me."

"I've still got the painting of Derillen to come," I whispered back.

Reading the other names on the paintings was impossible. We were being ushered along so quickly, but I made a quick note of the faces we were up against. There were so many of them. I was more than a little bit surprised when we came to the end of the corridor and hadn't seen Derillen's picture yet. I knew very little about the woman, but everything I had seen was enough to tell me that she liked glory.

The double doors at the end of the corridor opened into a huge entrance hall with white marble floors. I knew this place. I'd been here before with my parents. It was the Government building. This was where the laws of all the kingdoms were passed.

On the back wall, almost covering it, was the largest painting I'd ever seen. Derillen smiled down at us, wearing her customary purple and black. I looked away in horror. Just looking at her painting was enough to give anyone the creeps. In single file, we were marched through the atrium to the main front doors of the building. As we headed out, a line of people was waiting to get in. Each one had a wand waved over them to test for hidden magic—workers, perhaps, or members of the public waiting to get a tour of the building. A smart woman at a counter greeted each one as they passed. Inside, the government building hadn't changed much, but outside was a different story. The huge square that sat in the very center of Urbis was usually a vibrant area filled with people from all the kingdoms going about their business. I remembered cafes and restaurants bustling with people, but now, the square was almost empty of people, and the cafes were closed. Black and purple banners hung from every lamppost, and the famous Urbis Tower had been painted black to match, with the window frames a deep shade of purple.

"What now?" Fallon asked as we were marched along the wet cobbles in the direction of the train station.

"Follow my lead. I know this area."

The train station was almost as quiet as the square had been, but there were enough people to hide amongst. As our train to Northern Urbis pulled in and people began to disembark, in one swift movement, I pulled the white robe off and threw it under the train. Fallon saw what I was doing and shifted his appearance to that of a young woman. We turned quickly and joined those heading out of the station. Behind us, a man shouted. Fallon grabbed my hand and pulled me further into the crowd, walking as quickly as both of us could without seeming obvious.

Footsteps running behind us filled me with panic. Once we were out into the empty streets, we'd be caught for good.

Fallon hurled himself back first into a wall then pulled me into him. He grabbed my waist and pulled me into a kiss.

The guards ran right by us, not paying the slightest

bit of attention. When they were gone, we slipped through the door of another train and found an empty compartment. Fallon closed the door, locking it behind him.

"Well, that was gross," I announced, wiping my mouth with the back of my sleeve. The dirt from earlier made a long black mark.

"I'll have you know that a great many women have complimented me on my kissing. I'm quite well known for it."

"Were any of those women also your sister?" I asked dryly.

He waved his hand at me and shifted his appearance from the young woman to his normal self. "I saved us, didn't I? What did you think of kissing a girl?"

"If I had anything to throw at you, I would," I said, pulling the blind down, plunging us into near darkness. All our belongings had been taken from us at the government building, so we literally only had the things we wore.

Below us, the train began to rumble and then slowly pull out of the station.

Fallon sat back in his seat. "We need to find the others. If they did cross the border, which I suspect they did, they would have been caught."

"There's an easy way to find out. We'll pick up a newspaper when we get off the train. Do you know where this train is going, anyway?"

I shrugged. It didn't matter where it was going. It only mattered that we were heading away from Derillen's people. "We'll get off at the next stop before they come asking for tickets. Charlotte lives in a small apartment in Inner Urbis. We'll head there and then make plans."

Fallon reclined against the wall and pulled one leg

up to the opposite seat. "Remind me who Charlotte is again."

"She's a friend and the only person I know well enough in Urbis to casually drop in on."

"She hot?"

"She has a boyfriend, and you have a girlfriend remember?"

I closed my eyes, not wanting to answer any more questions. My head was reeling at the problems we faced. We'd gone from fourteen to two. Fifteen if I counted Eliana's mother. I had no way of knowing if she'd crossed the border with the others.

As soon as the train came to a stop, Fallon and I jumped out. I ran to the shadows as Fallon, looking like a kindly middle-aged lady, asked some passers-by the way to Charlotte's address. Getting on a train again was not a wise idea, so we walked, keeping to the backstreets so I wouldn't be recognized. Not that my own parents would recognize the dirty, shorthaired rat that their daughter had become in the months since leaving the castle.

It was late into the evening when I finally knocked on the door of the address that Charlotte had given me.

A man with long white hair and amethyst eyes opened the door. When he saw who it was, his mouth curved into a leering grin.

"Well, well, well, look who's finally here. I wondered when you'd show up."

"So did I," a man with shaggy hair said, stepping out from behind Caspian. "Flipping heck, Azia. What have you done to your hair?"

SEPTEMBER DERILLEN

Eight people sat around the massive oval-shaped oak table that was usually reserved for meetings with kings, queens, and the ministers that made up the Urbis Cabinet. There wasn't a law in any of the kingdoms that hadn't been discussed around this table.

"I'd like to welcome Queenie Heart into our little family," I said, my arms open wide from my place at the top end of the table. "She's been helping us with our little problem from the Forge. The ninth monster is currently being dealt with. Queenie brings with her an army of mechanical means, which I'm assured will do anything she asks of them. They are currently at work in The Forge but will be able to do our bidding once their work there is done."

A small smattering of applause went around the table.

"Can we get back to the matter of finding the missing brats?" Rumpelstiltskin asked, drumming his fingers on the table impatiently.

"I've already told you, we don't need to go and find them. They will come to us, and you know what we have in store for them here."

"I just don't see the point of waiting. Every time they find another brat, their strength grows."

I sighed. "Yes, that does pose a problem. The thing is, I don't know where they are. They are not using public transport."

Rumpelstiltskin tsked. "So? You are the president now. Pass some laws or something. Use it to your advantage."

"Hmm. I'll send a messenger out to every police station in all the kingdoms to keep an eye out for them." I turned to a small quiet woman in the corner. "Erika, please send a message to the editors of all the Urbis newspapers. In fact, send a message out to all the main newspapers in all the kingdoms. Use a photo that we have of the brats and tell them that they are wanted criminals."

"Yes, President Derillen." Erika curtsied and practically ran out of the room.

"That suit you, Rumpelstiltskin?" I asked, my lips pursed.

"It's a start, but I think it would be better if I went to find them."

"I'm not having you gallivanting about all over the countryside. I need you here. You are too important. I promise that if the brats ever find each other, I'll let you go look, but let's leave it for now. We have a lot to prepare for if they do eventually get here."

Rumpelstiltskin crossed his arms and pulled his features back into a sneer, but he didn't question me.

Momba, with her pointed hat and a green tinge to her complexion, raised a hand. A winged monkey jumped from her shoulder and circled the room.

"Yes, Momba?"

"What will Queenie's job be?"

Derillen raised her eyes to the air in concentration. "With her army of mechanical cards, let's make her commander of the army."

Momba raised her hand again.

"Yes?"

"I also have an army." Momba pointed out. The winged monkey landed softly back on her shoulder.

"Your turn is yet to come. Have you decided what your plans are with Dorothy's brat yet?"

"I was thinking it would be the easiest thing to have him thrown in Urbis Prison. That way I won't have to worry about him. The guards there can do their jobs."

Derillen nodded as she considered this. "Having one less of them to worry about will certainly be to our advantage. How will we get the guards to listen to us? I've only been President for a short amount of time and have yet to visit there."

Momba waved her hand. "The prison is guarded by ogres, stupid creatures at the best of times. I'll pay them a visit and tell them you sent me. I'll explain that they now have to do your bidding."

"Then it's settled," Derillen said, clapping her hands together. "You shall hereby be known as Keeper of the Jails and Chief of Urbis Prison. Cordel here is in charge of the security here, but you shall cover the kingdoms."

Momba adopted a self-satisfied smirk as she winked at Rumpelstiltskin. Rumpelstiltskin grimaced in reaction.

“Is there anything else?”

The members of the board shook their heads.

“Right, Edwin. I’m putting you in charge until I get back. I’ve got to pay a visit to Skyla to meet with a pirate with a hook for a hand.”

16TH DECEMBER
AZIA

"Will you get off the end of my bed. Don't you have a girlfriend to go and bother?"

Caspian held his hand to his heart. "Are you suggesting I'm here to try and seduce you?"

"It wouldn't be the first time," I retorted. "It didn't work back then either, if I recall." I pulled my sword out from under my blanket and held it to his neck.

The corners of his mouth pulled back into a grin, and his amethyst eyes sparkled.

"Just like old times, I see. I only came to ask you if you wanted breakfast." He stood up, holding both hands in the air.

"I'll be down soon," I promised, keeping the sword

exactly where it was.

"As you please."

When he'd left the room, I jumped out of bed and pulled on the clothes that Charlotte had brought for me.

Fallon's head popped up from the floor at the side of the bed, where he'd spent the night on top of a folded blanket. His hand covered his eyes.

"Safe to look yet?"

"Yep. All dressed."

"He's a crazy one, isn't he. What was he talking about seducing you for?"

I rolled my eyes. "He's always like that. I was supposed to marry him at one point."

Fallon jumped up onto the bed. "In all these months we've spent together, you never thought to tell me you were betrothed?"

"I wasn't betrothed...not really. To be honest, I've done my best to forget about it. Are you coming down for breakfast or not?"

Fallon never had to worry about new or clean clothes. Not since he'd honed his magical ability of changing his appearance to include the clothes he was wearing too.

In the kitchen, Charlotte placed a plate of pancakes with maple syrup on them in front of each of us, then passed us a black coffee each.

Castiel was already there, munching on an undercooked steak.

"It's not in the papers," she said, throwing today's edition of the Urbis newspapers on the table. "I checked through each one thoroughly. Not a mention."

"Does that mean they haven't been caught?"

"Either that or they aren't publicizing it," Castiel replied between bites.

"You still haven't told us how you ended up here," I pointed out.

Castiel swallowed the last of his steak and wiped his mouth on a napkin. "Same as you, I expect. I crossed over into Elder and magically ended up under the government building. They figured me out right away. Two guards started to take me to see Derillen, but I turned into a wolf, bit the pair of them, and escaped into the streets. They didn't have a hope of catching me."

"But how did you get here?"

"You told us all this address so many times I knew it by heart. I knew I'd never get back to you, but I hoped you'd find your way here. And look. You did."

"Not all of us," I sighed. "I don't even know if they crossed the border. I told them to, but they might have decided to wait for Fallon and me. We could have gone right past them and not even noticed."

"It wasn't her fault," Fallon said, pre-empting my pity party. "The fact is, we don't know if they are in The Vale or here in Urbis. If they are in Urbis, the likelihood is that Derillen has them. Getting Azia out in disguise was one thing. Getting the rest of them out with a purple dragon and a full-sized unicorn would be impossible."

"Charlotte," I began, taking a sip of my coffee. "Do you know where Derillen would keep them if she had them?"

Charlotte shook her head. "I don't. The government only tells us what they want us to know. The media is controlled by Derillen now."

Of course, it was. "She's probably not even back from The Vale yet. She can't just transport herself from one place to the other like Rumpelstiltskin can."

"She managed to transport us pretty well, not to

mention the thousands of other people."

"I think she had Rumpelstiltskin's magic to thank for that. I bet he's the one setting up the portals. I'm pretty sure she's traveling the old-fashioned way. She'll want to be seen. The Urbis Express from Elder will take time. There's a chance she hasn't even gotten to Urbis yet." I stood up, but Caspian grabbed my arm.

"I'm not letting you go to the government building without a plan. If she's not back already, she will be soon enough. You'll be walking into danger."

I pulled my arm from his grip. "You don't get to tell me what I can and can't do," I snapped.

"He's right," Charlotte said. "Going back there would be madness right now. If they do have them, they'll be locked down tight. We need to have some idea of what to do next. It's not going to be easy. The streets around here are full of guards, day and night. I'm surprised you didn't see any on your walk here."

"We saw a few," I admitted, "but they didn't recognize me with short hair. I think they thought I was some kid with his grandmother."

"Mother," Fallon piped up. "I didn't look that old."

"Derillen's pretty much brought Urbis to a standstill since she came into power. Most things are closed," Charlotte continued. "Any form of entertainment such as bars, restaurants, theaters, and the like are on strict curfew and have to close at eight every night. A lot have gone out of business. Shops are allowed to open, but most don't anymore because the guards are always checking in on them, which scares the customers away. The university has shut down because the staff and students tried to keep Derillen out of power. I've had to get a job, but it doesn't really pay the bills."

"You don't have to work," Caspian said, holding her

hand. "I've told you that a million times. I have plenty of money. I have a much bigger apartment we could go to."

"And I've told you a million times, I don't want to be a kept woman. Besides, I like it here. It's just around the corner from my new job."

"What about Morpheus?" I asked. "Have you found out anything else about him?"

Charlotte's eyes lit up. "Actually, I have. A lot of bars and clubs are floundering with the restrictions, but there are a few in Inner Urbis that are flouting the rules. They are open at all hours, letting people in. Word around town is that Derillen has been seen at some of them."

"And Morpheus?"

Charlotte shook her head. "No sign, but I can't think of any other reason Derillen would keep these places open. She doesn't seem the type to socialize for fun."

"You think she's meeting him there?"

"I think so, but I have no way of knowing for sure. Morpheus doesn't just walk in and out the front door. He gets to these places through a portal from the world of the gods. And these clubs. They aren't open to just anyone. You have to be a member of Inner Urbis's elite to even think about stepping foot inside."

I rested my head in my hands and thought through all the scenarios we had to deal with. We had to find the others, figure out what, exactly, it was that Derillen wanted, find Morpheus so we could get into the Dream World to find my mother and possibly Snow White. Then, we had to solve all the kingdoms' problems, all without being caught and killed by a gang of magical psychopaths and misfits.

"I don't know what to do first," I admitted.

"I have to go to work. It's just around the corner. Why don't you come with me, and Caspian can see what he can find out at the government building. He still works there, albeit in a diminished capacity."

"What about us?" Fallon asked.

"You can come with me," Caspian said. "You can change your appearance. They'll never know it's you. Castiel can stay here and get the blood out of the carpet."

Castiel looked down to where he'd spilled the bloody juice from his steak on the floor.

"Sorry, I'm not used to eating indoors on carpet. My cabin doesn't have one, and I've only started liking raw meat since I've been able to turn into a wolf."

"We'll meet back here this evening," I said, grabbing the last slice of toast, "hopefully, with a plan and some more knowledge."

Charlotte worked in a small art studio, not a hundred feet from her apartment building. Along the wall were pots of paints of every color imaginable. Weird statues had been left in a messy pile on the floor.

"Be careful you don't step on the costumes," she said, stepping over them.

"These are costumes?" I said, looking back down at the pile of what I thought were statues.

"Yeah. I work for the theatre doing costume and makeup. Or at least, I did until most theaters were shut down. The royal theater in the center is still showing performances, but that's the only one. Those costumes are for a show opening next week."

I stepped over the costumes and picked my way through the room to the far side where Charlotte sat at a desk.

"Why don't you go through there?" she said, pointing

to a door. "There's a stove. You can make us both a coffee, and we'll have a chat. I have to get this sewing done for tonight. I'm making a dress for the leading lady."

Through the door was a small kitchen with a couple of tables strewn with designs, most of which had coffee stains on them. Putting a pot of water on to boil, I rested against a work surface and looked out of the window. The snow hadn't reached Urbis yet, but the sky was dark and gloomy, and the cobbles were wet with rain. The weather matched my mood perfectly. I'd spent months dreaming of the day I'd finally get into Urbis to fight Derillen, but now that I was here, I felt further away and more lost than I ever had. My magic had dwindled, and my brothers' and sisters' magic was lost to me. I had no idea where they were, and with all the magic floating around the city, thanks to Derillen and her crew, I couldn't even tell if they were near.

Part of me itched to summon Nyre. But to do that, I'd have to send a beacon of magic up into the air for her to see. Not the most practical solution.

After making the coffees, I took them back and put one next to Charlotte on the table.

"I have you to thank for this job, you know."

I raised my eyebrows. "How so?"

"I never cared about make-up and dresses, but when your maid Dahlia did mine that day at Draconis Castle, I fell in love with how I felt. I came back here and taught myself how to sew and how to do makeup. Then, I landed this job. There are a few of us that work here, but as most of the theaters are closed, we've cut down our hours and only work the occasional day."

"The dress you are making is beautiful," I pointed out. I'd never much liked wearing dresses, preferring clothes I could fight in, but I missed my mother chattering away about clothes and how nice I'd look if I put in some effort. At the moment, I looked like a guy, with my hair cut at all lengths by Fallon's knife and the clothes Charlotte had picked out for me.

"I have an idea," Charlotte said excitedly, putting down the half-made dress and picking up the coffee instead. "Come with me."

I followed her back through to the kitchen and then through another door. Inside the room, the wall was covered in mirrors, next to which was a long table running the length of the room and some chairs.

"This is our dressing room. Sit down. I'm going to give you a makeover. We have a hundred different dresses in our wardrobe left over from past productions. There is bound to be something that would fit you."

"Thanks for the offer, but I can't have a makeover. I have to find the others. I have to save my mother."

"And a makeover might help you with both of those things," she replied cryptically. "Now sit down while I get my tools."

I sat at one end of the table and looked at myself in the mirror. I was barely recognizable to myself.

My hair stuck up at all ends and was so short that I'd lost my curls. My face had been cleaned in the bath at Charlotte's house that morning, but my skin was sallow with black circles under my eyes. I looked like a girl who hadn't had a good meal in months, which was pretty much exactly what I was. I was a ghost of my former self. Even the gold rings around my irises had dimmed.

"I'll start with your hair and explain my plan as we go," Charlotte said, pulling a tray of scissors and combs toward her.

"What about the leading lady's dress? I thought you had to finish it today?"

"Meh. The show doesn't open until next week. This is more important. It's not like I get paid enough to do this anyway."

I sat back in the chair and let her do her job. I kept silent as she recited her plan to me. It was a good one. Not perfect by a long shot, and I could think of a million ways I'd get caught, but it was better than any plan I had.

The dress she brought out to me was like nothing I'd ever seen before. I was used to beautiful ball gowns and pretty summer dresses, thanks to my mother, who always liked me to look nice, but this was something else entirely.

"This is a dress?" I asked as Charlotte helped me squeeze into it. "An actual dress that people wear outside? In public?"

Charlotte grinned at me. "Only if they want to look sexy and stylish."

"Or get paid by the hour," I quipped.

She shooed me away. "Don't be silly. The Inner Urbis elite all dress this way."

I looked down at the flaming red scrap of cloth that clung to my body. My cleavage was pushed right up, and the dress, if I could call it that, barely covered my ass. My pale legs seemed to go on forever in such a short dress. They were also covered in bruises and scrapes.

"I'll have to get you something to cover your legs."

"Like a pair of pants or a blanket?"

"I was thinking pantyhose. You'll need shoes too."

She came back with the items and waited until I'd shoehorned myself into both. The towering shoes belied belief at the sheer height of them, making me tower over Charlotte.

"Woah, lady. I think I went a bit far. All eyes are going to be on you. Mind you, you look nothing like Azia, Princess of Draconis anymore."

She turned me around and stood me in front of the one full-length mirror in the room. I sucked in a breath as I caught sight of myself. I'd had hundreds of makeovers in my time. Every time there was a royal occasion or a ball or a photoshoot, my mother had made me dress up, but this was something else.

Charlotte had cut my hair into a pixie cut that framed my face perfectly. The weight I'd lost from months of walking and barely eating had slimmed my waist and made my legs more shapely than I'd ever seen them. Charlotte had given me red lips to go with the dress, which gave me a look of wanton sexuality. I smoldered. The woman looking back at me was sure of herself. She could have any man she wanted, and she could do whatever she wanted without asking anyone's permission. If only I felt the same way as I looked. I could take over the world.

"You are going to want to keep Caspian away from me looking like this," I murmured, twisting my body to get a view of my back.

"Don't worry about him. I'm going to get dressed up too, and we're both coming with you. There's no way I'd let you go out alone looking like that."

"What time should we set out?" I asked, suddenly nervous. The woman in the mirror furrowed her brows, and the Azia I knew was back. It didn't suit the gorgeous woman. I rearranged my features and tried to look sophisticated, rather than downright terrified.

"Darling. The elite never go out before midnight."

DECEMBER
DERILLEN

"How are the queens?" I asked pleasantly. Something had changed between Morpheus and me, and I didn't like it. I never thought there'd come a time that I'd have to resort to small talk with him, but here we were.

Morpheus yawned. Actually yawned as though I'd become boring to him.

"I feel like you kind of duped me on that count, Derillen."

I swirled the ice around in the whiskey he'd poured for me. "What do you mean, duped you? I promised you the two most beautiful women in all the kingdoms, and I delivered. Are they not still in your...care?"

However much it galled me that he was using Briar

Rose and the queen of Enchantia as his own personal playthings, I needed him to be at least partly interested. Letting them go at this crucial point would overturn all my plans.

"Of course, they are. I might be a lot of things, but I never go back on my word."

I tapped my toe on the carpeted floor out of frustration. This was not how this meeting was supposed to go. I'd not seen the man..sorry, god, in months. I'd planned to sweep into his private club and have him take me to his private room and lavish me with praise about how magnificent I was, not to mention lavish me with other things, namely his body. Instead, we'd got to the point where it felt like I was having afternoon tea with my mother instead of afternoon delight with the sexiest person I'd ever met.

"So, what exactly is the problem?"

"They are both beautiful; there's no denying that. I'd even go so far as to agree with you that they are more beautiful than any other woman I've met, but they are both miserable. Both are wandering around, moping about missing their husbands and children. The pair of them are about as sexy as dishrags and twice as dull."

A small smile came to my lips. I sipped on the whiskey and leaned forward in my seat, letting my cleavage show. I might not be as beautiful as the two queens, and youth was not on my side, but I had something that I knew Morpheus liked. I had spirit. I had power. I was the president of the whole of Urbis and, therefore, the whole of the kingdoms. All the kings, queens, mayors, and ministers of all the kingdoms had to bow down to me. I was the most powerful person on the entire planet. And beauty? I still had it. Sure, I was not a young woman anymore, but thanks to magical help,

I was still more beautiful than ninety-five percent of the population. And that included the young bimbos he liked to surround himself with. Oh, he liked his fun with them, but not a single one could hold a conversation. He needed more than that. He needed me. I just needed to show him.

"I've decided to hold a ball in the government building to celebrate my presidency. I'd like you to come as my special guest." Not entirely true. I'd only just thought of it, but to be seen with me on his arm, he'd soon realize that we were meant to be together. I'd make sure that all the newspapers in all the kingdoms had people present.

Morpheus shook his head. "You know that's not my thing, Derillen."

"Not your thing? Elegance, dancing, the beautiful elite, champagne. I'd think it's exactly your thing."

"Being seen?" He stood up and nursed his own whiskey. I noticed that he'd not touched it since I walked in. "I'm a god. I can't go to parties. Why do you think I spend my time in the dark? Very few people know I come to the human realm, and I'd like to keep it that way. The second it gets out that a god is hanging around with humans is the second that I'd never get any peace again. I'd have to stay in the land of the gods. And let me tell you, they might have power, but they have no life. It's dull there. Everyone is perfectly perfect. Perfectly boring, and you know how I feel about boring."

"The ball will be anything but boring," I said, shooing away his concerns. "Since when have I been dull, Morpheus? It will be everything you hoped for, and no one has to know you are a god. Wear dark glasses to cover the gold rings around your irises, and you'll be a human just like everyone else. You'll be my mystery man. Everyone will wonder who you are. It will be a fabulous mystery. I'll get the prisoners to serve the food. It will be a delicious game. Just a quick spell to erase their memories for the night is all I'll need. Such fun."

"Your idea of fun is not the same as mine. I'm sorry Derillen, but I'm not interested. You have your ball, play your games, and I'll stick to my life. Now, if you'll excuse me."

He put his untouched whiskey down on the table and left me alone in the room.

I hated how desolate he made me feel. How unwanted. I wished I hated him, but with everything he'd said and done, I didn't have it in me. Morpheus was my one weakness, and I hated weakness above all else. I'd still hold my ball, and I'd make sure that only the most beautiful were invited. I'd find someone even more beautiful than him and make sure that my photo was on the front cover of every newspaper. I downed the last of my whiskey and left his stupid private room. He hadn't seen the last of me. I'd make him so jealous that he'd be eating out of my hand in no time.

17TH DECEMBER
AZIA

"Are you sure you'll be able to get us in?" I asked nervously as the carriage whisked us to the central part of Urbis in the dark. Somewhere, a clock struck midnight, signaling the clubs to open, according to Charlotte.

Caspian raked his eyes up and down my legs. "Looking like that, you'll be able to get in, no problem. We'll just follow you."

"You do know your girlfriend is sitting next to you, right?" I asked, glancing over at Charlotte.

Charlotte only laughed. "He's a cad, but he's my cad."

I tried hopelessly not to roll my eyes as I wondered if she even knew the meaning of the word cad. Scum bucket was a better definition, but she gazed at him with adoration in her eyes, and he was looking at her in a similar vomit-inducing way.

"Do you know what to do?" I asked Fallon, tearing my eyes away from the couple in front of me.

Fallon looked quite debonair in his stylish suit and styled hair. He'd complained about changing from his normal self, saying that he was good-looking enough already to get into the top clubs. But when I reminded him of the reward on his head, he changed into someone else, his friend from back home, Kalmin, something or other.

"While you and Charlotte are looking for a portal, Caspian and I will head to the men's lounge and see what we can find out about where our siblings might be."

I nodded. "And you," I said, talking to the robin that had just landed on the carriage window. "You stay nearby and keep an eye out for trouble."

Castiel cheeped and flew off.

The carriage came to a stop, and the driver opened the door for us.

"See how nice things are when you let me spend my money?" Caspian said, stepping down.

Charlotte ignored him.

"I don't know if Morpheus will be in this club, but it's the most likely one. It's one of his favorite haunts, and it's only just opened back up after being closed a while."

"What if he's not here?" I whispered, feeling both self-conscious and cold in the barely-there dress.

"Then we go home and try again tomorrow."

"I can barely walk in these shoes now. I can't do this again tomorrow. I knew I should have worn my boots."

"Dirt encrusted leather was so last year," Charlotte quipped, taking my hand in hers.

Breathing was hard enough in the skin-tight dress, and holding my breath was even harder as we came to the doorman.

"Names?"

Caspian opened his jacket and showed the man something. "I think you'll find I'm a member here."

The man folded his arms.

"I didn't ask if you are a member. I asked what your names are. This is an exclusive party."

"And I said you should check my membership card," Caspian asserted, pulling it from the inside of his jacket and handing it to the man.

"You're free to go in," the man said, changing his stance. At first, I thought that Caspian had done some kind of mind magic on the man, but as he handed Caspian's membership card back to him, I saw him surreptitiously pocket a hundred dollar bill.

Inside, the club was dimly lit and thick with cigar smoke.

"This isn't a normal club," Caspian whispered. "Music is played in the basement, whereas this floor has a number of gambling rooms. Upstairs, there are private rooms for meetings and on the floor above, more private rooms for personal pursuits." He winked at me, and I mimed puking. The quicker I got away from Caspian, the better. If I'd thought that he'd get better with a girlfriend, I was wrong. If anything, he was worse.

The dimly lit corridor reeked of wealth and cigar smoke. Thick carpet below our feet softened the sound of the pulsating music from the basement below.

"You two go upstairs. If he has his portal to the

dream world open, it will be out of sight, away from people. Fallon and I will head in here and play a few rounds of poker and see what we can find out."

Sounds of people talking filled the air. The thrum of music vibrated from below. The laughter of male voices came from rooms leading off the corridor, and above it all, the beat of my heart thumped erratically in my ears.

Ahead of us, stairs led to the upper floors. Caspian and Fallon disappeared into the first door leaving Charlotte and me alone.

"Let's get this over with," I said, taking a step toward the stairway. Beside me, Charlotte muttered in agreement, but I could sense her excitement in just being here. To her, this wasn't a necessity to get back her mother like it was for me. It was an adventure, the thrill of a lifetime, a culmination of years of research into one man—Morpheus.

To me, he was the person who took my mother away from me and locked her inside her own dreams. To Charlotte, he was a god. Something to be coveted.

It was fair to say that she was more excited than I was to be climbing the stairs in this weird exclusive club. Excitement practically radiated from her as she bounded up the stairs, taking them two at a time. I couldn't have done that even if I'd wanted to with the skin-tight dress, practically locking my legs together at the knees. I had to make do with stepping as quickly as I could in the dress and heels to keep up with her.

The next floor was similar to the one below, with a long, dimly-lit corridor culminating in another set of stairs. More voices came from closed doors, though this time, I heard women's voices in the mix.

"I wonder what's going on behind these doors!" Charlotte whispered as we hastened past them.

I shrugged. Whatever it was, I didn't care. I was here to save my mother and, with any luck, Kelis's mother too. The comings and goings of Urbis's rich and famous held no interest for me. One of the doors opened, causing Charlotte and me to stop still. I held my breath as an extremely large man with a cigar strode out. He walked toward us and tipped his hat as he passed. The stench of his cigar was barely noticeable over the cologne he wore.

"Ladies." He offered us a small smile as he hurried past. I let out a breath I hadn't realized I'd been holding. This was a club, and I had just as much right to be here as anyone else...kind of. And yet, I felt out of place as though everyone in the place would see me as a fraud or, worse still, recognize me as the princess I was.

"Come on," I hissed, grabbing Charlotte's hand. "Let's get this over with."

The third floor was much the same again, but this one was much quieter. I could no longer hear the music from the basement, and the hushed tones from the people behind the closed doors were now silent.

"This is as high as we can go," I observed. "Where would Morpheus keep a portal?"

Charlotte shrugged. I sensed disappointment in her, now we'd gotten to our destination. I'm sure she was hoping that we'd magically bump into Morpheus by chance, and he'd invite us to his private party. I held the opposite wish. Meeting Morpheus was the last thing I wanted to do. I wanted to find the portal, rescue my mother and Queen Snow, and get out of the place without Morpheus knowing we'd even been here. If Caspian and Fallon could find out where my brothers and sisters were being held, then even better. It seemed to me that they were much more likely to meet Morpheus than the two of us creeping about on the top floor, but I kept the thought to myself.

Charlotte opened the first door.

Inside was a grandly decorated room with a small drinks cabinet at one end and a couple of velvet chaise lounges and a side table at the other.

The next room was similarly decorated but with a long, dark, wood table surrounded by executive chairs.

"None of these rooms look like the kind of place where a god would keep a portal to the dream world," I observed as we carried on checking the doors one by one.

The whole place exuded elegance and sin and money. With each room we checked, my hopes of finding my mother diminished.

"It's not here," I said as I closed the second to last door.

"Ladies. Can I help you?"

I turned quickly to find a man standing at the top of the stairs. Dressed in a blatantly expensive suit with slicked-back hair, I wondered if Charlotte had gotten her wish, after all. I had no idea what Morpheus looked like, but this man was close to what I imagined. Good-looking, elegantly presented, and standing proudly as though he was exactly where he was supposed to be. He could be a god, but there was something disappointing about him, as though he didn't quite live up to the hype.

"We were...er..."

The man strode toward us. As he came closer, I was able to see him much more clearly. Good-looking but not beautiful. Not the ethereal sexuality that Charlotte had talked about practically nonstop since I'd known her. Still, I was at a loss for words. I had no business being up here, and no excuse came to mind for why I would be. Charlotte remained silent beside me.

The man looked me up and down as though he was appraising me, though there was nothing lascivious about it. I didn't see anything in his eyes other than curiosity as his gaze went from my shoes up to my hair.

It was then I realized that this couldn't be Morpheus. This man had warm, brown eyes with no hint of a gold ring around the iris. He was a human.

"Would you like to follow me? There is someone I think might like to meet you."

"I don't think so. We were just looking for our friends and got lost so..."

A sharp prod in my back had me silenced.

"We'd love to," Charlotte said.

The man glanced over at her as though he'd not even noticed her existence before that very moment.

"Very well. If you'd like to follow me..."

He showed us to the very first room we'd looked into. "If you'd like to make yourselves comfortable, please feel free to pour yourself a drink. He'll be up in a minute."

"What's going on?" I asked once he'd left. Charlotte had already skipped across the room and was pouring two drinks into crystal glasses.

"Don't you see what this is?" she asked, passing me one of the glasses. I sniffed it—whisky.

"Not really. It's not a portal, is it?" I said, gesturing around the room.

"It's better than a portal. That guy must have been one of Morpheus's lackeys. He's bringing him to meet us. It's well-known that he uses members of his staff to pick out pretty girls and bring them to his private room."

"That's so gross," I said, screwing my nose up and putting the glass down on a nearby side table.

"Women fall at his feet. If he went to the club in the basement, he'd be swarmed. This way, he gets to meet women without having to fight off all the ones he isn't interested in. He gets the pick of the bunch."

"Great. I'm beginning to feel like a banana."

Charlotte screwed up her face. "Don't be silly. This is a great opportunity. Do you know how many women actually get to meet Morpheus?"

"The way I hear it, plenty."

"Well, yeah," Charlotte admitted, "but in the grand scheme of things, only the most beautiful. I knew I should have worn that dress myself. Still, I'm here too. I can't believe it."

She jumped up and down on her feet, spilling her whisky as she did.

"I don't want to meet Morpheus. I want to find my mother. I think we should leave."

"No!" Charlotte cried out. "We can't go yet. We checked the rooms. His portal isn't here, but maybe if we ask him, he'll tell us where it is."

I rolled my eyes. "Sure. I can see it now. Mr. Morpheus, sir, please can you let me into your dream world. My mother just happens to be trapped in there, and I'd like to let her out. He was the one that trapped her in there in the first place, remember? He's hardly going to tell me how to get her out."

"Oh, crap. I forgot. He'll figure out who you are. Here, put these on so he can't see the gold in your eyes." She handed me a pair of dark glasses, which, if I were to wear them in the dimly lit room, would probably render me blind, not to mention ridiculous looking.

"I can barely see as it is. I'm sorry, Charlotte, but we have to go. I know how much you want to meet him, but I'm not doing anything to jeopardize my mother."

I reached for the door handle, trying not to look at Charlotte's crestfallen face, but the door opened before I had the chance to open it myself. I jammed the glasses on my face as the most beautiful man I'd ever seen walked through the door.

His eyes found mine almost instantly, or they would have if I'd not been wearing dark glasses. My heart almost stopped, and my legs turned to jelly as he fixed me with a penetrating gaze. My mind blanked, and my breathing hitched as he looked me up and down in much the same way his manservant had done minutes earlier, except when Morpheus did it, I felt completely exposed, as though he could see every inch of me.

His manservant followed him in and whispered something in Charlotte's ear. Her face fell as she was led outside. The door closed firmly behind her.

"Where is my friend being taken?" I demanded.

"She's not being taken anywhere. My man thought she would prefer to see the club downstairs, that's all."

"It's very presumptuous of him. It's very presumptuous of you to think I'd not like to see the club too. You know neither of us."

"That's true, but how can I get to know you if you leave?"

"I'm not in the habit of being plucked by men for the benefit of others, sir. I'm not a plaything or toy to be used."

He reached past me to the door handle, brushing lightly against my side as he did. My breath hitched in my throat at his nearness. His face was only inches from mine. If I didn't already know he was a god, I'd have thought it anyway. The gold rings in his eyes were almost illuminated around the near-black of his irises. And yet, there was a playfulness to them and the way he smiled, his mouth slightly higher at one side than the other. Heat poured through me as I found myself wondering what his lips tasted like. I took a step back, bringing Milo to the forefront of my mind. I had a man I loved. This guy was my enemy, not someone to desire.

"I can take you down there if you'd prefer." It wasn't a question, though he'd worded it that way. He knew instinctively that I wouldn't go back through that door, just as he knew the hold he was having on me, as he probably had on most women. I forgot that I was supposed to answer him and just stood there blankly.

"Would you like to join me for a drink instead, perhaps? To show you I'm not the man you think I am. I'm not here to...how did you put it? Pluck you." He held his hand out to one of the chaises, and I felt almost compelled to sit there—almost, but not quite. When he saw that I wasn't moving, he walked over to the drinks cabinet and poured himself a whisky from the same bottle Charlotte had used. He poured another and handed it to me, not noticing or not caring that I already had one glass on the side table. He took a seat on the chaise and raised his eyebrows in askance.

"Are you going to sit?" he drawled in a rich, deep voice. "Or shall I be forced to conduct our conversation in this subservient position?"

There was nothing subservient about him. Nothing at all. He could have been lying on the floor at my feet, and still, he'd be in charge, and he knew it.

Clutching the whisky in my hand, I walked over to the other chaise and sat on it purposefully.

"Do I get the pleasure of knowing your name?" he asked lazily.

"Dahlia!" I replied, giving him the first name that came to mind, that of my maid back in Draconis.

"Dahlia." He rolled the name around, repeating it on his tongue, as though I'd said something sensuous. I half expected him to tell me that a dahlia was his favorite flower, but he didn't.

"So what brings you here, Dahlia?" He lounged back on the chair and nursed his glass, rubbing his forefinger along the rim. I dragged my eyes away from it and back to him. "My man said you were lost, but you don't look like the type of woman that doesn't know exactly where she wants to be."

I bit back a retort about he didn't know me at all. "I came with friends. I'm not from Urbis, and my friends brought me here to show me the nightlife."

His eyebrow quirked up, and he leaned forward, his eyes not leaving mine for a second. I tried to remember if the glasses I was wearing were mirrored and wondered if he was peering at himself. His gaze penetrated mine as though I wasn't wearing glasses at all. "And are you enjoying your stay in Urbis?" he drawled.

I shrugged. "It's ok."

His eyebrows lifted, and he tilted his head slightly. "Just ok?"

"I didn't come here by choice," I replied. "I was brought here by magic, as was my brother, who is downstairs. All we did was cross the border into Badalah, and we somehow ended up in the basement beneath the government building."

"Ah," Morpheus said, sitting deeper in his chair. "And that displeases you. You'd rather be back home in Draconis." Not a question. He spoke as though it was a fact.

"Who said I was from Draconis?" I asked bewildered. He could read my mind now? The way he looked at me, it wouldn't surprise me.

"If you crossed the border into Badalah, you either came from Draconis or Aboria. I hazarded a guess, but forgive me if I'm wrong."

I let out a breath slowly. He was observant, that's all, not a mind reader. He didn't need to know that I'd actually crossed from The Vale to Elder.

"You are right on all counts, Morpheus," I replied, trying to match his level of sophistication. I sipped on my whisky, feeling the burn in my throat.

His eyebrows shot up. "You know who I am?"

Shit! Hadn't he told me when he walked in? I tried to recall the last few minutes, but my brain was in a whirlwind. Charlotte had told me time and time again that there was something about him, but she never adequately described the pull I was feeling in the pit of my stomach or the desire to move from my chair and sit next to him just so I could see what he smelled like. Milo! I repeated over and over in my head, reminding myself of my wonderful, faithful man back home. I had no business feeling attraction to another man. A man who had torn my family to shreds, no less.

He sat waiting for me to answer, and I realized I'd forgotten what he said, my brain too caught up in how he looked.

"I've heard of you," I blurted, finally remembering his question. Dragon crap, I wasn't cut out for this. I was wearing a dress made for sin, hiding a trembling body with mush where my brain should be.

I could see he was trying to figure me out. I shifted uncomfortably in my seat, wishing I'd just left when I had the chance. This was not how I wanted the night to go, terrified that anything I said would give me away. He was the enemy, I reminded myself—he and Derillen.

"It's not often people know of me. I like to keep

knowledge of myself to a select few. It seems I'm not doing a very good job." He smiled again, and I had to look away, not to think of his lips.

"I assure you that you are," I replied, inserting a confidence I didn't feel into my tone. "It just so happens that Charlotte is studying you at university, or at least she was until it shut down. She was the one who said you might be here."

"Charlotte? Your friend downstairs?" If he felt smug about being a person's life work, he hid it well.

I nodded.

"And do you study at the same university?"

"No. She studies here in Urbis. I just want to leave and go back to Draconis to my family. I'm not here for a long visit."

He nodded thoughtfully and stood. I watched as he walked back over to the drinks cabinet and refilled his glass. He brought the bottle back and refilled mine. I hadn't even noticed I'd emptied it

"Urbis isn't always like this," he said, lingering a little longer than necessary. "There have been a lot of changes recently."

"Yes. Derillen has taken over and is keeping people locked up against their will."

Urgh, why was it I couldn't keep my mouth shut? This guy was in cahoots with Derillen. He would hardly take kindly to me dissing her. If I wasn't careful, I was going to get myself killed. Morpheus was a god and an evil one at that. I was playing with fire and, queen of dragons or not, if I wasn't careful, I was going to get burned.

"Ah, Derillen. She is a personal friend of mine."

I opened my mouth in surprise. I'd not expected him to admit to such a thing.

"I can't say I agree with everything she is doing, but she has her reasons. The escaped murderers, not that you have anything to worry about. I hear she has captured most of them, and I daresay it won't be long before she gets the rest. She always gets what she puts her mind to. You might not like her, but she's tenacious."

I straightened my back in my effort not to squirm as he unknowingly talked about me. I looked nothing like my photo in the papers. With my new hairstyle and skin-tight dress, I was a million miles away from the bedraggled scruffy woman I'd been.

"Do you know where the prisoners are?" I asked, nonchalantly, as he draped his arm over the back of the chaise, the whisky bottle still clutched in his hand he'd used filling his whisky glass up as a way to move to my chaise. It was a sneaky move and one more becoming to a teenage lad on his first date, but unlike a teenager, there was no hesitancy. He knew exactly where he wanted to be, and damn him, I couldn't move away. His finger brushed against the top of my arm, sending a tingle shooting down my spine. I sipped at my whisky as a way to distract myself from the way my body was betraying me and responding to his touch.

"In the government building, I assume," he said, bringing me back to the conversation. "She has the ridiculous notion of using them to serve drinks at a ball she's holding."

"She's using prisoners as servants?" I asked with surprise, forgetting to keep the interest out of my voice.

"Ludicrous, isn't it? She'll slip them some kind of memory potion before the ball so they don't remember who they are. I think it's her way of showing the world just how powerful she is. She told the world that she'd find them. What better way than to parade them to the elite?"

"It's barbaric. Who is she to do such a thing?"

He had the gall to laugh at me. "What made you so angry? Do you have a vested interest, perhaps?"

Double dragon shit!

"No. I just believe in the presumption of innocence until being proved otherwise. The way I hear it, these prisoners haven't even had a trial."

He regarded me curiously. "I've never known a woman to be so interested in politics before. It makes a refreshing change."

"Maybe you've not known women interested in politics because you have women from nightclubs brought to you for your pleasure. I assume you don't usually listen to what they have to say."

"You think you know me, don't you? You've made an assumption about me, and you have no interest in learning otherwise."

"Am I wrong?" I countered, wondering why I was getting into this argument. "That's exactly how I came to be in this room with you."

"I'd like to prove to you that I'm not the picture of me you have in your mind. Derillen invited me to the ball. I'd like to take you as my date. I want to show you who I am."

"I thought you liked to keep yourself hidden," I whispered, gulping back my surprise.

"Contact lenses or glasses like yours will keep my identity secret." He leaned forward and made a motion to take the glasses from my face. I jumped up quickly before he was able to expose me.

I ran to the door, suddenly desperate to get away. I was tired, and being close to him was messing with my senses.

"I have to go," I said, grabbing the handle and ripping the door open. "It's late."

"You'll go to the ball with me, though?" He stood up to follow me. I had a feeling that he wasn't used to women running from him.

"I'll think about it," I said, racing through the door. I needed air. His presence had my head reeling.

"Where shall I pick you up?" he shouted after me as I raced down the stairs.

"The Urbis Royal Theater," I shouted back. Another flight of stairs later, I practically bumped into Caspian and Fallon as they emerged from one of the rooms as cigar smoke wafted out after them.

"What happened? Are you alright?" Fallon asked, catching my alarm.

"Where's Charlotte?" Caspian added, glancing over my shoulder with concern written on his features.

"I think she's downstairs. Can you find her? I'll meet you in the carriage outside in five minutes."

I dashed outside and sat on the step of the club, taking deep breaths of freezing air. My skin developed goosebumps, and I shivered. Minutes later, we were all in the carriage on our way back to Charlotte's apartment.

"Are you going to tell us what happened or what?" Charlotte asked impatiently

I closed my eyes and leaned against the inside of the carriage. I was going on a date with a man I hated. With a man who made my body feel on fire just by sitting near me. With a man who wasn't my gorgeous sweet boyfriend back home. I was saving my siblings, but at what cost to myself?

"I'll tell you tomorrow," I murmured. I wouldn't know

how to articulate my feelings about the evening, even to myself. I'd never felt so wrong in my whole life. I was throwing myself to the sharks and hoping I didn't get eaten alive.

18TH DECEMBER
DERILLEN

"What a pleasant surprise!" I enthused as Morpheus strode into my office. I hated anyone invading my personal space beyond the servant that brought me coffee, but exceptions could be made. Exceptions were always made for Morpheus.

"What brings you here?" Not that I cared about his reasons. He was here. That's all that mattered.

"The ball," he said, cutting straight to the point. "When is it?"

The truth was I'd given up on the spur of the moment idea. I'd told him that I was having it so that he'd be with me instead of those insipid bimbos he chose to surround himself with.

"I hadn't quite finalized the date," I lied. "I was thinking maybe I could have it for the winter festival. Decorate the building with magical snow. It will be magnificent."

"I was thinking I'd like you to do it before that. It's not for the winter festival. I thought you were holding it to celebrate your presidency? Don't dilute it with winter celebrations."

"The winter festival is in just over a week's time," I pointed out. "People will be celebrating already. Exactly how quickly do you want me to put this thing on?"

"Actually, I was thinking about tomorrow."

"Tomorrow?" I gulped. "I need to prepare. I haven't invited anyone."

"So invite people. You have a whole building full of staff to help you."

I closed my eyes at the sheer magnitude of what he was asking me to do. I needed food, decorations, music, a dress! Then I imagined myself in a purple dress being spun around the dance floor in the arms of Morpheus. This was the first time in all the years I'd known him to show any interest in doing anything for anyone else. Not once had he asked me to do anything with him away from the clubs he frequented. Nor, to my knowledge, had he ever taken one of his floozies anywhere except to his bed. I was the first!

"Fine. Tomorrow at nine. I'll see you there. Would you like to stay for a drink? I have some coffee brewed or some whisky if you prefer?"

"No, thanks, Derillen. You have enough to do without me taking up all of your time. I'll see you tomorrow night at nine."

He breezed out of my door as casually as he'd breezed

in, completely unaware of what he'd done to me. I'd woken up in a foul mood, what with the mess Urbis was becoming and the reports of people complaining about all the foreigners beings transported here via my boundary portal. I hated people. They were so stupid. I was capturing murderers as far as they were aware. What was a little inconvenience compared to being safe?

What was I thinking? Who cared about what the idiots thought? I had a party to plan. I was going on the very first date of my entire life. His first date too! I needed to plan what I was going to wear.

18TH DECEMBER AZIA

I barely slept a wink, worried that if I dreamed, Morpheus would find me within them. Could he find me through unconscious thought and see me for who I really was? Was that how it worked? Charlotte had talked to me about Morpheus on many occasions, but not once had I thought to ask her about this. Maybe she'd told me, and I'd forgotten?

I headed downstairs, bleary-eyed and still in pajamas to find the four of them already enjoying breakfast.

"Want some?" Charlotte asked, pushing a plate of toast in my direction. I sat down and laid my head in my arms on the table and groaned.

"Hangover much?" Caspian chirped in an unusually chipper manner.

“She didn’t drink that much. She’s probably not slept because of Morpheus, right?” Charlotte asked, nudging my arm. I could almost hear Caspian’s eyes rolling.

“Actually, that is it, but not in the way you think. I was worried that he’d be able to come to me in my dreams, and then he’d figure out who I was.”

A look passed between Fallon and Castiel. They obviously had been thinking the same thing.

“Did you tell him anything about you that would give him an idea where you are?” Charlotte asked, suddenly serious.

“No. I told him my name was Dahlia. I didn’t tell him where you live. He figured out I was from Draconis, but no more.”

“Morpheus has to know where to find you in real life if he wants to find you in dreams. He knew exactly where your mother was when she was pulled into his world, Snow White too. They are both queens living in castles. He knew exactly where to find them.”

“Oh,” I yawned, suddenly feeling foolish but better at the same time.

“Did he tell you where the portal is?”

“Did he try and kiss you?”

“Did he mention your mother?”

I blinked, trying to unravel all the questions being thrown my way. Castiel passed me a coffee, and I stared up at him gratefully. The caffeine cleared my head slightly.

“No, no, and no,” I answered all three at once. “I didn’t ask him about the portal because then he’d know who I am. Same about my mother. How could I ask him? He doesn’t know that I know he has her.”

I picked up a slice of toast and began munching on

it.

"You didn't answer my question," Charlotte pointed out, a twinkle in her eye.

"I said no. There's really not much else to add to that. I have a boyfriend. I have no interest in kissing some immortal guy."

Her face fell as though I'd done something terrible.

"He kidnapped my mother. And Snow White."

"He didn't really kidnap them," Charlotte cajoled. "I mean, you know exactly where your mom is. She's in her own bed."

I leveled what was left of my toast at Charlotte. "My mother's body is in her bed. Her mind, her soul, is running around some weird wasteland looking for a way to get home, but she can't because the man you are so interested in me kissing has her locked inside."

"I'm sorry... I didn't mean to..."

"I'm going on a date with him soon."

All around the table, the sound of spoons clattering suddenly stopped. I casually continued eating my toast as the four of them stared at me.

Castiel was the first to regain his composure. "You are doing what? Are you completely insane?"

"You all heard me. He invited me to a ball. I said, yes. Actually, I said I'd think about it, but I'm going to go. Charlotte, you and your team are going to have to do a brilliant job of making me look like anyone other than me. Everyone who is anyone will be there. Not to mention Derillen herself. I can't be recognized."

"I hate to repeat myself," Castiel growled, "but in this case, I'll make an exception. Are you completely insane?"

I finished my toast and downed my coffee. "Actually, I think I'm pretty clever. Derillen is using our brothers and sisters as servants for the night, using some kind of memory potion to stop them from running away. While I'm dancing with Morpheus, you guys are going to get them out."

Comprehension dawned on Castiel's face, splitting it into a grin. "You are a genius! How did you manage to get an invite?"

"I have my charms," I grinned, standing up from the table. Last night had given me a confidence I hadn't known was within me. Milo loved me, and Caspian had, at one point, developed an obsession with me. Over a thousand men had applied to a competition to become my husband, but none of that compared to the feeling of having a god lusting after me. I cared not one fig for him, but knowing a god that so many women wanted, wanted me had given me an ego boost.

"So when is it?" Charlotte asked, standing up to follow me out of the small kitchen.

"I..."

I didn't know when it was. Morpheus had left that little detail out. Suddenly, my ebullient mood came crashing to the ground. It served me right for feeling so high and mighty. "I don't know exactly. I figured it would be mentioned in the newspapers."

"You got asked on a date, and you don't know when?" Caspian laughed. "Are you sure he wasn't messing with you? He's known for treating women like shit. I think you fell for one of his lies."

"It wasn't a lie," I said, changing trajectory and heading back to the small table. I grabbed the newspaper from Castiel's hands and began to rifle through it for any mention of a party at the government building.

"Tell me," Caspian began, lazing back in his chair, his arms folded and an amused expression on his face.

One I would have quite easily slapped off if I didn't think it would upset Charlotte. "Did he, by any chance, offer you a drink while he was talking of this swanky ball? Did he tell you how beautiful you'd look in a ball gown, and even more so out of it?"

"Shut it!" I snapped, trying to find any details of a ball. It was nearly The Winter Festival. Surely, any ball would be before then? Or for the new year, perhaps, which would give us two weeks to prepare instead of one.

Caspian sat back in his chair, clearly amused by the direction the conversation was taking. "I read the papers every day, and I'm telling you now that there's been no mention of a ball. I don't know why you didn't just sleep with him and use that to your advantage."

I shot him a scathing look and stormed out of the kitchen, the paper still in my hand. Charlotte followed right behind me.

"Sorry about him. He can be a little uncouth at times."

"He's a total ass, and you can do better," I shot back, then felt bad as her face fell. "There is going to be a ball."

"I believe you, but without knowing when, what can we do? You didn't give him my address so how can he get the information to you?"

"I told him the name of the main theater in Inner Urbis. I figured that you go there for work, and he could leave an invite at the box office. It was the first place that came to mind."

Charlotte clapped her hands. "I'm going to have to call my friends in to work before the ball. We are going to give you the makeover of your life. There's a ballgown at the studio that we used for an opera last year. It's a subtle shade of pink—lots of layers, a hint of sparkle. It's absolutely beautiful, and I've always thought it was a waste that it's just hanging in a closet. It will be perfect for a ball."

"I'll need colored contact lenses," I added, not caring what I'd wore to the damn thing. I was going to free my siblings. Something told me that Charlotte was not the best person to plan that part with. "Can you tell Castiel and Fallon to meet me in my bedroom in twenty minutes? We need to figure out what we are going to do once we get there, and I don't think we'll have long. It might be as close as a week away."

Her face fell when she realized she wasn't invited to my planning session, but she quickly perked up. "Sure. I'm going to the Royal Theater today to drop some costumes off. I'll let the girl at the box office know to expect an envelope with your name on it."

"With Dahlia's name on it," I reminded her.

She gave me a grin and headed back into the kitchen.

Twenty minutes later, I was sitting on my bed wearing my own clothes. However unsophisticated they were and unsuitable for wandering around Inner Urbis where only the best fashions and business attire was worn, I'd become accustomed to the comfort they provided. My sword was at my side in its sheath.

"Planning on a sword fight?" Fallon joked when he saw it attached to my belt.

"No, but I feel better with it near. Charlotte is heading to the Royal Theater today to wait for the invite. I think we have a week, at most two, to plan how we are going to get the others out without anyone noticing."

"If they are serving food, we could wait until the dancing starts." Fallon offered.

"I don't think it will be that easy. Derillen isn't using

them because she can't afford staff. She knows people will be watching. It's her way of proving how powerful she is. Morpheus mentioned a potion to erase their memories. I don't really understand how erasing their memories will make them all want to serve food. There has to be more to it, but I got the feeling that he wasn't quite sure himself. I didn't think questioning him on the fine details would be a good move. If I was over-eager, he'd get suspicious."

"I can head to the government building and see what's going on," Fallon said, his mouth set in a grim line. "From what I could tell when we were escaping, they were still open and doing tours. I could take one and try and slip away to the kitchens, maybe. See if Derillen already has them working there?"

Even though Fallon could change his appearance, having him so close to the fire worried me. Derillen could detect magic. No disguise would conceal that.

"We are going to have to use the shield when it comes," I admitted.

Castiel furrowed his brows. "What shield?"

"I asked a friend to post a shield to this address. It blocks everyone's magic but Derillen's."

"I don't get it. Why would we want to block our magic? Let's face it. It's all we have."

I sighed at the sheer magnitude of what we were getting ourselves into. "Derillen can sense magic. If she senses it in us, it will put us on her radar. Don't forget, it's not just she who'll be there. We have all the others to contend with too. Rumpelstiltskin, Hook, the sea witch..."

Castiel looked at me as though I was insane. "All the more reason that we don't inhibit our magic."

"It will inhibit theirs too," I pointed out. "It's only

Derillen that it doesn't work on as it is her charm on the shield."

Castiel closed his eyes and pinched his nose, letting out a long breath from his mouth. "It also means that Fallon can't change appearance, and I can't shift into animal form. Having Charlotte make you over to the extent that no one recognizes you is going to be a push as it is, but to do it to all three of us and expect no one to notice... it's insane."

"How about we move past that bit for now and work it out later?" Fallon interjected, getting between the impending argument between Castiel and me. "How do we get half the serving staff out of there without anyone noticing? It's not as though we can just walk out of the front door with them. What about Zacharina? What about Queen Renee? What about Nyre? Not only do we have to get the most wanted criminals out from under the noses of twelve of the most powerful sorcerers of all time, we also have to get out a unicorn, a dragon, and the Queen of Vale. Even if by some miracle we do manage to not be noticed by the people wanting to kill us, I'm pretty sure someone there will wonder why a group of people is wandering around inside with a unicorn!"

Castiel looked at me as though he was waiting for me to come up with an answer. He had an infuriating expression of smugness on his face, which reminded me a little of Caspian from earlier.

"I don't know!" I huffed. "It's impossible. The whole thing is completely impossible, but what is our alternative? Go into hiding for the rest of our lives while monsters rule all the kingdoms using our brothers and sisters as slaves? That is if they don't kill them first."

Castiel's face softened at my outburst. "Sorry, I

forgot we were on the same side there for a second. Being cooped up in a house is getting to me. I'm not used to the lack of freedom, and it's making me antsy. You found a way in, which is amazing in itself. I think what Fallon said before makes the most sense."

Fallon's eyes widened in surprise. "What did I say?"

"You said we could head to the government building and stalk it out for the next week or so. Doing that will give us a little insight into what we are up against. Hopefully, with the knowledge we glean, we'll be able to come up with a plan that might work. Who knows? This might be our opportunity to overthrow the lot of them and fight back rather than just escape to go into hiding again."

However much I liked Castiel's sudden change of heart, overthrowing a government full of corrupt evil sorcerers whose only mission in life seemed to be to want us dead with only a week or two of planning was a little far-fetched. No, it was bloody insane.

Downstairs a doorbell rang as Fallon changed his appearance into that of a young girl of no more than nine years old or so.

"Fallon. What are you doing?" I queried as his hair lengthened into pigtails tied together with ribbons, and his shirt lengthened into a dress.

"I figured a school girl would attract way less attention than anyone else. Who would suspect this..."—he held a hand up to himself—"of scouting out how to break out wanted murderers? I could latch onto someone in the line for the guided tour, and people working there would think I was their kid."

"How you gonna get there, dummy?" Castiel asked. "People might start asking questions if a school-aged kid is wandering the streets during school time."

"So, I'll go on a weekend," Fallon shot back, pouting. The expression that was uniquely Fallon looked strange on a nine-year-old girl.

"We need to stop arguing," I said, slamming my hand down on the bed and making the pair of them jump as Charlotte opened the door to the bedroom. "We only have two weeks to get this plan down. Maybe one. We don't have time to mess around."

"Sorry to interrupt, guys," Charlotte said, handing me a rectangular white card. "A friend working at the Royal just brought it. It had my name on the top next to yours...well, Dahlia's. It looks like you have less planning time than you thought."

"What do you mean?" Castiel grunted, clearly pissed off with the whole thing already. "When's the party?"

I gulped as I read the date on the invitation.

"It's tomorrow night. It looks like our planning session is over. We are going to have to wing it."

"What a surprise," Castiel grimaced, standing up from the bed. "When has anything we've ever done gone to plan?"

19TH DECEMBER
AZIA

"I'm taking it, and that's final!" I demanded as Charlotte and her workmates collectively sighed in exasperation.

"The dress has nowhere for a sword to go!" Charlotte argued as though she was talking to a toddler. She held the pink, layered dress up. "It has a skin-tight bodice that needs lacing up, not to mention the layers and layers of fabric."

The dress was beautiful. It was something else entirely, with patterns of crystals glittering along the neckline and hand-embroidered flowers dotting it. It was the most perfect dress I'd ever seen for a magical fairytale ball. My mother, if she were here, would practically shoehorn me into the thing. But she wasn't here, and she'd never be able to corral me into wearing fluffy pink dresses again if I didn't survive the night.

"Morpheus met me when I was wearing a skin-tight red dress. Give me a plain black dress that I can run in. One that I can wear my sword with because I'm not going into that building without it."

"You heard her," Charlotte sighed, looking more disappointed than I'd ever seen her. "Find a black dress."

The group of stylists and designers hurried back into the massive closet, muttering to themselves as they went.

I looked over at Charlotte's disappointed face. "You know, if I don't wear this dress, it's free for someone else to wear..."

Her eyes lit up as she ran her fingers along the outer layer of pink material. "I can't wear this. I'm not..."

"Tall enough? You have a whole group of people right through that door that could shorten the hemline for you."

"I was going to say good enough. This dress is for a princess or a goddess or both, like you."

I picked the dress up and held it in front of her. "You will be a princess in this dress. I think it would suit you perfectly."

"Great. It's settled." Castiel huffed. "Charlotte has the pink dress, Azia gets a black dress, everyone is happy. Can we stop talking about dresses and come up with a damn plan. We are heading to the heart of the beast with at least twelve people that want to kill us, and you two are busy jabbering about what dresses you want to die in."

"No one's dying tonight!" I insisted with less confidence than I felt.

"So let's figure out how not to because if I have to listen to another conversation about the differences in silk and satin, I'm gonna kill the pair of you myself. I don't understand why I even need to be here. I could be at the government building now, trying to figure out our next move."

"We don't have time. We need you here to make a plan."

Eight hours later, I found myself waiting outside the Royal Theater, wearing an ankle-length, skin-tight, black dress with a split up the leg where my sword rested against my skin. My hair had been slicked back with fake black and silver butterflies nesting in it. It was the one concession I had made to Charlotte, who had wanted to dress me up like a pink cupcake. My makeup was like nothing I'd ever worn before. My mother always preferred elegant understatement. Charlotte and her friends had gone the opposite way, making me into a femme fatale. We'd argued and argued about the best approach. Castiel would have been happy with me wearing a sack and dowdy hairstyle so I could hide. I wanted to look as normal as possible to blend in, or I did until Fallon pointed out that my picture had been splashed across the front pages of every newspaper for months. It was a fine line between being caught and having Morpheus recognize me. In the end, I'd found myself in front of the mirror looking back at a beautiful stranger. If Morpheus didn't recognize me, he'd certainly be interested in me. I let my hand fall to the sword by my side. It was the one part of the outfit I had argued with everyone about—all except my brothers. Charlotte's workmates had told me time and time again that a sword was not a suitable accessory for a ball gown. Caspian had proclaimed it sexy, and Charlotte herself had shaken her head and pretty much given up on me by that point. The only ones on my side were Castiel and Fallon. It hadn't been spoken by any of us, but there was a chance that we wouldn't be able to go back to Charlotte's small apartment after tonight. In fact, I couldn't think of a single outcome that would have us going back there, and there was no way I was going without it.

The others had gone on ahead in a carriage, leaving me alone on the wide steps of the stunning building behind me. The government building was so close that I could have walked, even in heels, but I felt as though I was a million miles from anywhere or anyone.

My stomach lurched as the sound of carriage wheels on cobblestones filled the air. I gripped the small handbag Charlotte had lent me and waited for the carriage to come around the corner. Pulled by two of the most beautiful pure black horses I'd ever seen, Morpheus's carriage came to a stop right in front of me. The door opened, and I found myself peering into darkness.

Two golden rings were all I could make out in the gloom. Morpheus leaned forward, his face moving into the illumination of the street lamp. I held my breath as he held his hand out to me.

"You take my breath away," he said as the carriage lurched forward. "I have to tell you a secret. I've never been on a date before. This isn't quite what I imagined." he said, his eyes skimming the bare flesh of my thigh.

"What did you imagine?" I blustered, sitting back into the black leather of the seatback and trying not to lose it completely. My outside looked to be the type of woman who could eat men for breakfast. My insides had a long way to go to catch up.

"I don't know exactly, but not a sword-wielding beauty. I'm almost terrified of being alone in here with you."

The way he spoke with quiet confidence told me that being alone in here with me was exactly what he wanted. He'd planned it, after all.

I took a deep breath to compose myself and reminded myself of how I looked. Turning into a burbling wreck would spoil the whole image Charlotte and her workmates had created.

"I assure you, Mr. Morpheus. You are very safe with me." I twisted my mouth into what I hoped came across as a self-assured, sexy smile and rested my hand on my knee.

"More's the pity," Morpheus said, his mouth curling up into a smile.

I concentrated on the rhythm of the cobbles, trying to keep my composure. This man was pure evil and more powerful than anyone I'd ever met. One wrong move and he'd swat me like a fly without batting an eyelash. I closed my eyes and pictured my mother stuck in his monstrous dream world. It hadn't been part of the plan to try to get him to talk about how to get into his dream world. Tonight was all about freeing my siblings, but I knew that this was my only chance. After tonight, who knew where I'd end up. Even if I ended up dead, I knew I had to take Morpheus with me. It was the only way I knew of to get her back unless I could get him to tell me where the portal was. I was just thinking of a way of asking about it when the carriage came to a stop.

The door opened, and we stepped out to the most magnificent scene. The government building was lit up with magical purple light and a long purple carpet with golden ropes at either side to keep the public out. My heart nearly bounced out of my chest as I took in all the people. Thousands, if not tens of thousands of the public had turned out to see the Urbis elite walk into the party. At the far end, just before the huge golden double doors that marked the entrance to the government building, there stood a roped-off area filled with photographers. I clutched at my throat, feeling the panic rising. Why had I thought this was a good idea? I was one of the most wanted criminals in all the kingdoms, and, as amazing as my makeup was, I couldn't expect to get past so many people without someone recognizing me. Even if the people of Urbis didn't place me, my photo would be out there for all to see.

Morpheus held what I'd thought was a cane into the air and pressed a button in the handle. Seconds later, a large black lace parasol opened out. He took me by the arm and held the parasol over our faces as he hurried me down the purple carpet.

"I do so hate the media," he said by way of an explanation as we reached the very end. He bundled me in through the door and put the parasol down.

"My friends are here," I blustered. "I hope you don't mind. I said that you could get them in."

Morpheus laughed. "What are their names?"

I gave him Charlotte and Caspian's names along with a couple of made-up men's names for Fallon and Castiel.

I hadn't seen them, but then again, I'd not had much time to see anything as we'd rushed through the crowd.

I took a minute to gaze around the huge entrance hall that looked nothing like it had the last time I'd seen it. There were no lines of people waiting for a tour of the building, and no prisoners quickly being led out in the opposite direction. The hall was full of people dressed in their very best. I noticed a good number of them glance my way and then speak to their friends in hushed tones, though I only saw judgment on their faces, not recognition. I also saw no sign of any of my siblings, though there were a number of people dressed in the purple and gold uniform of the government staff. I looked into their faces, wondering if they were really prisoners under Derillen's spell, but if anything, they all seemed happy to be there to mingle with the elite.

My breath hitched in my throat as Morpheus came back to me and whispered lightly into my ear that Charlotte and the others would be let in shortly. It wasn't the feel of his breath on my neck or the heavenly smell of his cologne that had me holding my breath. It was the sight of Derillen appearing in a long, flowing purple dress at the top of the sweeping staircase.

Her eyes bored into me, and her expression was one of shock.

I'd been caught, and I was barely through the door. My instinct was to run. I'd take on ten thousand members of the public over Derillen a million times over, but Morpheus chose that moment to pull me toward the base of the stairs.

My pulse rate increased with every step she took toward me, her beady eyes boring into mine. I held my breath as she reached the bottom and turned her attention to Morpheus.

"Morpheus...A word."

"Derillen, I'd like to introduce you to my date for the evening. This is Dahl..."

"I said a word. In my office. Now!"

"I don't want to take you from your own party Derillen. I'm sure that whatever you have to tell me can wait."

If expressions could kill, the pair of us would have been dead within seconds, but Morpheus seemed not to notice nor to care. He whisked me away from her through the crowd of people.

She had been standing so close to me. If she'd wanted, she could have killed me on the spot, but she hadn't. Why? Even if she didn't want me dead, for whatever reason, there were plenty of guards in their purple and gold uniforms to come and take me down into the basement or wherever it was that she kept her most-wanted criminals.

I was saved from my own mind by the arrival of Charlotte, Caspian, Fallon, and Castiel.

"You alright, Azi...Dahlia?" Charlotte asked, looking gorgeous in the pink ball gown I'd turned my nose up at. "You look like you've just seen a ghost."

I moved away from Morpheus, who was in deep conversation with someone.

Keeping my voice low, I spoke to Charlotte. "Derillen's seen me, but..." I cast my eyes back to the other side of the entrance hall, but I could no longer see her in the throng of people.

"But what?"

"I don't think she recognized me. She looked right at me as though I was a piece of trash that had wandered in off the streets, but she didn't do anything. I was right in front of her."

"I don't like the sound of that," Fallon cut in, his pale grey eyes unnerving me. They were the only part of him that Charlotte had worked on. His golden rings had been covered with colored contact lenses, as had Castiel's and mine. The rest of him had been changed by his own magic, but he was no less handsome than usual. "Let's see if we can find the others and get out of here before realization hits her."

"I couldn't have said it better myself," Castiel added, looking increasingly uncomfortable in his tuxedo. Charlotte had really gone to town on him, giving him a short stylish haircut, a close shave, and even doing his nails. Of all of us, he looked the least like his former self, and yet, the expression of annoyance was still all his. The way his eyes skipped from person to person and place to place reminded me that he was a hunter, but this time, we were the prey.

"Let's do this," I said, gripping the end of my sword. I cut through the crowd of guests and headed to the place I thought my siblings were most likely to be.

Two large doors at the end of the entrance hall opened out to a huge ballroom. In the corner, an orchestra provided music to which no one at the moment was dancing. The room, just like the entrance hall, was filled with people talking, smiling, and chatting. Each of them more beautiful than the last. I recognized a couple of famous actors chatting with an even more famous singer. A politician I'd been introduced to once when I'd come here on a royal tour chatted animatedly with a couple of women in beautiful ballgowns. I made a note to stay away from his side of the room. I'd been so worried that Derillen or one of her cronies would recognize us that I hadn't thought of the people that worked here. The people that ran Urbis, or used to, before Derillen took charge.

"There's Cordel," Castiel whispered into my ear as he discretely pointed out the woman with curly, black hair who was in charge of the cells below us.

She, like me, had opted to wear black, but unlike my skin-tight dress, hers was a puffed out black ballgown that reminded me of a dead rose.

"If she's here, it's safe to assume the rest of them are too. Remember that Rumpelstiltskin can change appearance. He could be anyone here. Stick together and talk to no one."

As I spoke, a shiver of strong magic passed through me. I turned to see a tall man with tanned skin and a thin face ending with a goatee walk past.

Gaia's sorcerer!

The whole place was filled with magic, which was both good and bad. Good because ours mingled with everyone else's, so those that could detect it wouldn't be able to pinpoint us as the source. Bad because the chances of us escaping unscathed were slim enough as it was without adding the most powerful sorcerers in the world to the mix.

"There's Ivy," Fallon hissed, grabbing my sleeve.

I followed his line of gaze, and sure enough, she was there with a blank look on her face and a silver tray in her hand. She wore the same purple uniform as the other staff, and her blonde hair had been slicked back into a sleek ponytail. It was the first time I'd ever seen her without a hat on. I wouldn't have recognized her at all if I wasn't looking for her. She came our way, stopping right in front of us.

□Canapé?□ She asked, holding the tray toward us. Her eyes showed no recognition at all.

"Ivy?" I prompted, but she remained silent. She didn't know who she was, let alone who I was.

□Hmm, don□t mind if I do,□ Morpheus said, leaning over and taking a canapé from the tray. □Hmm, delicious. Where did you run off to? One minute I was talking to an old friend, and the next, you□d disappeared.□

"I found Charlotte and my other friends."

"Ah, yes, Pleased to meet you all. I'm glad you got in

ok."

Charlotte gazed up at him with a slightly dazed expression on her face and a soppy smile.

I thought she was going to keel over on the spot when he took her hand and kissed it.

"How about you introduce me to your friend," I said, taking Morpheus's arm in mine. "You guys can mingle, and we'll meet up later," I said pointedly. I couldn't look for my siblings while Morpheus was pretty much attached to my side, but the others could.

"To be honest, I don't really know that many people here, but I must say, it's nice to get you alone. Why don't we have a drink of champagne and find ourselves a cozy corner to chat in?"

I nodded eagerly. My heart jumped as Morpheus grabbed us a couple of flutes of champagne from a passing waiter, who just happened to be Deon. As Morpheus guided me to where he wanted to be, I discretely pointed Deon out to Charlotte, who was still looking our way with a slight hint of green about her face. Poor Charlotte. She did tend to fall for the wrong sort of men. First Caspian and now Morpheus, neither of which I could stand but both of which had seemed to take an interest in me.

"Beautiful party," I said absently for want of anything else to say. My eyes scanned the room as I spoke, looking out for the purple uniform of the palace staff.

Morpheus' hand touched my face, moving it away from everyone else and toward him. "It's beautiful because you are here."

Any other woman would have melted at his touch and at his words. My own body was beginning to betray me as he let his hand linger on my cheek. A shiver of lust went through me, which I quickly damped down.

The guy was an asshole of the highest kind, not to mention an evil piece of shit. There was no way I was going to fall for him. Not a chance.

"Thank you," I replied, taking a sip of my champagne.

"There's something about you that I can't quite put my finger on. You're different from the other girls I've been with."

"Of which there are plenty, so I hear."

"This is my first ever date."

"So you told me in the carriage on the way here."

He nodded, then leaned in to me. "And I'm as giddy as a schoolboy."

I stepped back before he did something I would end up regretting, like kissing me. "So you only take women to your bed and nowhere else?"

"Is that such a bad thing? I don't lie to them. I don't pretend it's something that it isn't. You're the first woman I've met that I've ever wanted to have a conversation with."

"You do realize that makes you sound like a sexist prick."

Morpheus laughed loudly, causing the people nearest us to turn and look our way and me to turn my head away from them.

"I like you, Dahlia. I like you a lot. You've got me pegged completely. I'm an oaf, but tonight I'm trying to be better. Don't give up on me so quickly."

"Ladies and gentlemen," a voice rang out. I turned to see a man in uniform standing on a dais. "May I present our President and the host of tonight's party, Derillen."

A smattering of applause filled the room as she took to the small stage. She looked magnificent in her long purple dress.

"Thank you all for coming here tonight. It's an honor

to be here. Tonight is about eating, drinking, and dancing, all of which we'll get to shortly. Before we do, there are a few people I'd like to invite to the stage. Without them, I would not be here.

"My most trusted team: Cordel..." The heavy-lidded woman took to the stage and bowed politely. "Momba..." A tall, thin woman with a sharp chin, green tinged skin and cheekbones followed. The audience gasped in delight at the small, winged monkey on her shoulder. "Edwin..."

As more people took to the stage, my nerves heightened. So much evil. I waited for Rumpelstiltskin's name to be called, but it never was. The last few were the man who'd passed me earlier, whom I learned was Hook, A miserable-looking woman in a ridiculously over the top ballgown, which was only eclipsed by the last woman on stage, Queenie Hart. Queenie had opted to come in a white ball gown with red hearts embroidered all over it. Her cleavage was pushed almost right up to her chin with the tight bodice she wore.

I counted nine, including Derillen. That meant there were three missing. Rumpelstiltskin was one. Just because he wasn't on stage didn't mean he wasn't here somewhere, lurking amongst the crowd. The sea witch was also missing, which made sense. There was no water here for her to swim in. Castiel's enemy was also missing, but as we didn't know exactly who that was, it was pointless worrying about it. I was in no doubt they'd make their presence known at some point.

The applause had increased steadily as more people took to the stage, but I noticed it wasn't exactly enthusiastic.

"I have a little surprise for you all before we start the merriment," Derillen continued. "You might have noticed our staff here tonight. You can tell who they are by their uniforms. What you might not have noticed is that nine of them don't have the gold trim like the other staff members. That's because they are not the palace staff at all. They are the murderers you've seen on the front pages of the newspapers."

She paused as the crowd gave a collective gasp and began looking about them as though a murderer might just jump on them at any second.

"Now, please do not worry!" she continued. "You are all safe. I have them all under a spell. They do not know who they are. They are here for your delight and as a reminder that any wrongdoing against me and the government will be punished to the highest degree. The men and women you have serving your food will be punished by death within the next few days. This is my way of giving them a last hurrah. Come to the stage and let everyone see you!" she clapped her hands loudly, and one by one, my brothers and sisters and Nyre in her part-human form trooped onto the stage.

"Line up!" Derillen said, and they complied. "Now, turn on the spot."

I watched in shock as my brothers and sisters each turned three hundred and sixty degrees in unison as though they were no more than puppets on strings.

"This is so like Derillen," Morpheus chuckled quietly next to me. "She does like to have her fun."

"Dance!" Derillen commanded, throwing her hands up into the air. My brothers and sisters danced as she asked, but in the most ridiculous way, throwing their hands about and performing jerky and uncoordinated movements. The only one not dancing was Jakon, who stood there stiffly, staring forward.

The audience laughed at the performance.

"It's disgusting," I hissed.

"They are wanted murderers," Morpheus replied. "I know she shouldn't be having her fun like this, but they do deserve everything they get if they think it's okay to murder innocent people."

I wanted to ask him whom exactly they were supposed to have murdered. I wanted to scream out for Derillen to stop it, but that would only give me away. I could only watch on in horror as people laughed at my siblings for their own sordid entertainment.

"Now!" Castiel whispered in my ear as he grabbed my arm, tearing me away from Morpheus. With one swift motion, he pulled my sword from its sheath and thrust it into my hand as he jumped onto the stage, changing from his normal form to a lion.

It took me a few seconds to understand what was going on. There would be no planning, no secretly trying to persuade my siblings to leave through some secret back entrance to the building. Despite the most powerful sorcerers in all the kingdoms literally standing right there, we were going to fight. Caspian was already on stage, his own sword out held up to Derillen's neck. Castiel roared as I began to push Nyre toward the stairs she had just come up from. She barely budged against my full force.

"Come on, Nyre, It's me. We have to escape." I'd planned for them to not recognize me. What I hadn't thought of was the fact they might not want to go with me. Why would they? They didn't know who they were. Nyre stared at me blankly. I shrugged at Fallon, who was at the other end of the line trying to get Blaise to follow him off the other side of the stage.

Someone in the audience was screaming, and a quick glance told me that the government guards were closing in on us. Behind my siblings, the shock of what was happening was beginning to wear off. Derillen, using magic, flung Caspian away from her. Flying monkeys suddenly appeared from nowhere. I carried on pulling at Nyre's sleeve as chaos erupted around me. Fireballs flew through the air, causing the crowd to begin to run. Except there was nowhere to run. The doors to the entrance hall were open, but there were so many people fighting to escape the madness that they were tripping over themselves. I thrust my sword at Queenie Hart, who ducked back. Hook dodged forward and tried to pull the sword from my grip with his hook. I reacted quickly, pulling back and sending the hook flying over people's heads. Nothing made any sense. Magic whizzed around my head, and there was nothing I could do but duck when a bolt of it flew by. Castiel was somewhere nearby. His roars sounded out over the commotion. I had to let go of Nyre, who still hadn't budged when I spotted a flying monkey pull Gaia into the air. I jumped up on Momba's back and grabbed at Gaia's legs. Momba shrieked and struck out at me, but it was too late. I was already sailing through the air, holding onto Gaia's leg. Below me was a mosaic of mess and confusion. Above all the noise, I heard Derillen screaming, though I couldn't see her in the commotion.

I was going to kill Castiel for this. We'd had no time to plan, but in all the schemes that had run through my mind, trying to get our siblings out in the most public way possible was not something I'd considered.

I grabbed Gaia's leg further up and began to climb up her. She didn't even look down as I lifted my hand to her belt and pulled myself up. Her mind was well and truly gone. Her expression was blank even though she was being whizzed around by a flying monkey over a room full of people, screaming and fighting and throwing magic, while her sister used her as a ladder. When I was high enough. I jabbed my sword toward the monkey. I hit its thigh, causing it to screech and drop Gaia and me right on top of Morpheus, sending all three of us to the floor.

"This is all rather exciting," he said, pulling me to my feet. "I almost didn't come because I thought it would be boring. I wish you'd told me about this earlier, though. I'd have come more prepared. I do have access to a number of swords."

"Help me get her out of here!" I hissed. If he wanted excitement, he could have it.

"My pleasure," he said, conjuring a portal. He picked Gaia up and pulled her through.

For a second, my mind could barely keep up with what was happening. Had he taken her to the dream world? "No!" I shouted, dashing through the portal as it began to close. Suddenly, I felt a lot colder. Everything was dark

My heart pounded as I took in my surroundings. We seemed to be in a yard of some kind.

"Get off me!" Gaia yelled, punching Morpheus in the face and scrambling down from his arms.

"Gaia!"

She turned, and when she realized who was speaking to her, she ran into my arms, pulling me into an embrace.

"Azia, what's happening? Where are we?"

"You were under Derillen's spell. We're in Morpheus's dreamworld. I'm sorry. I didn't mean to bring you here."

Tears began to prickle at the corner of my eyes. I'd let my sister down. I'd taken her from the pan right into the fire.

"Dreamworld?" Morpheus asked as he held his nose. Blood poured from it. "We're at the back of the government building. I thought you wanted to escape?"

"We're not in the dreamworld?" I asked, suddenly feeling foolish. Sure enough, I could still hear the sound of commotion coming from the nearby building and see the different colors of magic lighting up the windows.

"Why would I take you there? How do you even know of such a place?"

"Because you took my mother there and won't let her out!" I snapped.

I grabbed Gaia's hand and began to run back to the front of the government building. Behind me, all I could hear was Morpheus laughing.

Around the front, we had another problem I'd completely forgotten about. The tens of thousands of people that had turned up to see the elite were still there. We ran up the purple carpet as people in ball gowns and tuxedos were being ushered out of the front doors. Flashes of light filled the night sky as the hundreds of photographers that had turned up to the event got a lot more than they bargained for.

People were coming out of the main entrance in droves now, and pushing past them was impossible. There were just too many of them.

"Gaia?" I turned to her for help. I could bring my sword out and try to get through that way, but the likelihood was that an innocent would get hurt in the melee.

The gold rings around Gaia's irises began to glow, quickly followed by the rest of her body until she was completely consumed by flames. I felt the warmth of them where she held my hand, but it did not burn. It was only the illusion of fire. The crowd soon parted, and the two of us were able to get back into the building. The second we crossed over the threshold, Gaia's flames extinguished, and she stood stock still, her face blank and expressionless. I waved my hand in front of her eyes, but she didn't even look my way.

□Would you like a canapé?□ she asked politely.

Derillen's spell was still in force, but it seemed it was only concentrated on this building. If I could only get my other siblings outside, they'd know who they were. They could use their own magic to help us get out of here. I dragged Gaia the few inches back through the door to the outside, and the light came back to her eyes.

"I can't take you back in," I shouted above the noise. "There's a spell on you that only works inside. I have to go get the others. Stay out here and try and think of a way to get us through all these people once I get everyone out. Make sure Morpheus doesn't see you. I don't want to have to rescue you from him, either."

She nodded as I dashed back in.

Inside, it was complete pandemonium. I cursed Castiel once again as I dashed back into the ballroom.

It was no better than it had been before. Strangely enough, my siblings were still on stage where I'd left them in a long line. Castiel had disappeared somewhere, but I could see Caspian sword fighting with Hook, who seemed to have found his hook. Most surprisingly, Fallon had Derillen in a neck hold. She'd either completely forgotten how to use magic, or he was hurting her enough to ensure she couldn't use it. I grabbed for Nyre again and tried dragging her from the stage. Queenie Hart saw what I was up to and slapped me in the face so hard that I fell to the floor.

I closed my eyes, trying to think of a way out of this. There wasn't one. Getting Gaia out had been a fluke, but now that Morpheus knew that I knew about him, it wouldn't take long for him to put the pieces together and guess who I was. There would be no helping me then.

"Take them out of here!" screeched Derillen, who had found her magic again and used it to levitate Fallon upside down above her head.

She clicked her fingers, and my brothers and sisters began to follow her. I grabbed hold of Nyre's leg, and nearby, I saw Caspian grab hold of Elaina's hand to stop her from going. A huge bird swooped in and took hold of Halia in much the same way as the flying monkey had earlier. It pulled her into the air, but Momba caught hold of her and used a bolt of magic to send the bird reeling through the air.

The sorcerer kicked Caspian's hand away from Eliana so that he could pick her up. All the while, Nyre carried on following my brothers and sisters as I tried to pull her back. Cordel saw me and pointed a finger my way before letting out a bolt of magic. The instant it hit, I knew something was wrong. I was alive, but my fingers and toes became numb. I looked down to see the skin under my nails turning grey. The grey crept up past my wrist making everything numb.

This was the curse Deon had told me about. It had taken his plants, his flowers, and eventually, his kingdom. It had almost taken his queen, starting at the very tips of her hair and creeping up to the roots where it had almost killed her. I couldn't see my hair anymore, but I had no doubt it was turning grey along with the rest of me. I didn't have the luxury of extra-long hair like Rapunzel had, and since Charlotte had gotten hold of it, it was now shorter than ever.

I cried in frustration as I tried pulling my sword from

its sheath once again. My hands couldn't grip it. The bird flew to my side and pushed my arm up using its head.

"Castiel?" I asked, looking down at the bird. It blinked and nodded its head. When it pulled its head out from under my arm, my hands fell uselessly to my side.

"I can't stop it!. I can't move now."

Castiel used his beak to pull back on the lower part of the dress, where the split was revealing my leg. The grey had traveled all the way up to my thigh.

"I'm sorry," I whimpered as I fell to the floor, no longer able to support myself.

Suddenly it wasn't Castiel as a bird looking up at me anymore. It was Castiel, the man lying on the ground next to me naked as the day he was born.

"What just happened?" he said, looking down at his arms. "I didn't change myself back."

"I don't know, but look." My legs and arms were turning back to their original color. Quicker than it had spread, the grey was completely gone. I jumped up to see that it wasn't just Castiel and I that had changed. The flying monkeys had dropped out of the sky. The balls of fire had stopped, as had the blasts of magic.

Everyone stopped what they were doing to look about them to see why everything had stopped. Even the evil ones on the stage looked confused as silence abounded.

Derillen was the first to regain her composure. "What are you doing?" she shrieked at her team. "They are getting away!"

Sure enough, my brothers and sisters had come to their senses. Nyre, whom I'd been struggling to get off the stage almost since the start, almost bounded right past me, only stopping when she saw me.

"Azia!" she squealed in hushed tones.

"Follow me!" I said, pulling myself up. I had no idea what had happened, but all the magic had stopped—both ours and that of the other side. I ran through the crowd of people with Nyre and the others behind me. As everyone in the room rushed to the door, I pushed through in the opposite direction. Derillen must have figured out what was happening by now, even if she didn't know why. Which meant getting out through the door would be impossible. If we were going to leave, we were going to do it through a window.

Through the noise and panic of people racing for the door and the screams of Derillen at the other end of the room, I was sure I could hear someone calling my name.

Ignoring it, I pulled on the window latch. A blast of freezing winter air hit my face as I yanked the window open.

"Get out. Run to the front and find Gaia!" I said to Nyre, who jumped out into the darkness. Jakon came next, followed by Ivy, Kelis, Deon, and Castiel.

"You'll be able to change again once you are outside," I told him. "You might want to. Get everyone to the front of the building if you can. I've already told Nyre."

He nodded and jumped from the window ledge, turning back into the eagle.

Finally, Fallon, Eliana, Halia, Lyric, and Blaise jumped through the window. I climbed up to follow them, but someone caught hold of my dress, stopping me. Without thinking, I pulled on my sword and spun around, ready to attack.

Charlotte's eyes widened as the tip of my sword came within inches of them.

"Sorry, Charlotte," I said, lowering the sword.

"I brought this," she said, holding her hands out. In the center of them lay a shield with a letter D molded onto it. I recognized it immediately. It was the magic impeder that we'd taken from the police station I Leodis, the one I'd given to Ms. Clarington and asked her to send to Charlotte.

"How did you..."

□When I saw one of your brothers handing out canapés, I realized that the spell wouldn□t hold with this. It came this morning. I was so busy, I forgot to tell you. I□d left it at the theater. I ducked out and ran through the streets to pick it up and bring it back.□

"You are a superstar!" I said, kissing her cheek. "You take it. You are going to need it more than me now. Make sure you keep it by your side at all times. I think it's time that you move into Caspian's house. It will have more magical protection than yours."

I handed back the shield.

"Please stay safe!"

"Promise!" I replied, then dropped down out of the window. As my feet hit the floor, a strangled scream rang out.

"Derillen isn't too happy," a voice I recognized said. I didn't need to wait for my eyes to adjust to the darkness to know who it was.

"Morpheus!"

He had hold of Gaia's hand. She struggled against him.

"Let her go!" Deon said but made no move to get any closer. A gold circle of magic kept him and the others out.

"You heard my brother. Let her go," I said, holding my sword toward his face.

He conjured a portal and threw Gaia through.

"I don't understand any of this," he said, grabbing Jakon through the circle and pushing him through the portal after Gaia. I tried to follow but was bounced back by the magic. He grabbed Eliana and Blaise next and threw them through.

There was nothing I could do but watch him throw my brothers and sisters, one by one, through the portal, where they disappeared.

He grabbed Halia's arm and yanked her into the circle so that there was only me left on the other side. Halia pulled against him, but she was no match for his magic and strength.

"I wish I understood what was going on," he said, eyes on me. "I really have no idea, but I think you think I'm involved somehow."

"Oh, please. Don't play the innocent with me," I replied as Halia kicked him in the shin. He barely flinched. "I know you and Derillen are in this together."

"There you are!" Derillen screamed, her head peering out of the window. As Morpheus took my hand to let me through his magical field, a bolt of purple magic skimmed my ear, hitting Halia right in the chest. Her mouth opened in shock as she fell to the ground.

My eyes couldn't comprehend what I was seeing. Halia's eyes looked up sightlessly, the gold ring around her irises turning black.

"She's dead," Morpheus said, pulling me closer to him. The last thing I saw as he shoved me through the portal was the stars reflected in Halia's unseeing eyes.

Somewhere the sound of bells rang out, signaling midnight. A train blew its final whistle as my siblings and Nyre looked at me, waiting for Halia to jump through the portal behind me. But the portal was gone, and so was she.

My sister was dead, and there was no going back to save her.

19TH DECEMBER DERILLEN

"What are you trying to do to me?" I shrieked the second Morpheus entered my office. I stalked around him and slammed the door loudly.

Morpheus took a seat and crossed one leg over the other. "I didn't do anything to you, Derillen. They escaped. I'm sorry. I know it wasn't what you wanted, but I had nothing to do with it. You didn't have to kill that girl, though."

My blood boilcd, and I had to grip the office desk to not unload every inch of magic I had. I probably would have if I didn't think he'd just conjure one of his portals up and skip out of here.

"Nothing. To. Do. With. You?" I said slowly and as calmly as I could muster in the current situation. "Nothing to do with you? Ignoring the fact you conjured a portal and helped them through, you brought the girl here. You actually brought her here to my party."

"Dahlia? She was my date."

"Your date?" I shrieked, dropping the calm tone entirely. "Your date? You happened to find the one person I've been searching for, for the past year, and instead of coming to give me a heads up, you decided to bring her to my party. My party! You were supposed to be my date!"

His eyes widened in surprise. "Is this what this is about? You are pissed because I brought her as a date?"

"I'm pissed off because you helped all my prisoners escape, you ignorant fool. It has nothing to do with which whores you chose to be seen with."

"Now hang on, Derillen," Morpheus said, standing up. "You can't use that word. I invited her to your party, not my bed."

"Well, that would be a first," I muttered

"I'm sorry about the prisoners," he continued, ignoring my comment. "I really have no idea why she wanted to help them escape. I helped her because I was afraid you were going to do something stupid and hurt her. It's a fair assumption considering what you did to that other poor girl."

I gritted my teeth. Was he really that ridiculously stupid, or was he playing with me? I stared into his eyes. "You really don't know, do you? You actually don't know."

"Know what?"

I laughed. What else was there to do? The man in front of me was a literal god. He could come and go between both the realm of the gods and his own self-created dream world. He had more power in his little finger than I could hope to ever possess in my entire lifetime, and yet above all that, he was a man. A stupid man. A total and utter imbecile.

"She is Azia. Heir to the throne of Draconis. The same Azia that I've spent the last twelve months of my life trying to find to kill. The very same Azia whose birth destroyed me."

His mouth formed a perfect o–shape, and then, he had the gall to grin. His beautiful mouth twisted up in glee, making me want to punch him in it. "Wow. You've got to admit Derillen, that girl has some serious balls coming here." He chuckled and shook his head.

"Get out of my sight," I screamed, not caring who heard. Let everyone in Urbis hear my anger. I had twelve monsters to find and kill. I needed to be angry!

20TH DECEMBER
AZIA

I sat in silence as the train chugged on. I had no energy left to speak. I wasn't the only one. My brothers and sisters sat solemnly, only speaking when they had to show the conductor their tickets.

Where we were going, I had no idea. It had been Gaia that had purchased the tickets. I don't know where she'd gotten the money from, neither did I care enough to ask her.

Halia was dead. I didn't need Morpheus to tell me. The second the blast of Derillen's magic penetrated her heart, her own ribbon of magic was severed. Even when we were far apart, I could feel my brothers' and sisters' magic, like cotton threads weaving around my own. Now though, twelve had become eleven. We were weaker than we had been an hour ago.

We also had nothing left—no money, no tents, no backpacks. All we had were the clothes on our backs—one skin-tight, black dress with a split to the thigh, two tuxedos, and nine purple uniforms...eight purple uniforms. Halia's was back at the government building with her body.

A thought occurred to me. "What happened to Zacharina and the Queen of The Vale?" I asked.

Eliana answered, her eyes full of tears. "Zacharina flew her home before we crossed the border. She's safe."

It was something. I didn't have the heart to ask if there had been any sight of Fae. Eliana had enough on her mind. We all did. At some point, we'd have to come up with a plan and find somewhere to change into different clothes, to sleep, and to eat, not that I was hungry. For now, I was content to rest my head against the train window and watch the lights of Urbis houses pass us by. Every time we slowed at a station, my stomach clenched, worried that one of Derillen's team had found us. Or Derillen herself. But nothing happened.

All I could think about was Halia. She'd saved all our lives a couple of weeks back when wolves had attacked us. With her guitar and melodic voice, she could calm any beast, and yet, she'd not managed to calm Derillen.

It was almost dawn before the conductor called last stop somewhere in Middle Urbis.

We all stepped off into a lonely station. A few others stepped off and drifted away to their homes or places of work.

I felt that I should say something, tell the others where we should go or what we should do, but my mind was a blank. Exhaustion wound its way around the heaviness of the grief and the feeling of utter hopelessness.

Thankfully, Gaia took the lead.

"I've been here before," she said, ushering us to a back street. "I'm hoping they'll let us in."

I didn't question her as we roamed the small cobbled alleyways. She stopped in front of a hotel, pushed at the glass doors, and walked in. We all traipsed in behind her. The man behind the desk squealed in delight when he saw her.

"Princess Gaia!"

"Alex," she greeted him warmly. "My brothers, sisters, and I have gotten into a spot of bother. I was hoping you'd let us have a room for the night. Once things return to normal, I will, of course, reimburse you."

The man's eyes widened as he took in the rest of us.

"Princess Blaise of Atlantice," he gasped. "And Prince Fallon of Aboria and Pri..."

"We are rather tired, Alex. I'm sorry to be a nuisance."

"No problem at all. This is literally the most exciting thing that has ever happened to me!" he clapped his hands together. "I have the royal suite empty this time. There are three bedrooms in there, each with its own private bathroom and double bed. I also have a number of smaller suites on the floor below."

Gaia did a quick count. "I'll take the royal suite for my sisters and me, and if you could show my brothers to the other rooms, I'd be eternally grateful."

Alex couldn't get out from behind the desk quicker if he tried. He practically raced up the stairs, barely waiting for us to keep up. The second I was shown to a bed, I fell onto it without bothering to undress or shower. I probably looked a mess, but I didn't care. Beside me, I felt someone else get into the double bed.

"Goodnight, Azia," Blaise whispered as she pulled the covers over herself. In the next room, the murmured conversation between Gaia and Alex floated through the walls, but I was too tired to try to make out what was being said. I drifted off into sweet oblivion.

Later on, I woke up to the smell of food and the sound of people talking. I opened my eyes to find that Blaise had already gotten out of bed.

Hauling myself up, I took a quick shower in the ensuite bathroom and washed the makeup off from the night before. When I looked at myself in the mirror, I hardly recognized the girl that peered back. I looked older and still tired, despite the sleep. I took the hotel's white fluffy robe and pulled it on, strapping my belt with the sword and sheath to my waist. I looked ridiculous, but I couldn't bring myself to leave it in the bedroom. It was the only thing I had left.

In the lounge area, most of my siblings were tucking into a banquet of delicious food.

I counted them, balking as I manually deducted one from our number. Only Eliana and Lyric were missing from the group.

"They're still asleep," Gaia said, answering my unasked question. Everyone but her was dressed in exactly the same way as me. All of us matching in white robes with the hotel's insignia embroidered on the right breast pocket.

Gaia was wearing a beautiful yellow dress that complimented her skin tone and ability. She really did look like a queen of fire.

"I ordered lunch," she continued. " I thought we better eat while we can. I really think Alex has outdone himself. I never got food like this last time I was here. I think I survived on sandwiches the whole stay when I came to find out where we were born."

"I'd like to go there," I mused, taking a cup and pouring myself a coffee.

Gaia raised a brow. "To where we were born?"

I nodded. It was where this story had started. I needed to see it for myself.

"I feel that if we know where we came from, we might be able to stop this mess."

Gaia shook her head and took my hand in hers. "I felt the same way when I went, but there's nothing there. It's just a house in a poor district. Maplechase Lane, it's called. But I'm telling you, it sounds a lot prettier than it is. You'll be disappointed. A young family lives there now. They didn't even know the midwife that delivered us, let alone our mother."

"Nevertheless, I want to go. Where else can we go at this point? The only people I know well enough to stay with in Urbis are Charlotte and Caspian, and we can't go back to them."

"I was thinking we could stay here for a few days and make a plan," Gaia said. "It's as good a place as any."

I couldn't explain it to her, nor to any of them why I didn't want to do that. Staying still in any one place felt dangerous, now that Derillen knew we were in Urbis. "How can we stay here? We have no money." I looked down at my robe. "We don't even have any clothes." I literally had a dress and a pair of heels.

"We'll figure something out. This is Middle Urbis. We are right in the central shopping district. There are hundreds of clothes shops on the main streets."

I sipped at my coffee and closed my eyes, feeling the beginnings of a headache coming on. "How will we pay for clothes?"

Gaia paused for a moment then brought her hands

to her ears. She took out the gold earrings she wore and put them on the table.

"We have jewelry!" she remarked. "Everyone, give me what you've got. We need to go on a shopping trip!"

As everyone began pulling off bracelets and rings, I took my coffee and headed outside to the small balcony to get a breath of fresh air. I had no jewelry beyond the broach I'd received from the government to let me cross a border. I thought back to the ruby necklace I'd left around my mother's neck—my adopted mother, Briar Rose. Charlotte had told me at the time it was a necklace made by the gods. I'd completely forgotten about it until now. My real mother was a goddess. That's how it came to be in her possession. She'd given it to me as the eldest of all her children, not that it mattered. The magic in it was the only thing keeping Sleeping Beauty alive.

Down in the alley below, a small man walking past peered up at me. I blushed when I realized that I was only wearing a robe. Turning around, I headed back inside.

There wasn't much jewelry on the table. It seemed that Gaia had provided most of it, but one ring stood out. I picked it up and held the ornate ring made to look like intertwined vines, rubbing it with my thumb.

I handed Deon his wedding ring back. "I think we have enough without this."

He nodded and gave me a grateful smile before slipping the ring back on his finger.

"So here's the plan," I started, throwing my broach onto the pile. "Gaia. Can you go downstairs and arrange for this lot to be sold or exchanged for clothes. All of us need something to wear. We'll also need backpacks to carry the leftovers of this meal because we won't be able to afford to buy much in the way of food from now on."

The irony of the fact that we were among the wealthiest people in all the kingdoms and yet couldn't afford a meal didn't escape me. "We will need other stuff too. Weapons. Do you think your friend at the front desk will be able to get us what we need?"

Gaia shrugged. "Alex doesn't strike me as the type that knows where to buy weapons, but I can ask. He'll be able to help with the clothes situation, though. He's quite the fashionista."

Fashion wasn't exactly one of my biggest concerns, but I was grateful for any help we could get.

I sat and picked at the food while Gaia took the jewelry and headed out.

"We need a plan. Last night was a complete disaster. I don't want to..."

A scream from across the room interrupted my words, and seconds later, I saw Kelis diving for me. She jumped so hard into me that the chair I was sitting on toppled over, sending the pair of us to the floor.

"Kelis! What are you doing?" I asked as she fought to pull my sword from the sheath.

I gripped the handle to stop her, but she fought like someone gone wild.

"Kelis!" I shouted, trying to pull myself away from her. Some of the others had stood and were trying to pull the two of us apart.

"The sword!" she gasped. Both of her arms were pinned back by Deon, who had managed to drag her off me. "It's Jakon. He's not...I mean, he's Rumpelstiltskin."

My eyes went over to where Jakon had been sitting moments before. He was still there looking on in astonishment, as was Ivy, who sat next to him.

I closed my eyes and pulled my sword, striking him

right through the middle.

Next to him, Ivy paled, and someone screamed as Jakon stared at me with shock. Blood poured from the wound as I pulled my sword back. His eyes closed, and he slumped back on the sofa

"What the fuck did you just do?" Castiel bellowed, running over to our brother's body.

The world seemed to slow and then stop completely, and everything became silent. I'd killed Jakon. It felt my own heart would stop in shock, but then Jakon's body disappeared into a puff of pink smoke that wafted into the air and out of the window.

I collapsed on a chair in shock.

"It *was* Rumpelstiltskin," Castiel said slowly.

"I told you it was," Kelis said, finally pulling herself free of Deon. "I saw a premonition. He was about to strangle Ivy."

Ivy's eyes widened.

"So if that was Rumpelstiltskin, where is the real Jakon?"

"He must still be in bed. I'll go and check," Fallon said.

"What's going on?" Lyric said as she emerged from one of the bedrooms, Eliana behind her.

"We had Rumpelstiltskin here, but he's gone now," Fallon said, heading to the door. "I'm just going downstairs to bring Jakon up."

"Don't bother," I said, misery filling my every pore. "He's not there. He's already dead." I'd known it as soon as I'd plunged my sword into Rumpelstiltskin's heart. In my panic of wondering if I'd actually killed my brother, I'd scrambled around inside myself, sifting through my magic. Jakon's string of magic, just like Halia's the night before, was not there. I didn't even know when it had left, but it wasn't there now. Not even faintly. Wherever Jakon was, he wasn't alive."

~

"What do you mean dead?" Gaia asked when she returned a couple of hours later with bags full of clothes.

"As far as we can figure out, Jakon never made it out of the government building last night," Ivy said, bringing her up to speed. "In the chaos, Rumpelstiltskin must have switched places with him then, assuming his appearance."

"He was alive when the train left the station. I felt his magic. By that time, Rumpelstiltskin had already taken his place. He probably wasn't at the party at all. When you were all on stage, Derillen made you all dance. Jakon was the only one not dancing. I think he was already Rumpelstiltskin at that point, and Jakon was somewhere else in the building. I didn't think to check my magic again before I killed Rumpelstiltskin, but when I did check, Jakon wasn't there. They must have killed him back at the government building at some point last night."

"Not that we actually did kill Rumpelstiltskin," Deon pointed out. "He was projecting himself again. He wasn't even here. Azia thinks she saw him. The real him earlier."

"For Rumpelstiltskin to project, he needs to be nearby. I thought about this a lot when Roberta was with us in the forest. Eliana held her. She felt real. It wasn't just an image he projected. Same with Jakon. Ivy passed him some food, and he took it. It was almost like he was really in the room, but he wasn't. Do you have any idea how much magic that would take? I've never known anything like it before. Rumpelstiltskin is probably the most powerful of all of the bad guys. More so than Derillen."

"But you saw him?" Gaia asked.

"I saw a small man on the street below the balcony. I didn't think much of it at the time, but I think it was him."

"And we told him exactly where we were going to go next. You even mentioned the address, Gaia."

Gaia paled. "Well, obviously, we aren't going to go there now."

"Actually, that's exactly where we are going to go."

The madness of what I was proposing was not lost on me, but Rumpelstiltskin was one of the most powerful of the people after us. The most powerful, probably. He might not have the drive that powered Derillen, but in a fight between the pair, I would have bet what little money I had left that he would win. I gave a sigh. If only we could think of a way to pit them against each other.

Gaia and Alex had done a great job of buying clothes for all of us. Dark, unassuming outfits that, most importantly, were comfortable and hard-wearing.

They'd even managed to get sizes that fit us. I picked up one of the thick coats that Gaia had laid out on the sofa for us and pulled it on. The fur-lined coat would keep me warm for the winter. I wondered how much of the winter I'd need it for or if I'd survive the winter. It was a solemn crew that left the hotel room. One coat remained on the sofa. One that would have been Jakon's. I couldn't bear to look at it. Of all of us, he had people that depended on him. His brothers and sisters depended on him. They'd already lost their mother. One day, when this was all over, and if I survived, I'd make the journey to Oz and tell them of their brother myself.

It was the least I could do.

No one spoke as we made our way to the train station. Snow had begun to fall, coating the cobbled streets. It was a blessing in disguise as we could pull our fur-lined hoods up, giving us some anonymity. I didn't care much anymore if any of Derillen's people found us. I hoped they did. I'd kill them without a thought, but we were still wanted people. Probably more than we were before. I had no doubt that our pictures would be splayed on the covers of every newspaper. Being cornered by a brave member of the public or a local policeman would slow us down. I didn't want needless bloodshed anymore than I wanted distractions. I set my mind on Rumpelstiltskin as I boarded the train that would take us to Outer Urbis.

There'd have been more of us if I'd taken Nyre into consideration. Twelve brothers and sisters and one dragon shifter. The other side had twelve. We should have been beating them, but our numbers were now eleven. I wouldn't rest until I evened the score.

"I didn't think I'd be making this journey again so soon," Gaia mused. I looked up at her. Her face was partly obscured by her hood, but she looked so beautiful as she gazed out of the window, the late afternoon sun illuminating her face.

We'd all lost so much, but I wasn't planning on losing any more.

Two hours later, we pulled into a station.

"This is our stop," Gaia said, standing up.

We trooped out after her into a rundown area with higgledy-piggledy houses and shops. It wasn't anything like what I'd expected. I was born near here. I expected more. Something different. Something special. There was nothing special about this area. Nothing to tell that twelve demi-gods had been born here, changing the world. I trusted Gaia as she strode purposefully through the streets. She'd been here. She knew the place.

Eventually, we came to a street full of terraced houses. I thought I'd instinctively know which house we were looking for, but it could have been any of them. I stayed to the back as Gaia knocked on a door.

The door opened. A young woman raised her eyebrows as Gaia greeted her and re-introduced herself. I waited while they talked for a couple of minutes, keeping my eye on the people in the street. It was fairly quiet, but there were a few people milling around.

"Everyone, this is Kate."

I nodded with a faint smile as she stood back and let us into her house. The kitchen was small but bright.

"I'll put a pot of tea on, shall I?" Kate said, looking mildly flustered to have so many strangers in her kitchen. As there were only four chairs around the table, the majority were standing.

"That would be lovely," Gaia said, taking one of the seats. "Tell me, how is Elsie?" She looked about her. "Is she here?"

Kate shook her head as she filled a kettle with water and placed it on the stove.

"She's very well, thank you. She's out with her father at the moment. They'll be back soon enough."

Gaia smiled widely, but when Kate turned her back to get out some cups, she gave me a pointed look.

I took the seat next to her as she nodded at Fallon and pointed to Kate. Fallon took the hint and struck up a conversation about the tea plantations in Aboria.

"It's not Kate," Gaia whispered. "Her daughter is Elise, not Elsie."

I wasn't surprised. In fact, I'd expected it. Kate was Rumpelstiltskin. I couldn't think where the real Kate was, nor her daughter. Killing the fake Kate wouldn't help. She wasn't real. Just as Roberta hadn't been when Eliana used my sword to kill her, and just as Jakon hadn't been when I'd struck him in the heart. Kate was a projection, which meant that the real Rumpelstiltskin was somewhere close by.

"Keep her talking. Don't let her notice I'm gone," I whispered back.

Gaia stood and went to help Kate with the tea. Between her and Fallon, getting outside was easier than I expected.

I had no idea how Rumpelstiltskin's powers worked, whether he would look like himself or if he would have yet another persona. I would imagine his concentration would be on what was happening inside Kate's house, but I couldn't underestimate him. I'd done that one too many times.

The sun had all but gone from the sky, but the thin blanket of snow twinkled in the streetlamps giving the whole street an otherworldly ambiance. I shivered, whether from cold or magic, I wasn't sure.

Moving away from Kate's house, I hid in the shadow of the doorway next door and scanned the street. A few people were walking through the snow. A couple, hand in hand, a woman with a baby carriage and an unruly toddler, and a number of people who looked like they were returning home from work. I discounted them all. Not one of them was paying any attention to the house I was born in, though a number of them passed it.

Then I saw him, further down the road. He'd had the same idea as me and was using a shadowed doorway to hide. He was crouched down, his head almost resting on his knees as he perched on his toes. Surprisingly, his eyes were closed. Maybe he needed to be that way to become Kate inside. I knew then what I needed to do. I needed to kill him before his version of Kate realized I was missing. The snow dampened my footsteps as I crossed the road to where he was.

Revulsion filled me as I peered down at him. His mouth moved wordlessly, and his fingers twitched. The puppet master to the fake Kate inside. He hadn't actually killed anyone, and yet he was responsible for so much pain. Baby Fae was still missing; Jakon was dead. Everything he saw and heard went straight back to Derillen. My first instinct when I pulled my sword was to just kill him. Get it over with quickly, but as I lowered my sword to his balding head, I changed my mind.

Instead, I grabbed his head, pulling it back so I could hold my sword against his neck. His eyes shot open, and his mouth pulled into a toothy grin.

"Where is she?" I demanded.

"Where is who?" he asked, his voice slippery and high pitched.

"You know damn well who I mean. Where is Fae?"

"Oh, the baby." He spoke as though he was already bored by the way the conversation was heading. "Does it really matter?"

"It does if you want to keep your head on your shoulders," I growled back at him.

"You are going to kill me no matter what I say. I can see into your heart and your mind. I have no reason to tell you anything."

"I will kill you. I'll be happy to do it. I might make it quick and painless if you tell me where she is first."

He shrugged as much as he could. "I'll do you a deal.

I'll tell you where she is if you promise to let me go."

"Didn't you just say that you knew I'd kill you anyway? I'm not refuting that."

His eye ticked a little, and then I knew what he was up to. I'd heard enough from other people to know a little about him. A promise with Rumpelstiltskin was magically binding. If I made a deal with him, any kind of deal, it would have to play through whether I liked it or not.

I pulled the sword back, pulling hard on the blade. Blood spattered out, creating patterns in the snow below him. His eyes opened wide, but he was no match in strength against me.

"I don't care for your deal," I said, watching the life drain from his eyes. "I know where she is. Derillen has her. Derillen has always had her."

He couldn't confirm or deny it. He was already dead. I let his body fall to the ground. Somewhere behind me, someone screamed.

"Murderer! Police! Help!"

I turned to see a group of people heading my way. Normal people. Bystanders who just happened to be passing. I leveled my sword out in front of me, stopping any of them from getting closer. I knew how I must look to them. My hands and the sword dripped in blood, and though I couldn't see the expression on my face, I knew how crazed I felt. Behind the screaming woman and the group who were getting closer, I saw my brothers and sisters pour out of Kate's house.

"Go to the perimeter wall!" I shouted to them, sending a beam of pink light into the air. Seconds later, Nyre was in her dragon form, circling the pink light. She swooped in and pulled me into the air.

We followed the path of the others, running through

the streets below us, losing the crowd quickly. Not that losing them would help. I'd shouted out exactly where we planned to go. Urbis was no longer safe for us. We didn't just need to get to the wall; we needed to get over it.

By the time midnight struck, Lyric and Nyre had managed to fly all of us over the wall and out of Urbis.

I sat with my back to the wall, looking out over the body of water that separated The Forge and Floris.

With the death of Rumpelstiltskin, our chances had evened slightly, but we were a long way from where we needed to be. Almost as soon as the thought had crossed my mind, a green light engulfed the walls, throwing me forward and harshly depositing me in the inky black sea. Blaise and Deon scrambled over the rocks to pull me out of the frigid water.

"What just happened?" I asked, shivering with the cold.

"I don't know, but I think we can safely assume that getting back into Urbis is going to be a lot harder than it was getting out."

Lyric took to the air and flew above the wall that we'd just come over. As soon as she came into contact with the green glare, she was knocked back as I had been. Her wings were the only thing saving her from the same wet fate that had happened to me.

"That's it," she announced. "There is no way in unless the north entrance is still open."

I looked along the huge wall that surrounded Urbis. We were on the south side. Once again, we were faced with the prospect of walking for weeks. But this time, I was dripping wet, and the ground was covered in snow.

21ST DECEMBER DERILLEN

"What is it?" I snapped at the maid who had the audacity to wake me at one o'clock in the morning. It had taken me long enough to get to sleep as it was after Morpheus's betrayal. I'd turned it over and over in my mind. I'd been very clear that I expected him to be my date and not only did the bastard came with another woman, he came with *her!* "Someone better be dead!"

The maid shifted uncomfortably on her feet.

"Actually, yes, Ma'am. Word has come through that Rumpelstiltskin was killed an hour or so ago in Outer Urbis."

"Who did it?" I bellowed, jumping out of bed and pulling my robe on.

“There’s no word yet exactly, but a number of suspects fled the scene. It does look like it was *them*.”

Of course, it was them. I pushed the girl out of the way and stormed out of my chambers.

“Edwin!” I called out. My voice echoed down the spacious hallway, causing a number of people to come running, none of whom were the one I wanted.

“Where is Edwin?” I screamed at a passing servant who cowered under my glare.

“I’m here,” Edwin said, harrying up the corridor.

“Why was it left to a maid to tell me about Rumpelstiltskin?”

“I only just found out myself, President. I assure you that had I known sooner, I would have told you the news myself.”

“It doesn’t matter. Get everyone into the conference room immediately. Bring the child.”

“But, president, don’t you think...”

“I said, bring the child.”

Edwin bowed slightly, then scurried off down the corridor from whence he had come.

Of all of my team, Rumpelstiltskin’s death was a tough pill to swallow. He was my strongest man and my ears on the ground. Without him, I’d have to find other means of finding out what they were up to.

“You!” I screeched, pointing at a passing servant. “Get all the newspaper reporters here quickly. I’m doing a press conference in the great hall at three am precisely, and I need everyone there.”

“I don’t work in the media office,” the boy said. He soon moved when I glared at him. “Yes, ma’am. I’ll go and tell them.”

I didn’t need Rumpelstiltskin telling me what the monsters were up to. I was going to draw them out.

Bring them to me instead of me chasing them, but this time when they came, I'd be ready for them, and it wouldn't just be two of them that perished under my hands. They all would, and as I took Briar Rose's brat's last breath from her body, I'd look her in the eyes, and she'd know it was me that caused her downfall. I suddenly felt better at the prospect of it.

21ST DECEMBER
AZIA

I missed Jakon. In that very moment, with freezing water turning to ice on my clothes, I missed the brother who could conjure wind and control the weather. He could blow-dry my clothes for me using the elements. Instead, Gaia conjured up a fire that we all sat around as we came to terms with the prospect of another grueling walk ahead of us. I was tired. Tired to my very soul. I'd never envied my mother's never-ending sleep until that point, but I could happily have drifted off into the dream world and never come back. I pushed the thought away. Thinking of Morpheus only made me angry, and I had enough anger to add him to the mix.

"I could try and fly higher," Lyric suggested. "The

green light can't go on forever. There must be a top to this wall somewhere."

I didn't even look up. There wouldn't be a way over the wall, no matter how high Lyric flew.

Nyre muzzled her head under my hand, and I patted her on the head. "I don't think either of you could do it, but try if you like."

The dragon took to the sky, closely followed by Lyric. I watched as they flew directly upwards. They got smaller and smaller until they were mere dots. Eventually, they both flittered back down, unsuccessful in their quest.

"There must be another way in," Deon said. "Perhaps we could talk our way in through one of the closer entrances. Fallon can change his appearance and sweet talk his way in."

"Thanks, bud," Fallon replied.

"It won't work," I pointed out glumly. "Even if Fallon does manage to fool them into thinking he is someone else, how will the rest of us get in? Besides, the gates will be shut. This green wall is controlled by Derillen or someone else in the government. There will be no one at the gates for Fallon to sweet talk."

We were all silent for a second, each of us wrapped in our own thoughts. Despite our individual magic and our collective magic, I couldn't think of a way for us to use it to get through or over the wall.

"Kelis? I don't suppose you've had any more premonitions?"

Kelis shook her head. "Sorry. Nothing. My brain feels a bit numb at the moment. I can't see anything."

"I'll do it!" Blaise announced suddenly, standing up.

I peered at her. "Do what?"

"I'll get us in. I've not done anything to help our cause up until now. Now, it's my time to do something."

I wasn't sure what she meant until she pulled her top layer of clothes off and dove into the icy sea.

"I'll be back soon!" she called, then dove back under until there was nothing left to see of her.

"She can breathe underwater, remember?" Ivy said, draping her hand over my shoulder.

I nodded. I hadn't forgotten. I knew Blaise was as at home underwater as she was on land, but I also knew that her abilities only came to her this year, and it wasn't like she'd had plenty of time to practice. She'd barely ever been in the water without her mother or her boyfriend, Fish, nearby, and the pair of them were merfolk.

I waited with bated breath for her to re-surface, but she never did. Hours later, when the first tendrils of the sun's rays turned the inky black sea to pink, then red, and finally to a deep, blue-green color, and she still wasn't back, I felt sick to my stomach.

The others took leftovers from the meal we'd had at the hotel and passed them around, but I wasn't hungry. I'd held hope that we'd be able to walk into Urbis, fight the bad guys, and restore the kingdoms to how they used to be. We were magic, after all. Except we'd failed at every point. Two of my siblings were dead, we were no closer to finding Fae, and the problems in the kingdoms were as bad as ever. I'd actually been on a date with Morpheus and still not managed to find a way to bring my mother back. I'd never felt more of a failure in my life.

Kelis passed me a granola bar, which I took and picked at just for want of something to do. We needed to make a plan, but I couldn't think of one. The prospect of walking for more months exhausted me.

I was just contemplating asking the others if they

had any idea what we should do next when there was a disturbance in the water.

My first thought was that it was Blaise returning, but it soon became apparent that wasn't the case. The sea roiled and bubbled as men...or at least approximations of men began to surface. Hundreds of ugly green beasts began to crawl out of the sea and stumble over the rocks toward us.

Our impromptu picnic was abandoned as more of the beasts started toward us. They kept coming, and with each step they moved toward us, we took a step back. Fighting was not an option. There were thousands of them. All the magic in the world wouldn't keep them at bay. All I could do was keep stepping backward, swiping my sword in front of me as I tried to think of a way to kill these creatures. I managed to swipe through one. Seconds after me cutting it in two, it disappeared, turning into blue smoke and dissipating into the air. Pretty soon, we were surrounded, our backs to Urbis's wall. My mind went through all the magic we had, but nothing came to mind to help us in this situation. Gaia threw fireballs at them, causing them to shriek in pain before exploding into blue smoke. In the distance, the sound of laughing permeated the air. I looked up over the army of sea creatures to see Blaise held over the head of the sea witch.

"I have your precious Blaise," the witch shrieked, turning the sound into a giggle that didn't suit her at all.

"Let her go!" I shouted with more confidence than I felt.

She laughed again, an evil chortle that rang through my ears.

"I don't think you are in any position to make

demands, do you?" she cackled. "Now, do I kill the lot of you first and let Blaise here watch, or do I kill Blaise and watch all of your faces fill with sadness. Either way, you'll all end up dead, and I'll be happy, so don't take too long in your decision making."

"I can't see them properly," Blaise shouted out.

I furrowed my brows at her. What was she doing?

"Oh, so you want to watch your siblings die, do you? Ha! What a coward having your siblings die before you do. Or are you trying to be brave and spare them the agony of watching you die? Agony. It's such a nice word. Rolls off the tongue, doesn't it? So which is it?"

I watched as the sea witch levitated in the air above the sea. She moved closer to land to give either herself or Blaise a better view.

"Get her!" I whispered to Nyre. Nyre, still in her dragon form, nodded and took to the sky. I could only watch in horror as the sea witch batted her out of the sky, sending her crashing into the wall using magic. Blaise kicked out, trying for the sea witch's head, but she was in such a position that her leg ended up kicking air.

Still, the Witch moved forward. She didn't step out of the water onto the rocks. She floated about a foot above them, surrounded as she was by her army.

She closed in on us, leering over us, knowing she had us trapped.

Lyric spread her wings and flew into the air before I could stop her. She had no chance of saving Blaise if Nyre couldn't, but it didn't stop her from trying. I waved my sword at the creatures, killing the odd one, but I wouldn't be able to keep them at bay for long. There were just too many of them. For every one that Gaia and I killed, a hundred more popped up out of the sea.

They weren't real, but that didn't mean they couldn't hurt us. It only meant that we couldn't hurt them. The only one we could hurt was the Sea Witch, but she was surrounded by thousands of her creatures.

Lyric swooped down to grab Blaise. It felt as if time had slowed down, and I could only watch on helplessly as the Sea Witch raised her hand to fling Lyric to the wall as she had with Nyre. But Lyric remained in the air. The sea witch disappeared in an instant along with all her creatures. Blaise fell, only to be caught by Lyric just before she landed on the rocks.

Everything became quiet in an instant. No one moved, unsure of what had just happened.

A groan took my attention to Nyre. She pulled herself up from the ground at the base of the wall where she had landed, dusted herself off, and blew a small puff of fire indignantly.

"What just happened?" I asked as Lyric lowered Blaise gently onto the rocks. Beyond her, the sea was calm and, once again, a soft blue.

"Exactly what I wanted to happen," Blaise grinned. She shook her hair, sending droplets of water over all of us.

"Let's finish that food," she said, moving to the picnic site, which had somehow miraculously been left unscathed. "I'm starving!"

"Are you going to tell us what just happened?" I asked as she took a seat on the flat bit of ground and picked up a sandwich. Next to me, Gaia started the fire again.

"My plan had been to find a way into Urbis under the wall. I figured that the waterways in Urbis had to have a way out. I hadn't expected to bump into the sea witch almost as soon as I got through."

"You were gone hours," I pointed out, interrupting her story.

"I had to let her chase me. If I'd have come straight back to you, she would have figured something was up."

I was completely lost. "You wanted her to chase you?"

"Yep," Blaise replied, a self-satisfied grin on her face.

"And you planned to bring her out to us?"

Blaise nodded. "Yep, on both counts."

I glanced at the others, who looked clearly as confused as I was.

"But why? You know our magic. We had nothing that would get past an army of sea monsters."

"You didn't have to. I had something I knew would kill her instantly. I didn't really need any of you at all."

I must have looked perplexed because she carried on explaining.

"When I jumped in the water, I crossed the border from The Forge into international territory. No one kingdom owns the sea. When she carried me out of the sea onto land, I crossed the border again, back into The Forge. Just before that happened, I dropped the broach you were given by Cordel down the back of her neck. I took it earlier when you told us what it was. I thought it might come in handy. The broach didn't know or care who was wearing it. It only knew how many times it had crossed international borders. The second time it crossed, it killed the person wearing it, just as you told me Cordel had said it would."

I opened my mouth in wonder.

"You killed her using Derillen's magic?"

"Technically, Derillen's magic killed her. I didn't do anything. I only dropped the broach. How was it my fault that it happened to fall into her clothes?"

"You are a freaking genius!" Castiel said, bringing her into a sideways hug and kissing her roughly on the temple as she grinned back at all of us.

"There's a tunnel from the sea to the other side of the wall," Blaise continued, a grin on her face. "It's not too far. All of you should make it without much problem. I'll swim with each of you to make sure you get through unscathed."

"We can't!" Ivy said. "Blaise was able to cross the border because she had the broach. The rest of us will end up back in the government building dungeon."

"That will save us walking there," Fallon pointed out.

I shook my head. "No. The borders aren't restricted anymore. Rumpelstiltskin is dead. So is his magic. The portals were always his. The broach was powered by Derillen's magic. That's why it worked. We'll be able to cross into the sea without being transported."

I had no idea if my theory was right, but it felt right. No one questioned it as they stepped one by one into the cold water.

It was only when it was my turn to swim through that I realized that we had done what I'd set out to do when I woke up the previous morning. We'd evened the score. Two of our side were dead, but two of theirs were too.

Fallon and Ivy pulled me from the icy water on the inside of the wall. A quick glance around told me that we were at some kind of dock. A couple of boats sat on the almost frozen water, but otherwise, it was deserted.

A ball of fire enveloped me, making my clothes hiss with the evaporating water, but otherwise leaving me unscathed.

"Thanks, Gaia," I said as the warmth seeped through

harmlessly without burning me.

As we were only blocks away from where I'd killed Rumpelstiltskin, my first thought was to get us all out of here, as far away from the scene of the crime as possible. Hours had passed since I'd stabbed him, but the street where we'd all been born was bound to still be full of police.

"We need to get away from here, and we need to get out of this snow," I said, beckoning the others toward me.

"Where?" Castiel asked. "There is nowhere we can go. Our photos will be on the front of every newspaper after what just happened. No cafes, shops, hotels, or restaurants will let us through the door without calling for the police. We don't know anyone here except Charlotte and her loser boyfriend, and we wouldn't make it onto a train without getting caught."

While we'd had our faces plastered over every newspaper for months now, Castiel was right. People had actually seen me committing murder. Not that we'd been safe before, but we were in an impossible situation now.

"Let's find shelter. Anywhere. Look at this place. It's all run down. There must be an abandoned building we can break into. We'll come up with a plan from there."

"A plan?" Castiel responded. "Like we've ever managed to make a plan."

"There's a first time for everything," I snapped back. I was cold, tired, and in no mood to argue with Castiel.

We trudged through the backstreets, keeping our heads down. The bad weather was on our side, just as it had been in Leodis. Not many people ventured onto the streets, and those that did kept their hoods up and their heads down against the swirling snow.

After about an hour of trudging along the snow-covered cobbles looking for cover, I was almost about to give up.

While there were plenty of dilapidated old buildings to chose from, none of them were empty. The weather had gotten worse with the wind picking up and the snow falling heavily

"How about we go down into the subway?" Kelis suggested. It was the first time she'd spoken since getting back into Urbis.

"Subway?" Deon questioned.

"Subway, yeah." Kelis pointed to a sign over a set of steps that disappeared into the ground.

"What's a subway?" Castiel asked.

"It's an underground train system."

"There's no subway system in Urbis," Ivy pointed out. "They have them in Enchantia where the trains run on magic. It was thought about a number of years ago, but the government decided against it, saying it would be too expensive to build and too dirty to run."

"How do you know that?" Gaia asked, looking impressed.

Ivy shrugged. "The Steam Guild in The Forge was brought in to assess whether it was possible. I remember desperately wanting to join just so I could work on the trains."

I took a step toward the station entrance. "It looks like they built at least one station. Even if it comes to nothing, at least we can get out of this god-awful weather."

The steps down were dark and uninviting and smelled faintly of pee. It was a far cry from the hotel we'd spent the night before last in, but it was dry. And though I couldn't say it was warm, it was a lot better than the snowstorm we'd just come out of.

"Gaia!" I shouted back. "Can you come here?"

Seconds later, Gaia appeared at my side.

"Can you produce some light? I can't see a thing."

Gaia lifted her hand and produced a ball of light. Before us, the stairs seemed to go down forever. We continued on, getting deeper and deeper into the earth until the only light we had was the light produced by Gaia. Eventually, we came to a platform. At least, I assumed that's what it was. There was only a wide expanse of paving with a lower part that went from a tunnel on one side to a tunnel on the other.

"This is weird," Ivy said, coming up next to me. "There's a tunnel, but no tracks."

"If they only started the project and never finished it, maybe they didn't get around to putting the tracks down."

Ivy shook her head. "But the station is finished. Why go to the expense of making a station with an entrance open to the public if they weren't going to put tracks down? I don't like this one bit. I think we should go back up and see if we can find somewhere else to hole up."

I agreed, but when I turned back to the stairs, I was greeted with a brick wall where the stairs had been.

"What just happened?" I asked, pushing through my siblings to the wall. It felt cold to the touch and merged exactly with the other walls of the station.

"Shit!" Castiel murmured. "There never was a subway. This was put here as a trap, and we just walked right into it."

All of a sudden, the whole place lit up. Gaia extinguished her flame as we looked around. One of the tunnel entrances I'd seen was blocked off, but the other gave out a green glow.

An invitation laid out by Derillen herself.

And it was the only way for us to go. There was no going back now.

KINGDOM OF EVER AFTER

23RD DECEMBER
AZIA

Fear rippled through me as we walked along the glowing tunnel. Beneath our feet, long-forgotten tracks ran the length of the tunnel, dark and dirty. The tunnel gave up a musty smell of neglect and misuse with an overwhelming odor of urine, although had it been used for the reason it was built, it wouldn't have smelled any better. The walls, though dark, were free of soot, telling me that the Urbis Subway project had been given up long before the tunnels had been used for their purpose. Every so often, beyond the green glow, I spotted graffiti, probably made by the same people that had given the tunnel the urine smell. People had been down here. I wondered where they were and what had happened to them. The only sound came from the crunch of dirt under our feet, making the whole thing even more ominous. Fear swam through my veins, and I had my sword ready for attack, but it was an attack that never came. We walked hours along the tracks, most of it in silence, each of us caught up in our own thoughts.

My stomach growled, reminding me that I'd not eaten all day, but we had nothing left to eat. We had nothing left at all but each other.

"I'm hungry, Boss," Lyric finally said, breaking the silence after long hours of walking.

"What do you want me to do?" I snapped, coming to a standstill. "Cook you up an omelet? Take you out to a fancy restaurant? If you haven't noticed, we are currently in a tunnel. Not a lot of fine dining choices."

"I only meant..." she was cut off by Deon, who came between us.

"I was going to tell everyone tonight, but I have a few bits of food leftover from the hotel. Nothing fancy. Just some cookies and a few apples. I held them back when we had our picnic by the sea. I figured that we might need something later."

He held an apple out for Lyric, who took it gratefully.

"Maybe we should stop here for the night?" Deon suggested. "We've been walking for hours, and I don't think anything is going to happen. Derillen obviously wants us to come to her, and she knows we are here. She'll wait as long as it takes."

Before I had a chance to reply, everyone sat down along the sides of the tunnel. Deon handed each person a cookie or an apple.

Anger and guilt swam together in a maelstrom of emotion in my gut. Lyric had only voiced what everyone else had been thinking. I carried on walking up the tunnel. A few minutes later, Deon arrived at my side, panting as he tried to keep up with my brisk stride.

"That wasn't very nice," he said, running alongside me.

I shrugged, not slowing my pace. "I know. I don't feel particularly nice right now. Everyone wants me to make the decisions, but when I do, they complain or argue that I've made the wrong one. Then they just do what they want anyway."

"Who is doing that?"

"Everyone," I huffed, coming to a standstill.

Deon looked at me. I could see confusion in his eyes.

"Back there," I added for clarity, pointing back down the track to where the others sat eating.

"Nothing happened back there beyond you shouting at Lyric for no apparent reason."

I sucked in a breath then wished I hadn't. The urine smell we'd long since left behind. No one traveled this far along the unused tracks, but, despite the vents in the top of the tunnel every so often, the air was thin and gritty down here. I swallowed it back. "Lyric is always asking me what to do. I want to keep moving. There's no reason to stop, and yet everyone just sat down when you told them they should. Everyone listens to you."

Deon clapped a hand on my shoulder. "Azia, I love you. You know that, but sometimes you can be so bloody ridiculous. For starters, I only suggested we stay there for the night, not commanded it. Secondly, you never suggested otherwise. I didn't know you wanted to carry on until five seconds ago when you told me. You can't expect us all to be mind-readers. What is this all about?"

I felt tears pricking the corners of my eyes, but I

refused to let them fall. “I can’t do this, Deon. Everyone is looking up to me, and I don’t know why. I couldn’t keep Halia or Jakon alive. I can’t bear it. What if any of the others die? That will be my fault too. Part of me wants to sit in this tunnel forever so I don’t have to face what I know is coming, and part of me wants to keep going just so we can get it all over and done with and be dammed if we all die in the process.” There, the truth was out—my reasons for being so whiny and petulant. Every time I closed my eyes, I pictured my brothers and sisters dying in more and more horrific ways, and the worst part about it was that some of them probably would die and maybe in worse ways than my mind could imagine.

Deon pulled me to him, and I felt myself quivering in his arms. So much for not letting the tears fall.

He smoothed my hair with his hand while I used his jacket as a snot rag.

“No one blames you for Halia and Jakon, just as they won’t blame you if anything happens to the rest of us. We are in this fight together, just as we have always been. It’s not just your fight that you pulled us into. We all have reasons to be here.”

I could have stayed in his arms all day. Deon, always the one to pull me from the brink. To give me wise words, not always to comfort me, but to slap me back to reality too.

“I don’t think I’d have gotten this far if it wasn’t for you,” I mumbled.

“And none of us would be here without you. Take me, for example. Had you not come into my life, I’d have spent the last few months enjoying my honeymoon with my beautiful bride and then learning how to be a prince. Probably a dead prince, thanks to the plague ravaging through Floris, but a prince, nonetheless. "

I slapped his shoulder playfully and snorted, sending more snot in his direction.

"I'm a selfish asshole, I know. I should go back and apologize to Lyric."

"You really should," he agreed. "Here, eat this first and decide what it is you want. You want to stay here for the night or keep moving? It's hard to tell with the lack of light, but I think it's only early evening. We could probably walk a while longer." He handed me a chocolate chip cookie, which I took gratefully.

I looked up at the never-ending tunnel where the green faded into darkness. It would take us weeks of walking to get anywhere close to Inner Urbis. What were a few more hours?

"We'll camp out for tonight and set off early in the morning."

Deon nodded in the big brotherly way he always did, despite being younger than me. "Come on." He took my hand, and I let him lead me back to the others. He nodded to Lyric, then sat at the opposite side of the tunnel.

"Hey, Lyric."

She looked up at me, her eyes full of sadness. She looked so young, but so weary.

"I'm sorry, Lyric. I shouldn't have snapped at you back there. I'm an ass." It wasn't nearly enough of an apology, but it was all I had.

She gave me a watered-down smile. "You know, when I first joined you guys, you all reminded me of the lost boys back home. A family that had kind of come together from other places. Not you. You reminded me of a mother. I never had a mother. I guess I let you fill that void, and maybe I shouldn't. You never asked for it."

My heart swelled ten sizes, but the guilt increased too.

"All the more reason I should be better, huh? May I sit beside you?"

"You're doing better than you think you are. I'd really like you to sit next to me."

I took a seat beside her and draped my arm over her shoulder. She snuggled into me and closed her eyes. From the other side, Nyre narrowed her eyes slightly, but when Fallon turned to chat with her, she soon forgot I existed. I'd known for a while now that she had a crush on him, though she'd never told me. The flush in her cheeks every time he looked her way was a giveaway in itself. She knew as well as I did that he had a girlfriend, but in that moment, as she rested her head on his shoulder, echoing how Lyric was sitting with me, it didn't seem to matter.

I had a feeling Fallon saw Nyre as a rather annoying younger sister, and there was no way he was going to give Veda up for anyone, but he let her rest against him all the same. In that moment, between the light and the dark, not knowing what tomorrow would bring, or even if we'd survive it, we all needed the comfort each other brought.

I felt my eyes drooping as I rested my head on Lyric's. Soft, slow breaths told me she was already asleep. It might have been only early evening, but dragon-fire, I was exhausted. The walking and lack of food had me tired to my bones. I let myself drift off into a cold, uneasy sleep.

I woke sometime later to complete chaos. Derillen's green magic that had illuminated our path was now flickering like a candle in the wind, casting ominous shadows before plunging us into darkness, then flickering back on again.

Howls and screams echoed down the tunnel as I pulled my sword, steadying myself to fight. Confusing images flashed in the light. My brothers and sisters, Nyre. Something was attacking us, but I couldn't get a grip on what. There was too much movement, not enough light. The hairs on my arms stood on end as I frantically tried to make sense of what I was seeing. In the chaos, all I could see were shapes and snatches of faces, of arms. And above it all, a low growling. Then came the sound of flesh being ripped as the thing, whatever it was, tore into someone. Who, I didn't know, but the scream that came from their mouth would haunt me forever.

My instinct was to lash out, to thrust my sword at anyone near me, but in doing so, I would no doubt hurt someone I loved. I stood, rocking on my heels, my heart hammering in my chest as the screaming continued. Someone, I think Fallon, shouted out Blaise's name, but she didn't answer, which led me to believe she was the one screaming. The terrible noise gave way to guttural moans and then petered out completely until there was nothing but silence. And still, I couldn't tell what was happening.

"Everyone stay still," I shouted as the growling continued. "I need to see what happened. Is everyone alright? Blaise?"

"I think something got her," Fallon shouted out through the darkness. The green light flashed again, and I made out two figures on the floor. One laid out flat, the other hunched over.

"Fallon?" I asked, heading toward them.

He turned, his face contorted with grief. The green

light flashed again, giving me enough time to see Blaise on the floor, blood everywhere.

"She's dead," he whispered. I barely heard him over the ominous growl.

"Watch out!" someone called out. I turned to the source of the voice, but in the darkness, I wasn't prepared for the thing crashing into me. We both fell to the ground with it on top of me. I say 'it' because fur covered most of its body. It growled as we tumbled over the rocky floor until we came to a stop next to one of the tracks. It was then, I realized that I'd dropped my sword as I fell. Whatever this thing was, it was stronger than me. I pushed against it, trying to keep its teeth from my neck. I didn't want to end up like Blaise. It growled again, and I realised that it wasn't the source of the low growls I'd been hearing. That meant there were two of them. Or more.

I kicked upwards at the creature. It yelped as my foot connected with its body, and I was able to roll myself away from under it. I scrambled to my feet and to the wall, feeling my way along it. Somewhere another scream rang out. Another growl. Another growl that wasn't the low growl that hummed through my brain. It seemed that guessing there were two of them was wishful thinking.

The light flashed again, and I saw the creature briefly. Its head was facing away, but it had hair more human than creature. Long red hair that fell down its back. However, its body was covered in thick red fur with remnants of clothing ripped off of it. It also had a pair of wings, and though I hadn't seen them, I was willing to bet it had a wicked set of fangs. It was facing away from me. I tiptoed slowly away from the creature with the hope of finding my sword before it spotted me, but luck was not on my side. I tripped over a loose rock, falling backward. The noise alerted the creature to where I was, and it was on me before I had the chance to right myself. I'd gotten it right about its teeth. I didn't need to see them, to feel the prick of two fangs piercing the skin through my clothes on my shoulder. It bit down, sending a searing pain that rippled out through my body, even through the thick coat I wore. It pulled back and snapped its jaws at me again. This time it went for my neck where there was no coat to save me. It growled, sending spittle down my neck. All around me, I heard growls and screeches and screams straight from my worst nightmares. I wasn't the only one fighting these monsters. I kicked up again, but the thing was already at my neck, waiting to snap its jaws. With every ounce of strength I had, I pushed upwards, moving the thing's face from my neck to right in front of me. Someone shouted out my name, but I could only groan in answer. Everything else was too painful and required too much effort. The light flashed again, and the strength went out of my arms. Shock numbed the pain as I took in the sight in front of me. Although the light lasted only a couple of seconds at most, what I saw was guaranteed to feature in every nightmare I was to ever have again. The creature, the monster, wasn't a monster at all. It was Lyric. Her beautiful face was contorted with an anger I'd never seen in her, and her teeth were elongated into the fangs I'd felt earlier. Her long hair draped at the side of my face, and below her chin, her body was twice the size it usually was and covered in fur. Her ears had moved upwards on her head and tapered to a fine point. Not that I had much time to process any of it. There was a flash of silver and her face, along with her head, pointed ears and all, sailed completely away from her body, spiraling into the darkness, leaving what was left to collapse in a heap and pin me to the tunnel floor. Blood dripped down over my face. I clenched my jaw shut to stop it from seeping into my mouth. Bile rose to my mouth, so I had to turn my head to the side to vomit.

I pushed up with both my arms and legs until Lyric's body rolled away. Then, I dragged myself to the side of the tunnel and sat there, my head in my hands. The pain ripping through my shoulder was excruciating, but I'd live. If it wasn't for my coat, Lyric would have killed me for sure, and if it wasn't for the person wielding my sword, she'd have ripped my throat out just as she had done Blaise's.

Shock had me rooted to the spot. I barely noticed when the noise stopped completely, and the lights stopped flickering and came back on.

When they did, I wished they hadn't. The scene was even worse than anything I'd seen in the moments leading up to it.

Blaise was in a puddle of blood, her neck completely obliterated down to the bone. Next to me, Lyric's body lay prone, still covered in that ghastly hair.

Ivy sat further down, my sword at her feet, her eyes unblinking, staring out in front of her. She was blood-free, and I could just about make out the rise and fall of her chest, so I knew she was alive. She was in shock, just as I was. Her coat had claw marks, ripped into it. Further down still were another two bodies. One had a huge body covered in fur but with Kelis's face. Her body was charred beyond recognition, but clumps of fur still clung to it. The one furthest still was a wolf—a giant wolf. I looked around to see if it could have been any of my siblings, changed into a wolf. Castiel was the first that came to mind, but he was standing with his back to the tunnel wall, his head in his hands. Opposite me, Eliana was comforting Nyre, who was in her human form, naked and crying.

The rest of my brothers and sisters were alive, though I couldn't say any of them were well. Deon dry heaved as Fallon sat next to him, shaking his head. Eliana sobbed softly, as did Ivy. Gaia was the only one moving, doing something productive. I watched as she picked her way over Kelis's body to the wolf. She kicked it gingerly with her boot, but it didn't move. It couldn't move. It had a hole ripped right through its stomach, and half its guts were littering the tracks.

"Do you know this wolf, Castiel?" she asked softly.

Castiel nodded, then shook his head. "I wondered. All this time, I wondered."

"Wondered what?" Gaia asked, picking her way over to him.

"I don't know the wolf, but I think I know what happened here. I recognize the signs." His voice came out between agonized gulps. "This is the curse. Kelis and Lyric were changing. They had become like the feral wolves that turned my people into monsters. Unlike my friends, Kelis and Lyric weren't wolves, to begin with. Their bodies were partway through changing. That's why they look so strange." He glanced over at Kelis's body, then shook his head away quickly. "The curse made my friends into killing machines. They were hungry all the time, even after eating. They would eat anything—animals, people, their own children."

I thought back to how harsh I'd been with Lyric when she'd told me she was hungry earlier. She'd never been one to complain before. I should have known something was up. The curse had already begun to get its grip on her.

Castiel continued through husky breaths. “The curse had blighted the wolf shifter population in Aboria for many many moon cycles. It went away when I was born, but as you know, it came back. Everyone just thought it was a plague, a disease, but it wasn’t. It was a curse. Except no one ever knew who had cursed us. I’m guessing it was that fellow there.” He nodded toward the dead wolf. “Derillen must have figured out who was behind it and hired him like she hired everyone else.”

Another three dead for Derillen and another one dead for us. We were uneven again, with Derillen in the lead.

It was easy to figure out what had happened if what Castiel said was true. The wolf had come to kill us, to literally tear us apart. Instead of doing the dirty deed himself, he turned both Lyric and Kelis into monsters to do the dirty work for him. Ivy had found my sword and killed the wolf before lopping Lyric’s head off. Judging by the state of Kelis, Nyre or Gaia must have killed her by fire when she went for Fallon.

“We can’t stay here,” I decided, standing up.

“What about the bodies?” Deon asked, nodding toward Blaise, Kelis, and Lyric. “We should bury them.”

We should. Leaving them to rot would be despicable, but what if another horror was on its way to meet us? We needed to move. I needed to move, to get away from the harsh scent of charred flesh.

“We’ll come back and bury them when this is all over, but for now, we need to keep on our toes.”

No one argued as I picked up my blood-stained sword from Ivy’s feet and helped her up. She walked by my side, her hand in mine, away from the carnage with everyone else following behind silently.

24TH DECEMBER
AZIA

Jakon, Halia, Kelis, Blaise, Lyric. I recited their names in my head--one name for every footstep, repeated over and over again. I hadn'T killed Lyric, but I would have if Ivy hadn't found the sword before me. She was hungry, and I'd been her meal. I replayed how I'd spoken to her yesterday over and over in my mind, and my heart ached with it all. I'd apologized, sure, but it wasn't enough. She'd practically told me that she was coming under a curse, and I hadn't noticed. Oh, I knew what Deon would have said if I'd have told him my thoughts. He'd have said that there was no way that I could have known, that any of us could have known, and he was probably right. But I'd had enough of platitudes and clichés. Goddammit,

I should have known. She was my sister. I'd felt her magic in me as I felt those left behind. Why hadn't I felt the disease in her, in Kelis? It was no way for either of them to die. I gripped Ivy's hand hard, knowing how she must be feeling. She had killed Lyric to save me. Same with Nyre, who had used fire to save Fallon. I turned my head to see how my friend was, but she was nowhere in sight.

"Where's Nyre?" I asked, suddenly looking around the sea of desolate faces.

"She's here, with me." Fallon walked up from the back. He carried Nyre in his arms. Even in his big coat, she looked tiny compared to him. "She's fine. Asleep. I thought it kinder to carry her."

I nodded and gave him a sad smile. Maybe he did know about Nyre's crush on him after all. Maybe he was just being a nice person. There was love for her in his eyes when he looked down at her. It might not be the romantic love she wanted, but she was lucky to have him looking after her.

I turned back and continued to trudge onward. We'd all changed so much since we started out, Nyre, probably the most. The cute scrappy, ready-for-anything dragon was now just a child with no energy to continue. I knew exactly how she felt. We'd walked for hours, just as we had the day before. There was no night and no day down here, only darkness and green light. Misery was the only thing that drove me on. I was too tired for any other emotion. I should have been angry, vengeful, but I didn't have it in me anymore. I was as broken as Nyre was. The only difference being I was still putting one foot in front of the other... barely.

Every part of me hurt. My feet felt like lead weights, and my shoulder stung with every movement of my arm. The others had injuries too. I'd seen the blood. And I'd made them carry on. And they had followed me quietly.

"Stop," I said after a while.

Just hearing the word come from my mouth sent a shiver down my spine. We'd been fine yesterday until we stopped. Derillen knew we were down here. She'd somehow managed to plan this all along. I don't know how she knew, but yesterday's attack told me enough to reinforce the thought.

We sat in a circle close together. There was no food left, nor did we have any first aid kits. All our carefully packed things had been lost to us when we came through the portal to Urbis, and we'd somehow never managed to restock.

"I shouldn't have moved us on," I admitted. "Not without seeing the extent of our injuries. I'm sorry."

"I'm not hurt," Ivy whispered. Maybe not physically, but I could see the haunted look in her eyes.

"Me either," Gaia said, "Ivy saved my life."

"Nyre saved mine," Deon said. "I've got a couple of teeth marks in my leg, but nothing that won't heal."

"She saved mine too," Fallon added, looking down at the sleeping girl in his lap. She was still wrapped up in his coat, completely naked underneath. I opened my bag and pulled out a clean top and pants. When she woke up, she'd have to get dressed. I would help her. He stroked her hair, and she smiled in her sleep.

"I've got a few cuts and some bruises," Eliana murmured. "I'm fine."

I looked over to Castiel. He was the only one left to speak.

"Castiel?"

"I'm ok," He muttered, pulling his thick coat around

him. But he wasn't ok. How had I not noticed before? His face was ashen. His usually tanned skin was almost grey.

"Let me look." He pulled back as I stood up to walk over to him. As I got closer, I noticed a thin coating of sweat on his forehead and upper lip. He pulled back, not letting me near him.

"Ok, my ass!" I said, hand on hips. "Let me look, Castiel."

Slowly he peeled his coat back, flinching with the movement. Underneath it, blood soaked his t-shirt and had seeped through to the inner lining of his coat. I gingerly pulled his t-shirt up to find his entire stomach and chest a pulpy mess of claw marks and teeth marks.

"Castiel," I choked out in a whisper.

"I said I'm alright," he grunted, pulling away from me.

"Ivy, look in my bag. I have an extra shirt in there. Could you throw it to me?"

I ripped the shirt into lengths and tied it together to make bandages. It wasn't going to do much. He needed stitches at the very least, not to mention antibiotics, but it was all that I had. It would have to do. He gritted his teeth as I carefully wound the bandages around him. Blood poured from him, soaking through the flimsy bandages almost as soon as they touched him.

"We shouldn't have carried on," I said again quietly. Tears prickled at the corner of my eyes. "I'm sorry."

There was no way he was going to survive this. If we were in a hospital, maybe, but not underground miles from anywhere. I didn't even have any water to give him. I had nothing.

He grabbed my wrist and spoke quietly to me so the others couldn't hear. "We were right to carry on. We should always carry on. Promise me that when I die, you will go on. Staying around will only put you in more danger."

The guilt I felt at leaving my sisters' bodies pulled at my very soul, and now, he was asking me to do the same for him.

"You aren't going to die," I whispered back. "I won't let you."

He grunted. "You know you have no choice in the matter, right? You do have a choice about what you do after. Keep fighting, Azia. Promise me."

"But..."

"Promise me." Despite the pain he must be feeling, his gaze was firm. I nodded my head.

"I promise."

Almost as soon as I got the words out, the lights began to flicker again. My heart almost couldn't stand it. We were under attack again, and I didn't know by whom.

"Hold my hand," I instructed, grabbing Castiel's hand. With my free hand, I didn't go for my sword. Instead, I reached out for Ivy.

"Everyone stay together." I couldn't bear the thought of what happened last time when I didn't know where everyone was. We huddled closely, then turned so that we were all facing outward. Castiel remained in the center of the circle, as did Nyre.

Something small hit my face, almost knocking me over. I clawed at it as it attacked my face.

"Flying monkeys," Deon shouted out. "Jakon's witch is here."

Momba! The Wicked Witch of the West as he'd called her. I remembered her from the framed pictures on the government building's wall. She was difficult to miss with her green-tinged skin. I pulled the monkey from my face and slammed it to the ground, bringing my foot down hard on it. They were small and not very strong, but what they lacked in strength, they made up for in numbers. There were hundreds of them. No sooner had I killed one than another took its place. I swiped my sword ahead of me, killing them one by one as Gaia sent fireballs at them. Their high-pitched screeches filled the cavernous void in my brain so that it was all I could hear. Just like the flickering, green lights, they had been sent here to confuse us. My siblings could have all hot-footed it out of here, and I wouldn't have noticed, not that I thought they had. The noise and lights and Gaia's fire all contributed to the overload of my senses.

And they just kept coming and coming out of the darkness, lit up by the green light until we were plunged back into darkness again.

One flew at my face as I dealt with one biting my arm. Gaia flung her magic at it, and it spiraled through the air, a raging, screaming fireball.

Then, there she was. Tall, painfully thin with a hooked nose and a self-satisfied smirk on her face. She even wore a black pointed hat in case the flying monkeys and green skin didn□t get the point across that she was a witch. What a cliché.

The monkeys flew from behind her, still coming so that I could barely see her through the mass of wings and tails and monkey arms, legs, and teeth. I closed my eyes, ignoring the monkeys using my body as a chew toy, and walked toward her, pushing against the influx of monkeys.

"Azia," Ivy cried out as I left the outward-facing circle.

I don't think the witch expected it. She had enough faith in her monkeys to not have any other form of protection. I drove the sword into her heart and watched as she fell to the floor, surprise covering her face. The monkeys flew away. As soon as she was dead, she no longer had them in her spell. I watched as they flew en masse down the tunnel the way we had come. I wondered idly where they would go or if they would lose their wings now that the magic binding them no longer existed. But I found I didn't care as long as they were gone. The green light went back on, and I was faced with yet another bloody mess. This time, no one had been left unscathed. Everyone had scratches and small teeth marks all over them. Maybe not enough to kill them, but enough to scar them all for life.

"I guess I'm not going to be winning cutest royal for the sixth year in a row this year," Fallon quipped, his face a red pulpy mess of claw marks and teeth marks. He looked at the rest of us. "Although I might have a chance with the ugly lot of you as my competition."

His words were ridiculous, and yet, it broke the mood. We'd killed another one and survived the attack mostly unscathed. Castiel and Nyre were no worse than they had been before the monkeys attacked.

I laughed along with the others. None of us were happy. None of us had anything particularly to laugh about, and there was no way Fallon's joke was funny, but we needed the release. I wiped blood from my face on my sleeve, wincing as it passed over the cuts. Just like the others, I'd survived. At least, for now.

The lights began to flicker again, and my heart seized. Another one? I wasn't ready. None of us were ready. We'd only just gotten rid of the flying monkeys.

This time it was Cordel. She walked up to us slowly,

extending her hand to us. I could only watch as she sent out a bolt of magic, hitting all of us. Immediately my fingers started to tingle and then go numb. I knew this feeling. I'd had it before at the party.

"This is the blight!" I shouted out. "Deon. What do we do? You've dealt with this already."

"I don't know," Deon shouted back, his eyes locked on his greying hands in horror.

The blight crept up my arms quickly, and within seconds, it was at my shoulders. Once it touched my heart, I'd be dead. We'd all be dead, and at the rate it was spreading, it wouldn't take long.

"Not today, Bitch!" Castiel roared, jumping up from his position on the floor. He leapt toward her, turning into a tiger mid-air.

She didn't stand a chance. He knocked her to the floor and sank his giant teeth into her neck. Seconds later, it was all over. Cordel was dead. Just as they had at Derillen's party the previous week, my arms began to turn back to their normal color as the grey of the blight receded.

"You did it!" I shouted as the lights stopped flickering and once again became solid green. I ran to my brother and flung my arms around his big furry neck.

He didn't move. His eyes were closed. I ran my hand down the sleek striped coat on his back to feel movement, but there was none. My heart seized as I desperately felt inside myself for his strand of magic, but it wasn't there. Cordel's last act had been to kill Castiel. Castiel's last act had been to save us.

I collapsed on him, not caring that Cordel's body was beneath his. He'd given up his life to save us. Shifting into a tiger had taken everything he had left.

One more to Derillen. One more to us.

My body heaved with sobs. Castiel wasn't supposed to die. He was the strongest of us all. If I'd had been honest with myself, I'd have thought I'd go before him. If I could have had that choice, I would have taken it. He was so much better than me. He was the only one that never took my shit.

Someone, Deon, I think, pulled me softly away from Castiel's body.

"You want to bury him?" he asked as I sobbed into his shirt for the second time that day. The poor guy was a walking, talking handkerchief.

I thought back to the promise I'd made Castiel. It was the last words I'd spoken to him. "No. We must go on. I promised Castiel."

And so we did. I left another brother behind to rot away. Another sibling we didn't have time to mourn. Another shard of glass deep in my heart.

We'd not walked much farther when the green light became something else. My first thought was that there was another of Derillen's cronies here to attack, but this time the light was pure white.

Snow flittered down onto the tracks from above.

"A vent has had a partial cave-in," Deon said, looking up. "We can get out of here."

"Oh, sweet blessed dragons!" I mumbled beside him. The sound of singing filled the air, though the sky was black, telling me we had once again walked all day. Yet light shone down bright enough for me to see the fat flakes. Not natural light but the light from the street lamps and thousands of flickering candles. I went first, helped by Deon lifting me onto his shoulders. I found myself in an alley. The alley itself was dark and nothing to call home about, but the square it opened out onto was full of people singing. Each held a candle and what appeared to be a songbook.

I recognized the song too. It was a traditional Winter Festival carol. I hurried over to some of the people at the back. "What day is this?"

A woman turned. She blanched when she saw me. Not that I could blame her. I was a mess of blood. My clothes were ripped and dirty, and it had been so long since I'd had a shower, I didn't even want to think about what I smelled like.

"I asked what day it was," I repeated.

The woman held her nose in the air and ushered the two young children by her side away from me.

"It's just gone midnight," a kindly man said, nodding at a clock tower at the other side of the square. "It's Winter Festival Day."

He passed me a candle and lit it, using his own. "Happy Winter Fest."

My brothers and sisters crowded around me. Someone handed them each a candle, and we stood with hundreds of other people singing songs we'd all grown up with. Anyone else might think it was strange, us deciding to stop and sing in the middle of the war of our lives, but my soul needed it. We all needed it. I sang for Castiel, for Lyric and Blaise and Kelis, for all of my brothers and sisters who were no longer here to sing for themselves. For an hour, I forgot the horrors we'd left behind and the horrors that I knew were about to come.

25TH DECEMBER
AZIA

The sound of so many people singing reminded me of Halia. She would have loved this. She would have made her way to the stage and strummed her guitar, and everything in the world would have been at peace. But she wasn't here, and the beautiful melodies filling the night only masked the unrelenting fear and misery I felt.

Those of us left sang because what else was there to do? We had nowhere left to hide. Derillen knew where we were. It was only a matter of time before she came for us or sent another one of her henchmen or henchwomen to get us. This might be our last night of living. Might as well enjoy it.

The sound of clanging interrupted the song. At first,

like most other people, I thought it was part of the music, a new percussion, but it got louder, nearer. At the other side of the square, people began to move toward us, causing a surge. We pulled back into the alley as the song quickly turned into the sound of screams.

"What now?" I murmured.

"I know what this is," Ivy replied to me, her mouth set in a grim line. "That sound has haunted my dreams for too long not to know what it is. Queenie Heart's Army."

"The giant metallic blood-crazed robots?" I knew we'd have to face them at some point, but I wasn't ready. From what Ivy had told me about them, they were a force to be reckoned with. And unlike people made of flesh and bone, they were impervious to swords, arrows, and most magic.

Ivy gritted her teeth. "This is my time to shine. I've spent way too long watching the rest of you use your magic. This is where I come in!"

I had no idea what she planned to do, but instead of running through the crowd to get to the giant hulking beasts, she took off in the opposite direction. I watched her frizzy blond hair above the crowd as she ran along the street to a parade of shops. From where we were in the alley, I watched her as she slammed her elbow into the first shop window and managed to stick her arm through to open the door to the inside.

"What is she doing?" Deon murmured in my ear.

I shrugged. The shop sold fine jewelry. "Maybe she wants to die in style?"

She came out of the shop, her pockets bulging, then proceeded to do the same with a bicycle shop next door. Five shops she went in, and each time, she came out loaded with more items, which she threw on an old abandoned cart. People were still running past, desperate to be away from Queenie's metallic henchmen. I could see them now, spilling out into the other side of the square, trampling people who hadn't gotten away fast enough.

Eventually, Ivy came to a stop at a hat store. When she didn't come out, I beckoned the others across the street to see what she was up to.

We found her surrounded with what looked like junk. It was a mess of cogs and wheels and bits of machines that I had no idea of what they could be used for. In the middle of the junk, she'd already begun to work on a bike she'd picked up. Her hands moved so quickly, she was a blur of motion.

The shop had elegant hats on busts, though one of them had found its way onto Ivy's head.

"What's going on?" I asked, amazed at the array of junk around her.

"I've found an old steam bike," she explained, stopping for a second. "How long before the Hearts get here?"

Hearts. That's what she called them. It was altogether too nice of a name for the huge killing machines.

"About ten minutes at the speed they are going," Deon called back from the open doorway.

"What are you doing with the steam bike? And all this other stuff?"

"I'm making something," she replied cryptically. "All this stuff, I need. Can one of you go out into the back alley and see if you can find some old pipe or some tubing? I also need a tank of some kind."

I looked at her in baffled amazement as she once again began working in a flurry of activity. Her hands moved so quickly I could barely see them.

"A tank?"

She nodded. "Doesn't have to be a tank. Anything that will hold lots of snow."

"On it!" Gaia called out.

"Put whatever you find on that," she said, pointing to the old cart she'd brought into the shop.

Gaia headed out of a back door with the cart, helped by Eliana.

Fallon ducked out of the front door of the shop with Nyre hot on his heels.

"What are the hats for?" I mused aloud. The rest of the stuff I could understand, but I couldn't think of why she'd need to be in a hat shop.

She stopped for a moment. "For my head," she explained with a wink. "Actually, I do need them for something. When Gaia and Eliana find a tank, I need it filled with snow. Can you and Deon grab a hat each and use them to collect snow? The more, the better."

I didn't question her. The girl knew what she was doing. Instead, I grabbed a hat like she'd asked and headed outside.

Gaia and Eliana were in the back yard of the shop. The small rectangle of cobbled stone had a wall around it with a gate leading to an alley running the length of the shops and out into the square.

"We couldn't find a tank, but we did find a water barrel and a garbage can," Gaia explained over the sound of screams and the ever-approaching footsteps of the Hearts.

Both receptacles sat on the old cart tied together with a bit of old rope. Eliana carried a massive length of pipe back into the shop as I handed Gaia a hat and told her to look for snow.

The snow on the main road out front had been

trampled to mush by the onslaught of people racing away from the Hearts, so we set about scooping up what we could from the back alley. My fingers were stiff from the cold, and the thunk, thunk, thunk of the Hearts got ever louder as we worked together to fill the two containers with snow. I couldn't wrap my mind around why Ivy would need snow, but I needed to trust her. In the whole time I'd known her, she'd desperately wanted to help and had always felt that she wasn't as good as the rest of us. Or that her powers were somehow less than ours. She needed this.

A steaming mince pie was thrust into my hands. I looked up from my task to see both Fallon and Nyre with armfuls of the sweet snack.

"We found a bakery," Fallon said, passing the pies around. "This is all they had."

I swallowed the small pie almost whole, devouring the sweet taste with a hint of alcohol. Nyre passed me another, and I ate that one too. I'd not realized just how hungry I was, and the small bite-sized pies tasted out of this world after so long without food.

"They are nearly here," Deon yelled from the gate to the alley, though he didn't need to. I could hear them. Like a relentless heartbeat, they marched in unison, controlled by the Queen of Hearts herself. With each step that thundered through the air, my nerves increased. Ivy had fought them before, but that was when a whole city had risen up against them. Now, there was only us and whatever it was that Ivy was building. Six people and one dragon shifter. And how many of them? Too many to count. We were still hopelessly outnumbered. And though Ivy, Gaia, and the people of The Forge had won the battle last time, we were the ones fighting the war. And there were a lot fewer of us.

My heart thumped loudly with every step of the Heart's feet. And as the footsteps got louder, the anticipation in the yard rose. The six of us kept on doing what Ivy had asked, ducking out into the alley to find whatever clumps of snow we could until both containers were filled to the brim.

Then Deon yelled two words that almost brought the pounding of my heart to a standstill.

"They're here."

"Just in time," Ivy said, her lips pulled into a determined line. She pushed a steam-bike out through the back door and hooked it up to the cart before pushing a tube into the water barrel. Another trailed along the ground as she pushed the whole thing out through the gate into the back alley.

The Hearts were almost upon us as she drew the bike up to the side of the row of shops.

"Stay back," she warned as she kicked the bike into gear. A puff of black smoke engulfed her, then dissipated in the air. I had no idea what she was up to, but whatever it was, she had determination written all over her face.

She jumped off the bike and put the other hose in the garbage can full of snow along with a bottle of something she emptied into it. The other ends of the pipes ended at the front of the bike, where they pointed upward and slightly forward-facing.

We were surrounded. Up close, the Hearts were more intimidating than I'd realized with their massive height and width. It was like being attacked by a wall.

"Take that!" Ivy yelled as she pressed a button on the bike. It roared for a second, followed by a chugging sound.

"What's happening?" Eliana whispered, grabbing

my hand.

It soon became apparent what Ivy had built. The steam bike was heating the snow, melting it, and sending it out through the tubes to the cards.

My excitement at seeing Ivy's invention working soon turned to horror. She'd miscalculated. Instead of jets of water pulsing into the Hearts to knock them over, the water was falling like a deluge of rain above them.

And still, they came forward, blocking us from going anywhere. We backed up to the end of the parade of shops until there was nowhere left for us to go. There was no way we could fight them. They were too big, and there were too many. They were twenty feet away from us. Ivy's invention wasn't stopping them at all. Still, they moved forward as the water cascaded down upon the tops of them. Fifteen feet, ten feet.

I held my sword out in front of me, though I knew it was pointless. It wouldn't slice through metal, and even if it did, taking down just one of the giant metallic playing cards wouldn't help us. There was a whole army of them, all intent on killing us. Programmed to do so by the Queen of Hearts.

I increased the grip on my sword. If I was going to go down, I was going to go down fighting.

Five feet now, three feet, two... and there was nowhere to go. One of the hearts reached out to me with a mechanical arm. I had no chance. It grabbed a handful of my coat and lifted me from the ground, pushing me into the wall behind me.

My lungs struggled to fill with air as I looked down on the robot that was going to take my life. It didn't have a face, as such, though it had arms and legs. It was nothing more than a rectangle of metal with robotics inside it. A red light on the top blinked.

Then a small wisp of smoke emanated from the top of the rectangle, and the red light went out with a pfzzt.

Its grip on me loosened, and I fell to the ground as its arm fell.

"What's going on?" Eliana shrieked as another made a slow whining sound and came to a stop.

I opened my mouth in surprised realization. Ivy wasn't trying to knock the Hearts over at all. That had never been her plan. She was effectively killing them by getting water into their mechanical parts. With all the technology they had inside of them, they weren't waterproof. One by one, they came to a stop as the horrid screech of soaked mechanical parts filled the air along with a number of whirrs and bangs.

When they'd all come to a stop, and the last one had burnt out, Ivy jumped down from her steam bike and untied the now empty water containers from the cart. She pushed them both off.

"Come on," she yelled to us as she hopped back up onto her bike. "We have a war to win."

The others hopped onto the cart as I jumped up behind her and wrapped my arms around her middle.

She wove slowly through the Hearts until we got through the last of them and rode through the square.

"Why would the Queen not make them waterproof?" I wondered aloud as we left the broken metallic beasts behind.

"They probably were waterproof, but I added something in the water that I knew would get through."

"Oh?" I asked, flummoxed.

"I found some fast-acting corrosive in the bicycle shop. It was heavily diluted in the snow, but I only needed to get through the thin layer of metal on the top. The Queen of Hearts would have needed to make it thin enough to receive her signal so she could control them. Once the corrosive ate through, the Heart was done. You might not have seen, but the metal garbage pail was a mess of holes from the stuff."

I marveled at her. I would never have thought of something like that in a million years.

The square was now empty, though the bodies of those that had been trampled still lay on the ground along with discarded candles and songbooks.

"To the government building?" she asked.

I nodded. There was nothing we could do about the dead here. We'd defeated The Queen of Hearts' army, but we hadn't defeated her, and there was still a long way to go.

We'd not even made it out of the square when a man on a carpet flew into it. He was tall with gold and purple robes and a golden hat on his head. His pointed chin ended in a long goatee, and his eyes were kohl-rimmed. He was an imposing character if ever I saw one.

"The sorcerer!" hissed Gaia. "And he has my flying carpet!"

He sent a ball of fire our way. Gaia blocked it with one of her own, but the heat of so much fire singed my hair.

"Run!" I yelled, jumping off the back of the bike. A few seconds later, a fireball hit the bike, sending it up in an explosion of fire. Deon ran past me as fireballs filled the square. The stench of burning flesh overwhelmed me, and thick smoke clogged my lungs, causing me to stop to throw up. Someone, I didn't see who it was, grabbed my hand. I let them pull me through the chaos. The air around me was black, punctuated with flashes of red and orange. My eyes burned from the acrid smoke, and I couldn't see anything through the tears that stung my eyes.

We came to a stop near the back of the square where we'd first emerged from the disused subway.

Everything in me wanted to fight, but without being able to see, fighting was impossible. Gaia had this. I could just make out her screaming voice through the noise.

I huddled back against a building with Deon, who was the one who'd taken my hand. Seconds later, Eliana joined us, her face black with soot and tear tracks down her face.

"It's not just the sorcerer," she muttered between coughs. "Lyric's pirates are in there too. I caught sight of the one with a hook for a hand, but there are more."

I drew out my sword. Fireballs I couldn't fight, but pirates with swords. That's what I'd spent all my time training for. I drew out my sword and made to run into the melee, but before I could, I was scooped up and sent hurtling through the air. I crashed to the ground, which was much further down than I remembered. Suddenly everything was quiet.

A small glow appeared, showing me that I was back down in the subway.

Gaia held the glow in her hand. It illuminated her face that was equally as dirty as Eliana's and most probably mine too.

"I killed him." She spoke quietly and deliberately. "I think I got the pirates too. I didn't know what to do, so I called the flying carpet and brought us all back down here. I thought it was the safest course of action until we figure out what to do next."

I looked around me. "Where's Ivy?" It was then that I realized that the tears streaking Gaia's face were not from the smoke. They were emotion-filled tears.

"She never made it off the bike."

The words sounded hollow and empty, just like my heart did. Up until that point, I'd felt courage and hope. The thought that we'd beat Derillen had never wavered in me. I'd known it as sure as I'd known my own name, but the horror of the past few days finally caught up with me. There were five of us left, six including Nyre. In the space of days, we'd gone from a thirteen-strong team to six. Twelve demi-gods. We had all the strength in the world, and yet, we were being cut down like we were nothing. Nearly nineteen years had passed since we saved the world the first time—nineteen years since twelve babies had been born and unwittingly banished evil from the world. But evil had returned, and it had gotten its revenge.

"Where's Nyre?" I screamed. Circling around. Not Nyre too. I couldn't bear it. A small voice came from above me.

"I'm here."

She dangled her legs over the hole.

"Thank all the gods, you are alright," I whispered, holding my hand up to her, but she wouldn't come down. "Nyre, come on, I've got you. It's not much of a fall."

But she wouldn't budge. All I could see of her now were her legs from the knees down, but I could hear her sobs. They cut through me like a knife—screaming agony. She'd not cried like this for the others. She'd done the opposite—gone quiet, but now, her pitiful screams rent the air.

I climbed up through the hole to grab her, and it was then that I saw what had made her cry. Fallon's head lay in her lap, his eyes closed. Blood pooled around his body.

"He saved my life," she moaned, rocking forward and backward as the tears ran tracks down her dirty cheeks. "One of the pirates," she added.

"He's gone, Nyre," I said as delicately as I could after feeling for a pulse in his neck and not finding one.

It took all of us to encourage her to come back down into the subway. She didn't want to leave him, and I couldn't blame her. The light in her eyes had finally gone out. She clung to his coat as she finally let go of him and joined us in the subway.

"How did we win the first time around?" I sobbed. "We were babies, and we beat these people. We didn't even know what we were doing. We didn't know anything. So how is it that they are finding it so easy to kill us now?"

I sank to the floor and let the grief wash over me. Deon wrapped his arms around me and pulled both Nyre and me into a hug.

"We didn't win last time. We postponed the fight, that's all."

"And it hasn't been so easy to kill us," Gaia added, joining in the hug along with Eliana. "Two more of their side are dead. I've fought the sorcerer before and not managed to hurt him. This time, I knew I could. I took Ivy's strength and used it. She didn't die in vain, Azia. Neither did Fallon. They died so that we could carry on."

I wanted to believe it, but how could I? They'd died. They'd died because some evil sorcerer and some pirates with a grudge had wanted them dead. It was that simple. It didn't matter that the sorcerer and pirates were also dead now.

I couldn't say how long we sat there in the dark. Time had no meaning anymore. I'd not slept in what felt like forever, and I couldn't even remember the last meal we'd eaten apart from the mince pies Fallon had stolen for us. A small part of my brain reminded me that the playing field had once again evened out. Five of us left to five of them. Ivy had killed Queenie Heart's robotic playing cards, but she hadn't killed Queenie herself. She was still out there along with Edwin, Kelis's step-grandmother, Halia's old landlady and boss, and of course, Derillen. It all came back to Derillen. It didn't surprise me in the slightest that we'd not seen her yet on this trail of destruction. But she was here. The walls of the subway had begun to glow green again. That was all her. I figured the sorcerer and Hook were where they were to drive us back into the subway system. She'd planned it this way, and I knew exactly where we'd end up if we followed the tunnel. She was leading us to her, thinning us out as she did. This had always been about me and her. Everyone else was nothing more than pawns in her deadly game. She never cared for the people she recruited. They were just a way to get her what she wanted—and what she wanted was me.

I stood up and wiped the tears from my face with the back of my sleeve. I was going to give Derillen exactly what she wanted, but I was going to do it on my own terms.

"Where are you going?" Gaia asked as I began to climb back outside.

"Walking to Inner Urbis will take us forever. We have no food. We've not slept in forever. I'm getting something that will make our journey a lot faster."

The smoke had cleared considerably by the time I got to the square. I ignored the charred bodies and what was left of the steam bike and hurried to the parade of shops where Ivy had found her bits and pieces for her invention. She'd made the snow thrower herself, but the base of it had been a steam bike, and if she'd found one, there was bound to be another. I found what I needed in the bicycle shop. There were two left, two steam-bikes, inventions from The Forge. I took one and jumped on the back, turning the key in the ignition and letting it growl into life. At the entrance to the subway, Eliana and Deon lowered it down as I went back for the other.

"Gaia, you take this one, I said, passing her a bike. Deon, Eliana, you take the other."

Deon stared at me as though I was crazy. "What about you?"

I glanced over at Nyre. "I'm going by dragon."

Nyre had lost a lot of what was essentially "her" since Fallon's death. Her eyes perked up when I mentioned the pair of us flying.

"No carrying me in your talons," I said as she bounded over. "You're big enough now to carry me on your back."

She nodded solemnly and let me jump up on her. And then we were gone in a blink of an eye to the sound of two bikes and one dragon's growls.

We rode and flew for hours along the weird, green-lit passageway. Lack of food and sleep were taking their toll on all of us, but the determination to get to Derillen never wavered. I'd had my moment of self-pity. Now I only felt anger coursing through my veins and a determination to kill the woman who had killed my siblings. Even at the speed we were going, it would still take us a week or more to get to Inner Urbis. At some point, we would have to stop for food and rest, but sheer adrenaline kept me going. Nyre always had more stamina than me. It came with being a dragon, but I could see the fire in her eyes. She felt the same way I did. The others, too, all of us bolstered by the thoughts of defeating the greatest evil ever known.

The mental image of plunging my sword right through Derillen's heart took up my concentration, so when we saw the giant mirror filling the subway in front of us, it was already too late. Deon, Eliana, and Gaia zoomed through it first, followed a second later by Nyre and me. I waited for the glass to crash down on us, but the crash never came. The tunnel, however, changed. Gaia skidded her steam bike to a stop, and Nyre flew us both to the ground.

"What was that? Another portal?" The mirror was still there, blocking the tunnel, filling it entirely. Another one blocked us from going further. Everywhere I looked, I could see us—five exhausted, filthy beings. I hardly recognized myself in my own reflection.

"It's a portal, alright, but there's something weird about it," Gaia replied, walking up to the mirrored surface. She put her finger to it, and the smooth mirror began to ripple. Quickly, she pulled back. "It's swimming in magic."

It was plain to see that we'd traveled a lot farther than we should have. The tunnel, which before had had roughly hewn walls, now had smart off-white tiles covering the surface.

"We're in Inner Urbis!" Eliana exclaimed, pointing to a mosaic sign, almost hidden under the years of dirt and grime. The sign bore the name of one of the Inner Urbis train stations. One we'd passed through days before. "I guess they planned to open up the subway to the main stations. It must be right above us."

As if on cue, a rumbling filled the tunnel, and the ground beneath our feet began to shake. "A train?" I asked. We all waited with bated breath, waiting for the rumbling to end. Eventually, it did. I let out a long breath. "We should be at the government building in a couple of hours if we really are directly under the train station on the sign." I made to walk through the mirror blocking our way, but Gaia stopped me.

"What are you doing?"

"I'm going to the government building. What do you think I'm doing?"

Gaia shook her head. "It's a trap. Can't you see that?"

I shrugged, not really caring anymore. "The mirror we just came through helped us. It brought us closer to where we need to be. Maybe walking through the second one will get us right there."

"And what if it doesn't?" Gaia challenged.

"Well then, we're screwed because the way I see it, we have to go through one or the other of these mirrors. The stairs to the train station above us haven't been built yet, and in case you haven't noticed, there's no other way out."

I was snappy and irritated. I could see that Gaia had a point, but going backward wasn't an option.

Suddenly, a face appeared in both mirrors. A huge disembodied face, looking down at us from both sides with a look of bemusement. "Goodness me, the lot of you really are as stupid as Kelis. And, though I hate to say it, you've got even worse dress sense. Ugly and gross is so last season."

Filled with anger, I drew my sword and slashed out at the head. My sword cut through the mirror like butter but did no damage at all. What was the point of a mirror if it was impossible to smash it? I'd have taken seven years' bad luck, just to shut the guy up.

Gaia stepped forward. "Kelis's step-grandmother's

mirror, I assume?"

"Not as stupid as you look after all. Shame you look like you've been dragged through a hedge backward."

"I assume you are here for a reason and not just to insult us?" I growled.

It pouted. "You're no fun, but yes. I'm here for a reason. I have a game for you."

"Great," I huffed under my breath. "The future of all the kingdoms hangs in the balance, and your master wants to play games."

The thing pulled its face into a frown. "I don't know who you think my master is, but I assure you I don't have one."

"Kelis's grandmother!" I cried out in exasperation.

"Oh, darling. Do you ever have it wrong! That old bat died long ago. She had an ego the size of a planet. Always 'who is the prettiest of them all?' I have to say, it was a glorious day when I could inform her that her stepdaughter, Snow White, was prettier than her. She didn't like it."

"She's dead?"

I'd been waiting to face up to her. The way Kelis had said it, she was a powerful witch that had tried to kill her mother a long time ago.

"Yes. So long ago, alas. She went to her grave, knowing that she wasn't as beautiful as she thought she was." He twisted his face into an evil grin.

I thought back to Kelis's story. "But someone brought apples to Snow White. Kelis told me. It was why she ended up falling asleep."

The mirror rolled its eyes. "Goodness me. Id' have thought you'd have figured out who did that by now. Isn't it obvious considering your own wretched history?"

"Derillen!" I'd counted her as a separate person, but

it was she who had helped Morpheus take Snow White into his realm. I should have figured it out.

"Bingo!"

"So that means there are only four of them left. We outnumber them again!"

The mirror pulled its face into a frown. "I don't think so. Aren't you forgetting someone? I might not be a witch, but give me some credit."

"You are a mirror," I shot back. "What can you do?"

It began to laugh. A high-pitched laugh that sent a chill right through me.

"Have you already forgotten our game? Oh, you are so going to love it."

I sucked in a deep breath and gritted my teeth. "I don't have time for games."

"Nevertheless, I have one, and you're going to play it. The only way out is through one of my mirrors. You can go forward or back if you prefer. If you go alone, you will die. If you go hand in hand with someone, only one of you will die, the other will survive. If you go in a foursome, two of you will die, and if you go in a five or a three...well, anything could happen."

I stared at it in shock as it grinned maniacally.

Anger coursed through me. "You were the one who set up the portals throughout the kingdoms."

"Ah, I wish I could take credit, but that wasn't me. It was Rumpelstiltskin. It was my idea, though. A very good one, I thought."

"What if we stay here?" Eliana asked, putting her hand on my arm as though I was going to combust on the spot without her sense of calmness to hold me back.

"I can survive forever without food and water," it grinned. "How long do you think you can last?"

I sat on the ground and closed my eyes, trying to figure a way out of this. My sword had not harmed it at all. "Gaia. Throw fire at it."

She produced a fireball and aimed at it the thing's smug face. It passed through the mirror harmlessly.

Deon tried next. Coaxing weeds up from the ground, he attempted to cover the mirror, but there was nothing to grip. The mirrors were not made of glass; they were made of magic. Nothing Eliana or I could do would help.

"There's only one option as far as I can see," Gaia began. "Two of us will go through. The one that survives gets help."

I shook my head. "That way, someone dies."

"Every way I look at it, someone dies. This way, only one of us does."

"No!" I cried out. They were ahead of us at every step. I turned to the mirror that was still watching us. "Why not kill all of us and get it over and done with?"

It chuckled. "Oh, but where's the fun in that? I had thought about letting you all starve to death in here, but I figured letting you decide who gets to die would be more fun."

"And how do you decide which one lives and which one dies if two go through together?"

It winked at me, actually winked. "It's completely random. Who knows who shall live and who shall die?"

I balled my hand into a fist and rammed it down into the dirt between the tracks, stifling a scream as I did.

Gaia was wrong. Going through with two people wouldn't work. There was no help waiting on the other side. We had to sacrifice two or even three of us to give us the best chance.

"We're all going to die," I finally said, my voice low. "We never had a hope of getting out of this alive. All the way through, I've been harboring this ridiculous notion that we could beat them. With each of them that died, I took it as a personal win. When Ivy and Fallon died this morning, I realized that we can't. That fire, or whatever it was inside me that kept me going, went out. But then, I changed my mind. There were five of us left. Five of us and five of them. We were evenly matched, weren't we?" I shook my head. "But we aren't evenly matched. They know where we are. They know our limitations. They've known about us from the start. We can't win this."

Eliana brought her hand up to my shoulder. "You don't know what you're saying."

I looked her dead in the eyes. "I know exactly what I'm saying. We can't win, but we can take down as many of them as we can before we lose. Hopefully, someone, sometime in the near future, will take up our fight and when they do, let's give them as few of them to deal with as possible. I'm willing to give up my life to help bring this to a close. I'm going to die anyway. Even if I survive the mirror, there'll be another of them waiting to kill me. Who else is willing to come with me?"

The five of us sat in a circle. Five dirt-streaked faces that had seen more pain than anyone should have to in a lifetime. My mother was still trapped in Morpheus's world. Fae was still with Derillen. There were so many things we hadn't accomplished yet.

Gaia nodded her head and held her hand out to the center.

"Me too." Nyre's hand joined Gaia's. Every part of her body was filthy. She was done. We all were. Silently Deon joined them. All eyes were on Eliana. Going through the mirror meant that there was every chance she'd never see her daughter again. It meant Fae would grow up in Derillen's care.

“Please promise me that you’ll save her,” she choked out. “I don’t care about myself. Just save her.”

I brought my arms around her as she sobbed loudly into my coat. “If it’s the last thing I do, and if I survive the mirror, I’ll save your daughter. I’ll take her back to The Vale and to your parents.”

She nodded and grasped my hand. Together, we added our hands to those in the center of our circle.

We lined up next to each other, hand in hand, fingers entwined. Nyre was to my left, wearing my coat that I’d just passed to her. Gaia took my hand to my right. Next to her, Eliana grasped her fingers, and Deon took the end. Together we took a step forward and walked through the mirror.

26TH DECEMBER
AZIA

As I walked through, Nyre's hand tightened its grasp on mine, but Gaia's hand disappeared in my own. One minute she was there, and then she wasn't. There was no agonizing death. She just ceased to exist. I already knew she was gone, but my heart held hope that Deon and Eliana had made it through. When I turned my head to the side and saw that they weren't there either, my heart ripped into a thousand pieces.

Dying wasn't the worst part of this; surviving was. The grief was insurmountable. I'd known that the mirror would take at least two, but I'd held onto the hope he'd stop at two. Why was it I kept doing this to myself? Hoping that something good would happen when all the evidence suggested it wouldn't.

I couldn't breathe with the force of it. My entire body was wracked with pain. I was the only one left. Out of twelve siblings, I was the only one remaining. Nyre stalked past me. I looked up when I heard the smashing of glass.

The mirror, the real one that had been placed on the tiled wall of the subway, now littered the ground, shards of glass twinkling in the eerie green light. The two mirrors behind us vanished, leaving nothing but the long tunnel disappearing into the darkness behind us. Deon, Gaia, and Eliana were gone. No bodies. Nothing.

I was numb with grief. So numb that I couldn't even muster up any sadness for them. For Deon, who had been my voice of reason this whole journey. For Gaia, who was the cleverest of all of us. And for Eliana, who'd come all this way to find her daughter and fallen at the final hurdle. It should have broken my heart, but my heart was already destroyed beyond salvation. All that was left was Derillen. Sure she had a few more of her people for me to get through, but they were dispensable to her. Putting the mirror up on the inside of the subway tracks was enough to show me that she never cared for all these people she sent out to fight us. There were three of them left. Three people, I'd expected to meet before I came face to face with Derillen—Edwin, Queenie Heart, and Halia's old boss, Madam Fontaine. As far as I knew, of those, Edwin was the only one who had magic. Queenie's magic was in her way with words and her way with machines. Without her army, she was nothing. The question was, without my siblings, was I nothing too?

With Nyre at my side, we walked. One foot in front of the other. There was nothing left for us to do. It was either walk or give up, and somewhere in our souls, we were not ready to do that yet. I held her hand. It was so small. She was not much younger than I, but I felt responsible for her. In her human form, she appeared even younger than when she was a dragon. I didn't even tell her to get dressed. I had no clothes left to give her anyway. She walked, naked apart from Fallon's coat, filthy, cold, and hungry, but mostly, bravely. She'd seen more in her short life than most people did in their lifetimes.

Neither of us was surprised when Queenie Heart appeared in front of us. Nyre ran right to her and jumped at her. Maybe it was the shock of having this tiny, almost naked, person jumping on her, but she fell to the ground. Nyre pummelled her with her small fists. She was like a wild animal gone insane as she rained down blow after blow on Queenie's face. The queen's face was already pulp by the time I was able to deliver the final blow with my sword. A small box fell from her hand—a remote control of some kind. Whatever it was she was planning to hit us with, she'd not accounted for Nyre's speed. I brought my foot down on the box hard. It sputtered, and the small light on it died.

And now, there were three—two to go before Derillen.

It didn't take long before the green light illuminating our way began to flicker again. I didn't have the energy to feel fear. Death didn't scare me anymore. Nyre stopped and tugged on my hand. "Edwin or Fontaine," I croaked. It didn't matter which one.

"It's Derillen!" she whispered back.

For the first time in hours, I felt something. Grief had rendered me numb, but seeing Derillen in front of me, the rage that had been building in me for months came back with a vengeance

"Derilllen!"

"Azia, how nice to finally meet you." She stood about thirty feet ahead of me. Just her. No magic, no army at her back. She'd thinned the herd. Now, I was hers for the taking. She wore her black dress and purple robe, a headdress on her head fashioned into horns. Evil practically radiated from her.

Nyre screeched loudly and ran toward her in much the same way she had done with Queenie. Unlike Queenie, Derillen was ready for the attack. She was also magic.

It only took a wave of a hand to send Nyre skidding into the tunnel wall. Her head struck the wall with a sickening bang, and she crumpled to the ground.

I ran to her. She was still breathing, still alive but unresponsive.

"Why?" I screeched out, leveling my gaze on Derillen. "I'm here. You could kill me without breaking a sweat. You didn't need to hurt Nyre."

She narrowed her eyes. "I find it strange that you are under the illusion that I care about your filthy friends. I would have thought, going by my previous actions, you'd have realized that I don't. It's almost depressing what an unworthy opponent you've been. Sure, you can fight. I'm sure that were I to let you charge me with that sword of yours, you'd beat me hands down, but you should know by now that I'm not going to do that. However much of an anti-climax this is going to be for me, I think I'll get this over and done with quickly."

She held fire in her hand—green fire made of magic. Pulling her hand back, she threw it right at me. I dodged and watched it fly past me harmlessly.

"Oh, so you want to play?" she teased, throwing another fireball my way. This time, I hit it back at her using the flat part of my sword. It missed her by a few feet, but the smug look fell from her face.

Maybe I was a worthy opponent, after all.

“Don’t underestimate me, Derillen. You’ve taken everything away from me that I care about. I have nothing to lose. That puts you in a dangerous position.”

“Is that so?” She grinned back, sending another fireball my way. I batted that one back to her, too, taking a step forward. She began to throw them at me, thick and fast. Each one, I sent spiraling back to her. I might not be fighting a human with a sword, but I was quick and precise. Derillen had to duck more than once. With each of her spells I batted out of the way, I took a step closer to her.

When I was five feet from her, she finally stopped. A spell from her at this range would either kill her or kill me.

The tunnel fell silent as we glared at each other, neither of us speaking.

There was so much hatred between us, but only one could survive. I held my sword out in front of me and screamed as I ran forward. There was a flash of green, and then everything went black. All I could hear as I fell to the ground was the sound of my scream echoing back to me.

And then I couldn’t hear that anymore.

The war was over. Derillen had won. I was dead.

27TH DECEMBER
AZIA

A feeling of euphoria filled me, and for a second, there was nothing but serenity, peacefulness, and an all-encompassing feeling of wellbeing.

Then the light came. It pierced the darkness, filling me with light, and that, in itself, was beautiful. Or it was in the brief moments until my memories came back. They came crashing in on me in a deluge of grief.

"I guess I owe you ten dollars," Fallon quipped, bringing me to my senses.

I opened my eyes, blinking a few times for the picture in front of mc to clcar.

"Hey, Boss," Lyric said, grinning at me from ear to ear. Her head was back on her shoulders without a mark to show where it had been lopped off.

I closed my eyes and shook my head, then opened them again.

"Aren't you supposed to be dead?" I asked, rather stupidly. I looked beyond where Lyric was gazing at me to find my brothers and sisters. All of them. Plus some other people I didn't know. All in a white room that went on forever with no walls or ceiling. Just whiteness and light.

"Aren't all of you supposed to be dead?"

Fallon pulled his pockets out to show that they were empty.

"Don't be silly, Fallon, darling," said a stunningly beautiful woman with long, flowing, black hair. "There's no money here. You'll have to pay your brother back another time."

Fallon nodded and high fived Castiel.

"Does anyone want to tell me what's going on?" I asked, pulling myself into a sitting position from the floor where I'd been lying.

"I bet Castiel that you'd make it to the end and kill that bitch," Fallon announced. "Castiel thought that you wouldn't be able to without us there. It seems that he was right. I owe him ten dollars."

I tried to take everything in. The white surroundings, the people, my dead brothers and sisters who were quite plainly alright. "But you can't pay him yet because...we are dead?"

"That's right, sis," Fallon said. "But I'm sure he'll remember and ask for it later."

"Later?" I asked, still confused. "We're in heaven, right?"

The afterlife, any afterlife was not something I'd ever believed in. I'd not been brought up with religion, so finding out I was a demi-god had been a shock enough in itself. Ever since I'd found out my heritage, I'd wondered if there was something after, someplace we all went when we die, but my actual life was too busy for me to contemplate it much. Yet here I was with my family. It felt weird, and I wasn't sure how to feel.

The woman that had spoken to Fallon before moved forward.

There was something so serene about her, so perfect. She lowered herself down to my level and took my hand.

I knew instinctively who this was without her having to tell me.

Her touch filled me with hope and happiness and joy, and all the emotions I'd not felt for a very long time. I tried to remain stoic. This woman had given me away as a very young child after all, but I felt my bottom lip begin to wobble. Every emotion I'd ever felt came crashing out of me, and I gave in to it, feeling the tears pouring down my face. I'd finally found her. My mother. I expected her to draw me into a hug, although I wasn't sure I could bear it. She didn't. Instead, she squeezed my hand and let me cry.

"Azia. I'm so proud of you. So, so proud. I've been told by your brothers and sisters what you have been through. I know how hard your fight has been."

My heart felt like it was being pulled through a wringer. I'd lost the ability to speak, so I could only nod through my tears.

"This is not heaven. That is not a place I have ventured, nor will I ever. You, my darling daughter, will also never see heaven, nor will you see hell beyond the nightmare you have experienced in the human world. This is the Realm of the Gods. This is my home and yours too now if you want it to be, although if what I'm told by your siblings is correct, I think you might not want it to be just yet."

"I died and ended up here?"

She shook her head. "You forget who you are. Half of you is human, but the other half is a god. You cannot die. You are an immortal being."

I shook my head, trying to rid myself of the confusion I felt. "But I died. Derillen killed me. I'm here," I said, finally looking around the place. The bright whiteness had taken shape. It looked like we were inside a huge white palace.

"You came here through death, I suppose, but you are not dead. Your body in your world will have disappeared not long after death, turning to smoke, then to nothing. It then came here. You are flesh and blood just as you've always been."

She squeezed my hand again as if to prove her point.

"I still don't understand."

She smiled and ran her hand down the side of my face, wiping the tears away with her thumb.

"You are immortal. Death, as you call it, brought you through a kind of portal. It is not the only way between the human world and the world of the gods. There are other ways. I myself ventured to the human world once, but you already know that."

She looked to the side for a second, her eyes wistfully looking into the distance.

"Morpheus! He uses a portal to go between worlds." How had I not thought of it before? I'd been so fixated on the portal he used to get to his dream world that I'd never really thought about the other portal he used frequently.

"Morpheus does indeed flit between realms as the mood takes him. I do not know him very well, but I hear you do?"

My stomach clenched, and my cheeks colored as I remembered the date we'd been on. "Briefly," I said, then closed my eyes as a sickening thought popped into my head. "Please tell me he's not my father."

My mother laughed. It was a glorious sound like the melodic tinkling of the high notes on a piano.

"No. I already told you that you are a half-human. Your father was a drunken mistake. One which I both regret deeply and relish because it produced you. I don't even know who he is. I'm sorry. Even gods make mistakes, and I made the worst kind. I suppose you could say that it was partly due to Morpheus, although he was absolutely not to blame for my actions."

"How?" I asked, suddenly desperate to know everything about my own history.

She sat down on the floor and clasped her hands together. "I've lived here in the place of the gods my whole life. My job sounds beautiful and wonderful. I'm the goddess of love. I've sprinkled love down on the world for the longest time. All kinds of love. Romantic, brotherly, friendly, the love a mother has for her children," she said, now stroking my hair. It was like being kissed by rainbows and sunshine. "Passionate love. I did it all. For centuries and centuries. but then I became bored."

She cast her eyes downward as though she had a shameful secret she was about to unload. Behind her, my siblings had drifted away slightly, no longer interested in the story my mother was telling me. They must have all heard it already.

"I stopped doing what I was supposed to do. I stopped caring about humans." She pulled her hand away from me and drew it to her head. "I never got to see the joy that love brought to them. It all became so meaningless."

"A hundred years ago?" I asked, thinking of the time in Draconis's history when Derillen put my adoptive mother to sleep. When the history books said, the world went dark.

She nodded. "About that time, yes. I know that my actions, or should I say, lack of action, brought about sadness to the world. I deeply regret it, but to me, nothing had changed."

"There were wars."

"I know," she replied, pulling at her bottom lip with her teeth. "I was told such things, but why should I care? They didn't affect me. I know how selfish and callous that sounds, and it was. I was."

"So, what changed?" I asked her.

"I saw Morpheus heading out into the human world, Something, my father, would not let me do. He always seemed so at peace with himself and happy. The other gods thought him frivolous, but he had something we did not. He had a life. He had fun. I'd thought that by stopping doing what I was created to do, I'd have time to do things for me, that it would make me happy, but it only made things worse. I was bored and restless. Then, about nineteen years ago, I slipped away from my father and did what I'd seen Morpheus doing. I headed out into the human world."

She laughed a small melancholy laugh. "It terrified me and excited me at the same time. But I wasn't Morpheus. He'd been going to the human world and partaking in its pleasures as long as humans existed. I was hundreds of thousands of years old, and yet I felt like a child. I was lost, scared, and thrilled all at the same time. My plan had been to find Morpheus and hang around with him for a while, but very quickly, it became obvious that I wasn't going to find him. The people of Urbis had never heard of him, and I'd not thought to simply follow him through his portal. It was late, I was alone, and I knew no one. Part of me wanted to flit right back through the portal I'd made and go home, but a stronger part knew this was my chance to actually see something, to experience it. I went into the first bar I saw and ordered a drink for courage. Morpheus had mentioned being a lover of whiskey, so that's what I ordered. It was the only drink I knew of, and I was too scared to ask for anything else."

Hearing my mother talk about her foray into the human world fascinated me. I'd thought about how she'd left me and my siblings often, but her journey to get to that place hadn't crossed my mind much. Now she was telling me about it, I let every detail soak in.

"I hadn't exactly accounted for how potent that stuff was. I only knew I liked the way it made my throat burn as I swallowed it. Later, I liked the way it made me feel. It didn't take long for the bartender to ask me for money in exchange for the drinks. That was something else I hadn't thought about, but by then, I didn't care. I was already tipsy and having a great time. So I used my power to make him fall in love with me. I told myself it didn't matter, that it was only for one night and was only for free drinks. Of course, it did matter. I was doing something so awful for my own gain. I was playing with someone's feelings. I got free drinks as long as I wanted them."

"The bartender was my father?" I asked.

"No, he was but the first of many people I used my powers on that night, and that was just one of the bars I ventured into. The drunker I got, the more reckless my behavior became. By midnight I was making people fall in love with other people all over the place. People that had no business loving the people they fell for. I dare say I was the cause of a lot of failed marriages that night, not to mention the cause of a lot of pregnancies. Which brings me to the next part of the story.

"I didn't even know his name. I didn't care. I'd made so many people fall in love that night, and they all seemed so happy. I wanted to try it for myself.

"I'm ashamed to say that your father could have been anyone. He just happened to be a man at a bar. I made him fall in love with me, and then, I made myself fall in love with him.

"For the first time in my entire life, I finally understood my power. I was besotted with him, utterly under his spell, although in reality, it was just a spell. At that point in time, he was the most beautiful creature to ever walk in the human world. I wanted him, no, needed him, and he felt the same way about me."

She laughed again, but there was no joy in it. "Of course, he did. I'd made it so. I couldn't keep my hands off him, and when he kissed me, I could barely breathe with excitement. We found a room in a nearby inn, and I slept with him. It was my one and only night of knowing a human connection like that. It was ironic. I was the goddess of love, and I lost my virginity to a man I didn't know. And oh, how I enjoyed it. I'll never forget the heat that ran through my veins that night. It was the most magical night of my life.

"But, like so many others before and after me, the spell wore off. I woke up alone in a cheap hotel bed with a hangover. I never saw your father again, and before you ask, no, I never looked for him. I had nowhere to start looking, and to be honest, I was so ashamed of myself and my actions that I didn't want to see him again."

Hearing how ashamed she was made me feel sad. "You did nothing wrong. So you got carried away. It happens." I thought back to the time, not so long ago, when I almost kissed Morpheus. The temptation had been strong, and I could so easily have given into it. If I'd been as drunk as my mother had, then maybe I would have.

"I did everything wrong, my sweet child. The man only wanted me because I made him want me. Had I been sober, he would merely have been just another face in a bar. But I wasn't, and what was done was done. I immediately came back to the Realm of the Gods and vowed to be better. To start my job again, and this time, to take care in how I did it. I finally understood the power of what I did. "That had been the plan, except then, I found out I was pregnant. It hadn't crossed my mind. Like so many other things, I suppose. My father would have been livid if he found out. I'd already gone against him by sneaking out that one night. I'd gotten away with it, but I wouldn't get away with a pregnancy. There was nowhere in the Realm of the Gods to hide, so I went back down to the human world. This time, I vowed not to drink any alcohol. I had no money, so I had to find any job I could just to survive. For nine months, I hid, living as a human in the cheapest part of Urbis, doing whatever I could to survive. I didn't dare use my powers again. I became friends with a midwife who looked after me. She was the only person I ever told the truth to. She knew who I was, and she knew my story. On the morning of the first of January nearly nineteen years ago, she helped me bring you into the world, dear Azia. You were the first true love of my life. I knew it without having to use my powers. It was a stronger love than I had ever known, and it blew me away with the force of it."

She brought her hand to my cheek again, and this time I brought my own hand up to cover it. Tears began to form in her eyes as she spoke. I remained silent as she continued her story.

"I knew I was having more than one child. I was ridiculously huge. I had to spend the last three months of my pregnancy in the midwife's own bed because I couldn't move. She slept on the sofa all those months without complaining. Blaise was next, then Castiel. With each child, the midwife wrapped you all up and put you in bassinets, then in drawers when the bassinets became full. She told me to expect four or five babies, but they kept coming. I don't know who was more shocked, her or me, but I ended the day with twelve beautiful, perfect, darling babies. Twelve beautiful babies that had no father and nowhere to live. I couldn't keep you with the midwife. Her house was tiny. Nor could I take you back to the Realm of the Gods. My father is a brutal god with a fiery temper. I was afraid that he would kill you. I thought about raising you in the human world by myself, but the truth was I could barely afford to feed myself when I was pregnant. There was no way I could afford to keep twelve babies alive."

"So you gave us up!" I said. It came out much more harshly than I expected it to.

"No. I spent a week trying to come up with ways to make it work. I was going to stay in the human realm and bring you all up, but then the world began to change. Really change and for the better.

"I couldn't ignore the changes. The midwife brought me newspapers daily, showing me how all the kingdoms were beginning to thrive. How wars were coming to a close. I didn't want to admit that it was because of you. You were born from the goddess of love. A goddess that had been neglecting her job for years. All the love I'd deprived people of for so long came flooding back into the world because of you. You sent it out there without trying, all of you. Eventually, I had to listen to the midwife. She knew that if the people saw a huge difference in the world, my father would eventually notice too. I had no choice. If he found out about you all, he'd have killed you for sure. The midwife and I came up with a plan. It was her idea to give you to the kings and queens of each kingdom. All twelve had overcome some strife recently and come to peace. You'd done that. Of course, it wasn't only the royals that came to peace that week. It seemed that everyone did. There were a lot of marriages that week and a lot of new relationships. I don't think you twelve were the only ones throwing love out into the world. I was so absolutely full of love for the twelve of you that I'm sure some of it must have leaked out.

"So we set out in a carriage to the twelve kingdoms. It fit perfectly—twelve kingdoms, twelve children needing a home. I dropped you off first. I didn't need to use my power to have your new parents fall in love with you. I could see it in their eyes from the very first second they saw you. However much I hated to admit it to myself, I knew you'd be happy there. Those few weeks were the lowest point in my life, and when they were over, I scuttled back to the Realm of the Gods and started my job again. Always sending out love, never seeing how it affected people. But it had affected me. I never forgot you. Any of you. I never told a soul of your existence beyond the midwife. Gaia told me that she died at the hand of the witch named Derillen."

"We think that's the case, yes," I admitted. "We can't be sure, but it sounds like it was her. She was the one who killed me."

"You are not dead," she reminded me. "I had nothing to do with what happened to her all those years ago, to any of the bad people. I couldn't have known that your birth would grip the blackest of hearts and render them useless. Nor could I have known that as you grew up, the magic I inadvertently gave you at birth would dwindle one day so your real powers could shine."

"So that's what happened? My powers of love diminished enough so I could control Dragons?" Not that I'd ever really controlled dragons. Nyre had a mind of her own, but she always did what she had to, including trying to protect me from Derillen. That wasn't some kind of god magic. That was love.

"Your powers of love will never diminish, my child, but essentially yes. The power you have now is your own rather than remnants of mine. Your powers grew from the environment you were raised in. You were raised in a kingdom with dragons; therefore, you have the ability to control them. Blaise was raised by a mermaid, though she didn't know it. She got the power to breathe underwater and so on and so forth."

Dragon! Just saying it sparked something in my mind. "Nyre!"

I stood up quickly in a panic.

My mother's eyes widened. "Nyre?"

"She's my dragon. She was with me when Derillen killed me. She's not a god or a demi-god. If Derillen kills her, she'll be dead...really dead. There's no coming back from death for dragons."

"Your siblings were waiting for you. I didn't want them to leave without you. But now, you are all here."

She made a wide circle with her hand forming a swirling light that I'd come to recognize as a portal. "Go together and stay together and know that when you come back here, I'll be waiting for you."

I wanted to fall into her arms and let her hug me, but there was no time. I'd wasted so much of it already, hearing her story. I knew I'd see her again.

I gave her a quick nod and jumped through the portal back to the underground tunnel. Back to the war.

Derillen was no longer in the tunnel, and neither was Nyre. My heart hammered as I took in the familiar place, now empty. My brothers and sisters piled out of the portal behind me. I thought I'd lost them, that I'd never see any of them again. My magic had dwindled to one strand, but now I felt the strength inside me. Twelve swirling strands of magic intertwined and another smaller thread. Fae was still alive.

"I can feel her," I said, turning to Eliana.

She nodded, her face set in a grim determination that softened into a brief smile. "I can too. Let's go and get her."

She pushed right past me toward the dark tunnel that I knew would take us back to the government building.

I made to follow, but someone tapped me on the arm. I turned to see Lyric with her broad grin on her face and my sword in her hand. "Hey, Boss, I found this on the ground. I thought you might want it."

"Thanks," I replied, taking my sword and placing it back in its sheath by my side.

28TH DECEMBER
DERILLEN

"What's this?" Morpheus demanded, throwing a copy of the Urbis newspaper down on the table in front of me. "And while we are at it, what's that?"

I looked down to where his gaze was held. The child snuggled sleepily in my arms.

"I think it's quite obvious what this is," I snapped at him. "It's a baby."

"Very droll, Derillen. Why do you have it?"

"Shc was crying. I picked her up to rock her to sleep in my arms, not that it's any business of yours."

"Is it hers, Derillen?"

I was a little confused by the question to begin with,

but then it dawned on me. He was still fawning after that little bitch, Azia, and everything was about her, even the child.

"No. She did not come from that brat. Why are you here, Morpheus? Or did you just want to shout at me for no reason?"

"No reason?" he bellowed. I didn't think I'd ever seen him so angry. Gods, he was beautiful when he was angry. So beautiful, in fact, that I barely took in the drivel he was spouting out of his beautiful mouth. "You killed her!"

"So? I told you I was going to. She was a murderer."

"Bullshit." He slammed his fist down on the table, making the child squirm in my arms. I had to jiggle her to lull her back to sleep.

"You'll wake the baby," I admonished.

"I don't give a crap. You had some weird thing happen to you years ago, and you've centered all your rage on Azia. She was a baby, too, when it happened, if you remember. She did nothing to you."

"She did everything to me!" I raged back, making the child wake up properly this time. She squeezed her tiny hands into fists and bellowed loudly, her cheeks turning red in the process. I cooed to her, holding her up to my face so I could rub my cheek against hers. Immediately, I felt the rage melting away. "Her grandfather cheated on me with her grandmother. Then there was Briar Rose, the woman *you* agreed to lock away in your dream world, I want to point out. You are hardly innocent in all this."

"I never killed anyone. I made mistakes, and I admit that. I let her go. Snow White too."

I felt my anger rising again but then realized it didn't matter anymore. I'd killed Briar Rose's daughter.

Having her back in the real world would bring her fresh pain that she wouldn't have experienced in Morpheus's dreamscape. "You do what you have to do and let me do what I have to unless you have anything of interest to tell me."

"I have plenty to say. You had no right to kill her. How is having her dead going to help you anyway?"

I sighed. The man was a fool. "For one thing, I don't have to worry about her coming for me anymore. For a second, I have plans. I kind of like being the president of everywhere."

A sudden thought popped into my mind—something so utterly dangerous and wonderful at the same time.

"President is such a dull term, don't you think? I want to be queen, but there is no king."

I placed the child back in her bassinet and walked around the desk until I was face to face with Morpheus. He was so stunningly beautiful that I could barely breathe. He was an idiot, and yes, he was mad at the moment, but it would pass. He'd get over her, just as he got over every woman he'd ever been with. Not one of them had stood by him as long as I had. We were meant to be together. He just needed to know that.

"Why not forget all this nonsense and rule with me. You could be the king. The king of everything, and I could be your queen."

I whispered the last part in his ear, making sure I brushed my lips against his skin. Oh, it was exquisite misery being so close to him and not being able to touch him as I wanted to. He was mad, but I felt his body stiffen at my words. Whether good or bad, he was reacting to my breath on his neck, and he'd not moved away from me. I moved closer so that my body rested against his and looked up into his eyes. "Come on,

Morpheus, we've been playing this game for too long now. Let's not waste any more time."

He grabbed my arm and looked down at me, anger filling his eyes. "I'm not a king, I'm a god, and I do not need a queen."

"Well, get out then," I spat at him. "I don't need you either."

He let go of my arm and turned away from me. I watched him walk away from me and wondered if it was for the last time.

28TH DECEMBER
AZIA

We'd walked so far over the past couple of days that I was actually surprised when we finally ended up under the government building only hours after coming back to the human world.

The tunnel ended at a door, which opened out into a place I recognized very well, despite only spending one night there. We were in the basement of the government building where Derillen kept her prisoners. Except there were no prisoners here now. The whole place was empty and quiet.

"Where is everyone?" Halia whispered. Her melodic voice echoed off the walls.

"We were caught and killed," Deon said quietly

behind us. “There’s no need for the border portals to bring people here anymore.”

“Not to mention the fact that it was Rumpelstiltskin that ran them,” Eliana added.

So the portals had stopped working either because of Rumpelstiltskin’s death or ours. Derillen had no use for hundreds of prisoners once she had us, and so, therefore, she had no use for the guards that held them.

I half expected Cordel to step out from behind a pillar even though I’d seen her die with my own eyes. I knew there was no reason for guards to be down here anymore. Derillen thought we were all dead, but that didn’t stop my fear that we were walking into a trap. Nothing about this felt right.

I fingered my sword, pulling it from my scabbard.

As if on cue, hundreds of guards began to filter out into the underground chamber, led by Edwin. Our last adversary with magic apart from Derillen. Derillen’s right-hand man.

“I knew you’d be back,” he shouted out. His voice echoed around the chamber. “Fallon, how lovely to see you again.”

“I’ve waited a long time to kill you, old man,” Fallon said, racing toward him. “When you’re dead, your magic will fade, and my father will cease to be a beast.”

As he ran, he changed his appearance. He was still a man, but now he was huge. Biceps ripped his arms, his broad shoulders grew so quickly, his top shredded and fell to the floor. He was magnificent. I was only sad that Nyre wasn’t here to see this particular transformation.

He attacked Edwin using his own bare hands. Now that I knew he couldn’t die, I didn’t waste any time worrying. Instead, I drew my sword and began to fight.

To my left and my right, my brothers and sisters fought alongside me.

Castiel turned into a lion and cut through the guards. Chaos abounded around me as I grabbed Eliana's hand. I'd made a promise to find Fae, and I was going to make sure Eliana was with me when I did. We ran through the guards, my sword ensuring we made good progress. I'd always been good with my sword, but it was amazing how knowing I was invincible helped. For every thrust of a sword in our direction, I was able to parry back, ensuring Eliana and I made it up the stairs to the main part of the government building.

Behind me, flashes of light filled the space. Some, no doubt, from Edwin and his magic, some from the fire created by Gaia and magic created by Kelis.

It seemed that Derillen had been busy creating an army of her own, now that both Queenie and Momba's armies had been defeated. Except this army was human. We were outnumbered by ten to one, but we had magic.

Everywhere I looked, magic flew around my head. Hook and some of his men had been killed in the square, but it turned out not all of them. As my brothers and sisters fought, I had only one thing on my mind. Derillen. Wherever Derillen was, Fae would be.

Eliana never left my side as we hunted for the pair of them. We continued to search for Fae, but after hours of looking, we were finally pulled apart when I found myself fighting four pirates at once.

"You keep searching," I shouted to her. She nodded and ran up the main stairwell of the building as I knocked one sword away after another. Above me, Lyric circled, occasionally throwing anything she could find at our attackers.

Then, as though it couldn't get any worse, Derillen

herself appeared at the top of the magnificent staircase. She let out a jet of green light. The floor beneath me began to shake as the magic got closer. It grew until it would encompass us all but then changed shape into that of a giant arrow. An arrow pointed right at me. It sped up and shot toward me; I wasn't quick enough. She was going to kill me for a second time... But then, a portal opened up in front of me. The magical arrow shot through it harmlessly.

"Morpheus!" Derillen screamed, her face like thunder as he took up the fight next to me. I'd never seen her so angry. She certainly hadn't been so angry when she'd fought me the first time. She whipped her cape around her and disappeared into thin air.

"She won't have gone far," Morpheus said as a dozen guards ran toward us, their swords aloft.

I fought alongside him, doing everything I could to keep the guards at bay, but there were too many of them.

Just as it looked like we were going to be defeated, the huge main doors to the government building opened. I was almost stabbed as I paused for a second to take in the sight in front of me. Hundreds of people ran in, led by none other than Caspian. A bird with glorious fire-colored wings flew over them, landing on Gaia's shoulder. It was followed by a blast of blue magic that killed all the pirates around her.

All around me, there were gasps of recognition and names I'd heard from my brothers and sisters called out. The guy with the blue magic was undoubtedly Gaia's genie.

Then, everything fell away as I was yanked into the air.

Below me, I saw the scope of the fighting. The huge

entrance hall was filled with people. The flying monkeys had returned and were clawing at everyone. I saw Halia below me with an ugly woman in a huge dress in a headlock. Another ugly woman dressed similarly screamed next to them. Morpheus was using his magic to shield Ivy, Blaise, and Jakon from a couple of nasty pirates with huge swords. My heart leapt when I saw Nyre fighting alongside Fallon. She was still wearing his filthy coat, and she had a smile on her face bigger than any I'd ever seen. It was a beautiful sight.

"What are you doing?" I yelled as Lyric pulled me high above everyone else.

"I heard a baby crying."

She flew me down a corridor that was mostly free of fighting and dropped me outside a door. I didn't hear the baby's cries that Lyric had heard, but Fae's strand of magic inside me was the strongest I'd ever felt it.

"Go find Eliana," I said to Lyric, drawing my sword. Outside, the giant government bell in the tower struck twelve. Midnight. We'd been fighting all day. I held my hand out and pushed the door open. I entered with my sword in front of me.

29TH DECEMBER
AZIA

"Do it!" Derillen yelled. "You've wanted to kill me from the moment you were born."

I held my sword closer to her throat, watching how it pushed against her skin slightly. It would take so little movement from me to push it forward and slice her throat.

"I didn't even know you existed until you made your presence known," I shouted back at her. "You could have lived out your miserable existence in Draconis, or anywhere for that matter, and I wouldn't have known about you at all. The reason I'm here to kill you is entirely because of everything you've done."

She glared at me in such a way that made my blood run cold. She was my greatest foe, but at the end of the day, she was mortal, and I was not. One of us was always going to kill the other. I think we both thought it was going to be her doing the killing. She had done the killing first. When I killed her, there would be no coming back.

Next to her, Fae began to cry. Derillen didn't move, but I noticed her eyes shift down to the bassinet.

The little girl was way too big for it now. She looked big enough to crawl out of it, though she seemed more content crying and waiting to be picked up.

For the first time since I'd stepped into the room, I saw fear in Derillen's eyes. She didn't care when I held the sword to her throat, she didn't flinch when I told her I was going to kill her, but the sound of Fae's cries had thrown her.

I wasn't about to hurt Fae. Derillen knew that, and yet, I saw something in her eyes, I never expected to see.

Without thinking, I stepped back slightly. Derillen didn't hesitate. She ran straight to Fae and pulled her into her arms. Fae immediately quietened down and snuggled into her arms.

I stood there, astounded at the tenderness she showed Fae, and unable to process my next move. Killing her would have been so easy just moments ago.

"Kill me if you have to, but let me take her outside first. Give her to one of my staff."

"She has a mother," I pointed out. Eliana would be here as soon as Lyric found her.

Derillen nodded and closed her eyes for a second. I watched as she inhaled the baby's scent and held her tightly.

With a shock, I realized I was looking at love. Pure love. Derillen had done countless despicable things over the past twelve months. She'd killed, tortured, and hurt so many people, but she'd essentially been Fae's mother since the day Rumpelstiltskin had brought her back here. It was a sobering thought. Fae was about eight months old, and Derillen was the only mother she'd ever known. I'd had many thoughts about how this would all end. At first, I'd expected to die, and then when I thought I'd died, I thought I'd kill Derillen, and this would all be over. Not for a second did I expect this.

I couldn't kill her. Not anymore. In those brief minutes as she consoled and cuddled Fae, I saw something in her I never expected to see. I saw redemption.

I let her be and walked to the door instead. It was much quieter now. Magic still lit up the hallway, but with less frequency. I looked around, trying to find the one man who could save us all.

"Morpheus," I called out when I saw him fighting a woman I recognized as Madam Fontaine at the other side of the hall. He hit her with a spell that sent her crashing into the wall, then came bounding over to me.

"What is it?" he said breathlessly. "She'll be up again in a few seconds."

"It's ok, old chap," Caspian said, darting past, his sword held high. "I've got her."

Old chap? It seemed not even a slimy fae git was impervious to Morpheus's charms.

"Derillen is inside. She has Fae. I need your help with something."

As if she'd been listening out for the sound of her daughter's name, Eliana appeared seemingly from nowhere.

"She's in there?" Eliana's face streaked with tears, but they were tears of anger and of determination. She tried to push past me, but I stopped her.

"She's totally fine. Derillen has her."

It was the wrong thing to say.

"So let me in! Now, Azia!"

I pleaded with Morpheus with my eyes to help me. I knew that letting Eliana into that room with Derillen would only spell trouble. The witch had a heart full of hatred for me, but I was willing to bet she had more love for Fae. If she was forced to give her up to Eliana, who knew what she was capable of.

Morpheus looked at me with curiosity, but he took hold of Eliana and pulled her back from me.

I spoke to her as calmly as I could, given the situation. "I'll go in and bring her out to you. It's the only way I can do this."

"She's my daughter!" Eliana growled. "I need to see her."

"You will see her—very, very soon. Please trust me, Eliana. I'll bring her out to you in a few minutes. I need you to trust me."

She fought against Morpheus for a few seconds then went limp in his arms. "I do trust you, Azia. I always have, but you've got to bring her right out to me. I'll give you two minutes, and then I'm marching right through that door after you, and nobody will be able to stop me. Not even a god."

"Noted," I said, giving Morpheus a slight nod. He let go of Eliana. I opened the door and let him walk ahead of me into Derillen's office. Eliana's face contorted into shock that I was allowing Morpheus in there and not her, but I didn't have time to explain or argue. I had two minutes. I walked inside and shut the door behind me, leaving Eliana outside.

"What are you doing here?" Derillen snapped, seeing the both of us together, her mouth lowering at the corners. “Come to announce your engagement?”

“I’ve come with a proposition for you. For both of you, actually.”

Morpheus raised his brows in surprise. “For me?”

I nodded grimly. I’d barely noticed the clock on the wall before, but now that I did, it was all I could hear. The tick, tick, tick counted down the seconds I had left before Eliana barged through the door.

“Give me Fae, and I’ll let you live,” I said, looking directly at Derillen.

“Why should I believe you?”

“Because you love Fae, and I know you want what’s best for her. I also know that you never wanted this.” I held my hands up, indicating the ornate room about us.

“Revenge, yes, but the power you held was never your primary objective, was it?”

“I don’t know what you mean,” she sneered.

“This started because you were jilted by my grandfather all those years ago, but he was never your first love. This has only ever been about Morpheus. You are in love with him. You’ve been in love with him your entire life.”

Morpheus’s mouth dropped open, but I ignored him. It was Derillen I was most concerned about. Who knew if I was right or if I was way off the mark on this one, but I’d seen the way she looked at him when he’d come to my rescue earlier. It was the same look she’d given me when I’d shown up to her ball on his arm. It wasn’t because I was Azia. She hadn’t even recognized me at that point. It was because I was Morpheus’s date.

“Is this true, Derillen?”

For the first time since knowing her, I saw uncertainty in her. “Well, I…”

"Why didn't you just tell me?" He moved toward her.

"I told you a hundred thousand times. You were just too stupid to realize it. There was always one more pretty face you were wrapped up in." She turned to me. "Don't think you were the first. You won't be the last either."

I sat on the edge of the desk. "I think you have it wrong about Morpheus and I. I'm in love with a man called Milo. When this is all over, I'm going back to Draconis and marrying him. Nothing ever happened between Morpheus and me."

"It's true," Morpheus agreed. I held my breath, hoping he wouldn't tell her about the almost kiss we shared. While I'd never been interested in Morpheus like that, the same couldn't be said about his interest in me. An interest I'd literally just killed for him by mentioning Milo.

"Give me Fae and let her go back to her mother," I said quietly. "Eliana is waiting outside for her. She loves her so much. You don't have to worry about how well Fae will be taken care of. She'll grow up in a castle in The Vale surrounded by meadows full of unicorns. What more could a little girl want?"

"And then what?" Derillen sneered. "You slice my head clean from my shoulders?"

I smiled. "I have a better idea." When I told her the full plan, I was surprised at how eager she was to go along with it. I was even more surprised that Morpheus agreed to it, but then maybe he did have more love for Derillen than he realized. She was the one woman he'd spent more time with than any other.

Derillen handed over Fae into my arms. The baby cried as I took her away. I walked through the room and out to where Eliana was waiting.

I'd planned to usher them both to safety, but the fighting had come to a stop. The building was still.

I stood there as Eliana held onto the child she'd lost all those months ago. Fae didn't remember her, but in time she'd forget Derillen, the woman who'd raised her for her first few months of life. I hadn't lied to Derillen. Fae would grow up to be the happiest little girl surrounded by the most loving family a kid could wish for.

"Did you kill her?" Eliana asked eventually.

I shook my head. "No, but we won't hear from her ever again. She's out of our lives for good."

I opened the door to her office again to find Derillen's sleeping body on the floor and Morpheus gone. I'd need to move her at some point. Somewhere safe, just in case Morpheus ever got bored of her and let her out of his dream world. For that's where she was. With the man she loved. She gave up everything for him. The power she held, her magic, the child she'd come to love as her own. I only hoped, for her sake, it would be worth it.

I closed the office door once more and went to find my brothers and sisters in what was left of the building.

As we stepped outside, hand in hand, a cheer went up. The green glow that had surrounded Urbis was finally gone. It was no longer magic that illuminated the building but the light of thousands of candles.

Edwin and Madam Fontaine were dead. Killed at the hands of my siblings and friends. I would spare no sorrow over them. They weren't the conductors in this symphony of hate, but they all played in the orchestra. None of them would be missed.

Nyre flew into the sky as big fat flakes began to drift down around us. Tonight was a night for celebration, but it wouldn't last long. I couldn't remember the last time I'd slept in a bed. I'd never known exhaustion like this.

"We will rebuild," I shouted out to the people. Kelis waved her wand at me, and immediately, my voice got louder. "You're getting really good at that," I said, nodding toward her wand and giving the crowd a giggle in the process. I turned back to them.

"Derillen is gone. Her people are dead. From now on, Urbis is a free city. You may come and go as you please."

A roar went up, making me smile. I had ideas for Urbis. Big plans, most of which involved getting at least one person from each kingdom to be part of the cabinet. The kingdoms needed to learn to work together peacefully, and they couldn't do that if they didn't have a say in how their own kingdoms were run.

Next to me, someone placed their hand on my shoulder. I turned, expecting to find Deon or Gaia, but it was my mother. She'd come from the Realm of the Gods.

"You can give a speech tomorrow," she whispered. "The people will survive another day without you. You are tired, and there is someone I'd like you to meet."

I nodded and stepped back into the building, following the others.

My mother, the goddess of love, conjured up a heart shape portal. Before I stepped into it. I grabbed a passing member of staff that had somehow managed to get caught up in the fight.

"Derillen's body is in her office. Please take it down into the cellar. Once you've done that, find someone to make a glass coffin for her. One that is magic proof."

The servant nodded his head, looking dazed.

"And then go home and get some sleep. We all have

a lot of cleaning up to do tomorrow."

My mother took my hand as we stepped through the portal into the Realm of the Gods. Before it closed, Nyre zoomed through, finally changed back to her dragon form.

"You can't be here!" I said as she touched down on my shoulder.

My mother patted her on the head. "I think we are all past what is allowed and not allowed at this point. Nyre will come to no harm here. I promise. I'll conjure up a new portal for you all to go back to the human world once I'm happy you've had enough sleep."

Sleep! As gods, my mother and Morpheus didn't need it, but as a half-god, half-human, I was ready to pass out and sleep for a month.

"So this is them?" a voice bellowed.

"Yes, Father. This is them. Your grandchildren and your great-granddaughter."

A man...a god, twice as tall as me and scarier-looking than anything I'd encountered back on earth, came over to us. He had a long, red beard that flowed over his naked muscular chest.

"I told my father everything this morning. I've lied and concealed you all for so long, but once I'd met all of you, I knew I couldn't live like that anymore."

"It was quite a shock, I'll tell you," the man bellowed. "I'm only a few millennia old. Nowhere near old enough to be a grandpa."

His size was enough to have me trembling in fear and the square cut of his jaw and long, fiery, red hair that made it look like it was ablaze all added to the effect of someone not to be messed with...ever.

He shook the hands of my brothers and sisters, eventually coming all the way to me at the end of the line. His eyes widened at the sight of Nyre on my shoulder, but he didn't make a comment about her.

"You will all, of course, do as I say," he continued, his voice coming out as a roar.

I wanted to argue back, to tell him I didn't do anything because someone told me to, but his face broadened into a smile. "And I say that you are welcome here anytime you like. I will bestow on all of you the ability to create your own portals so you can visit when you like. They will work in the human world for getting from place to place too, so you can visit each other without having to rely on public transport. Aphrodite, my daughter, tells me it's terribly unreliable."

31ST DECEMBER
AZIA

I stepped up to the palace gates, wondering what I would find. Getting home had been a lot easier, thanks to Zeus giving me the ability to cross through portals. But in a way, it had been harder too. I'd set out a year ago, a young girl with no knowledge of the world beyond royal tours and palace life. At many points, I'd not known if I would ever see this place again. A year ago, I was a different person. Now, I was literally a goddess with eleven siblings, another mother, and a grandfather. They would never replace the family I was coming home to, the one I grew up with, but they would be an extension of it.

"Ma'am?" one of the guards said. As I'd walked up, I'd hoped it was Milo in one of the palace guard uniforms, but it wasn't anyone I recognized.

I opened my mouth to speak, but the other guard beat me to it.

"Bow down, you idiot. It's Her Highness, Princess Azia."

I turned to the older man and smiled. "Jack, I'm so pleased to see you!" I ran to the grumpy old guard and flung my arms around his neck, kissing his cheek for good measure. Jack's cheeks reddened, and as I pulled away, he mumbled something.

"The lad's really missed you, girl."

He'd never called me girl before, but then again, I'd not kissed him before.

"Is he here?" I asked. I'd thought of Milo every single day since leaving. Knowing I was just about to see him again after eleven long months had my stomach in knots.

"He is, but you have some other people you might want to talk to first." He nodded through the closed portcullis to the main palace doors. Running across the cobbled yard, my mother ran toward me, her arms open wide and tears streaming down her face.

"Come on, lad, let's get this portcullis open," Jack huffed at the younger guard. The pair of them disappeared into the gatehouse and began winding the mechanism that worked the portcullis.

The second the gap below it was high enough, I ducked under and ran toward my mother. She almost knocked me over as she barrelled into me, flinging her arms around my neck. I fell into her, inhaling the scent of her perfume as I buried my head in her neck. Behind me, four more sets of arms surrounded me, pulling me into a five-way, royal sandwich.

"Aza Ba'" Remy said, behind me. I turned my head

as best I could in the squish I was in and looked my eldest brother in the eye.

"That's right, Remy. I'm back. I missed you so much. I missed you all so much."

My family pulled back so I could hug them all individually.

"I'm proud of you, Azia," my father said, placing his hands on my shoulders. My father, who never ever cried, looked down at me with damp eyes. "I'm not sure if you want it, but there is a place in the Draconis Army for you. I was thinking head of the new Dragon division."

"There's a dragon division?" I asked, full of surprise. The Dragons were not known for working for others, especially for the king of Draconis.

"I've had many talks with Vasuki since you left."

I raised my eyebrows.

"We've become something of friends. Anyway, we both realized that we need to work together. We might be Dragon shifters and humans, but we are all Draconian."

"Bout time you figured it out," I said, giving him a friendly nudge. "I don't think I'll accept your offer, though I thank you for it. I do know someone who would be amazing for the job, though."

I thought of Nyre, who had traveled through the portal with me just ten minutes earlier. She'd flown back up the mountain to see her parents Vasuki and Emba. If anyone could command an army, she could. As long as she could learn to put some clothes on when she shifted into her part-human self.

Ash and Hollis were next. I hugged them both tightly. Both of them looked so handsome in their uniforms. And each of them had grown at least six inches since I last saw them and now towered over me. Another year or two and they'd catch up with Remy in the height department.

"Remy," I said, turning to my eldest brother. "How about a sword fight later?"

He jumped up and down, a grin splitting his face. "Capa?"

"Caspian? You want to fight Caspian?"

He nodded eagerly.

"You're in luck. Tonight, we are all having a big party in Urbis, and everyone is invited. Caspian will be there along with Charlotte."

I turned back to the rest of my family. "Will you come? It's a New Year's Eve party to celebrate the union of the twelve kingdoms and Urbis. I'm hoping the other royals will come so we can spend a few days rebuilding the government. The kingdoms are broken and have been for a long time. My brothers and sisters would like to bring them all together. Oh, by the way. I have eleven brothers and sisters if you'd like to meet them."

My mother pulled me back into her arms. "Of course, we would like to meet them. I can't wait."

As much as I wanted to be with my family, there was someone else I wanted to see.

"Is Milo around?" I asked, trying to sound more casual about it than I felt.

"You might want to go into the woods behind the castle," my mother said with a grin. "Make sure to take your sword with you."

I kissed her cheek. "Thank you."

So many thoughts rushed through my mind as I opened the small gate that led from the castle gardens to the copse of trees.

I treaded lightly, the snow on the ground dampening my footsteps.

I found him in the training circle he'd set up all those months ago. He swiped his sword at an imaginary opponent. My plan had been to call out his name, but seeing him fighting thin air gave me a better idea. I slowly pulled the sword he'd given me from its scabbard and held it out. When he turned in my direction, I jumped out from the trees and into the circle. His eyes widened as he saw me, and he paused for a moment in surprise. I took the pause as a chance to parry, knocking his sword clean from his hand. Dashing forward, I kissed him.

He stood stock-still for a second, his lips not moving, his body rigid. My heart fell like a stone, wondering if I'd misjudged everything. We'd only been together a few weeks when I set off on my adventure. That had been eleven months ago. I'd thought of him every day, but that didn't mean he'd thought about me. He could have found someone new. He could be married by now, and here I was, jumping on him without even a hi.

But then he softened, pulling me into him. The kiss started out as a way to say hello after eleven months away, but then, it turned into something else. Eleven months is a long time to go without kissing, and the soft touch of lips turned feverish as our bodies meshed together. His hand pulled on my head, his fingers weaving through my hair as he held me to him, his other hand on my waist. My own hands went to his face, holding onto him as much as he held onto me, neither of us wanting to let the other go, to let go of the moment we'd both waited for so long. My thumb brushed against his hair and against his temple as I tried to remember every inch of him.

I wanted more. More of this, more of him, but we were in a clearing in the woods, and snow was falling around us. With great reluctance, I pulled away from the kiss. And then I couldn't help myself. He was so beautiful, his warm brown eyes drinking me in, that I leaned forward again. There was so much to do before the big party, but after eleven months away, what were a few more moments to get lost in his kiss? So I brought my lips to his, and that's exactly what I did.

BLAISE

The portal I'd created disappeared behind me once I'd stepped through it. It was going to take time to get used to being able to travel where I wanted when I wanted.

The palace, my home, was behind my right shoulder. I could have set the portal to take me there, but I needed time first. Time to process who I now was and how my life had changed. My mother, father, Emma and Hannah, and all the other people who were expecting me home would wait. They must have read about me in the newspapers. I sat on the rocks and stared out to sea as waves crashed around me, dampening my clothes. I inhaled the salty air and waited for the one thing I'd missed the most. But apart from a couple of seagulls in the distance, there was no sign of life. It was too cold, too choppy for any of the merfolk to be playing on the surface. They would be in the calm waters below.

Giving a last wistful glance at the palace behind me and the people inside who loved me and were awaiting my return (not to mention the fireplaces where undoubtedly the staff were keeping the fires stoked), I stripped down to my underwear. My skin puckered with goose-pimples, and a shiver ran through me at the freezing temperature. Jumping in the stormy water would either kill me or cure me of the cold. I picked my way over the sharp rocks to the sandy beach and waded into the water. The iciness of it took my breath away, but the further I went in, the warmer it seemed to feel. By the time I was completely submerged, my body tingled in a pleasantly warm way, and I thanked my lucky stars that my magic was sea magic.

Coming back to the ocean felt like coming home. I swam toward the entrance to the undersea kingdom that my grandfather ruled.

I was only halfway there when a group of merfolk spotted me. I waved my arm, but they retreated, swimming away.

I stopped, suddenly feeling nervous. The AML had broken up, and things were better than ever between humans and merfolk when I left. Had it started up again? Did they think I was part of it again? I floated below the surface, suddenly not sure of what to do. I should have gone home first and gotten myself up to speed with what was happening in Atlantice.

I wavered for a second, dithering about what to do, but then Abe appeared at the entrance to the underwater kingdom. I saw him before he saw me. I watched as his eyes raked his surroundings. He was looking for me. That's what the merfolk had been doing when they shot off. They'd gone to fetch him. His eyes finally found me, and his whole face lit up with emotion. So many feelings had been running through me as I'd been waiting for him. Doubt, fear, guilt for staying away for so long—all that melted away as he raced toward me, his eyes full of love. He pulled me into an embrace so hard that we toppled end over end over the ocean floor, his naked chest against mine. The stillness of the ocean below the stormy surface was the opposite of how I felt. I kissed Abe calmly while my insides churned with excitement.

And then I kissed him again, and the calmness dropped away to something else. I would go home to my parents and friends, but just for now, this time was all ours

CASTIEL

The walls we had spent weeks building were all gone. That was the first thing I noticed after passing through the portal. The second thing was, despite it being winter, the forest was alive with the sounds of birds and animals. Critters ran through the undergrowth when they should have been hibernating. If it wasn't for the cold, I would have sworn it was summer. Nine moon cycles had passed since I'd walked through these trees, but the smell of the pines brought me right back home as though I'd never left. The same couldn't be said for the wolf settlement. I'd left it in a state of ruin, surrounded by a wall. Now, the houses were better, bigger, and newer. The wood we'd used for the wall had been repurposed to build the village up again.

In the distance, I watched as Micco spoke to a couple of wolves in their human form. He looked so healthy and fat. When I'd left, his skin clung to his bones with barely any fat separating the two, but now, he was well-fed, and if the expression on his face was anything to go by, happy. I watched him for a few minutes as he went about his business, talking to the other wolves. Every single one of them was in their human forms. That was why I hadn't been spotted the second I came through the portal. Their wolf senses would have picked up my scent right away. I was glad I hadn't been spotted yet. It gave me the chance to see what this place had become. It was thriving. I even saw a number of tree folk ambling around, chatting with the wolves as though it was perfectly normal. Happiness settled around my belly. It was a far cry from how I'd left the place.

A scream rang out quickly, followed by my name being screeched. Grace ran toward me, grabbing my face in her hands and planting her lips on mine in a rather enthusiastic manner.

"You're home!" she squealed, a picture of excitement. My own excitement in being home abated somewhat when I saw Nikkan behind her, his hands on his hips and a stern look on his face.

Shit. I'd forgotten how jealous he was. He'd almost killed me when he thought I liked Grace in the same way he did. How he was going to cope with me kissing her was anyone's guess. I braced myself, setting my feet apart, waiting for the punch as he strode toward me purposefully. I almost closed my eyes as he reached forward. Thankfully, I didn't because he grabbed my head in much the same way Grace had and planted a kiss right on my lips.

"That was quite a welcome," I huffed, wiping Nikkan's kiss from my lips.

"Don't get too excited, dude," Nikkan grinned. "I'm a married wolf now."

Grace took his hand as a group of kids ran over. "And a father."

It was the children left without parents after the plague.

"And the plague?" I asked, skirting around the real question I wanted to ask.

"It's fine. All gone. we've never been healthier."

"And..." I couldn't bring myself to say her name. It still felt weird thinking of her as something other than my sister—adopted sister, whom I'd not really grown up with, but nevertheless.

Grace pointed out a lone figure in the distance

wearing a red cape and hood.

I'd not been asking about my mother, but it was good to see her all the same.

"I'll be back soon," I said to my two friends as I started walking toward Red. It was only when I came close that she spoke. She didn't even turn her head. She knew me by the sound of my footfall. She also wasn't Red.

"Sera?"

She finally turned and looked at me. I'd forgotten how attractive she was. She was no longer a little girl. Not that she had been when I left, but there was a confidence about her now that I'd not seen before. Not just the cocky confidence she used to possess but the self-assurance of a woman who was in charge.

"I thought you were my mother for a second. The robe." I said, pointing to the red cape she wore.

"Your mother is back at the village. She's very happy in her new role as a retiree."

"I never thought I 'd see the day," I replied

"Want to go see her?" Sera asked.

In that moment, I only wanted her. More than I ever thought I could ever want anyone. I wanted to whisk her into the forest and make love to her, and to tell her everything that had happened and all my thoughts about how Elder could change for the better, but most of all, I wanted to take her into my arms and kiss her like she'd never been kissed before.

"I'd love to, but first..." I stepped toward her.

"Race ya!" she said, pulling her hood down and giving me a grin. She turned and took off into the forest toward the tree village at high speed. She had almost disappeared by the time I came to my senses. I raced after her. She was going to make an amazing Red, but she was already the most exciting woman I'd ever met.

She was going to keep me on my toes, that one.

I raced off into the woods, hot on her heels. When I finally caught up with her, I was going to give her that kiss I'd promised myself I would. That was unless she finally figured a way to outpace me.

DEON

Even under a blanket of snow, the winter berries were already out, pushing through the white with their red berries. The evergreens that lined the palace driveway were back to what their name suggested they should be. Green.

I passed the sheds and then the greenhouses, which were full of plants. Live plants that were thriving. Hedley was inside changing the compost of some of the flutterberries, though he was so consumed with his job that he didn't notice me walk past. With me back, he could retire again, though, I doubted he would. I itched to go inside and take a look at what was growing, but Lillian appeared at the other end of the rose garden, her dogs running at her feet.

"Garden boy!" She called excitedly as she noticed me walking toward her. I smirked and pulled her toward me.

"I've missed you so much, Lils," I said, bending my head lower to taste those sweet lips of hers. I inhaled the scent of her shampoo and lost myself in the taste of her lips as the dogs yapped around our feet.

"I read all your letters," she murmured, happy tears streaming down her face. "They kept me going when things were rough. When the newspapers announced your death..."

Her expression became solemn, and the tears flowed more freely.

"I can't die, Lils. I'm a god. You'll never have to worry about me ever again."

"I'm never letting you go again!" she said, gripping my hand in hers. "Not without me, anyway."

I looked around the gardens I loved, "I'm not planning on going anywhere. Not without you, anyway."

"I love you, Garden Boy."

"Prince Garden Boy, I'll have you know," I replied, showing her the ring on my finger.

She took my hand, and her warmth cut through the icy cold. After the party in Urbis planned for New Year's Eve and the celebrations and work that was to follow, I would come back here and take up my official position of Prince of Floris. After that, I'd never leave again. I'd had enough adventures for one lifetime. The only adventure I wanted now was a lifetime of happiness with my wife.

ELIANA

Zacharina was the first thing I saw as I passed through the portal into the meadow. It was as though she knew I was coming home. Right behind her, Epiphany followed. She'd grown so much since I'd last seen her, losing the dappling of her baby hair.

"I'm sorry I wasn't with you on the last part of your journey," Zacharina said, nuzzling up to me, her voice coming through into my mind rather than through her mouth. "I tried telling Jay that I knew you were fine, but I wasn't sure he understood me. The poor lad was broken while you were gone. He's been through hell."

My heart, already stretched thin, almost broke at her words. He'd lost Fae, and then he'd lost me. I knew him well enough to know that not being able to defend me would have almost killed him.

"Take me to him, please." Zacharina lowered her body so I could jump onto her back.

The staviary was empty of even the palace unicorns and horses. There was a sadness about the place as though it hadn't been used for a long time. It was not the place I remembered it being, nor was it the place I wanted to bring Fae home to.

With fear in my heart, I spoke to Zacharina as I dismounted. "Where are the horses, the unicorns? Where is Jay?"

"They are all out in the meadow," a voice called.

I turned to find Jay running toward me, his face contorted into a sweet, agonized smile. "You found her!" he said, spinning the pair of us around. He kissed me. Not the long sensual kiss I'd wanted but a quick kiss so he could kiss Fae too. Then he came back to me and our second kiss was longer. Then he broke off and kissed Fae again. I handed her over for the first time since getting her back the day before. I'd slept with her body right next to mine, fearful that if I left her for a second, she'd be taken from me again. There was no fear in my heart as I passed my daughter over to her father. His eyes shone as he took in my sweet girl, hugging her closely. My eyes filled with tears, and my heart filled with hope at the sight of the pair of them together.

"Get your fill because her grandmother won't let anyone near her once she gets hold."

He stopped spinning Fae around and took my hand. "Then I'll turn my attention to you, but before that, look what I made."

With great excitement, he pulled me around the corner to show me a miniature carriage just big enough for a tiny little girl.

"She's only just started to crawl," I laughed. "Don't

you think she might be a bit young for that?"

"Nonsense," Jay said, putting her in the little seat. She sat in it, then brought her head around to chew on the back of it. "Okay, maybe a little young, but she'll grow into it."

He picked her back up and kissed her forehead again. She giggled as he tickled her side. It was the sweetest sound in all the world.

"I thought Epiphany could pull it around the palace grounds."

"Where are all the horses? The palace unicorns?"

He grabbed my hand and pulled me through the gardens around the castle to the meadow in front of the palace grounds. The meadow was full of horses and unicorns—more than I'd ever seen before in my life. Even the air was full of them.

I began to laugh at the magical sight, and as I looked upon them and then to Jay and Fae, my family, my heart and my home, and knew we'd never be separated again.

FALLON

The maid almost dropped the plates she was ferrying from the kitchen as I stepped out of the portal in front of her.

"Sorry," I said to her as she recovered from the shock of having the heir to the throne pretty much materialize out of thin air.

She curtsied awkwardly, balancing the plates in her hand.

"Let me help you with those," I offered.

She shook her head. "I appreciate the offer, Your Highness, but I think their majesties and Ms. Veda would like to see you. They've been waiting in the throne room all day for the delivery of the newspaper to see if you are ok."

"The throne room?" I asked, noting that she'd mentioned my father. Was he man or beast? Edwin was dead, but did his magic live on? I was too afraid to ask.

"Well, I think they are expecting reporters too. No one really knows what's happening. A couple of days ago, you were dead, and then you weren't, and then you were a hero. It's all been a bit confusing, to be honest."

"Yes, I suppose it must be," I replied idly. I thanked the girl and headed to the throne room. I almost pushed open the door when I had a better idea. Shifting my appearance to an approximation of a reporter, I knocked on the door then made my way in.

My father stood up from his throne. He was back to normal. No sign of the beast he'd become. By God, I'd missed him.

"What is the meaning of this?" he bellowed. Okay, maybe some of the beast still resided in him. "Who are you?"

"I'm a mere reporter from the Arboria Weekly News, Your Majesty. I'm here to do a report on the homecoming of His Royal Highness Prince Fallon."

My father furrowed his eyebrows. "How did you get in? This is most inappropriate for you to walk in here unannounced."

Shit! Months away, and thoughts of royal protocol had completely gone from my head. "Yes, well, I was told to come here by... er, a member of staff." No point putting anyone on the chopping block. I pulled out a pencil and notebook from my pockets.

"What can you tell me about Prince Fallon? Some would say he's a national hero."

My father relaxed and sat back down on his throne.

He pointed at a chair for me to sit in. I ignored his finger and carried on talking.

"The savior of Aboria, I've heard," I added, laying it on thickly.

My father eyed me, gruffly. "He's my son. I'm extremely proud of him, but then again, I've always been proud of him."

My mother reached over and placed her hand on his. He gave her a smile. I smiled too. It was nice to hear my father's thoughts.

"What about sexy?" I asked, turning to Veda. "He was voted the sexiest royal in all the kingdoms in more than one magazine. Surely, he's even more so, now that he's saved the kingdom."

To my surprise, Veda started to laugh. She let her head fall back and roared in amusement. I stood there perplexed, wondering what had gotten into her.

She stood up from her chair and walked over to me. I almost had a heart attack when she brought me into a kiss. It was a kiss worth waiting for, of that, there was no doubt, but she was delivering it to the wrong guy. My mind was screaming in protest that she shouldn't be kissing some random reporter that showed up out of nowhere, but my mind was overruled by my lips, which were enjoying the experience too much to stop.

"Fallon, you great goof," she said as she finally pulled away.

"You knew it was me?" I looked down at my pretend body and clothes. I looked nothing like me.

"No one... and I mean this with all the love in the world, no one thinks you are sexier than you do yourself." She paused for a second with a wicked glint in her eye. "Except for me."

She brought me into a kiss again, and I let my fake

self fall away until it really was me she was kissing. She might have had a point that I thought a little too much of myself, but with her at my side, I knew I was becoming a better person.

GAIA

Most of the others had all left Urbis to go home to their families. Only Kelis and I remained out of all the siblings. They'd all be back tonight for the big party, but someone needed to stay to organize the cleanup. Kelis had gone through a portal to see her parents and a young man named Topher, but she'd brought them back with her. Being the king and queen of the most magical kingdom of them all had its uses. Between the four of them, they cleaned up the Government building, restoring it to its former beauty.

As for me, I took over the President's office, now that Derillen's sleeping body had been removed to the underground chamber.

"What do you think of me running for president?" I asked, putting my feet up on the desk. I'd been thinking about it through the night. While the others had spent the night in the Realm of the Gods, I'd been here with Genie.

He pulled my feet off the desk then sank to his knees. "Gaia. I love you with everything that I am. I fought it for so long, which was foolish."He took my hand in his. "Will you marry me?"

My breath hitched in my throat. I'd had hundreds of marriage proposals in my time—thousands, probably. This was the first time I'd wanted to give an answer to one.

"Of course, I will."

He took me in his arms and spun me around

the room. "I know you would hate it if I asked your father's permission before asking you. You are way too independent for that, but he's my best friend."

I was just happy that my father recognized him again. Now that the sorcerer was dead, my parents could finally start to rebuild Badalah into the prosperous kingdom it once was.

"Let's go tell them the news," I grinned. "I'll let them know I'm thinking of becoming president while we are at it."

I conjured a portal, and Genie gripped my hand.

"I wouldn't expect anything less."

HALIA

"We're holding a party, right?" Tia said, precisely thirty seconds after me stepping through the portal into the bar. It was practically the first thing she said to me after flinging her arms around my neck.

"There is going to be a celebration," I said, grinning from ear to ear. "Tonight for New Year's eve. I was hoping you'd all come."

I looked at Mikka and Lorenzo, who, so far, hadn't been able to come close to me, thanks to Tia being the limpet she was. Lorenzo gave me one of his sexy smiles. There would be time for his embrace...as soon as I could pry Tia away.

"Please, tell me you're going to sing!" she squealed.

"I lost my guitar...and I don't know if there is a stage."

"Are you a god or not?" she exclaimed. "The papers said you were the granddaughter of Zeus, for goodness sake. Conjure one up."

I laughed. "My powers don't work that way, but I do have a sister that can do magic. Maybe she can get me a guitar."

"No need," Lorenzo finally spoke. "While you were gone, I had one handcrafted for you. Your parents... I mean, your adopted parents, the king and queen, were happy to pay for it."

He ducked into his office and came out with the most beautiful guitar I'd ever seen. He'd had it made in black wood and had flowers etched into the surface.

"It's perfect," I croaked. "But how did you know I'd survive?"

He took my hand in his. "I never doubted it for a second. Now let's go and get this stage set up. I've not heard you sing in six months, and I must admit, I've missed it."

As we all passed through the portal back to Urbis, he grabbed my ass. "Your voice isn't the only part of you that I've missed," he growled. I laughed, glad to be finally home where I belonged.

IVY

They were all waiting for me as I stepped through the portal into Alice's living room. Alice and Wit, Chesh and Pearl, even Dinah, the cat. There was only one person missing. One person that I'd left at the hospital.

"Where's Raven?"

"Darling," Alice said, bringing me into a hug. "Look outside. It's still daytime. He's perfectly fine, now tell us about your adventures."

I sat and told them everything, but as I spoke, I noticed they all looked somewhat preoccupied.

Eventually, I stopped talking. "What's going on? There's something I don't know? Is it about the stipend?"

Pearl waved my question away. "The stipend ended months ago. I have a job now."

My eyes widened. "A job? A real job?"

She laughed and nodded. "You're looking at the newest teacher at the Melfall Beauty School. And Chesh has been invited into the inventors guild, so we will be quite well off without the stipend; thank you very much."

"Is that why you are all grinning like Cheshire cats?" I asked, feeling a little unnerved by all the white teeth I was seeing.

"Wit and I got married," Alice finally admitted, holding her hand out to show me her ring. Beside her, Pearl squealed in excitement, even though she'd already known.

"I'm so happy for you!" I enthused. Alice had spent too much of her life on her own. It was about time she finally found some happiness.

"And I'm pregnant!" Pearl added, cradling her stomach and barely containing her excitement. "It's twins."

"Congratulations. I'm going to be an aunt!" I brought my sister into a hug. She'd changed so much since I'd last seen her. We both had.

"It's getting dark," Alice pointed out, nodding to the window. "You'd better get going if you want to invite him to the party. We'll be here waiting for you when you get back."

I hugged them all and stepped out into the night. There was a vampire out there that I needed to see. A beautiful, sexy man of the night, waiting for me. I rushed down the cobbled streets and knocked on the door to his hat shop.

When he opened the door, my breath caught in my throat. He was more beautiful than I remembered. "I'm back," I whispered.

"So you are," he said, pulling me into his arms. The

door shut out the whole world behind us, and that was alright. Until the party, at least, there would be only him and me.

Jakon

Five children ran at me, smothering me with kisses.

Meg, Frank, Chester, Ethel, and Lucy. I kissed them all in turn, pulling them all into a hug. Behind them, Scarecrow and Clement watched on.

"I missed you all so much."

"The newspaper said you have lots of brothers and sisters now," Lucy said, her bottom lip quivering. "Does that mean you don't need us anymore?"

I pulled Lucy up into my arms. "I need you five more than ever. I'll always need you, but they would like to meet you if you'd like to meet them? Tonight! There's a party in Urbis, and you're all invited."

"Even the purple dragon?" Lucy's eyes widened, and I laughed.

"Even Nyre. I dare say that she'll give you a ride on her back if you ask her nicely."

They all whooped and cheered.

"The Ferris wheel is working." A voice I'd waited months to hear cut above the din the children were making. I remembered the last words I'd spoken to Clement. I'd promised him a kiss on the top of the Emerald City Ferris Wheel.

"Ok, out of the way, the lot of you," I said to my over-excited siblings.

"What was it I promised you if we went to the fair? Cotton candy?"

Clement's face split into a wry smile. "That was one of the things, but not the one I was thinking of."

"Was this it?" I asked, taking his face in my hands. I touched my lips to his.

“I think that was it,” he grinned when we came up for air. “But let’s just try it again to make sure I remembered correctly.”

I kissed him again, and in the background, five children chattered excitedly about who would get to ride the purple dragon first.

KELIS

I waved my hand, letting my magic flow through the wand and into the building. Portions of the huge white government building had been destroyed completely in the fight, and now it was up to my mother, father, Topher, and me to put things right for the party tonight.

“A bit different from the magic competition,” Topher remarked, taking my hand in his. “Please tell me that you at least made some of these holes.”

I grinned. “I think it was mostly Edwin, but you never know.”

“You’ve come a long way from only being able to use your wand to brush your hair,” My mother added, coming up behind us. “I hear that the mirror was smashed.”

I nodded. “Nyre did it. I wasn’t there, but apparently, she smashed it to pieces.”

My mother nodded curtly, though I could tell she was pleased. She’d been wanting me to get rid of it for years.

“Good.”

She waved her wand toward the building, and huge pink and purple streamers erupted from the end, decorating the front of the building.

We’d almost finished clearing up the mess and decorating for the party when Halia appeared from a portal with three other people in tow.

"I need a stage," she panted, holding up a stunning black guitar. "Apparently, I'm going to sing tonight."

"I think that can be arranged." I held my wand up and visualized a stage. When I opened my eyes, a stage stood right in front of the government building just as I'd imagined it.

My magic really was coming into its own.

"Maybe I should go in for another one of those magic competitions?" I said to Topher.

"The regionals for the kingdom-wide championships are next week. I already signed you up."

I gave him a kiss and grinned. I was going to kick the other competitors' asses.

LYRIC

"Star boy!" I called out to the man sitting in the tree. He almost fell when he heard my voice. Skye flew right over to me when he saw me.

"Thank goodness you are back," the little pixie squeaked. "He's been a real grump since you've been gone."

"Windsong!"

Bay ran toward me, knocking us both right off the edge of Skyla's rim and sending us both hurtling to the ocean below.

"I missed you so much," he shouted as the wind sent his hair flying out above him.

I gripped him tightly then spread my wings, bringing us to a comfortable stop on one of Skyla's lower islands.

"That was quite a welcome," I grinned. "But you know, a polite hello and us not practically falling to our death would have worked too."

"A polite hello? Not a chance."

He pulled me to him and kissed me passionately

until I felt as though I was floating. Maybe I was. We lived in Skyla, after all.

"I didn't want Skye to see me do that," he said cheekily once the kiss was over.

"My brothers and sisters are having a party in Urbis tonight. I'd like it if you could come. We can get there through a portal."

He mused on my invite for a minute. "I had planned to attend the Lost Boys New Year party, but I guess we could all come with you instead. "

"We?"

"You, me, Skye..."

"Of course."

"Whisper, Tiger Lily, and of course, the..."

"Lost boys?"

He nodded. "The Lost Boys. Will we all fit into your party?"

I nodded, a grin on my face. "It's being held at the government building, so I should imagine so."

"My father?"

My grin fell. I'd been so happy to be home that I'd forgotten about Hook.

"He's dead. I'm sorry. I wasn't there to see it, but I was told that it was quick."

It wasn't exactly the truth. Gaia had killed him using her firepower, but Bay didn't need to know that.

He nodded and then went quiet. "Good," he murmured, nodding his head as though he was trying to talk himself into being ok with it. I held him close for a long time, but no tears were shed for Hook. He'd never really been a father to Bay.

"How have everyone's memories been since I left?" I asked, thinking of my own father, Peter Pan, and how he'd practically forgotten me before he died.

"Everyone's memories are fine," Bay assured me. "Except for mine. I distinctly don't remember kissing you yet."

"But we just kis..."

He cut me off by pressing his lips to mine.

EVER AFTER AZIA

Tomorrow would mark our nineteenth birthdays and the start of a new year.

I could tell you that we all lived happily ever after, but happily ever after is a cliché.

We lived like everyone else. We had our ups and our downs. We had adventures, we had children. We lived.

If you want to know what happened to me and the others, I'll tell you.

Blaise spent her life between the ocean and the land. She became known as the queen who brought together the two realms, and many statues were erected in her honor.

Castiel spent his life in the woods with Sera and their kids, of which there were many. And every single one of them could change into wild animals.

Deon and Lilian had three children, Rose, Poppy, and Daisy. All three had long blonde hair like their grandmother's and spent almost every minute of their lives outside in the gardens just like their father.

Eliana was the first to marry of all of us. She married Jay less than a year after Derillen was vanquished. Fae was their bridesmaid, and though she was only a year old, she managed to walk down the aisle on Epiphany's back.

Fallon and Veda never married, but they lived together until Veda died of old age. Now, he runs a yearly poetry competition for the people of Aboria, with the prize being a scholarship in Veda's name to one of the universities they set up together. The last time I saw him, he showed me a magazine with him on the cover naming him the sexiest senior in Aboria for the tenth year running.

Gaia and Genie are still alive and together now. After hundreds of years have passed, their age gap no longer looks so noticeable.

Halia became Arcadia's biggest singing sensation and spent her life touring the kingdoms, selling out stadiums wherever she went.

Ivy rebuilt The Forge, starting with the clock right in the center. She spent her whole life with a vampire named Raven.

Jakon went home to Oz, and along with his boyfriend, Clement, formally adopted all his siblings. After the older ones left, they carried on his mother's work and continued to adopt. In Clement's lifetime, they adopted and fostered over fifty children, giving them all a home in the Emerald City.

Kelis ended up marrying Topher and living a long and happy life filled with magic.

Finally Lyric. She'd had the adventure she'd spent her life craving. The second all the celebrations in Urbis were over, she flew straight home and hasn't left Skyla since. She had one son with her partner Bay. They called him Peter Pan.

As for me... Milo and I married on my thirtieth birthday after ten years of traveling the world and having adventures together. We had two children, Jess and Max, both of whom spent half their lives up the mountain on the backs of dragons. Nyre got over her infatuation with Fallon and became the Queen of Dragons, a title I was happy to let her take from me. She was the true leader of bringing Draconis back to peace.

I know you want to know about Derillen and Morpheus. Neither of them was heard of again, but every so often, a rumor would get to me that one or another of the nightclubs were having a very exclusive event—an event I was always invited to. I've never been to one...not yet anyway.

MEET THE TEAM

The Kingdom of Fairytales Series was a team effort. Below are the people that made it possible:

EQP Management: Rhi Parkes & J.A. Armitage

Our authors: J.A. Armitage, Audrey Rich, B. Kristin McMichael, Emma Savant, Jennifer Ellision, Scarlett Kol, Rose Castro, Margo Ryerkerk, Zara Quentin, Laura Greenwood and Anne Stryker.

Our Editor
Rose Lipscomb

Our Beta Team
Nadine Peterse-Vrijhof
Diane Major
Kalli Bunch
Stephanie Woodwood

Our Proof Reader
Tina Merritt

And to all the wonderful people who loved the world we created and reviewed our stories.
Thank you

READING ORDER

SEASON ONE
SLEEPING BEAUTY
Queen of Dragons
Heiress of Embers
Throne of Fury
Goddess of Flames

SEASON TWO
LITTLE MERMAID
Queen of Mermaids
Heiress of the Sea
Throne of Change
Goddess of Water

SEASON THREE
RED RIDING HOOD
King of Wolves
Heir of the Curse
Throne of Night
God of Shifters

SEASON FOUR
RAPUNZEL
King of Devotion
Heir of Thorns
Throne of Enchantment
God of Loyalty

SEASON FIVE
RUMPELSTILTSKIN
Queen of Unicorns
Heiress of Gold
Throne of Sacrifice
Goddess of Loss

SEASON SIX
BEAUTY AND THE BEAST
King of Beasts
Heir of Beauty
Throne of Betrayal
God of Illusion

SEASON SEVEN
ALADDIN
Queen of the Sun
Heiress of Shadows
Throne of the Phoenix
Goddess of Fire

SEASON EIGHT
CINDERELLA
Queen of Song
Heiress of Melody
Throne of Symphony
Goddess of Harmony

SEASON NINE
ALICE IN WONDERLAND
Queen of Clockwork
Heiress of Delusion
Throne of Cards
Goddess of Hearts

SEASON TEN
WIZARD OF OZ
King of Traitors
Heir of Fugitives
Throne of Emeralds
God of Storms

SEASON ELEVEN
SNOW WHITE
Queen of Reflections
Heiress of Mirrors
Throne of Wands
Goddess of Magic

SEASON TWELVE
PETER PAN
Queen of Skies
Heiress of Stars
Throne of Feathers
Goddess of Air

SEASON THIRTEEN
URBIS

BOXSETS

www.ingramcontent.com/pod-product-compliance
Lightning Source LLC
Chambersburg PA
CBHW020353310726
48979CB00015B/2582/J

* 9 7 8 1 9 8 9 9 9 7 8 9 5 *